THE GIANT AWAKENS

LEE JACKSON

THE GIANT AWAKENS

Severn River Publishing
www.SevernRiverBooks.com

This is a work of fiction based on actual events. Names, characters, places, historical events, and incidents are the product of the author's imagination or have been used fictitiously. Although many locations such as cities, towns, villages, airports, restaurants, roads, islands, etc. used in this work actually exist, they are used fictitiously and might have been relocated, exaggerated, or otherwise modified by creative license for the purpose of this work. Although many characters are based on personalities, physical attributes, skills, or intellect of actual individuals, all of the characters in this work are products of the author's imagination.

ISBN: 978-1-64875-222-3 (Paperback)
ISBN: 978-1-64875-223-0 (Hardback)

ALSO BY LEE JACKSON

The After Dunkirk Series

After Dunkirk

Eagles Over Britain

Turning the Storm

The Giant Awakens

Riding the Tempest

Driving the Wave

The Reluctant Assassin Series

The Reluctant Assassin

Rasputin's Legacy

Vortex: Berlin

Fahrenheit Kuwait

Target: New York

Never miss a new release! Sign up to receive exclusive updates from author Lee Jackson.

severnriverbooks.com/authors/lee-jackson/

PROLOGUE

December 7, 1941
Chequers Court, near Ellesborough, Buckinghamshire, England

Sir Winston Churchill, Prime Minister of Great Britain, stared emotionlessly at the radio on a console across from arched windows overlooking his garden. He had turned it on to listen to the nine o'clock evening news. On either side of him, US special envoy Averell Harriman and US Ambassador John Winant sat up to listen more closely. The majesty of the sun's waning glow, aided by a brilliant chandelier in lighting this exquisitely appointed dining room of the prime minister's official country home, was lost in the grip of the report. When the newscaster had finished, the two American diplomats exchanged inscrutable glances. Churchill's eyes narrowed into a fixed stare.

Minutes later, hunched over the desk in his study, his phone pressed to his ear, Churchill heard the familiar greeting of US President Franklin Roosevelt, whose voice was edged with strain. “What’s this about Japan?” Churchill asked.

"It's quite true," Roosevelt replied. “The Japanese attacked us at Pearl Harbor. We are in the same boat now.”

“Then I shall come there immediately. The king must approve, and I’m sure he will, and by the time you address Congress, we will have already declared war.”

December 11, 1941
Sark Island, English Channel Isles

“So, it’s done, is it?” Dame Marian Littlefield’s flat tone evoked grim acceptance of reality. “The US just declared war on Germany. The whole world is in the soup now.”

Her husband, Stephen, turned to look at her from his perch on three suitcases stacked together in a storage room at the back of their house. Inside an open trunk pushed against a wall, a radio whined and bleeped as Marian reached forward to shut it off. The contraption didn’t look much like a radio—just a small, square wooden platform with earphones attached to electrical wires that a technical person on the island had cobbled together. It was permanently tuned to the BBC. Their large radio had been confiscated along with those of all the other islanders. Marian and Stephen sat close together to share the earphones to hear this one.

“At least Britain is not alone in this war now,” Stephen remarked.

Marian sighed grimly. “If America can mobilize in time. If only she hadn’t disarmed to the bone after the last war—” She shook her head. “And now she faces veteran armies and navies on two fronts. Her fresh-faced recruits will fight against hardened warriors, and months will pass before any of them see combat. Meanwhile, our own regulars fight on in North Africa and Greece. I pray for those soldiers who will die, and for their mothers, and for the Americans too, when they join the battle."

"Don't forget the fathers," Stephen said, nudging her. "We feel it too."

Marian caressed his chin. "I know." She bit her lower lip to hold back tears. "I suppose your nephew will be involved now too. Isn't he in the US Navy?"

"He is," Stephen responded soberly. "In fact, the last I heard, Josh was assigned aboard the aircraft carrier *Enterprise.*" He grimaced. "I don't know what rank he is, but he must have been promoted a few times by now. It's been a few years since he graduated from Annapolis."

"And what about his siblings, Zack and Sherry?"

"I don't know. It's been hard to keep up since my brother died and this damnable war has kept us separated from the rest of the world. I'm sorry for Della. She must be terribly worried for her children and trying to handle everything alone."

Marian sighed. "I hope they come through all right, and our own family too. Every time I think of Lance in that cold POW castle, I shudder. And Paul. Where is he? No one seems to know." Unable to hold her tears back, they streamed down her face. She sniffed and wiped her eyes. "Claire must feel so alone in London." Fighting back sobs, she added, "And Jeremy, our youngest, escaped to Britain after Dunkirk, but what's he doing now?"

She took a deep breath, and together, they closed the trunk and began stacking mounds of suitcases on top of and around it. As they worked, their two white poodles barked wildly at the front of the house. The couple glanced anxiously at each other.

"Your alarm system works well," Stephen said, chuckling. "We'd better hurry along."

"I'll go," Marian said. "You finish up here. If it's the major, I'll bring him into the library, and you can meet us there." As she walked slowly, methodically through the halls, intent on giving Stephen enough time to hide the radio, she passed a mirror and stopped to straighten her hair. It had grown long and become unkempt, with white strands overcoming dark ones. Her normally robust face stared back at her with sunken eyes, gaunt cheeks, and loose skin hanging from her jaw. She wore a heavy overcoat, but it hung on her frame, now weakened and skeletal from months of meager rations.

As Marian approached the front of the house, her servant met her. Behind the hungry expression, a pretty face still showed, but the privations of German occupation had stolen the color from her cheeks and curves from her figure. "The *kommandant* is waiting for you in the foyer," she said.

"Bring him into the library. I'll wait for him there."

"Yes, mum." The girl curtsied before returning to the foyer.

"Ah, Dame Marian," Major Bandelor greeted her as he entered the library. "It's good to see you as always." Despite his jaunty demeanor, the stress of administering an occupied population manifested in a drawn face with furtive eyes and tight lips. "I imagine you've heard rumors and I wanted to set the record straight before they become too outlandish."

"I've heard nothing," Marian replied stiffly. "How would I or anyone else among our friends and neighbors? You allow us no radios under threat of death."

Bandelor eyed her skeptically. "And yet your people often seem remarkably well informed ahead of official news bulletins."

Marian shook her head and threw up a hand. "I wouldn't know anything about that. What news have you come to tell me?"

Bandelor frowned.

Stephen entered the room and extended his greetings to the major.

Bandelor cast Marian a piercing look. "I'll accept your protestations." Then he turned to Stephen. "She claims ignorance of news." He heaved a heavy sigh. "It's good that you're here. You should both hear what I have to say."

He hesitated, and when he spoke again, his reluctance was evident. "After extended effort, Japan broke off negotiations with the United States and attacked its navy at Pearl Harbor four days ago."

"I did hear that," Marian broke in, "from one of our fishermen who heard it from one of your guards. I dismissed it as rubbish intended to demoralize our people, but you're telling me it's true?"

Bandelor nodded and took another deep breath. "In the days since then, our *führer* obtained a classified copy of the American president's plan to enter the war with his primary objective being to attack and defeat Germany first, and then Japan. In light of that provocation and the state of war that already exists between America and our ally, Japan, *Herr* Hitler was forced to declare war on the United States."

He paused to take in the Littlefields' reactions but saw only blank expressions. "You're taking this calmly," he observed, and then continued. "Just before leaving my headquarters today, I received word that Germany had declared war on the United States. I am sure that in a very short while, the US will reciprocate."

Marian regarded him with a stony expression.

Bandelor alternated his attention between her and Stephen, who also remained implacable. "You don't seem surprised," he said.

"No, I'm not surprised," Marian said, and anger tinged her voice. "You and the Japanese have been hurtling toward this moment for years. Italy too. You conquer, subjugate, enslave, and destroy whole cultures. What did you think? That the United States would stand idly by and do nothing as the threat grew on both of her coasts?"

"And what did you expect?" Bandelor retorted. "The US cut off oil supplies and scrap metal to Japan, and they impounded Japanese financial assets held in the US, all crucial to their economic survival."

"You mean crucial to its continued conquests in the east. Japan's massacres in Manchuria are well known. What civilized country can countenance that?"

Bandelor regarded her through narrowed eyes. "You seem remarkably well informed for being isolated on this island."

Marian did not reply. Instead, she sat in a chair, resting her forehead in her hand. "So now, we're all in it. The whole world."

"Madame, I told you, the *führer* had no choice. Mr. Roosevelt threatened Germ—"

"Mr. Roosevelt threatened nothing," Marian retorted, taking to her feet once more and advancing toward Bandelor. "Hitler had no provocation to seize the European countries and these Channel Islands, and he had none to declare war on the United States. With the atrocities already ascribed to Germany, you're well suited to be allied with

Japan. Since a state of war already exists between them and the US, you would have entered that conflict with or without the declaration of war you claim as the reason for your action."

"Madame, I must remind you that Poland attacked Germany," Bandelor replied under apparent restraint. "We merely defended ourselves; and then Great Britain and France declared war on us. We had no alternative."

Marian barely repressed her disgust. "Do you think anyone in the thinking world believes that? Hitler had broadcast his intentions for years. He picked his moment, and I'm sure history will record that he fabricated the 'provocation' in Poland. Well, he's in it now, and so, unfortunately, is the rest of humanity."

Stephen had listened to the exchange quietly with increasing concern as his wife's vehemence grew. He stepped forward as if to intercede, but Bandelor stopped him.

"It's all right," the major said, and his face showed no anger. "I also came to bid farewell. My time in these islands has come to an end, and I am reassigned to the mainland." He regarded Marian with a smile bordering on warmth. "It has been my pleasure to know and work with you," he said. "The governance of this island is a peculiar arrangement—a British territory just off the coast of France, the last of the feudal estates where French is spoken as much as English, and now occupied by Germany." He turned to Stephen. "And you, American-born and senior co-ruler—"

"Only by right-of-wife, and that's an antiquated law," Stephen interjected. "I'm a naturalized British citizen and I defer to Marian on all governance decisions. She is the native of Sark in this marriage, and she inherited her title and rights."

"I know," Bandelor said. He regarded Stephen with a stoic expression. "And that might cause you problems in the future."

Stephen studied him intently. "What do you mean?"

"I can say no more." The major turned to Marian. "I admire your courage. You represent your people well, and you have always treated me with courtesy and respect."

Taken aback, Marian stared at him, wide-eyed. "I—I don't know what to say. What should I say to an uninvited guest who's forced his way into our homes, announces his departure, and then compliments us on the way out? Should I not mention the starvation conditions you leave behind?"

Bandelor forced a smile. "If our positions were reversed, I would feel the same."

Marian's eyes met his, and she studied his face. Bracing her shoulders, she took a deep breath and grasped his hand in both of hers. "I will say this, Major Bandelor: you have been an honest man and a fair one. You've done your best to treat our people with dignity under trying circumstances you did not choose."

Bandelor bowed his head slightly in acknowledgment. "Thank you, Madame." Once more, his demeanor became reluctant, and when he spoke, he chose his words carefully. "As you might imagine, with this turn of events, conditions will change on your island, and I can't say that they will improve. On the contrary, they will probably be worse. I believe that when Major Lanz was here, he informed you that at some point, the military will hand over control to a civilian bureaucracy."

Marian and Stephen both nodded.

"Regardless of what you might think of my country and our leadership, the German military is a professional one.

The same cannot be said—" He stopped himself and took a moment to reformulate his thoughts. "Let me just say, Madame," he continued slowly, his hands steepled in front of his mouth, "that you would be wise to hold your tongue and subdue your anger." He gestured toward two volumes displayed prominently on the bookshelves, *Sawdust Caesar* and *The House That Hitler Built*, both anti-Fascist books. "You might do well to put those books out of sight." Then he looked directly into Marian's eyes. "I should add that revealing to future administrators your knowledge of events beyond those provided through official German channels is not prudent. You know the penalties for being found with a radio."

Observing that Marian reacted with an increasingly stony expression, he bowed slightly. "I offer my advice with the friendliest sentiment, wishing only the best for you."

Marian's demeanor softened. Then she stepped forward and grasped his hand again. "I wish you safe travels, Major, and a brighter world for all of us."

1

December 12, 1941
Marseille, France

Madame Marie Madeleine Fourcade glanced around the terrace and gardens of her villa at the people relaxing and conversing in clusters. She moved about greeting them, exchanging comments, and enjoying their company. Bringing them together this way carried risks, but she had confidence in Maurice, her security chief, that early warning and other measures were in place to either keep them safe or give them time to escape from a raid, should it occur. Also, General Pétain, the Nazi puppet and formerly revered French hero of World War I who ruled Vichy France from a spa town by the same name, had not yet succeeded in sublimating the local *gendarmes* to his will, so she felt confident that she and her guests could enjoy the evening without dictatorial interference.

This gathering seemed worth the risk. Only yesterday, she had listened to the radio with a few of the others now present as President Roosevelt had broadcast his declaration of war against Germany following Japan's attack on Pearl Harbor. He had already declared war on Japan three days earlier, and the combination had rattled the nerves of everyone, despite that they welcomed the United States as an ally against Nazi Germany.

And the local group of Fourcade's French Resistance Network did have an element to celebrate. Last night had brought the reunion of Jeremy Littlefield and Amélie Boulier, two young lovers torn apart by the war who were also two of her favorite operatives. Thinking of them now brought a tinge of sadness as she fingered a note in the pocket of her dress.

Momentarily, she shifted her eyes to observe Maurice with affection. He was a huge man with bulging eyes and a fierce countenance that he somehow converted into projected friendliness with a broad smile. The vegetable vendor had brought his wife and three children with him. He was a key person in Fourcade's network, having organized much of the local Resistance. While his children played nearby, he engaged in light conversation with Sergeants Horton and Kenyon, both British survivors of Dunkirk and the sinking of the *Lancastria* at Saint-Nazaire eighteen months earlier.

Derek Horton had managed to escape to England and was shortly afterward dispatched back to France to liaise between Churchill's Special Operations Executive, the SOE, and Fourcade's Alliance, headquartered in Marseille. Horton's mother being French, he spoke the language well. He was a burly young man, barely in his twenties, and had played rugby in school.

Sergeant Kenyon, on the other hand, had chosen to stay in France after the *Lancastria* debacle. He was a demolitions expert who worked with the French Resistance, training members in his specialty and participating with them in sabotage against the Germans. He had arrived in France more than a year and a half ago speaking no French, but with ardent study and frequent use, he had become almost fluent, although with a heavy accent. Several years older than Horton, he was lanky and good-hearted.

While Fourcade watched the two Brits, another man joined in their conversation. Dark-complected, lean, and lithe, Pierre was the fisherman who had rescued them and a third Brit, Sergeant Lance Littlefield, when the *Lancastria* sank. After bringing them to shore at Saint-Nazaire, Pierre had housed and clothed them, and they, in return, trained a group that Pierre had organized. Then they joined them in a sabotage raid. During that operation, Lance had been captured.

Fourcade diverted her attention to a teenage girl, Chantal Boulier, Amélie's younger sister, entertaining Maurice's young children. She had a slight figure, auburn hair, and honey-colored eyes, and she served as Maurice's assistant for security and was already the best in the local Resistance for providing detailed surveillance and reconnaissance reports. At the moment, her gaze fixed glowingly on Horton.

He noticed but pretended not to.

Fourcade laughed in amusement and glanced toward a garden bench just below a set of stairs leading down from the terrace. The young lovers sat together, Jeremy and Amélie, holding hands, murmuring to each other, and laughing softly, oblivious to the others on the terrace.

She observed them quietly, and then sighed. Reaching into a pocket on her skirt, she fingered a scrap of paper and started toward them. Then she stopped herself. *Leave them together a while longer. They might never see each other again.*

Turning back toward the house, she saw a man come through the door, and her heart leaped. Léon Faye, a former major in the French Air Force, had been imprisoned in Algeria for opposing the Vichy French government and seeking to depose General Pétain. Upon his release, he had sought out Fourcade in Marseille, and now served as her chief of staff. Popular in military circles, he had recruited former senior air force officers who worked actively in the Resistance. Tall and dark with aristocratic good looks, he conducted himself with courtesy but with an undertone of mischief that Fourcade found endearing.

He approached her. "You look troubled."

She handed him the scrap of paper from her pocket. On it was scribbled a note. The message was simple: "Send Littlefield and Kenyon home on next flight."

Léon glanced toward Jeremy and Amélie. Shaking his head, he exhaled. "You want me to tell them?"

Fourcade shook her head. "Let them enjoy their evening. You can inform Kenyon." She cast her eyes toward Chantal. "We're going to break yet another heart this evening. We'll be sending Horton north to stand in for Jeremy until we get his replacement. Chantal thinks she's in love with the sergeant, but he sees her as a little sister. They're about three and a half years apart. She recently turned sixteen."

Léon followed Fourcade's glance. "This is a hell of a way for a young girl to grow up. Them too," he added, jutting his jaw toward Maurice's children. His tone took on a note of ferocity. "We have to win this war. For them."

2

Five Days Earlier
Opana Radar Site, Oahu, Hawaii

Private Joseph Lockard stared lazily at a blip on his cathode ray tube indicating a small flight of planes flying toward Oahu. A group of B-17 bombers intended to be stationed at Hickam Airfield was coming from almost due east and expected to arrive in roughly ninety minutes, so he made note of the blips and went on about his duties. He was hungry anyway, his shift would be over in an hour and a half, and the breakfast truck should arrive at any time.

Suddenly, a huge spike in the vertical light on the tube's screen dwarfed the earlier formation's smaller signal and morphed into an upright light band dancing across his screen. He stared, not believing what he saw: blips from the largest formation of aircraft he had ever detected flying from due north and three degrees east, one hundred and thirty-seven miles out, and closing—fast.

With growing nervousness, he squinted to check his vision. His early morning shift, begun before dawn, had seemed long. He blinked a few times and rubbed his eyes, but when he looked again, he was greeted by the same frenzied clutter on the tube.

He called across the room to Private Richard Schimmel, on duty with him. "Take a look at this."

Schimmel sauntered over sleepily, stared for a moment, and grunted. "Let's run a system check. It's probably nothing."

Moments later, having completed their diagnostics and seeing no decrease in the size of the dancing display, the two privates exchanged anxious glances. "We'd better call it in," Schimmel said.

Lockard nodded and called the Pearl Harbor Intercept Center.

Pearl Harbor sat snugly behind a natural, shallow inlet bounded by hills. When the fleet was in port, it was secured by the US Army. The commanding general of the United States Army Pacific, Lieutenant General Walter, had thrown himself into the task of building up the island's defenses against a seaborn attack. Conventional wisdom had ruled out the probability of an air assault because the vast expanses of the Pacific Ocean would have to be crossed to execute such a maneuver.

First Lieutenant Kermit Tyler took Lockard's call. He had drawn this duty for the night. Having newly arrived in Hawaii, he was still learning his specific duties. Eight of the nation's battleships had arrived from exercises to their home port at Pearl the prior day, and their crews had been out celebrating most of the night. As a result, he had received numerous calls from civilian authorities regarding high-spirited sailors reveling a bit too ambitiously on their return to shore amid the company of women. But that had abated as the night wore on, and as he glanced out the window, the first rays of sunshine reflected gold across the sky, promising a gorgeous day.

Now, as he took Lockard's call, Tyler recalled being informed that the headquarters had contracted with a commercial radio station to play a particular song when American military planes were inbound, to give the pilots a friendly homing signal as an electronic guide for the final leg of their long journey from the American mainland. He checked his logs and saw that the B-17 bombers were due in from California shortly, so he turned on the radio and dialed to the appointed station.

The designated music played.

"Good job, Private," Tyler told Lockard. "It's our own guys coming in. You can disregard."

After hanging up, and despite the casual dismissal, Lockard kept his eyes glued to the cathode ray tube. When the aircraft formation had grown even larger and come fifty miles closer, he called again.

"Sir, they're approaching. Fast. Two miles a minute."

Once more the lieutenant reassured him. Lockard hung up and shook off his uneasiness.

The vertical lines on the radar screen continued their dance.

An hour later, after one more call to Lieutenant Tyler, Lockard and Schimmel finished their shift, turned their duties over to a relief crew, and left for breakfast. The morning was glorious, the sky blue, and the weather perfect. "This is great duty," Lockard observed. "It's easy, the place is beautiful, we're at peace—"

Schimmel suddenly nudged him. "What's that?" he said, pointing in the direction of Honolulu.

Lockard shifted his view. There, far in the distance, juxtaposed against the clear blue sky and the verdant hills of Oahu, an ominous black cloud of unimaginable dimension rose into the heavens. Then, as they watched, they heard the low thud of far-off explosions.

Aboard the USS *Enterprise*, Pacific Ocean, East of Midway Atoll

Against the clatter and clang, the turbulent roll and smell of oil, machinery, and fighter exhaust aboard the huge aircraft carrier, and amid whistling wind and the salty air of the Pacific Ocean, Lieutenant Commander Josh Littlefield watched the two men before him on the ship's bridge. Rear Admiral "Bull" Halsey, commander of the Navy's Pacific Air Battle Group and Task Force Eight, and Captain Rutherford Browning, his chief of staff, spoke with their heads close together in a short, clipped discussion.

Josh was a trusted hand in the command's operations section. Tall and slender, he had dark hair, blue eyes, a straight nose, and a strong jaw. Approaching his mid-thirties, he had flown Wildcats until Captain Browning spotted his talent as a tactician and brought him into operations.

Browning signaled Josh to join them. "Tell the admiral exactly what you told me." He turned to Halsey. "I'm going to check on what else we can find out."

The admiral nodded and faced Josh while Browning departed. "Let's hear it."

"Yes, sir." Josh cleared his throat. "This morning at 0615, we sent out fourteen planes of Scouting Six and three planes of Bombing Six, plus the Air Group Commander to check the route ahead of us. They were to land at Ford Island."

Josh's voice caught, but he went on. "Ensign Manuel Gonzalez, one of Scouting Group Six's pilots, was one of them. They arrived in the vicinity of the naval station on Ford Island at roughly 0700 hours. Suddenly, Gonzalez' voice came over the radio, and he was frantic. He yelled, 'Don't shoot! Don't shoot! This is an American plane.' Then, seconds later, we heard him order his crewman, Petty Officer Joe Kozelek, to bail out."

Josh hung his head momentarily, and then straightened. "That's the last we heard of them. And Admiral"—his eyes narrowed in anger—"when Gonzalez' mic was open, we heard explosions, gunfire, and bullets impacting his aircraft."

As Halsey listened, his shoulders hunched, his arms crossed, and his face grew hard, expressionless. "You're sure of what you heard?"

"There's no doubt in my mind or among any of our guys who heard it. They're mad as hell."

"What's your assessment?"

"Sir, we searched the radio channels and listened to transmissions in Japanese mixed with those of our own stations. Ours were frantic, and again, we heard explosions and sounds of gunfire. There's no doubt in my mind: the Japanese just attacked Pearl Harbor."

Nine days earlier, under Halsey's command, the *Enterprise*, three heavy cruisers, and nine destroyers had sailed as "Task Force Eight" to Wake Island in an atoll much closer to Japan than to Hawaii. Ostensibly the task force was on sea maneuvers, but their covert mission was to deliver twelve Marine F4F Wildcat fighters to Squadron VMF-211 at the far-flung base. On reaching a safe proximity to Midway on December 2, the Marines had flown on to their destination while the fleet had turned about for the sixteen-hundred-mile return voyage.

Prior to leaving Pearl Harbor, Admiral Kimmel, commander-in-chief of the Pacific Fleet and Halsey's boss, had received and re-transmitted to his subordinate commanders a dispatch from the chief of naval operations in Washington, DC. In short, it read, "War warning," and further informed that diplomatic negotiations with Japan were reaching a dead end. An attack was expected within days. Kimmel ordered his commanders to proceed on a war footing.

Knowing the tenuous relations between Washington and Tokyo, and recalling Japan's history of starting a war with Russia in 1904 by sneak-attack three hours before delivering a war declaration to the Kremlin in Moscow, Halsey retained a visceral sense of the danger of his mission, and on receipt of Kimmel's directive, he immediately instructed his staff to check the shipping schedules for traffic in the sea lanes where his ships would sail. Finding that the way should be clear and anticipating the conflagration that was bound to follow a chance encounter with Japanese warships, he ordered, "Shoot and sink any vessel we encounter."

A mid-grade officer, Commander Bill Buracker, objected. "Sir, are you sure about that order? You can't start a private war. Who'll take responsibility?"

"Me," the admiral snapped. "If anything gets in my way, we'll hit hard, hit fast, and hit often." He turned to Captain Browning. "Draw up and issue my order."

Expecting that any Japanese assault would be against the US naval station on Midway Island, Kimmel had ordered Halsey to sail and defend there after completing the mission to Wake Island. Arriving at his second destination, and after days of fruitlessly sending out scout planes seeking any sign of a hostile naval strike force, Halsey's carrier group had begun the final leg of its return voyage to Pearl Harbor, expecting to anchor there on December 6.

Then, a storm had kicked up across the intended path, slowing the task force. Turbulent waves had tossed the ships, breaching one of the destroyers at the seam, and further impeding progress. But the morning of December 7 had dawned calm and beautiful as Task Force Eight continued what the crews had expected to be their last day at sea for this voyage—until overhearing those fateful radio transmissions.

At dusk two days after the Pearl Harbor raid, the men of Task Force Eight spotted lingering wisps of smoke over the horizon even before the Oahu coast came into sight. Fumes rose with intermittent thick black columns reaching into the sky.

A stench greeted them as the ships approached the shore and lined up to navigate the narrow channel into the harbor. Instead of the salty, fishy smell that usually accompanied the line where land met sea, the stink of burning oil, melted steel, and scorched carcasses assaulted their senses. Every man not engaged in running the ships crowded on deck, not believing the devastation and carnage inflicted on their fellow Americans that now assaulted their senses. Despite the hundreds of men aboard the task force, silence hung over the ships, broken only by the rumble of engines, the lap of wavelets, and occasional horns.

As they cleared the passage and entered the harbor amid a pall of smoke and fire, and steered past the wreckage of Battleship Row, the sight brought many stoic faces to repressed tears. In every direction, debris was strewn across the harbor, with exhausted workers swarming to rescue, repair, and salvage what they could.

The men of Task Force Eight took in the horror of what they had heard reported on the news. Spread across the harbor, ninety-four US naval ships had been attacked, and of the seven battleships parked there, all had been hit. At the back end of the row, the USS *Oklahoma* rested on its side, only its hull visible to the passing seamen. In place of the USS *Arizona* was an empty space with a black stream gurgling up from the depths. Still visible but sunk were the hulks of the USS *West Virginia* and the USS *California*. Only the USS *Pennsylvania*, in dry dock, escaped heavy damage.

Over two thousand people had been killed, and another two thousand wounded. As the *Enterprise* approached its moorings, the crew reeled from the myriad dark, dried blood marking where sailors, soldiers, and civilians had fallen.

Josh stood at the bridge rail with Captain Browning. On the other side of them, Admiral Halsey sat in his chair surveying the disaster, his face set in an angry mask. He swung around to Browning. "Have the ships provisioned and fueled tonight. We sail at dawn. We're going hunting." Then he muttered, "Before we're done, the Japanese language will be spoken only in hell."

3

December 16, 1941
Moscow, Union of Soviet Socialist Republic

Robert Anthony Eden, 1st Earl of Avon and now British Foreign Secretary for a second time, arrived in the Soviet capital to meet with Vyacheslav Molotov, People's Commissar for Foreign Affairs and Deputy Chairman of the State Defense Committee. Their purpose: to negotiate a treaty between Great Britain, the Soviet Union, and the United States in their common fight against Germany, Italy, and Japan. Their secondary objective: to shape post-war European borders.

London, England

A disgruntled Jeremy Littlefield, accompanied by Sergeant Kenyon, entered the MI-9 office in room 424 of the requisitioned building that had been the stately Metropole Hotel. A matronly secretary, Vivian, met them there.

"How good to see you, Jeremy," she exclaimed, "all safe and well." She hugged him, and then extended a hand to Kenyon. "We've never met, but I've heard so many good things about you."

Jeremy set his ire aside for the moment and returned the greeting warmly, as did Kenyon. He tempered his impatience as he said, "I'd like to see Major Crockatt as soon as possible. I really should be getting back to my group in France."

Vivian regarded him blankly. "He's been promoted. He's a lieutenant colonel now. There's a commando officer in there with him now, Lieutenant Colonel Newman." Her expression turned to one of concern. "Oh, dear. I suppose you don't know why you've been recalled."

Jeremy glanced at Kenyon. "We do not," he said, "but we'd like to, after being weathered in for two days and then that bumpy ride by moonlight in a small plane over enemy territory and the Channel."

"I'll let them know you're here."

Moments later, after greetings, introductions, and having taken seats, Crockatt said, "I'm sorry to have pulled the two of you back here."

He was a stern man, albeit with warmth residing just below the surface that manifested in genuine courtesy. He was tall and fit with dark, receding hair and piercing eyes over a well-groomed mustache. Jeremy knew him to be a valued mentor to Paul Littlefield, Jeremy's eldest brother.

"You've both been in and around Saint-Nazaire," Crockatt went on. "We'd like to quiz you on what you've seen and know about the area."

Jeremy and Kenyon looked at each other questioningly.

"I'm not sure I can be of much help," Jeremy said. "I came through the town when I escaped France, but I wasn't there long, and I had a guide to take me through. That was such a muddled time. I don't recall much." He gestured toward Kenyon. "He'd probably be more helpful. He's been on a few raids there."

Kenyon shook his head. "Like Jeremy, I came through the port to make my escape. After the ship was bombed, I was on a few raids with the Resistance, but that was on the outskirts of the town. I studied the routes to and from the objectives and some alternate routes, but I would hardly put myself forward as an expert on the area."

"Any information will be helpful," Newman broke in. He was also of medium height and build, in his late thirties, with close-cropped, receding hair, an oval face, a slight mustache, and a rugged look that came from spending many hours outdoors. His manner, though friendly, was no-nonsense. "Do you mind if we ask about what you *do* know? You might reveal some nuggets that we had not known before."

For the next two hours, Jeremy and Kenyon described their separate experiences on passing through Saint-Nazaire and its port, pointing out various streets and landmarks on a map that Newman had brought. He prodded their memories on several points, and finally said, "Well, thank you. You've been very helpful."

Once again, Jeremy and Kenyon exchanged glances. "Is that it?" Jeremy asked. "You risked our lives and limbs to fly through enemy territory for this?" He surprised himself with his directness, but he was still angry over his abrupt recall.

He replayed in his mind his conversation with Fourcade when she delivered the news. "Crockatt sent me into the

Loire Valley to organize Resistance groups, and the reception was initially not friendly," he had protested. "I've been there what—two months, maybe three, and he's pulling me out? Why?"

"I don't know why," Fourcade had replied, "but we can do it precisely because you have *been* so effective. The French leader you're leaving behind is capable and dedicated, and he understands our abilities and constraints. We'll send Horton to fill in for you, but he'll have more of a coordinating role than a leadership or organizing one."

Containing his anger, Jeremy had acquiesced and bid Amélie a sad farewell. More than being the woman he loved, she had risked her life to save his, going out into a storm to divert German soldiers away from where Jeremy hid. Her image flitted through his mind: her small figure, auburn hair, full lips, and honey-colored eyes.

In contrast to Jeremy and Amélie, Horton had been thrilled with his new assignment. Not so for Chantal, who was perturbed at the thought of Horton leaving Marseille.

Newman's chair scraping on the floor brought Jeremy back to the present. He cleared his throat while exchanging glances with Crockatt. "We'd like for both of you to join Number 2 Commando, which I command."

Stunned, Jeremy and Kenyon stared at him and then at each other.

"I agreed to this conversation with Lieutenant Colonel Newman on the proviso that I get you back," Crockatt broke in. "He's planning a particular raid that he'd like you both to be on, after which you'll return to MI-9."

"Let me clarify," Newman broke in. "There's a proposed raid that has been bandied about a few times, with starts and stops. It was originated by Lord Mountbatten, but since he has no assets to command, and the raid is not favorably regarded by the joint chiefs, it has not yet gained traction, but I suspect it will."

For a few moments, no one spoke. Then Jeremy said, "Of course we've heard of the commandos. Everyone has. But I believe they are a new organization, and we've been in France for months. Kudos on what you did in Norway, but Sergeant Kenyon and I don't know how you operate, where you're based, whom you report to—"

Newman interrupted. "Churchill had the idea to form the commandos. "The regular army opposed him, but he made the point in writing that only a small part of the *Wehrmacht* did the fighting in their *blitzkriegs*. They were followed up by a ponderous, even antiquated army to hold the ground the frontline had seized. For heaven's sake, eighty percent of their support travels on horseback or pulled wagons.

"The PM was impressed with what the small forward vanguard accomplished. Accordingly, he developed his idea of a highly independent, professional force where each man could end up being the leader due to casualties in any operation and still carry on, completing the mission. We get in, do our business, and get out."

Quiet descended again. Newman broke it. "I've studied your records. You both survived Dunkirk and a bombed troopship and stayed out of German hands. Captain Littlefield, you became a national hero when you saved a small child from drowning in that shipwreck and brought him home to England. As I recall from newspaper reports, you kept the child, and your sister cares for him. Since then, you've flown fighters in the Battle of Britain and night-fighters in the *blitz*, and then returned to France to work with the Resistance.

"Sergeant Kenyon, absent any other orders, you opted to

stay and work with a French Resistance group, training its members in demolitions and carrying out missions with them.

"You're both exactly the kind of men we've been recruiting, but you'd have to go through our full training and an additional school. There's just enough time to do that and insert you into No. 2 Commando in time for rehearsals for that raid."

"At Saint-Nazaire?" Kenyon inquired gruffly.

"How did you guess?" Newman responded with a wry smile. "Yes, at Saint-Nazaire. And the additional school you'll go to is for demolitions. Even though you're an explosives expert, we foresee a special application, and the participants must rehearse extensively together before the operation."

"Can you tell us anything more about it?" Jeremy asked.

Newman leaned back and exhaled. "You already know more than the commandos who will carry out the raid, should it be approved. I can tell you this. We must succeed, or we will lose the battle in the Atlantic, and if we do that, our people starve, and we could likely lose the war. Even with America joining us, overall victory would be far less assured. Since the war in the Pacific started up, we've had to shift a large part of our navy there, so we have less defense against German U-boat attacks on our shipping in the Atlantic."

Kenyon eyed him skeptically. "And you need the captain and me on the raid, or it won't succeed?" he said with a note of sarcasm.

Newman chuckled. "Hardly, but as I stated, this is a mission that must succeed, so it must have every incremental chance of success." His eyes twinkled. "You're a potential increment." Then he became serious again. "But that's a fair question. We're bringing together the best men we can find. I should tell you that we expect high casualties, probably better than fifty percent, and that's if we're lucky."

"Our odds are probably lower than that," Kenyon said, indicating himself and Jeremy. "We've beaten odds like that too many times. Eventually, fate catches up to you." He took a deep breath and grinned. "I'm skeptical of any organization that'll have me, but all right, I'm in." Shooting a glance at Jeremy, he asked, "You, sir?"

Jeremy folded his arms while nodding. "I must be daft, but I'll do it. I told Lieutenant Colonel Crockatt long ago that I'd serve wherever I could do it best."

A short silence descended on the room again. Newman broke it once more. "Thank you. I know this is not an easy request to accept. There are two more things you must agree to before we proceed."

He straightened in his seat and made eye contact with Jeremy and Kenyon in turn. Before speaking again, he inhaled. "If you join us, you'll be required to relinquish all rank at the beginning of training. You'll be promoted after that based on merit within the commandos."

Kenyon guffawed and turned to look at Jeremy. "Do you mean I get to call him by his first name?"

Jeremy harrumphed with mock disgust. "You've done that the entire time I've known you in France."

"But I always added 'sir,'" Kenyon said. He turned back to Newman. "With that, how can I refuse?"

"What's the other condition?" Jeremy asked.

Newman had been enjoying the banter, but his face once again became serious. "You cannot speak of this mission to anyone, and you can't reveal the location of this raid to the other commandos. They won't be apprised of where it's to take place until shortly before we execute. Only a few people know. Secrecy is imperative."

Jeremy regarded the officer with somber eyes. Then he clambered to his feet and extended his hand. "When do we start?"

"Immediately."

Jeremy gave a short laugh. "This will be one bloody way to celebrate Christmas and New Year's Eve."

4

December 22, 1941
Hampton Roads, Virginia

The HMS *Duke of York*, a British King George V-class 14-in gun battleship, plowed through the mouth of the Elizabeth River after dusk, escorted by destroyers *Faulknor, Foresight*, and *Matabele*. During the twilight, they berthed at the renowned Norfolk Naval Shipyard.

Once the vessel had docked, Winston Churchill disembarked with the closest members of his entourage, Admiral of the Fleet Sir Dudley Pound, The First Sea Lord; Field Marshal Sir John Dill, Chief of the Imperial General Staff; Air Chief Marshal Sir Charles Portal, Chief of the Air Staff; and US special envoy, Averell Harriman.

The eight-day ocean crossing had been arduous, particularly for a man who had just turned sixty-seven and carried the weight of a war-torn empire on his shoulders. Originally, the plan had been to sail north on a great circle route to Norfolk from the departure port at Firth of Clyde on Scotland's west coast. However, stormy weather and turbulent water had dictated a turn to the south past the Azores, a route that invited attack by German U-boat wolf packs roaming the Atlantic.

Roosevelt had initially discouraged Churchill from making the crossing because of the twin dangers of the weather and the U-boat threat, but Churchill was undeterred. The president conveyed his reluctance for the prime minister to take the voyage.

Churchill brushed aside those concerns, writing Roosevelt, "We could review the whole war plan in light of reality and new facts, as well as the problems of production and distribution." He added that the bigger danger lay in not meeting to coordinate strategy.

In response, Roosevelt had telegraphed, "Delighted to have you here at the White House."

Shortly after the ship moored, a plane lifted into the sky, transporting Churchill and his entourage to Anacostia Naval Air Station near the US capital. While it touched down and taxied to the terminal, President Roosevelt waited in his car.

"It's so good to see you," he said as the prime minister settled next to him in the car's rear seat. "Is that a cane you're carrying?"

"It is, sir," Churchill replied as the car drove away, "but not for the reason you might think. It's fitted with a light at the bottom." He demonstrated. "That's so we can find our way about during blackouts."

Roosevelt eyed the cane gravely. "Things are that bleak over there?"

"They are, but all is not lost. I suppose you heard that since attacking your fleet at Pearl Harbor, Japan sank our battleships *Prince of Wales* and the *Repulse*?"

Roosevelt nodded.

"Those are as hard as any blows we've taken throughout

this war," Churchill went on. "We had just been discussing detailing them to join your fleet when that happened. That leaves you and me and our countries with no capital ships in the Indian Ocean or the Pacific, aside from the survivors of Pearl that went back to California for repairs. Over that entire expanse of water, Japan now reigns supreme. They have full battleship command of those oceans for the moment."

He paused as he gathered his thoughts. "But this voyage was good. With no cabinet meetings, special committees, or events to attend, I was able to concentrate on my view of the war with a fresh mind and at length. You know, Napoleon promoted doing that as a key to success, and what I see after my long reflection is that we live to fight another day. I see the war laid out in front of me, with the priorities that must be met to gain and build momentum to final victory, and there are a few bright spots.

"Most important among them is that we're gratified to have your country as our ally; the Russians have racked up some significant wins at Leningrad, across the whole Moscow front. In the south of the Soviet Union, most of the *Wehrmacht* is in retreat—much of that thanks to your help with Lend-Lease in supplying the Soviets with arms, ammunition, transport, aircraft, and supplies.

"Our Foreign Secretary Eden is in Moscow negotiating with Stalin as we speak. I had a visit in London from Stalin's envoy, Molotov. Now there's a rough customer, quite hard-nosed, and he insisted that we hand over rights to Latvia, Lithuania, and Estonia as well as the eastern part of Poland per his agreement with Hitler. He was quite belligerent on the subject, and he was certain that Stalin supported his position." He laughed. "That was until Stalin cabled him to sign our Grand Alliance treaty without such a provision.

"Eden reports that Stalin has softened, probably because of German victories on his territory, and he knows he needs us to save his skin. He says Stalin is much more malleable right now but does not feel strong enough yet to take on Japan on his far east flank." Churchill chuckled. "I'll tell you honestly that I didn't think the Soviets would last beyond a month against the Germans. I saw the Nazi action as merely a prelude to attacking Britain again, so three days after the start of Operation Barbarossa, I ordered our defenses against invasion to be at orchestra pitch by September 1."

"That was wise," Roosevelt cut in.

"You know Hitler's troops very quickly reached Leningrad, the old Saint Petersburg," Churchill went on, "and he ordered the city razed to the ground, street by street, and building by building. Stalin wrote me in a panic, in his own handwriting, demanding a second front in Europe with thirty divisions. Of course, I couldn't do that. I don't have that many divisions in my whole army, and it's scattered across the world.

"But the Soviets held out, and the comrade thinks that by spring, he might have built his army back to the strength it was in the north before having to move so many elements west to confront the Germans. If that comes about, he might seriously consider declaring war on Japan.

"Meanwhile, our Battle of the Atlantic is finally manageable. It's been the only battle I've feared. Hitler abandoned the notion that he'd defeat our RAF over Britain, and with it the idea of invading us. But he's still intent on starving our people, and he'll do it if we don't defeat his U-boats."

Churchill paused for breath. "Hitler's submarines are still our major threat. In his Directive 21, he even specified that the Kriegsmarine should concentrate their resources in the Atlantic. But they avoid a pitched battle there, I imagine hoping to wear us down by attacking our supply lines. By February, they had sunk over half a million tons of cargo just off your own shores. But our losses are reduced significantly from where they were earlier this year, thanks to Lend-Lease and the protection of your navy. However, with increased demands for our warships in the Pacific, the Battle of the Atlantic still poses a major threat and could grow in scale again. Regardless of whatever else we might lose, we must win in the Atlantic, or we are lost."

Churchill glanced out the window as he gathered his next thoughts, seeing nothing in the darkness. "In North Africa, Field Marshal Auchinleck and our Eighth Army currently has driven that desert fox, Erwin Rommel, to retreat three hundred and fifty miles, though I suspect we'll still have heavy fighting ahead of us. Both the German army and our own face the problem of long supply lines, and time will tell if Auchinleck's initiative can be sustained."

The prime minister sighed. "We've been alone in our fight for a long time, Franklin, with only you, personally, as our principal ally. But now, four-fifths of the world is on our side."

Roosevelt nodded in acknowledgment. "Go on. I'm keen to know your view of how the war should be conducted." He chuckled. "I haven't had the advantage of a sea voyage and the time it affords to think."

Churchill eyed the president. "You've been kind to ask about our people, and I've been prattling on about news you probably already know. How are Americans faring after the attack on Pearl Harbor? You made an excellent speech in Congress. 'A day that will live in infamy.' That phrase will resound throughout history."

The president drew a deep breath and acknowledged the comment with a nod. "Billy Mitchell was right," he said, and then anger laced his tone. "He was an outspoken general that we crucified for daring to insist that we improve our air forces after the Great War. We court-martialed him and ended his military career."

"I've heard of him. He was a visionary."

Roosevelt nodded. "He was, and in 1924 he predicted the places—Pearl Harbor and Clark Field in the Philippines—the day of the week and time of day that the Japanese would attack. He was off by only twenty-five minutes." He tossed his head. "We're mad as hell, Winston, and ready to carry the fight all the way to Tokyo and Emperor Hirohito's hideout in Nikkō, Tochigi.

"We were still in official negotiations with the Japanese at the time of their attack. That raid focused American attention like never before, and we're fixed on avenging Pearl Harbor." He leaned closer to the prime minister. "Despite that you and I thought our entry into the conflict was inevitable, and after all the preparations we've taken, I'm not glad it's happened, but this is a war that we must win, or perish."

He paused, mulling his thoughts, and then went on. "We were caught by surprise, but our people at Pearl Harbor rose to the occasion." He shook his head. "Do you know that the battleship *Oklahoma* rolled over on its side, and sailors trapped inside could be heard banging the hull?"

Churchill nodded grimly. "I heard."

"Well, our frogmen ignored the second wave of the Japanese assault, suited up, and went down to cut through two feet of solid steel to rescue our sailors even as more bombs fell, more planes strafed, and more torpedoes struck." He shook his head in disbelief. "Those rescuers were magnificent. They demonstrated immediately the spirit of America." His voice caught. "We saved only thirty-two men trapped in the *Oklahoma*. We lost four hundred and twenty-four from that ship alone." He leaned back and wiped his eyes. "All told, we count over twenty-four-hundred casualties—over seventeen hundred of them from the *Arizona*—and sixty-eight civilians. Nineteen of our warships were sunk, including eight battleships."

Churchill nodded wordlessly as the president continued. "Everyone jumped in to help the wounded—nurses, doctors, corpsmen, civilians—I'm in awe. Men rushed out in their skivvies to man anti-aircraft guns; and when it was all over, some very brave pilots climbed into the cockpits of the few fighters we had left and went out to look for the Japanese fleet." He fell silent for a moment. "You know the Japs struck civilian areas too. Pure terrorism, like their ally, *Herr* Hitler, did to your cities and all across Europe. But I'm not sure they accomplished their objective."

The prime minister glanced at him in surprise. "How so?"

"Our aircraft carriers were out to sea. The *Enterprise* was delayed by a storm after a mission to defend Midway Island —and thank God it was. Midway is where Rear Admiral Kimmel expected the attack.

"The Japs took out our big battleships, but we'll re-float six of them; and anyway, I'm convinced, as are several of my advisers, that the day of the battleship is past. Our aircraft carriers are now our most lethal weapons at sea, and the raid didn't touch any of them." The president's expression became resolute. "We'll carry out offensive operations almost immediately. In fact, Halsey's crew killed a Japanese submarine three days into the war, and he's been carrying out harassing raids against Japanese-held islands since a few days after the attack."

Roosevelt took another deep breath. "You know it wasn't

just Pearl Harbor they hit. They also bombed and strafed Hickam Field, Schofield Barracks, Wheeler Airfield, and a naval service station at Kaneohe Bay.

"We had large fuel storage tanks at Pearl Harbor to service our fleet—an obvious target. The raid destroyed the island's defenses, so we expected another attack. Reports came in that their paratroopers had landed on Oahu, and the residents were terrified of invasion because of the unspeakable atrocities, tortures, and executions the Japanese carried out in places they've conquered. But those dangers never transpired.

"Now Hawaiians live under martial law, they've got bomb shelters built everywhere, and the fronts of their buildings are stacked with sandbags." His voice rose to exasperation. "At night, they live under blackout conditions. By day, children are carrying gas masks to school and crouching in hastily dug dirt trenches for bomb drills." He glanced at Churchill, sober awareness overtaking his expression. "But you've seen all this before, all across England."

The prime minister nodded. "For more than two years now. I don't wish it on you."

"Of course not." Momentarily overcome with anger, Roosevelt muttered, "The bastards. They don't know what's coming their way." Then, his jaw set, he added, "Our crews at Pearl Harbor are working twenty-four-hour shifts to repair our warships. We'll have those that are salvageable made seaworthy and take the battle to Japan faster than they can believe, with new ships and weapon systems coming behind."

He gathered himself and sought to raise the gloomy atmosphere. "What's it been, four months since we've seen each other?"

Churchill nodded. "Since August, when we announced

the Atlantic Charter aboard the *Augusta*. The whole world loved it—at least those countries allied with us did." He chuckled. "And neither of us even signed it. The press got only what was sent out by the radio operators on the *Augusta* and the *Prince of Wales*." He glanced at the president with a half-smile. "I don't have a copy. Do you?"

Roosevelt shook his head, and Churchill added more somberly, "We didn't get as much out of the charter as we hoped. It didn't sway the American people to join us in the war."

"No," Roosevelt replied grimly. "It took Japan to do that." Anger returned. "And as you well know, they hit us at Guam and Wake Island that day, too. They also attacked Hong Kong, Singapore, the Philippines, and Shanghai, and they invaded Thailand and Malaya. Since then, they've gone into Burma and Borneo."

He stopped and smiled wryly at the prime minister. "I don't mean to be a news reporter. I'm assuming your radio communications were difficult on the ship."

Churchill nodded. "We still got reports, but there's no harm in comparing notes."

Roosevelt chuckled. "Eleanor is put out at me. I told her of your coming only a little while ago. She feels like I should have informed her sooner." He glanced out the window and sighed. "Ah, well. Your whereabouts have kept the newshounds in fits. Sneaking out of London is not easy for a prime minister of the British Empire. Radio Berlin variously opined that you were in Washington and in Moscow. Then, four hours before you docked, they broadcast that 'diplomatic opinion is increasingly voiced that Churchill is in the Middle East.'" He gazed out the front window. "I should warn you that a gaggle will be at the White House to receive us on arrival."

Roosevelt's brow wrinkled as a thought crossed his mind. "I wanted to ask you about the raid you did in Norway last March. It must have had a point, but for the life of me, I can't figure out what it is."

Churchill's eyes twinkled. "Public relations," he said while reaching inside his jacket pocket to extract two cigars. "Do you mind? These are from the box you sent me." He offered one to the president, who chuckled as he took it. Then they both lit up, each opening his window a crack to let the smoke out.

"You're speaking of Operation Claymore, the raid at Lofoten," Churchill continued. "We started up a new type of military organization. We call its soldiers 'commandos.' I intend to use them on targets that deliver strategic value by the smallest possible force. We trained them over many months, but they had no mission to execute. I'd assigned Admiral of the Fleet Sir Roger Keyes to organize the group, and the regular army pressured him to either find an operation or disband—I'm afraid our regulars regard our commandos as spoiled brats.

"We train them for independent thinking and initiative. Two months ago, long after Lofoten, I put in Lord Louis Mountbatten as Advisor of Combined Operations, essentially replacing Keyes. He'll watch over our forays in the foreseeable future."

"He's young, isn't he?"

"Yes, but he's been in naval combat, captained ships, gone down with one under enemy fire... The men like and respect him, and he knows what he's doing. He's working on this new concept he calls 'combined operations.' It'll bring in elements from land, air, and sea forces to cooperate for maximum effect. He'll apply it on our next raid."

Roosevelt's eyes gleamed with interest. "How does it work?"

As the prime minister explained the idea, the president nodded enthusiastically. "That sounds tremendous, if you can effect the coordination."

"We expect difficulty, but it's similar in command and control to Sir Hugh Dowding's air defense system that won us the Battle of Britain, but this is Mountbatten's initiative. We're using the techniques offensively and the main difference is that we're bringing together all three military services on a single operation."

"Let me know the results. It sounds like a concept our own forces should study and perhaps adopt. Changing subjects, what happened to Admiral Keyes?"

"I'm afraid our chiefs of staff thought his ideas too outlandish. He's a good man, but he was always in a row with them. Called them cowards to their faces. I believe a new and younger figure might be in the public interest. I'm happy with Mountbatten. I told him he had two objectives: to keep up the commandos' spirit and harass the enemy. I told him that above all, in every possible way, he was to turn the south coast of England from a bastion of defense into a springboard for attack. He has a sterling record and will do quite nicely.

"In any event, getting back to Lofoten, it was a low-cost raid, ostensibly to destroy anything useful to the Germans, particularly the fish oil for the glycerin they use in manufacturing explosives and for the Vitamin A their U-boat crews need. They're deprived of it, you know, for the lack of sunlight." He cranked down the window a bit more to release a smoke ring and then raised it again. "In all, our chaps destroyed eighteen factories, scuttled eleven ships, and released eight-hundred-thousand gallons of fish oil into the harbor. But in reality, we wanted to showcase our new commando force.

"Our men were rather disgruntled when they initially encountered no Germans to battle; some went out in search of them. But the townspeople were thrilled to see our commandos, and even shared their scarce coffee and hoarded food. The good people of Lofoten were quite disappointed to learn that it was only a raid and our men would be returning to home base." He laughed. "There were even sparks flying between our commandos and the young women of the village. It turned into quite a social occasion."

"Hmm. That's interesting," Roosevelt interjected while savoring his cigar. "I've heard of your commandos, but I don't know what they're supposed to do. Certainly, Lofoten could not be the intended model."

Churchill chuckled. "No, but they did destroy several enemy ships and captured another cryptographic machine, one of the Enigmas; and they brought back three hundred and fourteen Norwegian volunteers, including some of those lasses who said they wanted to be nurses. They also brought two hundred and twenty-eight German prisoners and an official of the Norwegian Quisling puppet regime thought to be a collaborator. So I'd call the mission a success, even from a military standpoint. It took less than six hours onshore from start to finish. A German spotter plane saw them as they departed. Then a few *Luftwaffe* fighters showed up, but our navy kept them at bay.

"Public morale had been low in Britain. People were afraid of Germany's impending invasion. The BBC and the newspapers gave the Lofoten raid a lot of attention, billing it as a resounding victory, and it had an immediate positive effect.

"But you asked about our commandos. They are a

special force. I told Sir Roger to recruit men who would be ready to spring at the enemy's throat. They must be highly intelligent and physically fit. We take them to the wilderness in all sorts of terrain and train them differently than regular troops. Their job is to go after critical targets, meet specific objectives, and get out. The Lofoten raid proved the concept works. They are here to stay. Sir Roger did a brilliant job."

"What about the Germans? Did they retaliate?"

Churchill sighed. "Sadly, yes. We received reports of arrests, beatings, destruction... There is no justification for that, but we also learned that the Germans were embarrassed by being caught unprepared for the attack, so Hitler's moved thousands of troops to defend his positions in Norway. We don't yet have a good estimate of how many, but those are German soldiers our chaps won't face elsewhere, so I consider that to be another successful outcome of the raid."

Roosevelt pondered the comment a moment. "That's an impressive victory, but you said it was done mainly for public relations. Can you give me an example of a mission you expect your commandos to complete that would provide greater military benefit?"

"I can. Recall that the battleship *Bismarck* had a sister ship, the *Tirpitz*. She was making moves to break out into the Atlantic from the Baltic Sea before we sank the *Bismarck* last summer, preventing their linkup. The two together could have defeated our navy in that ocean, which would have been a cataclysmic disaster. Alone, the *Tirpitz* is still a major threat, and we believe that Hitler is still intent on sending her out there.

"Think Saint-Nazaire," Churchill went on. "It's an upcoming raid that will test the commandos and the combined operations concept on a larger scale." He explained the outline of the raid. When he had finished, Roosevelt sat back and whistled in amazement.

"If your commandos can accomplish that..." He left the sentence unfinished.

"I've already ordered it."

Shaking his head with incredulity, Roosevelt contemplated what he had just learned. "So, with that first raid, you wanted to showcase your commandos, and that's why you went into Norway—"

The prime minister interrupted. "We wanted to show the British people that we can carry the battle to the enemy. They've needed some morale boosting, what with food shortages, blackouts, and endless funeral processions. They'll see a lot more of our commandos in the near future. In fact, within a few days." He explained his comment.

Roosevelt reacted with excitement. "I'll be watching closely for the results."

"We'll watch for them together," Churchill replied. "I'll still be here in DC."

"Good, the analysis should be useful, and let me tell you that I have a surprise of my own being prepared as we speak —for the Japanese."

When the president had finished describing his objective, the prime minister nodded in admiration. Then Roosevelt said, "I'm glad you initiated the liaison arrangement between me and the British Security Coordination office in Manhattan. Your Bill Stephenson and our General Donovan work well together. The general is forming a new organization, the Office of Strategic Services, the OSS, with many of the same aims and capabilities as your Strategic Operations Executive. It should be up and running in June.

"Without the success of Stephenson and Donovan, we never could have accomplished what we did in luring Hitler to delay his Operation Barbarossa into the Soviet Union and diverting whole divisions to Greece and the Balkans, and now Norway. That will cost him dearly."

Churchill acknowledged with a nod. "It already has. Barbarossa was a dismal failure, so he's launched Operation Typhoon to try to regain the initiative, but all it's done is catch his troops in the grip of Russia's winter at the gates of Moscow. And they're not outfitted for it because the *Wehrmacht* expected to finish off the Red Army and be home in time for Christmas. So much for Hitler's vaunted *blitzkrieg* when it relies on an extended supply line in the dead of winter." He puffed on his cigar and removed it from his lips. "We should be seeing Stephenson and Donovan while I'm here—"

"And that young captain of yours, Stephenson's aide, what's his name?"

"Littlefield. Paul Littlefield."

"Yes. I remember. I was impressed with him."

"He was carefully selected."

"Getting back to the Soviets, what's your feel for Joseph Stalin? Will Eden get anywhere with him. He's not another Neville Chamberlain, is he?"

Churchill turned to Roosevelt sharply. "I hope someone else originated that comparison," he replied archly. "Whether you like Stalin or not, Joseph put it to the Germans. He was a little slow off the mark, but he's held them back.

"We understand what he wants: war materiel and an early second front in Europe. You're already providing him with ample supplies and weaponry, and you're doing the same for us. Now that America is in the war, my guess is that supplying your own military will limit what you can send to either of us. That being the case, and with the US still having to raise fighting forces for two major theaters, that early second front is unlikely in the near future."

"We'll have something to say about that—" Roosevelt broke in.

"Of course," Churchill went on. "But beyond supplies and the European front, Stalin wants to keep his borders as they were before Hitler invaded Soviet territory—and he won't admit it right now, but that includes Poland, or at least the part he seized while still partnering with Hitler. Right now, he's feeling like he has a strong negotiating hand, because Britain had been taking a beating in North Africa until Auchinleck's recent successes, and now you're taking one along with us in the Pacific.

"Meanwhile, Stalin stopped the German advance within sight of the Kremlin barely two weeks ago, and without our direct help. Now, he's essentially telling us that if we want a treaty with him, it's going to come at a price. Freezing storms keep Hitler's army pinned down—God help his poor soldiers. And his central and southerly campaigns aren't doing any better. The *führer* thought the *Wehrmacht* would be able to forage, but villagers burned their own crops and ran off their livestock ahead of the German advance. Now he has a long supply line through Russian snows, and the lack of winter gear is freezing his soldiers to death. Those who don't die are losing arms and legs to frostbite." Churchill's face had taken on his famous pugnacious look. "Our Norwegian and Balkan gambits worked."

Roosevelt listened intently. "So, what do you expect that Eden will accomplish in Moscow?"

Churchill shrugged. "We shall have to wait and see. My strict instructions are that we will cooperate in every way to expedite getting supplies to Stalin; that we are open to a European front, but not in 1942, probably not in 1943, and probably not until after we've driven the *Wehrmacht* from North Africa. In any event, we will remain true to our treaty and commitment to Poland so that their sovereignty over their territory is non-negotiable. That takes Stalin's territorial aims off the table, and he won't like that." He chuckled. "I have no doubt that Comrade Joseph will try to put them back on the table."

Roosevelt nodded solemnly. "I think so too. But my position is already firmly stated in Article Four of that elusive Atlantic Charter. This war is about democracy, and you can't have democracy if people aren't free to live where they choose. That principle is one we won't negotiate away."

"I quite agree with you."

The car turned onto 17th Street. To the left, the Washington Monument rose in ghostly splendor against the night sky. "Would you mind if we stopped for a moment?" Churchill asked.

When the car had halted, Churchill gazed through the windows at the monument and along the mall to the Capitol, captivated by seeing the American capital doused in the same blackout darkness of London. Then he turned to look in the opposite direction, past a reflecting pool glimmering in ambient light, to the marble stairs leading to a stately Grecian edifice in which, in the darkness, he could only imagine the statue of Abraham Lincoln sitting in eternal contemplation. Ahead of them, the White House stood, barely visible.

"This is such a grand city," the prime minister mused quietly, "a fitting capital for a great country, even if shrouded by a world at war. If my father had been American instead of my mother, I might have been here much sooner." As the car resumed travel, he added, "It's not lost on me that I'm visiting the house we Brits burned down a hundred and twenty-odd years ago."

"Let's keep history where it belongs, in the past," Roosevelt replied, adding, "so long as we learn from it." Then he turned to fully face Churchill. "Is there any other immediate issue you'd like to mention before the news gaggle descends on us?"

Churchill nodded. "I must visit Ottawa after we've finished our business here. My purpose is to acquire Canadian acceptance and support for whatever we agree upon here and work out any vagaries. That might require a return trip to Washington before I go home."

He paused and eyed the president matter-of-factly. "You know what is chief on my mind. I am concerned that we coordinate strategy to seize victory in Europe before turning our focus to Japan, which is not to say that we neglect the Far East. I fear that, due to America's understandable desire to avenge Pearl Harbor—and that was only two weeks ago—the urge will be to put all effort into defeating Japan to the neglect of the European theater, which includes North Africa. I feel that would be a mistake.

"Our people of the United Kingdom have been at war since October 1939—just over two full years. We survived the Battle of Britain and the *blitz*. We're weakened, but we set the battlefield by maneuvering to bog down many of Hitler's divisions in the Balkans and the Soviet Union. He's in a war he cannot win—unless the US focuses its attention on the Pacific war, thus allowing him to win in the west. And Britain can't defeat him alone. Jointly going after Germany first, we can then turn our combined attention to the east. But going after Japan first, I fear, would waste precious resources and prolong the war or lose it altogether."

The prime minister shifted in his seat to face the president more directly. "For all its naval and military prowess, Japan cannot threaten the homelands of the United States or Great Britain. But the German wolf still growls at our doorstep."

They rode in silence for a few minutes, and then Churchill said, "There is another action which I believe to be crucial but which I understand will be difficult for the United States to carry out at the moment."

"Shoot."

The prime minister took a deep breath. "I'd like to see you post up to six divisions in the north of Ireland. The shipping to get the troops and equipment there is a critically limiting factor, but that should be done as soon as possible to dissuade Hitler from advancing on the UK from the north and make him fear an invasion from that direction. We'll pin down more forces in that part of the world that our troops won't have to fight elsewhere. I doubt that your troops would see much action there, but stationing them that way would shape the battlefield in our favor."

He paused a moment. "I have three papers I wrote to my chiefs of staff committee while on the voyage. They contain my personal thoughts on the conduct of the war. I shall deliver them to you in the morning, if you like, for your perusal and comment."

Roosevelt listened intently, unblinking. "I'll read them immediately."

The car pulled in front of the White House gates. The president glanced at the stately mansion and then smiled at Churchill. "We've arrived."

A surprised world thrilled to see the two statesmen, familiar figures who had dominated headlines for years and now were formal allies, standing side by side at the White House front entrance, bathed in spotlights, and posing for the press. Roosevelt, even in his leg braces, stood a head taller than his counterpart.

Churchill, robust but weary and true to his love of military uniforms, wore a double-breasted peacoat and a cap with a Brotherhood of Trinity House crest, signifying his membership among the royal keepers of lighthouses and providers of pilots to navigate northern Europe's waterways. In one hand, the prime minister held his cane with the light at the bottom. In the other, he held his cigar out of sight at his side until news reporters' camera bulbs had stopped flashing. Then, as he walked with Roosevelt, who was now safely ensconced in his wheelchair, he put the cigar back in his mouth.

5

December 23, 1941
The White House, Washington, DC

Roosevelt and Churchill gathered in the late afternoon in a conference room with their military advisers. As dusk approached amid pointedly frank and open discussion, Churchill sensed a glimmer of hope for resolving his greatest strategic issue in the way he preferred: seeking victory in Europe first.

Last night, after retiring for the evening, he had looked out his window in the Blue Room, which was temporarily modified to be his living quarters. Instead of bright lights outlining thoroughfares and illuminating monuments, the city was cloaked in darkness, with only ambient reflections off the sides of buildings, dimmed headlamps on cars, and occasional Christmas lights, the result of wartime blackouts.

"The war finally touches you, America," he murmured.

At breakfast with the president and First Lady Eleanor this morning, he had turned to her when a meal that included two eggs was placed in front of him. "That's twice as many as our people see in a week these days," he said. Mrs. Roosevelt had refrained from open reaction.

Most of the day had been taken up in greeting well-wishers until the afternoon meeting where the historic strategic priorities of the newborn Grand Alliance had been hammered out. Then, earlier this evening, after leaving their meeting, and as the sun began to set, Churchill pushed Roosevelt's wheelchair through the White House.

"That was an early Christmas present for you," the president said. "We are agreed that victory in Europe must be our first aim."

Churchill smiled. "I'll take it with profound thanks, but obviously, we have much more to work out. Your chaps are still intent on an early cross-channel invasion of the mainland through France. I think that would result in a bloodbath for us and French civilians, not to mention the lack of ships, landing craft, and air superiority that are imperative to success. We should secure our position in North Africa first. Then we'll use it as a base to launch an all-out assault through southern France."

They passed through the Oval Office into the president's private study, and while Roosevelt wheeled behind his desk, the prime minister settled into a comfortable chair. "The German empire is like a crocodile," Churchill continued. "Its head is in Europe, with the brain residing in Berlin. Its tail is in the Middle East, and it's flailing, hoping to take Egypt and the Suez Canal. If that happens, our supply line from the Far East is cut off.

"Anyone can see that the most effective way to kill a crocodile is to attack its soft underbelly, and that's across North Africa, from Morocco to the Suez Canal, and that's where the fight is now, in Libya."

The president listened with one hand stroking his jaw

while he scanned a message awaiting him on his desk. "I understand your point, but we'd like to get this war finished and put to bed. You're talking about a protracted effort that could take years."

"Agreed," Churchill replied, "but I don't see any shortcuts that will bring an early victory. Our army has been fighting in North Africa since immediately after Dunkirk, a year and a half ago. If we invade Europe anytime soon, we'll leave a seasoned enemy on our flank, which will then be able to seize the Suez and launch a counterattack across the Mediterranean, because we'd have pulled our troops fighting in Libya and protecting the Suez to support the invasion in France. At present, Rommel still has the Libyan oilfields."

Roosevelt's jaw tightened as he listened, still holding the message in his hand. "I have another piece of news to share. This just came in. General MacArthur is vacating Manila with his headquarters and family, and he's moving them to Bataan." He met Churchill's troubled gaze.

"I don't understand, Franklin. Why were Douglas' air assets still parked on the ground? He had plenty of time to evacuate with all his forces to Corregidor before the Japanese attacked them."

Roosevelt sighed deeply. "I don't know. If he were anyone else, I'd probably have fired him. Maybe I leave him there because he's so popular with the public—they'd clamor loudly, and right now, he's the only hero we've got in this war." He grunted. "Or maybe because the three of us—you, me, and Douglas—share the same maternal great-great-grandmother."

Churchill eyed him without expression. "Hmph. It's probably good that we don't speak about that tidbit often.

This war can't be seen as a family affair. Getting back to it, Japan is making fast progress."

"As you say, Winston, we still have much to work out, and I'm sure that by now, Comrade Stalin has weighed in with Secretary Eden, pressing his views on the best approach to victory in Europe." He looked at his watch. "We still have time to freshen up before Eleanor and I distribute gifts to our staff and then light the Christmas tree. If you don't mind, I'd like you to say a few words to the American public at the ceremony. We'll be on the radio."

Thousands of people braved the wintry cold for the tree-lighting ceremony, straining to see the two statesmen together in silhouette against the warm background of White House lights within the South Portico. Accompanying them were members of the staff and the British delegation. People at the front of the crowds pressed against the security fences, recently increased from three feet to six feet high by the Secret Service.

Amid oohs and ahs, the president signaled, and the twinkling, colored lights flickered on. Then, he stood in front of the radio microphones and addressed millions in America and those listening across the globe. "Our strongest weapon against this war is the conviction of the dignity and brotherhood of man which Christmas Day signifies—more than any other day or any other symbol," he said. "Against enemies who preach the principles of hate and practice them, we set our faith in human love and in God's care for us and all men everywhere."

While Roosevelt spoke, Churchill stood at his side, and when he had finished, the president gestured for the prime minister to step in front of the mics. True to form and in his sonorous voice, Churchill addressed in profound terms the grim conditions and suffering brought on by the war. "I spend this anniversary and festival far from my country, far from my family, and yet I cannot truthfully say that I feel far from home... On this strange Christmas Eve, let the children have their night of fun and laughter. Let the gifts of Father Christmas delight their play. Let us grownups share to the full in their unstinted pleasure before we turn again to the stern tasks and formidable year that lies before us. Resolve that by our sacrifice and daring these same children shall not be robbed of their inheritance or denied the right to live in a free and decent world."

The crowds cheered, the statesmen, politicians, and staff waved, and after thirty-five minutes, the ceremony was over. Churchill retired to the Blue Room, and once more stood before the window, staring solemnly, with a cigar between his lips.

Christmas Day, 1941

Early in the afternoon, after the president and the prime minister had attended church services together at the National Cathedral and following a sumptuous Christmas dinner with all the trimmings, the two of them gathered with three other men in Roosevelt's private study next to the Oval Office. "At last, we get together," Roosevelt intoned, "the four of us." He glanced across his desk at British Army Captain Paul Littlefield. "Are we adding another member to our 'band of brothers,' and making it five?"

"I'll vouch for him," General William Donovan, the president's communications director, chimed in. "He performed well when he went with me to the Balkans back in February. If Little Bill doesn't want him, I'll take him." The general, dubbed "Big Bill" by the president and called "Wild Bill" by his friends, had earned the nation's highest military honor, the Congressional Medal of Honor, as well as multiple other awards for valor in the last war. Tall, muscular, with practiced military bearing, a square jaw, and white hair, he served as the president's eyes and ears on far-flung missions.

"Captain Littlefield gets muddled over moral dilemmas and sometimes lets his tongue loose ahead of clear thinking," Bill Stephenson interjected. The corners of his mouth turned up in a hint of a smile. "But I'll keep him around, for amusement, if for nothing else."

Stephenson, nicknamed "Little Bill' by the president for his small physique, sat next to Paul in a semi-circular row of chairs in front of the desk, but he loomed large in behind-the-scenes maneuvering of international affairs. As director of the British Security Coordination office that fronted as the British Passport Office, he was Paul's boss and the man who ran the vast British intelligence operation headquartered at Rockefeller Center in Manhattan, with appendages in every part of the world.

As a pilot and intelligence officer in World War I, he had forged a remarkable reputation for courage, tenacity, and competence. Because in subsequent years he had become a successful industrialist with world-wide interests in advanced technology, Churchill had asked Stephenson to establish the organization in anticipation of a German effort to invade Great Britain.

Through Stephenson and Donovan, the two heads of state had secretly cooperated since 1939 to prepare the United States for war with either Germany, Japan, or both.

Public opinion in America had been isolationist, and Roosevelt had campaigned for re-election on the basis of staying out of the war, but Churchill saw the conflict as unwinnable without the United States' military and industrial might. The attack on Pearl Harbor had settled the matter.

Stephenson had recruited Paul as a walking archive, to provide first-hand knowledge of Stephenson's activities in the event of the spymaster's incapacity or demise. Paul's position had gradually morphed to additional duties as an aide and confidante.

Now Churchill watched and listened with amusement to the banter at Paul's expense and observed the officer's stoic reaction. "He'll do in a pinch," the prime minister said as his contribution to Paul's discomfort. "Shall we move on?"

The president leaned back in his chair and chuckled. "The trouble with you, Winston, is that you have no sense of humor. All right, let's get down to business."

Paul breathed an imperceptible sigh of relief for the shift of the figurative spotlight. He had become accustomed to and sometimes joined in the banter between Wild Bill and Little Bill. But being the subject of that repartee, in front of the president and prime minister no less, was not his idea of fun.

Paul was of medium height and build, with brown eyes, dirty blond hair, a straight nose, and strong chin. Being that his assignment with Stephenson was top secret, his family had no idea of his whereabouts, and with their parents being isolated on German-occupied Sark Island, communicating with them had become all but impossible. He missed them.

"Well," Roosevelt said gravely, opening the discussion, "we are where we are in this war. The Japs surprised us, but we did well in maneuvering Hitler after he attacked Great Britain. He's already encountering our strongest weapon to date, the Russian winter." He fixed his eyes on Churchill. "So, Mr. Prime Minister, you got your priority for going after Germany first, and that wasn't an easy concession. The American people want to see Japan pay for its treachery."

"And I believe they shall. You can count on my country to pursue that end with all vigor. We will be better positioned for that when Hitler and his regime have been disposed of. The big question in front of us now is *when* do we re-invade Europe? You know my feelings. I don't see the possibility of that happening in the coming year or even in the year after that with any hope of success. Your military must re-build, train, and deploy. Ours must be re-supplied."

Churchill continued, "If we don't defeat Germany in North Africa first, we leave our southern flank wide open to attack. Our lifeline from the Far East through the Suez and the Mediterranean would be lost. Having then been victorious in North Africa, the *Wehrmacht* will be poised to counter us in Europe from the south. Our invasion on the Continent through France would be a bloodbath. In that scenario, military and civilian deaths are incalculable."

Roosevelt sat silently pondering the prime minister's words. Finally, he raised his palms in a placating gesture. "I understand your position. I don't necessarily agree, but I see the rationale. Our joint teams will study the issue thoroughly in the coming days.

But we need to talk about one aspect quite clearly."

The president took a moment to gather his thoughts, choosing his words carefully. "General Marshall, my army chief of staff, says that the shortest distance between two points is a straight line. He often refers to London and Berlin when he says that. He and most of my senior military advisers think that we can move in and make short work of the *Wehrmacht* in Germany, decapitate the snake in Berlin, and then turn attention to North Africa. I know Rommel gave your guys a rough time at Tobruk, but on the other hand, he was tied up there fighting you and now he's in retreat. If we can keep him occupied, then when we've mopped up on the Continent, we can reinforce in North Africa, finish that off, and move on to finish off things in the Far East."

Churchill took his time to respond. "As you say, Mr. President, our staffs will discuss matters thoroughly over the next few days. I'm not confident that we've heard the last of Rommel, and mark my words, any invasion through France will be a bloody, intense slugfest. It should occur only after we've marshaled every asset at our disposal and achieved air superiority over Europe."

Roosevelt took his time to respond, his eyes locked directly on Churchill's. He spoke slowly and carefully. "Yes, but there's an aspect that you should be aware of if you're not already: your insistence on engagement in the Mediterranean is seen as a possible diversion from the objective of freeing Europe, with your intent being to preserve the British Empire by preserving your dominance over Egypt and India. If you lose those two countries, the empire crumbles.

"From the perspective of those of my advisers who hold that position, the principle of fighting for freedom, which our citizens believe we are doing, is antithetical to the notion of one country holding imperial sway over four-hundred-million people on the other side of the planet. And don't forget that a people's right to self-determination is included as one of the fourteen tenets in the Atlantic Charter.

"At present, I take neither side about whether we invade North Africa or Europe first, and I won't take a position until we've had a thorough airing. But you should be aware of the views as I just outlined them."

For several moments, the prime minister and the president stared into each other's eyes with blank expressions. Stephenson and Donovan held their silence. Paul sat stock still.

At last, Churchill spoke. "Mr. President, I am, of all people, a believer in and defender of the good that the British Empire has brought to the world. But now we confront an evil which could bring down every foundation of every civilization on God's green earth. My comment to your advisers would be that the first consideration now must be defeating that evil. I don't question America's motives. I have made mine plain."

Roosevelt took a deep breath and let it out slowly. "I'll pass along your comments, and I'll remain open to both sides of the discussion until our shared strategy is firmly established. When that happens, we'll reasonably expect each other and our allies to support the strategy, whichever way it goes."

He leaned back in his wheelchair and, with a distant look, took in the understated trappings of power in his study while he gathered his thoughts. "Having said that, Winston, regardless of the path taken, please know that you have a personal friend in me. We are likely to disagree on many points throughout this war, and friendship must never sway our considerations except as they lend confidence in each other's good intentions and judgment, but after decisions are made, count on me for personal support, come hell or high water."

Churchill had sat hunched in his seat, listening without

expression. "You honor me," he replied, "and I reciprocate. Now, regarding the part of the Atlantic Charter you mentioned, how that tenet is interpreted and applied is still an open question. I've heard from Antony Eden regarding his negotiations with Molotov in Moscow. Stalin is taking a hard line. He's pushing for post-war borders to remain as they were when Hitler abrogated the non-aggression pact. That would leave him with half of Poland, and he won't entertain a discussion about the three Baltic states on the basis that Latvia, Lithuania, and Estonia joined the Soviet Union by plebiscite."

Roosevelt sighed. "We do have some bumpy roads ahead, don't we? Is a plebiscite valid when conducted at the point of a gun? All of that will have to be sorted out." He forced a bright smile. "But the war is still young."

Paul stirred in his seat; the implications of the drama he had just witnessed were not lost on him. The president noticed and, as if glad for a diversion, asked Paul, "Did you have a question?"

Not sure that the president had addressed him personally, Paul hesitated. Then when Roosevelt's eyes bored into him, he replied, "No, sir. I'm here to listen—"

"Speak," Churchill interjected, seemingly also happy for the departure from the high-stakes exchange. "If you have a question, let's hear it."

Paul glanced cautiously at Stephenson, who chuckled and nodded. "You've not kept silent before," he said. "Don't let this august gathering intimidate you."

Paul nodded and faced the president. "I'm curious about how you mobilized so rapidly, Mr. President. When the war started in Europe, America's army was ranked eighteenth in the world with antiquated and insufficient weaponry, no industry that supported wide armaments production, and a public that was completely opposed to being in the war. Lend-Lease passed only nine months ago, but almost immediately after signing it, you were sending Liberty ships to England loaded with supplies, and now you're arming Great Britain as well as the Soviet Union. Not even three weeks have passed since Pearl Harbor, yet you seem confident of your country's ability to conduct military operations on two fronts, far from home. How did you mobilize so quickly?"

The room was quiet when Paul had finished. Donovan was the first to speak. "That's a great question, and if Paul is to be a memory of these events for the benefit of future generations, then he should have a thorough answer." He turned to the president. "Sir, you've assigned me to do an inspection tour for you of our arms factories, supply depots, transportation lines and hubs, recruiting and training facilities, and anything else that contributes to the war effort. I'd like to take Captain Littlefield along so he can see for himself how we mobilized." He shifted his eyes to Churchill and Stephenson. "With your permission."

"I think that's a grand idea," Roosevelt enthused. He directed his attention to Paul. "Let me give a short answer to your question, and let's give credit where it's due. Your prime minister had a lot to do with the rapid construction of the Liberty ships." He gestured to Churchill, who accepted the acknowledgment with a slight bow of his head.

The president continued. "British shipbuilders provided the design and contracted with Henry Kaiser to have new shipyards constructed, the first one in California. Then the ships themselves. Kaiser used mass production and assembly line concepts used for consumer items, like automobiles. No one had thought to do that in shipbuilding before. He cut production time and cost to a fraction of what they had been." He shifted his attention back to Churchill. "Are you happy with the product?"

"Very," the prime minister responded, "and with the provisions they bring to our shores. They held off starvation for our people and kept us in the war."

"Good." The president turned his eyes back to Paul. "That project alone makes the point that the war will be won in the factories. The military that's backed by the fastest and greatest production of weapons and supplies will win. There's no combination of countries in the world right now that outproduces the United States, and I have other secret weapons besides Kaiser, including Bill Knudsen, K. T. Keller, and Don Nelson, among others." He gestured toward Donovan. "Wild Bill can fill you in on what I mean later." Glancing at Churchill and Stephenson, he added, "That is, if you'll allow the captain to accompany the general on his inspection tour."

"I have no objection," Stephenson said.

Churchill nodded his agreement.

"Good then," Donovan said, addressing a startled Paul. "We'll leave the day after tomorrow, early. Bring a bag. We'll be gone for a few days."

"Changing the subject," Churchill said to Stephenson, "how are the projects up in Canada? Are the Hydra and Camp X coming along as we'd hoped?"

"They are sir. The Canadian government provided all assistance. Our new spy school is in operation, as is our new communications capability. With Hydra, we can send and receive encrypted radio messages as easily between North America and Europe as we can between North and South America. There is no current communications facility that is its equal."

"I've observed the training at Camp X," Donovan broke

in. "It's patterned on the spy schools in England and Scotland. We know their success. This one in Canada should yield similar results. The FBI sends people there now, and I'll be doing the same with OSS recruits. And since the US is now *in* the war, I'll be setting up similar schools inside our own borders."

"Operations are being planned, trained for, and rehearsed there now," Stephenson interjected. "For purposes of deniability, I think I should say no more at this point, but when they occur, they will be notable."

For a matter of seconds, no one spoke. Then, Roosevelt, who had intermittently peered at Churchill with concern throughout the discussion, remarked, "Winston, you're looking tired. Are you feeling all right?"

Churchill brushed aside the observation with a wave of his hand. "I just did a long ocean voyage. I don't recover as fast as I once did."

"All right, gentlemen. Thank you for coming. We can adjourn. Enjoy the rest of your Christmas." He directed another searching glance at Churchill. "And Mr. Prime Minister, please get some rest. You've got that big speech before Congress tomorrow."

6

Late the following night, Winston Churchill heard his name called seemingly from a distance, as though through a mist. He opened his eyes and found his vision blurred. Looking wildly about, he focused on a face in front of him that he did not recognize but became clearer as seconds ticked by.

The face bore an anxious expression, but then moved aside, and Roosevelt leaned over him with Eleanor. "You've suffered a heart attack, Winston. The doctor says you'll recover, but you need relaxation."

Churchill lay still while the president's words registered. He remembered pain in his chest. It had been sudden and severe, but he recalled no details of the minutes before or after the onset. He struggled to sit up.

"Don't worry," Roosevelt admonished. "Your medical situation is known by only a few, and it's classified as top-secret. But you need time to get well."

"I can't," Churchill gasped. "Tomorrow—"

He found himself unable to speak and so relaxed into his pillow. Events of the day and evening floated through his mind. Only hours ago, he had been at the rostrum inside the chamber of the US House of Representatives, addressing the imposing body at a joint session of Congress. The floor had been packed, with extra chairs brought in to accommodate all legislative members, the president's cabinet, and senior staff. In the gallery, people had crowded together, and those on the front leaned over the edge of the balcony to see and hear, sensing history in the making.

Punctuated by loud applause and several standing ovations, Churchill had spoken for a little over half an hour. In his opening remarks, he reminded his audience of his American ancestry through his mother, and that despite his aristocratic lineage, he had been taught by his father to always be a man of the people with a duty to serve them, emphasizing his belief in the notion memorialized at Gettysburg, Pennsylvania, of a government of, by, and for the people.

"...here in Washington in these memorable days," he said, "I have found an Olympian fortitude which, far from being based upon complacency, is only the mask of an inflexible purpose and the proof of a sure, well-grounded confidence in the final outcome. We in Britain had the same feeling in our darkest days. We too were sure that in the end all would be well...

"...The forces ranged against us are enormous. They are bitter, they are ruthless. The wicked men and their factions, who have launched their peoples on the path of war and conquest, know that they will be called to terrible account if they cannot beat down by force of arms the peoples they have assailed. They will stop at nothing...

"...to me the best tidings of all—the United States, united as never before, has drawn the sword for freedom and cast away the scabbard.

"All these tremendous facts have led the subjugated peoples of Europe to lift up their heads again in hope. They have put aside forever the shameful temptation of resigning themselves to the conqueror's will. Hope has returned to the hearts of scores of millions of men and women, and with that hope there burns the flame of anger against the brutal, corrupt invader...

"It is not given to us to peer into the mysteries of the future. Still, I avow my hope and faith, sure and inviolate, that in the days to come the British and American peoples will, for their own safety and for the good of all, walk together in majesty, in justice and in peace."

Thunderous applause had erupted and continued seemingly interminably, and as Churchill made his slow way back through the House to the exit, members of the audience surged for a chance to shake the hand of this lion of a man. As for the prime minister, he felt growing fatigue, and was glad to finally escape from the House into the president's limousine.

"You look a bit piqued," Roosevelt observed as his convoy proceeded along Pennsylvania Avenue to the White House. "You've had some particularly active weeks. Maybe you should cancel plans for tomorrow and just rest."

That was when pain had pierced the center of Churchill's chest and spread down his left arm. After that, he remembered nothing until seeing Roosevelt leaning over him.

"You need rest," the president said flatly. "We're clearing tomorrow's schedule."

Churchill shook his head and once again struggled to sit up. Failing that, he grasped the president's arm. "Tomorrow. It's already tomorrow in London," he panted. "I can't be ill now. Tomorrow—today—our chaps, our commandos—go again. Into Norway. They're probably there now. This time, it's serious."

7

December 27, 1941
Vågsøy, Norway

Corporal George Peel peered over the rail of the small barge as it approached the island in the pre-dawn hours. Large swells splashed against the sides of the boat, heaving it in rhythmic motion with occasional erratic lurches. The starless sky closed in with early morning mists, and aside from the sounds of the sea, all was quiet. The vessel's crew had doused the engine and remained inside their cabin while the commandos waited in silence. Their mission would execute at dawn.

George was but one of five hundred and seventy fighting men from No. 3 Commando, two troops of No. 2 Commando, a medical detachment of No. 4 Commando, and a demolition party of 101 Troop from No. 6 Commando that would land by canoe, and a dozen interpreters from Norwegian Independent Company 1. They had departed their wardrooms, leaving Christmas decorations still hanging from their walls, and boarded the converted landing ships *Prince Charles* and *Prince Leopold* for the voyage. The Royal Navy's light cruiser HMS *Kenya*, with destroyers HMS *Onslow, Oribi, Offa, and Chiddingfold*, accompanied them for fire support. A submarine, the HMS *Tuna,* sat off the coast to provide navigational support. The Royal Air Force provided a squadron of bombers to round out the combined operation.

The crossing had been uneventful, with some commandos sleeping, some playing cards, some reading, and still more incessantly checking their equipment, each man dealing with the knowledge of the hair-raising operation that lay ahead. Twenty-two-year-old George had never thought of himself as a tough warrior or anything extraordinary at all. Nearly a year ago, he had answered a public call from Winston Churchill for five thousand volunteers for "special service of a hazardous nature."

Its objectives were mystifying, but the major qualifications were clear: the candidates had to be men of high intelligence, physical fitness, initiative, and spirit. The service took all comers, but performance was the discriminator, and those not able to meet training standards were returned to their units. The commandos called it being RTU'd, a humiliation that made even strong men cry when it happened to them.

The resulting organization became a cross-section of British young men: high-brow, low-bred, blacksmiths, clerks, some with minimum required education, others with advanced degrees—independent-minded men who would take the fight to the enemy. Many came from prison, granted reprieves in exchange for life-threatening service. All were stripped of rank on reaching their training locations and had to earn whatever rank they achieved. A solid requirement for advancement was that anyone being promoted had to perform better than those they led. Further, sergeants carried more than privates and corporals, and officers carried more than sergeants, expecting that they would all be doing the same fighting, side by side, a band of brothers.

Instead of barracks on bases, they were allotted a daily sum and told to find their own lodging, no simple feat in small villages where the only housing was with families having spare rooms that they were willing to rent out. Many villagers welcomed the commandos into their homes while refusing payment.

George remembered well his arrival for training; his troop set off immediately on a fifty-mile hike with each man carrying fifty-five pounds of equipment. That grueling exercise brought on doubts about his fortitude and courage. He thought he would die.

In subsequent days the troop had tromped mile after mile over rugged Scottish Highlands, scaled steep mountain peaks, and then rappelled off cliffs that plunged to pristine lakes or the seacoast far below. Often during such exercises, they wore their gas masks to become familiar with them.

Aiming to accomplish any task at twice the speed of the regular army, they developed endurance and learned orienteering and direction-finding. On many occasions, at the end of a long hike, they had been marched into the sea above chin-level before being ordered to turn about and return to the beach. Their endurance objective was achieved when they were able to climb a mountain at a rate of a thousand feet per hour.

On the ranges, they fired every infantry weapon in the British inventory, even shooting the Boyes anti-tank rifle from a standing position and two-inch mortars from their hips—with the attendant threats of shattered bones in their upper and lower regions. Then they punished each other's bodies in hand-to-hand combat, practicing disarming and dispatching a foe swiftly, frequently with his own weapon. Among other killing techniques, they learned to grab the front edge of an enemy's helmet from behind and jerk it backward so that the rear edge jammed into the base of the man's neck, snapping his spine. And they learned how to wield a knife against vital parts of the body to exact instant death. Among the techniques George had learned, the most efficient and silent method was to creep up on a foe from behind and slash his throat.

When he and his commando mates had mastered those and other military skills and exercised urban and rural tactics, they were sent on mock spy missions in the surrounding countryside, partly to hone their abilities and partly to keep themselves busy; roughly five thousand commandos trained and waiting without an assigned mission, until the public relations foray into Lofoten.

In one instance, the objective assigned to a small group had been to locate and waylay Earl Mountbatten's daughter. To provide physical proof of mission accomplished, she gave her "captors" a handkerchief.

In another mock raid, the commandos "captured" a brigadier general of the regular army. His senior commanders and staff were not amused.

Nine months passed without another mission since Lofoten. Until now.

Still waiting in the dark and staring across the expanse of water, George chuckled at the recollections, and then saw lights flickering on shore. He thought they must be from fishermen just getting up—or they could be German soldiers doing the same. He reached down and fingered his finely designed and machined knife. Its blade was long, slender, razor sharp; and it was black with a matching handle to prevent reflection from ambient light. It had been specially designed for commandos, and one each had been presented at graduation.

George also checked his "Tommy gun," the same model Thompson submachine gun favored by Al Capone, the famous American gangster in Chicago. One each had also been issued to every commando.

Although he had paid strict attention and practiced aggressively during the sessions on how to kill an enemy in a shoot-out or in hand-to-hand combat, he could not envision actually doing it. The thought of killing another man from a distance with a firearm seemed alien despite the many hours he had spent training to do exactly that. And despite the militarily unconventional freedom of training and the time that had elapsed after completing the course in an atmosphere of a highly spirited boys' camp, George could hardly envision using his lethal skills, particularly up close with his knife.

The commandos called their methods "dirty fighting," taking their foes unaware from the rear. An extension of the concept was establishing "killing zones" in which the commandos shot anything that moved. While some commandos trained their weapons on the killing zone, their comrades maneuvered along the perimeter to drive unsuspecting enemy into the field of fire.

George's thoughts caused him to wonder fleetingly

about the cruelty of war and his participation in it. Then images crossed his mind of dogfights over Britain and the horrors of the bombings during the many months of the *blitz* when whole cities, including London, Liverpool, and Coventry, were brought to ruin with the horrifying deaths of tens of thousands. His country had been nearly brought to her knees. *Our tactics are no dirtier than that.*

He reminded himself that a commando contingency mission existed to engage in guerrilla warfare against the Nazis inside the British Isles if and when they invaded. *We save our people by taking the fight to the enemy.*

So, here he was, in the dark, off the coast of Norway, on a wet, surf-tossed barge in freezing weather, preparing to attack German gun emplacements and engage in house-to-house street-fighting in the small town of Måløy, on Vågsøy Island. His commander, Captain Jarles, stood next to him. Neither spoke, nor did anyone else, everyone straining to hear the slightest sound that would signal that they had been discovered, or the start of combat.

Intelligence had informed that Måløy was garrisoned with unseasoned soldiers despite its heavily fortified gun positions. The guns protected a large fish processing plant producing glycerin and Vitamin A for the Germans. The gun emplacements and processing plant were to be destroyed.

Boom, boom, boom! Three massive rounds from the main guns of the *Kenya* arced high in the heavens toward Moldøen Island. They were joined shortly by the rounds from the main guns on the destroyers *Onlsow* and *Offa*. Accurate targeting blasted fortified gun positions that erupted in blinding explosions, lighting up the dark sky.

Moments later, a coastal battery on nearby Moldøen

Island returned fire, but it was quickly silenced by another onslaught from the *Kenya*.

Someone behind George muttered, "I thought this was supposed to be a secret bloody raid."

"One advantage we'll have over the Germans is that they are recovering from Christmas hangovers," someone replied, sparking low, nervous laughter. The slow progress of early morning light spread through the mist, revealing the outlines of the coast and surrounding hills and the line of landing craft in front of and behind the one George rode in.

Then out of the darkness, musical notes floated on the salty breeze, haunting in their tenor, uplifting in their source —the thin, reedy sound of bagpipes playing "March of the Cameron Men." Commandos stared about, exchanging tense glances.

In spite of his immediate danger, George smiled, albeit grimly. That would be the nutter, Lt Col John "Mad Jack" Churchill, the bagpipe-carrying, sword-wielding, second-in-command of the raid. He was tasked with leading a force to seize Moldøen Island. The rugged-looking officer had been a male model and magazine editor in Nairobi prior to the war. Though no relation to the prime minister, Mad Jack was a legend to his men: fearless in battle, hilarious at parties, and an inspiration to those in his charge.

"Do you see anything?" a commando queried from farther back in the barge.

Another one at a porthole replied hoarsely, "There's a truck coming along the road with its headlamps on, and it appears to have a gun of some sort, maybe a machine gun mounted on the rear." The man's voice jumped an octave. "It *is* a machine gun, and he's turning it toward us." Then, amid tracers and lead whizzing past overhead, the barge's engine rumbled, it kicked into gear, and with two other boats, it headed toward shore.

"That's the first enemy fire I've seen," someone called. "It's bloody ineffectual."

"I imagine it'll get better," another replied with a grim note.

The cold, gray dawn revealed other vessels in the raid. Group 1 of the assault force with fifty commandos headed toward the coast to seize a suspected gun position north of the southern tip of Vågsøy, a mile or so before the main objective in Måløy. Finding none, they headed toward Måløy on foot.

Kenya had already ceased its salvos, and Captain Jarles ordered the crew in the Group 2 landing craft in which George rode to fire a flare that signaled Hampden bombers, orbiting a safe distance away, to drop smoke bombs at the landing sites at Måløy and Moldøen. Group 2's objective was to neutralize an anti-aircraft battery, a task requiring the commandos to scale a line of cliffs.

Then, the first tragedy struck. As three boats headed toward shore, a Hampden bomber was struck by anti-aircraft fire. Damaged and losing altitude, it dumped its cargo of smoke bombs, and they dropped into one of the wooden landing craft, setting it on fire along with several commandos. Their agonized screams rolled across the waters while comrades watched in horror and beat out the flames.

When they reached shore, their commander yelled, "You can't help them. The medics are on the way. We have a mission to execute." Then, as wounded commandos writhed in the snow to cool their burns and an aroused enemy launched blazing machine gun fire at them, the remaining commandos rushed up the bank.

Group 3, led by Mad Jack Churchill, oblivious to the tragedy that had struck and still playing his bagpipes with a Scottish broadsword at his side, continued on to Moldøen Island to finish off any remaining enemy indirect-fire guns and crews that had not been destroyed by the *Kenya's* main guns. From there, they prepared to support the main force at Måløy.

Group 4 remained on the *Kenya*, held in reserve.

As George's landing craft turned sharply and headed toward shore, he gritted his teeth and tried to control his breathing, but he found himself panting despite his best effort. *This is no exercise. How will I do?*

He was a good-looking young man, taller than most of his peers, with a firm, angular chin, round cheeks, and a perpetually friendly demeanor that reflected how he treated people. He was from a small town, Knowle Bristol, and he had attended school at St. John's. Nothing in his experience prior to the war had led him to believe in his wildest dreams that he would be a commando in the lead element of the first-ever combined operation of the British army, navy, and air force.

Behind them as the smoke cleared, two destroyers, *Onslow* and *Oribi*, slid past in the narrow channel on the other side of Moldøen Island. Group 5 with seventy-five commandos rode aboard the *Oribi*, which was to offload them at the north end of Måløy. Their tasks were to establish a blocking position across the main road leading into the town from the north, cut the telephone lines, and prevent reinforcements from arriving.

As the two destroyers cleared Moldøen, they encountered withering automatic fire from a now fully awakened German force north of Måløy. Nevertheless, they continued to their objective, but with four wounded men and minor damage.

George had watched in horror when the smoke bombs dropped into Group 2's boat from the impaired Hampden. He heard the tortured screams of burning men, some still thrashing in snowbanks, and the shouts of the commander; and he saw the remaining comrades scrambling up the bank under the weight of their weapons and equipment.

Then his boat touched shore.

Commanded by Captain Jarles, his troop's task, after overrunning the anti-aircraft position, was to turn north and support seizing the German headquarters at the Ulvesund Hotel in the center of town. As the captain prepared to lead the way uphill, George was right behind him. The captain lurched up in front of his men to lead the charge. "Come on," he yelled.

A bullet struck his forehead. He fell dead.

George stared only momentarily. In a split second, he turned from being a boy on a dangerous adventure into a blooded fighter. Rage welled. *Those bastards!*

He rushed out of the barge, his teammates behind him, running uphill, dispersing, seeking cover and concealment. They lunged below the cliffs and halted, glancing at one another while taking stock of their position in the misty first light of day.

The plan they followed had been well rehearsed, and they quickly identified the routes that would take them to the gun sites. While providing covering fire, they alternated rushes from one cover to the next, hearing the tk-tk-tk of bullets striking the snow all around them. Far from an unseasoned enemy, as Intelligence had informed, they realized they faced a crack infantry unit of veterans complete with snipers who were savvy at city-street fighting. Then, as the commandos moved uphill into the town, Messerschmidt 109 fighters screamed down on them, delivering streams of machine gun fire.

London, England

Squadron Officer Ryan Northbridge of the Women's Auxiliary Air Force hurried through the underground corridors of Whitehall to a conference room. She knocked nervously and grasped the doorknob so as to open it as soon as bidden. Hearing a voice call, "Come in," she thrust it open and glanced around a long table with serious men until she spotted Lord Louis Mountbatten. She hurried to him and whispered, "Sorry, sir. You instructed me to inform you as soon as we have word from Norway. The reports are coming in, and I'm afraid they are not good."

Mountbatten looked up sharply and nodded. Then he excused himself and followed Ryan into the hall. "What's happened," he asked as they hurried along the corridor.

"We took some early casualties," she replied without breaking stride. "And apparently that resulted from our own bombing." She filled him in with as much as she knew. "Also, the German force there is much more proficient than expected. They're giving our chaps a real row."

They arrived at a door marked "Combined Operations" and burst through, moving past rows of intent men and women operating radios, typing on machines, or otherwise busily engaged. Ryan and Mountbatten headed straight for a huge map that took up one full wall at the opposite end.

"The Operation Archery raiding force arrived on time and without incident," Ryan briefed, not waiting to be prompted. "The naval guns took out the artillery on Moldøen Island as planned, the *Kenya* stationed properly, and the destroyers moved into position as they should have." As she spoke, she pointed out the various geographical points pertinent to the mission. "They've met stiff resistance and are now engaged in house-to-house fighting," she said on finishing her report.

Mountbatten listened intently, took in a deep breath, and exhaled. "What about the commando troop on Moldøen Island? Are they prepared to reinforce?"

"They are, sir. That is Lieutenant Colonel Churchill's command. As I mentioned, the naval guns took out those on the island and there wasn't much for him to do. He's regrouping to move onto Vågsøy now."

Mountbatten stroked his chin. "I wonder if he went ashore playing his bagpipes and waving his sword." He glanced at Ryan without breaking a smile. "Good report. Thanks for breaking into the conference, and please keep me apprised." He started to leave, and then turned back around. "You know, the prime minister himself recommended your transfer here from the Group 11 Fighter Command control room." He regarded her appraisingly. "Good choice. He also told me to watch out for you—that you were somehow connected to an army intelligence officer on special assignment."

Ryan froze and then blushed slightly. She took a deep breath. "Yes, sir. That would be Captain Paul Littlefield, but I have no idea where he is or what he's doing. It's all rather frustrating." She looked around, suddenly aware of curious glances at her from others in the control room, and added, “But no more so than the challenges every Brit faces these days.”

Mountbatten smiled. “Yes. Well, we have the Americans with us now, so perhaps that will change.” He glanced about the room. “Good job, all around. I regret that the news isn’t better.” He took one more look about, said, “Keep me informed,” and returned to his conference.

8

Vågsøy, Norway

Finding little resistance at the southwestern tip of the island, the troop of commandos who landed there had worked their way east along the coast to support the main effort, and Mad Jack's troop on Moldøen Island had crossed the narrow strip of water to Måløy for the same purpose. Farther north on the fjord, a cargo barge heading out to sea and unaware of the battle that had already raged for hours encountered the *Onslow* and was quickly destroyed. Crews on three other ships moored across the fjord tried to cast off quickly, intending to ground their vessels to prevent sinking. Two succeeded. The third was sunk where she lay, a casualty of heavy naval gunfire. Meanwhile, munitions dumps, fish oil factories, and houses and other buildings where German soldiers had sought refuge were in flames. Thick smoke combined over the town, creating a dark cloud. Måløy appeared to have encountered the apocalypse.

George lay on his belly in the snow atop an embankment overlooking a row of houses. A distance behind him, the Ulvesund Hotel burned uncontrollably. The German unit putting up unexpectedly stiff resistance had turned out to be *gebirgsjäger*, mountain troops, who had come to Måløy for rest and recuperation over the Christmas holidays. They had been on a hike when the commandos struck. Some were quickly killed or captured, the latter providing information under interrogation.

Those still in combat had fought fiercely, some barricading themselves inside homes, stores, office buildings, warehouses, and any other edifices that provided defensive positions. Reluctantly, the commandos resorted to setting the establishments on fire with guards posted near the doors to capture the Germans as they rushed to escape the flames. George had taken one of those guard duties, and when several enemy soldiers rushed out of a burning house with guns firing bursts from automatic weapons, he and a companion had dispatched them from the flank. None of the Germans survived. George was unscathed, but he emptied his gut into the snow.

Such had also been the fate of the *Wehrmacht* soldiers defending the headquarters at the Ulvesund. The hotel now smoldered in charred ruin.

George peered over the ridge of the hill where he rested. Heavy firing gave way to sporadic shooting in the village that lay below along the coast. Several nearby companions from his troop were also prone, surveilling the neighborhood. They had climbed through the town and fought hard against the *gebirgsjäger,* most of whom were now subdued. But George and his companions had worked up a sweat, and now, as they observed the incongruously tranquil scene, a freezing wind swept over them from behind.

George felt icy talons seeping through his combat uniform, moist from sweat. The moisture collected in wet rivulets coating his body, sending piercing cold through his skin to his bones. Soon, he was shivering, and then his teeth began to chatter. Glancing at his companions, he saw that they too reacted to the freezing weather.

Sweeping his vision across the landscape below, he studied the house closest to them. It showed no signs of life, but a wisp of smoke rose from its chimney, and its front door was on the near side. Getting to it required descending an exposed hill, clambering over a four-foot fence, and dropping an equal distance to a road below.

The risk seemed worthwhile. Staying where they were could result in frostbite, hypothermia, or worse.

Calling softly to the others and pointing to the house, he saw them nod in response. Forcing his aching body to his knees, he glanced about rapidly.

No enemy responded.

He tensed his muscles, sprang forward, rushing over the crest, and ran headlong down the hill. On reaching the fence, he vaulted over it and dropped to the road. Then, rushing across the street, he dived to the ground by the corner of the house and peered back the way he had come.

He had met no resistance.

He signaled back to his companions, and one by one, they followed his route until all were safe by the house. Then, exercising similar procedures and caution, they entered it.

All was quiet inside—and warm. They stayed low, lying on the floor, listening. From somewhere below them, perhaps in a basement, they heard momentary scuffling, and then whimpering, as if from a child. It quickly ceased.

A new and pleasant sensation wafted on the air—whiffs of Christmas spices and baking—and looking around, they gazed in awe on a cut fir tree adorned with wreaths, tinsel, and colorful glass balls, the decorations of a wondrous, globally shared celebration.

Above them on a dining table, a bowl of fruit sat near the edge. The commandos had not eaten in more than twenty-four hours and were suddenly famished. They ate the fruit and then found some cakes also on the table.

While downing an apple, George took in the room. Time had passed to mid-morning, but no lights were on, and the sun's angle left the room in shadows. Nevertheless, he noticed a tiny silver box resting on a side table. When he took a closer look, he saw a cross etched onto its lid. He reached for it and examined it. Turning it over, he noticed the word "Matthew" engraved on its bottom.

Suddenly, the day's horrors raced across his mind in vivid detail: the smoke bombs dropping into the landing craft and his fellow commandos writhing in the snow; his captain shot dead in front of him; his own taking of several human lives as the German soldiers had rushed out of a burning building he guarded. Overcome with revulsion of what he had seen and done, he opened the silver box. Inside were tiny slivers of paper, and on them were printed New Testament verses.

"I need this today," George muttered, slipping the box into his pocket. "This is for me."

Shortly, a rocket from the *Kenya* signaled that the raid was ending and the commandos should rally for departure at the harbor. That meant traversing the main street rapidly where German holdouts would likely train automatic fire on them. Nevertheless, the signal was a welcome sound, bringing a sense of relief.

George and his companions emerged outside and headed back toward the center of town. They moved quickly but cautiously, taking special care at intersections and around corners. Arriving near the center of town, they proceeded on, scurrying from cover to cover, and then came under enemy fire.

They dispersed quickly, and George darted into an alley. He was alone there, with no cover or concealment in sight. He kept going until he was out of the line of fire, and then hugged the near wall.

Moving along with his back to it, he came to a door and was about to bypass it when he noticed it crack open. Stepping back immediately, he saw it continue to open by millimeters at a time. *No civilian would do that.*

Glancing up the street again in the off chance of having missed some means of concealing himself but finding none, he reached down along his leg and gripped his black commando knife, removing it from its sheath.

Pivoting swiftly in front of the door, he kicked it open and lunged with his knife.

A shaft of daylight fell across the eyes of a very young German soldier in agony.

George had struck his blade upward from below the ribs into the soldier's heart. The soldier stared into George's eyes as the light in them faded, and then he fell onto his back, holding the knife's handle. His heels drummed the floor as life faded.

Appalled at what he had done, George left the knife. Having plunged it into the gut of another man, he found himself incapable of pulling it back out. The German continued to stare up at him, sightless. George stumbled out into the alley and worked his way alone toward the rally point.

9

December 28,1941
Washington, DC

"I hope you're feeling better today," President Roosevelt greeted Prime Minister Churchill as the two met for breakfast in the small dining room adjacent to the president's private study.

"Much better, thank you. Yesterday's rest did a world of good, and I appreciate the arrangements you made to keep my communications open with my staff."

Roosevelt cast him a sidelong glance. "You need to take care of yourself, Winston. I fear that this old world would fare sadly if you were to leave us at this moment."

Churchill chuckled. "Many would be happy to see my departure, including some among my countrymen." He reached for his cup of coffee. "But I can't leave just yet. I'm on to address the Canadian House of Commons in a few days, and they won't take kindly to being snubbed since I spoke in your House of Representatives."

Roosevelt laughed. "Your speech to Congress was well

received, and the American people loved it. I hear that in London, your people have another reason to celebrate—a tremendous victory."

"For the raid in Norway? Yes, it was a victory," the prime minister replied flatly, glancing at the president. "It should go far in boosting public morale back home. Unfortunately, we lost twenty-two good men including seventeen commandos. At one point, all the officers who were then leading elements on Vågsøy had been killed—four of them. Our chaps were technically leaderless for a time—"

"But they carried on?"

"They did. Other officers from the reserve came forward, and the raid succeeded."

"Then the commandos proved their worth."

Almost tearfully, Churchill nodded. "They did. Our magnificent chaps proved their worth." He paused to collect himself. "Brigadier Durnford-Slater, who led the raid, reported to Mountbatten that he could not be prouder of their actions and initiative." He paused as though reluctant to go on. "We had one chap, Forrester, an officer—"

The prime minister's voice broke as he struggled to speak. "The fighting around the Ulvesund Hotel had grown fierce. Those German soldiers were good and determined to hold that position. This Forrester chap took a grenade in each hand and charged the Germans along with a Norwegian fighter. Once in their midst, he detonated the grenades and killed them all, himself included."

Silence hung over the breakfast table. Then Churchill continued, "We suffered fifty-seven wounded, including four sailors; eight aircraft downed; and one cruiser lightly damaged. That's against a hundred and twenty Germans killed, ninety-eight captured, and ten of their ships sunk. We also captured another full set of *Kriegsmarine* codes and several Quisling collaborators, and we brought back over seventy Norwegian loyalist volunteers. We took out the major gun emplacements at Måløy and destroyed all the fish factories."

"You mentioned the Norwegian who charged the German position with Forrester. So, the Norwegians were in the fight?"

Churchill nodded. "They had a company of three commando troops with us. We trained them. They're fierce fighters, but their officer, Martin Linge, was killed too. We also took along some of their non-combatants as interpreters and to assist in keeping civilians out of the way. They helped us identify Nazis and collaborators too." He took another sip of his coffee. "Unfortunately, we incurred civilian casualties. That could not be helped. The Germans hid out in their houses and had to be rooted out."

Roosevelt eyed him. "You're holding something back; I can see it on your face." He gestured at the food on the table and chuckled. "I had poached eggs and toast done up special for you, with lots of butter and jam, orange juice, and a shot of whiskey right next to your coffee. If I've missed anything, let me know. Your cigar follows. Now, tell me the rest of it."

Churchill viewed him sagely. "I'm quite pleased with the success of Operation Archery and it'll get the lion's share of public attention, but it was a diversion. Our main raid, Operation Anklet, was carried out by a much smaller force of three hundred from No. 12 Commando, in the Lofoten Islands again. Our objective this time was to destroy two radio stations, capture two German garrisons, and sink as many ships as we could."

If Roosevelt had been caught uninformed, he gave no hint. "And did you succeed?"

The prime minister prodded his poached eggs with a fork as though testing them for viability. "That operation is still ongoing, but the reports we've received indicate that it is meeting its objectives. We landed them at Moskenesøya yesterday simultaneous with the operation at Vågsøy, and we picked the date figuring that the Germans would be still celebrating Christmas and we could catch them unawares—like George Washington did when he crossed the Delaware and surprised the Hessians.

"As of my last report, our commandos were unopposed, they occupied the towns of Reine and Moskenes, and they captured a small German garrison and a number of Norwegian Quislings at the radio station at Glåpen. We still have a larger garrison and another radio station to go, and some more ships."

Roosevelt stared at him and then laughed. "Well as my famous distant cousin Ted used to say, bully for you. Your boys have done a fine job."

The prime minister leaned back and fixed a solemn gaze on the president. "Beyond the immediate military objectives, we had two other overarching goals." He paused, choosing his words carefully. "We wanted confirmation of our commandos' effectiveness, and their ability to carry out large raids in geographically separated areas at once. And we wanted to test Mountbatten's combined operations concept."

Roosevelt had started to put a piece of toast in his mouth. Instead, he put it back on his plate and leaned forward. "And did it work?"

A shadow crossed Churchill's face. "I would be happy to say that it succeeded, and it did, but we have much to learn. Unfortunately, one of our aircraft dropped smoke bombs on our own men, causing burn casualties. Otherwise, yes, the concept is proven. We will be doing more combined operations, and I'd like to suggest that, while I'm here, we discuss a similar arrangement to command the actions of our two forces."

The president studied Churchill as though trying to see behind the man's eyes. "You're suggesting US and British forces under a single, combined command? What about our other allies?"

Churchill sighed heavily and put down his fork. "With so many competing interests between nations, that might be untenable. But I think that if our two countries agree on strategies, the others will fall in. I don't see any other way to get to victory without breaking down into provincialist squabbling. If we are to have a prayer of winning, we must have unity of command."

Roosevelt sat quietly mulling for a few moments. "How would that work?"

"The details, of course, would need to be worked out, but in broad stroke, we'd form a committee of the chiefs of staff from both of our militaries that would report to the two of us. It would be permanent for the duration of the war, headquartered here in Washington, and I'd leave senior officers from each service here for instant communications with their respective headquarters in London."

Roosevelt leaned back, his eyes wide. "You really were doing some deep thinking on your way over here." He slapped the prime minister's arm. "And you've given me plenty to ponder."

He started to go on, but Churchill interrupted him. "If I may say something about the two operations in Norway, Archery and Anklet, before we move to other subjects—we had an additional objective, and I'd like to report that we succeeded beyond expectations by a prodigious amount."

"You always like big words, Prime Minister," Roosevelt said, smiling. "Go on."

"As you know, we hoped to get Hitler to divert troops to Norway after Operation Claymore, our first raid on the Lofoten Islands. In fact, he sent thousands to Norway."

"I'm aware. Good job."

"We hoped these last two raids would get him to move more there. Word from our cryptologists at Bletchley is that he's in a rage and ordered an additional thirty thousand troops transferred."

"That's a respectable—"

"There's more." Churchill's eyes gleamed. "He's ordered construction of an 'Atlantic Wall.'"

"A what?"

Churchill smiled. "He's ordered massive defensive positions to be built along the Atlantic coast all the way from Norway to Spain."

The president stared at the prime minister in amazement. "Won't that slow down any invasion to liberate Europe?"

Churchill chuckled. "Maybe. The Maginot Line didn't do much for the French. Even breaching the Great Wall of China is a historical fact, recently repeated by the Japanese. And to build his Atlantic Wall, Hitler will have to divert incalculable numbers of men, and sew up vast quantities of materiel and money. With three quick raids, we've effectively denied him those resources for his eastern front and North Africa."

The president laughed. "Winston, you're incorrigible. You already got him to stall his invasion into Russia and face the winter storms outside Moscow, and you got him bogged down in the Balkans." He shook his head, regained a serious expression, and added, "I want to talk more about combined operations and this notion of a joint chiefs of staff committee to maintain unity of command."

"Do you think your senior military commanders and staff will go for it?"

Roosevelt smiled as he lit a cigar. "Leave that to me."

"Good. I discussed the concept with my own military chief of staff, General Alan Brooke, and he was deeply opposed to it." He smiled slyly while lighting his own cigar. "But note," he said as he closed his lighter with a metallic clink, "he is not here." He shrugged. "Someone had to stay in London to run the war in my absence."

10

Washington, DC

"How is the prime minister," Donovan asked as he and Paul settled into their seats aboard a government plane the next morning at the airfield at Anacostia.

"He rested yesterday, but he's insistent on keeping up with the raid in Norway. Fortunately, initial reports show it was a success, but details are still coming in. Regardless, the prime minister won't stay down. He's probably up and bustling about now."

"That was an intense meeting we had two days ago," Donovan said, clapping Paul's arm as the aircraft transported them into the heavens. "Are you fully recovered?"

Paul laughed. "What a way to spend Christmas. The lesson I learned is not to move even a hair when two national leaders are in a momentous discussion right in front of me. I had wondered about the rapid mobilization, but I had no intention of asking about it; at least not in that meeting, and particularly not after that exchange."

The general chuckled. "You asked a good question and look where it got you—on a lark." He looked down at his watch and became serious. "If my timing is right, your commandos should be smack in the middle of their mission in Norway about now, or close to finishing it up."

"They went in at sunrise, which that far north means around ten o'clock, and they expected to take six hours. They're twelve hours ahead of us, so they should be finished. Stephenson told you about them?"

"He did. I wish them Godspeed."

They sat in silence for a few minutes while the plane droned through the skies. Then Paul asked, "What can you tell me about the Detroit Arsenal?"

"We build tanks there. I'll explain about it when we get there. Listen, more people should be asking the question you did and taking note of the answer." He had to speak loudly above the engine roar and vibrating aircraft. "The fact is, when Germany invaded Belgium, President Roosevelt started thinking that America could eventually have a problem with that fascist regime. When the *Wehrmacht* steamrolled through France like it did in Poland, and then Dunkirk happened, things shaped up for an invasion of Great Britain. The president had already started action, first by allowing Churchill to establish your intel organization in Manhattan. Then he called me in to liaise directly between him and Stephenson, who, in turn, was the go-between to Churchill. That provided a short communications route for cooperation between your PM and our president without the whole world knowing about it.

"Roosevelt's problem, though, is that he campaigned on keeping the US out of the war. But he had early warning. Way back in 1937, your boss, Stephenson, got hold of a copy of a secret summary of Adolf Hitler's briefing to the German high command. It outlined the *führer's* plan to conquer Europe and control the British Empire. Bill got it to the prime minister, who shared it with the president."

Paul stared at him, aghast. "That was Hitler's original plan?"

Donovan nodded. "Sounds insane, doesn't it? Too crazy to be believed. It became more believable when the *Wehrmacht* occupied Czechoslovakia and entered Prague about three and a half years ago. Roosevelt appealed for peace, but Hitler snubbed him."

"I remember. I was already in intelligence, working out of Whitehall."

"Until then, Hitler's conquests had been accomplished by intimidation, without firing a shot." Donovan pursed his lips. "We'll grant that Austria wanted to be part of Germany. But when Adolf *blitzkrieged* into Poland, bombs dropped, tanks rolled, and civilians died horrific deaths—lots of them —and the world was awake and watching, but Hitler didn't stop."

"So, how did America go from having a tiny army with almost no weapons to the behemoth it appears to be in the space of what—weeks? The Japanese attacked nineteen days ago."

Donovan took a deep breath. "Like his politics or not, the president deserves credit for seeing ahead. Earlier in his career, he was the assistant secretary of the US Navy. In that job, he learned the ins and outs of government military procurement and how it interacts with private industry. He knew from experience the long lag times contracts can take, and that's before design and production.

"So, he did several things. You're intimately involved with one of those, allowing British intelligence to operate out of Manhattan. With the agreement to share intelligence, you Brits also delivered to us your radar technology. We were novices in that area, and now we're far down the road and developing even more advanced capability, which we share back with Britain."

"Germany didn't think much of radar when the war began," Paul broke in, "but they've figured out that we've used it effectively, and they're pouring money into it. If we had not put up our radar systems on Britain's coasts and then on board our aircraft for air-to-air contact, our country would already be history."

"Agreed," Donovan replied grimly.

The transport plane reached altitude, and Donovan stood to stretch his legs. "I'm going for coffee. You want some?" When Paul nodded, the general ducked down to look out one of the windows. "We're having a pretty smooth ride so far." He chuckled. "I don't want to spill it."

Once seated with their beverages, Donovan continued. "The president did several things starting in 1939 that put America way ahead in getting ready to at least defend itself —and don't forget that we're already arming the UK and the Soviet Union."

"I'm in awe, frankly. I truly am. I recall back in the summer when he signed the Lend-Lease Act. Roosevelt had Liberty ships on the way to us within days. I wondered then how he did that."

Donovan grinned. "That's a special case that I'll explain later, but then I guess they all are. You're familiar with Lend-Lease, so I won't cover that, but we had to have tanks, planes, trucks, etcetera, to lend and lease. We also needed a way to transport them across the ocean, and that means ships, lots of them, and we don't have nearly enough. When all is said and done, we need to take at least three and a half million men overseas with all the equipment and supplies to support them, and shipping is the bottleneck that must be fixed or all else fails. All of that takes raw materials, manufacturing, and distribution, So, Roosevelt called in his secret weapons, his dollar-a-year men."

"His what?"

"Dollar-a-year men. They're leaders of industry and commerce—they're patriots, movers-and-shakers, and they work for a one-dollar-per-year salary that creates an employment relationship with the government so they can act on its behalf. Roosevelt assigns them an issue, and they get things done.

"He already told you about one of them, Henry Kaiser. He mentioned three others too: Bill Knudsen, K. T. Keller, and Don Nelson. The president formed several boards a few months ago, including a War Production Board that Nelson runs. Together, the boards oversee resources, production, and distribution of all the commodities and products we'd need to win if we were attacked. And, of course, we were.

"Roosevelt put these men on the boards with charters to streamline and speed up processes. You'll see what I mean when we get to Michigan."

Paul's expression turned thoughtful, and he took a moment to formulate his question. "We've all just been through the Great Depression. Economists say the US came out of it only this year, and five years ago, your country was in the last part of the Dust Bowl. So, where did the money come from for your military expansion?"

Donovan laughed. "I'm in the military, so I'm walking on thin ice discussing that subject, but I'll give it my best shot and try to stay on the safe side of the line. I'm no economist, so here are my observations, and you can form your own opinions. You've heard of Roosevelt's New Deal?"

Paul nodded. "I know it pretty well."

"What I saw during that time was that business viewed government with hostility. They coped with tons of regulations and taxes because the president was surrounded by bureaucrats and politicians who thought that the means of production should be owned and controlled by the state."

"I thought that's what socialists, communists, and fascists do."

Donovan shrugged. "The label doesn't matter. When only a few people at the top are making all decisions about which products should be made, how, when, where, in what quantities and varieties, and reaping all the economic benefit, not much gets done by the common folk beyond what they need to subsist.

"I've heard arguments that the New Deal prolonged the Depression for those very reasons, and I've heard the opposite, that it pulled us out of the recession. Note, though, that the economy started rebounding as we prepared to defend against an attack. As I said, I'm no economist, but the fact is that during the Depression, investors weren't putting their money into new sources of raw materials, developing new products and services, or expanding existing ones. There's not much incentive when all the increased reward from investment is scarfed up by Uncle Sam through taxes and regulation.

"That all changed when the president perceived a national risk from a potential Nazi attack. The *blitzkrieg* through Europe and the Battle of Britain brought the point home. Suddenly, we needed smart industrialists and businessmen, and fast. So the New Deal went out the window, regulations were sliced, and businesses were encouraged to innovate, produce what we need, and make a profit. They came out of the woodwork and set their minds and capital to work. You're going to see the result."

"I thought Detroit was a big city," Paul said, looking out the window as they descended several hours later. "All I see for miles around are cornfields."

"The plant is called the Detroit Arsenal," Donovan replied with a chuckle. "It's located in the mighty city of Warren, population about five hundred and seventy, and you're right, it's in the middle of a corn patch twenty-eight miles northeast of Detroit."

Minutes later, they stepped out of the aircraft into blinding sunshine against a blue sky. Paul raised a hand to shield his eyes and saw a huge building dominating his immediate view several hundred yards away. "Is that it?"

"That's where we make our tanks," Donovan said, nodding. As they walked across the tarmac to a waiting car, he went on. "Fifteen months ago, there was nothing here but more cornfields."

Paul stared at the huge building. "Are you telling me you built that plant in fifteen months? How big is it?"

"About a quarter-mile long and a tenth of a mile wide. And we designed and built it in *six* months. We've been rolling out tanks here for the past nine months. Lend-Lease was signed about the time the factory opened, and the M3 tanks we've been sending to your army in North Africa came from here."

Paul gaped as he took his seat in the car for the short ride to the plant, whose enormous proportions became more evident as they drew closer. "How many tanks?"

"You'll see."

"Circle around it," Donovan told the driver. "I want our British visitor to see the scale of this thing."

Rising out of the cornfield, shimmering white to three stories, the building had a flat roof, and from a corner, the length disappeared from view into the distance. Even the front spanned almost two athletic fields. After they had driven a lap around the plant, Donovan directed the driver to stop.

"You couldn't put one of those on Sark Island," Paul remarked in wonder. "It would take up most of our one and only plateau."

Massive sets of wide-open doors revealed a cavernous interior alive with thousands of workers—and tanks, hundreds of them, in various stages of assembly. Men swarmed on them, emplacing the main guns and the machine guns, laying out tracks on the floor to be installed, and performing myriad other tasks.

"All of those are going to your army in North Africa," Donovan said.

"This is astonishing. I'm—"

"But there are problems."

Paul glanced at Donovan sharply. "Sir?"

"Notice that the tanks are held together using rivets. When your guys in the desert get hit broadside by a German panzer round, those rivets break under force and bounce around the interior. That's not healthy for your soldiers.

"Another issue is that the main gun has a limited horizontal traverse capability. To engage a target, the whole tank has to turn its general direction and make fine adjustments. That's bad if the target is another tank coming up behind or to the side of you and shooting. We'll fix that by producing a whole new tank, the M4 Sherman. The gun's bigger, and the tank is welded instead of riveted, which saves a lot of time and money—it's stronger and the turret will rotate three hundred and sixty degrees."

Paul grimaced. "That sounds incredible. How long before production starts?"

Donovan grinned. "We'll roll them out in March, three months from now. We expect defense department approvals by then—"

"But how?" Paul asked in amazement.

"That's where the dollar-a-year men come in. Had you ever heard of Bill Knudsen before the president mentioned him?"

Paul shook his head.

"Most people haven't, but he's had a huge effect on American life. He came here as a very young immigrant and went to work in Henry Ford's factory. He was talented, rose rapidly, and became a senior executive in the production end of manufacturing.

"He figured out that Americans like variety in their products and tried to get Ford to modify the company's production line, but he was refused. So, Knudsen went to Chevrolet, a subsidiary of General Motors, and made his pitch. They bought into his concepts, hired him, and it is largely he who developed mass production using standardized parts and nimble assembly lines as we know them. That's why people have a variety of cars to choose from now, even from a single manufacturer.

"The president tasked him with developing this plant and its production line. Our new Shermans will meet and beat anything the Germans have now. And here's some data for you. At the beginning of this year, before this plant opened, America was producing thirteen tanks a month. By year-end, the Detroit Arsenal will have manufactured three-thousand nine hundred and sixty-four of them. That's roughly fifty percent more than the Germans had produced this year at the time we broke off relations." He halted abruptly. "I have some business to take care of with the manager. The driver will escort you around. I'll meet you in an hour, and then we've got a long flight ahead of us—to California. That'll take most of the night."

11

December 29,1941
Richmond, California

"'Airplanes—NOW—and lots of them.' That's the order Roosevelt gave Hap Arnold at a White House meeting three years ago," Donovan told Paul as their flight winged west through the night. "We had only about one hundred and fifty fighter pilots at the time. The president perceived that we'd need thousands, and soon. He told his military chiefs of staff that he wanted to build fifty thousand warplanes a year.

"When we stepped into the last big war in 1917, we were completely unprepared, especially in the air. We were in no better shape this time around. When we went to war in 1918, we had thirty-five military pilots to fly fifty-five military planes. None of them was equipped or fit for combat. Europe had advanced in aircraft design far past us." He elbowed Paul. "Ironic, isn't it, since Orville and Wilbur invented the airplane?"

Paul agreed with a slight nod. "How prepared is your airpower going into *this* war?"

"Better, thanks to the president's forward thinking, the push from a pilot we got by the name of Jimmy Doolittle, and Hap's diligence."

"I've heard of Doolittle. He's a colonel, I believe. Some call him the greatest pilot in the world. Our RAF credits his development of one-hundred-octane fuel at Shell Oil with helping to win the Battle of Britain because of the added speed it gave our fighters. I'm not familiar with General Arnold."

"You're right about Doolittle. He's a terrific pilot. He was horrified by the military build-up he witnessed in Europe on a flying tour for the Air Corps, and he has the president's ear. He started the push to modernize and expand our own air capability.

"You'll hear more about Hap Arnold by the time this war ends. He was one of the first military pilots anywhere, one of the few trained by the Wright brothers, and he's a West Point graduate to boot. Class of '07. In addition to ramping up design and manufacture of bombers and fighters, he oversaw recruitment of pilots and mechanics." He chuckled. "You'd think a guy with his record would have been at the top of his class, but he was a hell-raiser. He still finished in the top half and took a commission in the infantry.

"You'll be happy to know that, in developing our air capability, he set as his first priority the task of building a strategic bombing force to support Britain. Six months ago, he was promoted to be chief of the Army Air Corps where he commands our air force combat assets. He has the VIII Bomber Command ready to be activated next month, and in the following month, February, his advance party will arrive at RAF Daws Hill in Britain to set up headquarters."

Paul regarded Donovan in amazement. "My head is spinning. It's only been three weeks since the Japanese attacked."

"They miscalculated," Donovan replied with an edge to his voice. "They thought we were sitting on our laurels. They don't know that we developed and now produce many types of aircraft, and we have in excess of twenty-five hundred of them. Our factories are churning them out. We have B-17 Flying Fortress heavy bombers and B-26 Marauder medium bombers, and we're working on a high-altitude B-29 Superfortress heavy strategic bomber, but that's still a few years off. We've also developed P-38 Lightning and P-47 Thunderbolt fighters. We've got a long-range, single-seat fighter in development, the P-51 Mustang. It'll give the Messerschmitt 110 and your Spitfires a run for their money, and we've built transports, observation and reconnaissance planes, trainers that double as fighters—"

"That's all well and good, sir," Paul interjected, "but who's going to fly them?"

Donovan glanced at him askance. "Excuse me?"

"You just told me that three years ago you had only a hundred and fifty military pilots."

Sudden air turbulence jolted them out of their conversation momentarily. They looked about, and as the aircraft settled back into comfortable flight, they resumed the discussion.

"We didn't waste those three years," Donovan said, continuing his line of dialogue. "Roosevelt prodded the Selective Service Act through Congress in September of last year and imposed the first peacetime draft in our history. In the past two years, we've gone from a hundred and forty thousand to a million and a quarter men in uniform.

"Roosevelt's charter to Hap Arnold corrected the situation of too few pilots. Hap got out and contracted with nine airfields located across the country to develop flight schools, the main one being at Randolph Airfield near San Antonio, Texas. We have thousands of pilots now, and they're all itching to get into this fight. Hap set up schools to train the mechanical and technical staffs too."

He leaned toward Paul and nudged his arm. "Look, running this war is a complex project, with lots of moving parts. You've been heavily involved in intelligence operations, and you know how crucial those can be. But the other elements of war fighting are just as important. If we don't anticipate the needs and address them, we'll lose this war.

"For instance, with Japan's moves in the Far East, we're about to lose our access to eighty percent of our raw rubber imports. And the war moves on rubber, millions of tons of it. Think of the trucks, airplane landing gear, cars, and other vehicles that roll on rubber. They carry men and equipment to the front, and they roll our fighters and bombers to takeoff speed and buffer their landings. We use rubber for washers in engines and in thousands of other uses. If we don't have rubber, we grind to a halt."

Paul peered at Donovan with a bewildered expression. "So, what do we do?"

"Synthetic rubber and reused rubber," the general replied with a grin. "'We gather up all the old tires sitting around in scrapyards, behind people's houses, and in barns, re-process them, and turn them into tires or whatever. In addition, we make synthetic rubber from petroleum. The president allocated seven hundred and fifty million dollars divided up between fifty-seven plants to make the stuff."

He grinned with mock malevolence and dropped his tone to a conspiratorial whisper. "Hitler needs the Romanian and Soviet oilfields, but we've got our own. And on top of that, the Germans invented synthetic rubber at one of their Bayer plants." He laughed. "We're using their own technology against them." He paused and straightened in his seat. "We're doing the same types of things in producing guns, ammunition, combat rations—

"The men on those boards I talked about earlier know how to get resources, how to produce, and how to distribute. Whether it's food or clothing for the population or for the front, they know how to get the products out to where they're needed." He leaned close to Paul again. "That's how we'll win this war, and what you'll see tomorrow will boggle your mind."

They landed in the early-morning hours at an airfield near Richmond, situated northeast across the bay from San Francisco. Having freshened up as best they could, they emerged from the airplane a bit disheveled, with sunken eyes from lack of sleep. A car and driver waited for them and drove them to the Kaiser Shipyard.

"The US might have been unprepared for Pearl Harbor," Donovan said as the car made its way through the maze of men, machines, and steel girders forming skeletal structures, "but we've been preparing for war for a long time. In the week after the attack, we launched thirteen new warships and nine merchantmen, some from right here." He gestured at the scene unfolding before them. "Two years ago, this was empty shoreland, but now, here and in other places, we have under construction fifteen battleships, eleven carriers, fifty-four cruisers, a hundred and ninety-three destroyers, and seventy-three submarines."

Paul gazed in wonder at the hive of activity. Even before

reaching the security gates, the driver weaved the car between columns of vehicles bringing supplies to the yard. Some of them were flatbed trucks transporting huge pieces of shaped metal with unrecognizable purpose.

"That's all impressive," Donovan added as the car continued toward the water, "but our army is still not up to speed in training, and we don't yet have the capacity to get enough of them 'over there.'" He took a deep breath and let it out slowly. "For the time being, the land war in Europe must be fought by the Soviets."

On entering the gates, the driver steered toward seven bays with tall scaffolds made of timber and steel, each stretching into the sky, and each in some stage of building a ship. In one bay, little more than large pieces of metal, like the ones that had been on the flatbed trucks, lay on a hard concrete surface in the bowels of the scaffolding. An army of ironworkers bent over them with hoods shielding their heads and eyes while sparks flew as they welded the pre-formed parts of a keel together.

"Kaiser broke the ship's design into sections," Donovan explained. "They're pre-fabricated in other plants around the country, and then brought here for assembly. We gain the advantage of using standardized parts developed by experts. Manufacturing, assembly, and maintenance costs become a fraction of what they would have been, and so does the time to build the ships."

In other bays, huge cranes swept their arms across the sky with massive sections of steel tethered to them by thick strands of cable and a heavy hook. In the cabin atop the upright girders supporting the cranes, operators in helmets and goggles steered the sections to their proper places, guided by sweaty men below, bellowing and waving hand and arm signals.

Amid the clanging, pounding, hiss of welding, and the smells of molten steel, Donovan and Paul followed the driver, who now acted as their guide, through the plant. "Your prime minister asked the president to supply Britain with cargo ships," Donovan shouted over the din to Paul. "At the time, the president was restricted by the Neutrality Act. So, Churchill sought a shipbuilder in the US. When he was told that they were all scheduled beyond the time that Churchill needed his ships, he offered to pay to build a new shipyard along with a steady supply of cargo ships. His engineers designed one which they expected to replicate, and the whole scheme went out for bid.

"This industrialist, Kaiser, was one of the bidders. He's the guy who built the Boulder Dam in Nevada, and that established his credibility despite never having built a ship." Donovan laughed and cast an incredulous look Paul's way. "He had never built a dam before either."

They reached a stairway and climbed higher for a better view midway along the center bay. From this vantage, Paul saw far through the scaffolding to the other bays on his left and right, and then to the floor far below where workers in yellow safety helmets and gray overalls scurried about on their various tasks.

"So, Kaiser goes to the Brits and tells them that he'll build the ships by their design at a fraction of the cost, but the shipyard and the ships had to be built his way. He convinced them that he could do the job and got the contract. He built this shipyard in record time, and introduced mass production, assembly line, and pre-formed manufacturing methods. The first ship took a year to build. Now they're turning them out at a rate of nearly twenty a month. The objective is to launch one a day."

While Paul regarded him in astonishment, Donovan

swept his hand to indicate the seven bays. "At that rate, you'd think these Liberty ships are small boats he's building. Far from it, they're four hundred and forty feet long with a fifty-six-foot beam, and they can carry ten thousand tons with a crew of forty-five sailors. They can take twenty-eight hundred disassembled and boxed jeeps, five hundred and twenty-five armored cars—"

"Also disassembled and boxed?" Paul asked, breaking in.

"Of course. We handle duce-and-a-half-ton trucks the same way. We've set up assembly plants around the world to put them back together." He chuckled. "Our most productive one is at Andimeshk in the Khuzestan Province of eastern Iran. It supplies trucks to the Soviets. The workers there can reassemble a truck in thirty minutes. They're putting them out at a rate of two thousand a month, and of course what that tells you is that we're producing a lot of jeeps and trucks—"

He stopped and looked around. "I won't bore you with more details. The long and short is that we're building a lot of cargo ships fast, and now we're building them for our own use too. And we can take almost any cargo, light tanks, heavy tanks, you name it.

"Kaiser is building three more yards here in Richmond and two more at Portland, Oregon, and one in Vancouver, Washington. His real magic is that he brought mass production and assembly line concepts to the job of building ships, and in so doing, he launches the ships at a fraction of the cost and time. We're applying the same concepts to manufacturing airplanes, so our fighters and bombers are rolling out of the assembly plants at record rates. And since we're playing catch-up in this war, Kaiser's and Knudsen's methods are exactly what we needed."

He gestured toward the car. "The driver can show you

around while I complete my business with the shipyard manager, and then we'll be on our way."

"You were right—my mind is boggled. I'm amazed," Paul said as their plane took off into beautiful flying weather with a clear blue sky. "Where to now?"

"We've been diverted," Donovan replied. "We're in for another overnight on the aircraft. You'll have to take my word that we also developed a rapid build-up of our manpower."

"I've seen men signing up for the draft and to volunteer. The lines stretched back for blocks. I've seen middle-aged and even old men in those lines. That started right after Pearl Harbor."

Donovan nodded. "And it's happening all over the country. The president signed the first peace-time draft legislation sixteen months ago as a precaution against attack; and a good thing too, but he might not have had to do it. You've seen how that attack enraged our people, and they responded by the millions.

"Our recruits are fresh and raw, but we'll get them in shape; and women are taking over farm and factory jobs so the men can join the military. We've had a similar response to everything needed to support the war effort, from producing bullets and tanks and artillery rounds to harvesting field crops and getting rations to our soldiers in combat. We'll be ready for the fight, thanks in large part to men like Kaiser, Knudsen, Nelson, and the others who brought their expertise to bear."

The two descended into silence. Paul scanned out the

window across the landscape far below. Donovan stretched, folded his arms, and closed his eyes.

After a while, Paul said, "You didn't mention where we're going."

"Camp X," Donovan replied, opening his eyes momentarily. "We were supposed to observe 7th Infantry Division training at Fort Ord down by Monterey, but the president wants to know the progress of the spy school in Canada. They opened the day before Pearl Harbor, and we were a bit distracted then. Roosevelt wants a feel for how effective the school is. He also wants me to double-check on Hydra's effectiveness.

"We'll get you down to see troop training at Ft. Benning some other time. It's where we train our paratroopers. You'll see them jumping out of perfectly good airplanes."

"Brilliant! I've been curious about that. Didn't you just experiment with the concept a few months ago?"

"We did," Donovan replied, nodding. "The concept works, and soon we'll have whole battalions of soldiers trained to jump into positions behind enemy lines. The mistake we made was that we showcased the jump, allowing foreign military reps to observe. That included Germans. We'll no doubt regret that somewhere along the way."

12

New Year's Eve, 1941
The White House, Washington, DC

Roosevelt and Churchill conversed alone in the president's private study. "Winston, my friend, you're still not looking so well."

"And of course, you feel compelled to point that out, Mr. President," Churchill grumbled. "This has been a long journey."

"It has at that," Roosevelt responded, "but an incredibly productive one. How was Ottawa?"

"Splendid. I gave my speech, and the loudest and most frequent applause was when I mentioned your name and the entry of the United States into the war and your full-fledged support."

"You're being overgenerous, Winston. I watched the film of the speech. Your greatest applause was your response to Hitler's bragging that he would defeat the British within three weeks and wring your neck like a chicken's. Of course, his boast occurred nearly two years ago, before the Battle of Britain and the *blitz*—and you're still standing, and he's reeling in Russia's winter storms. Your quip of 'some chicken—some neck' brought the house down."

"Yes, well, the Canadians are a good lot, and they've honored every obligation they hold under the commonwealth, and they are prepared to go the full distance to ensure victory. I explained to their authorities our concept of the combined chiefs of staff who will report to you and me, and they are prepared to support it."

"That's tremendous. We've prepared a document to be signed by the two of us as well as by the Chinese, the Soviets, and the other allies. I changed the title of the emerging organization from the Associated Powers to the United Nations. I hope you don't mind."

Churchill shook his head. "No. I quite like that. It has a better ring to it."

"Good, then we'll go forward with it. I'm also happy to report that the formation of the Combined Chiefs of Staff Committee has gone smoothly in our view. We'll have a single chain-of-command across all theaters that report to you and me, and the chiefs have developed an initial plan for responsibilities in the Pacific. I've already instructed General Marshall to ensure that only the least number of men and equipment be assigned to the Pacific while we concentrate on beating Hitler in Europe, and he's in full support of that course of action.

"With regard to operating in the Western Pacific, your country has the greatest experience there and is still the largest land and naval presence aside from Japan's; and the man with the greatest experience across multiple theaters is your own General Wavell, so we suggest that he take leadership as the Supreme Allied Commander in Southeast Asia within specific boundaries, and we'll subordinate our forces to his orders."

Churchill had listened intently and now sat back in surprise, mulling. "What are the boundaries?"

Roosevelt noticed his reaction. "You don't seem pleased." When the prime minister did not immediately respond, the president added, "We can work on the limits of the area, but they would probably take in the Malay Peninsula to include the Burmese front, extend to the Philippine Islands and southward to our logistics base at Fort Darwin and the supply line through Northern Australia. We refer to it as the Malay Barrier, and his task is to hold the Japanese back while we organize our units and supply lines. I don't see it as a long-term command, but it would include all forces of the United States, Britain and the British Empire, the Dutch, and any other allied forces in the theater."

The president studied the prime minister's face and, seeing no reaction, asked, "What do you say?"

After an extended moment of silence, Churchill said, "I'm surprised. That's a very generous gesture, given the enormous load of men and equipment that America will have to mount up to effectively meet the Japanese, even just to hold them in place. I would have thought that you'd prefer an American in that position. And I do have a pertinent question: are you overlooking that I relieved Wavell of command in North Africa for his failures there?"

Roosevelt took a moment to respond. "We don't regard that matter in the same way. Granted, we're removed from the issue by distance. Not then being *in* the war, from our perspective, General Wavell proved himself by rolling back the Italians in swift order, and then for much of the rest of his time there, he fought three separate battles simultaneously with limited forces.

"In Libya, he contended with Rommel's *Afrika Korps*. In Ethiopia, he cleaned out the Italians. In Iraq, he settled the local tribal uprisings near vital oilfields. And he did all that while preparing for potential attacks through Vichy-held Syria and Lebanon. In addition, he defended your strongholds in the Mediterranean, like Crete and Malta.

"He had his hands full, and he was in command for an extended time. He must have learned some useful lessons, and he was probably ready for a break."

Churchill listened intently. When he did not offer an immediate response, Roosevelt continued forcefully, "The object is to win the war. Your generals and admirals have been in the fight by land, sea, and air. Your experience is real. Putting Pearl Harbor and the other battles of that day aside, our know-how is theoretical, with our last engagements dating back to the last war.

"I'm supported in this choice by our own senior leaders from the army and the navy, in particular General Marshall. We have two men in mind as supreme commanders for separate parts of the Pacific theater, General Douglas MacArthur and Admiral Ernest King. But we need someone to go in now and keep the Japanese at bay. We think your General Wavell has the experience to do that, largely coming out of what he accomplished in North Africa."

As the president took a breath, Churchill leaned forward and interjected. "Let me speak plainly, Franklin. We have full confidence in General Wavell, despite that I relieved him. I just thought the theater was ready for fresh thinking. However, this year, 1942, is not going to be a year marked in victories. On the contrary, it will be marred by bloody defeat after bloody defeat, and I don't say that by way of using a British epithet. Real blood will be spilled, and the purpose is to keep Japan from further deploying its forces while we build ours and continue to defeat Hitler.

"General Wavell enjoyed a long and illustrious career, and he'll see his proposed battlefield exactly as I have described it—in failure after failure, with blood spilling over more blood. Essentially, we're asking him to enter into clashes he cannot win and to order men into combat knowing that a high percentage will not survive, and to do it for a victory that will be years down the road. His task to hold Japan at bay will only be accomplished at a horrific price in lives and equipment.

"Only a man with the highest devotion to country would take on such responsibility. I have no doubt that if asked, he will agree, and if the judgment of the combined chiefs is that he be offered that command, then I'll put it to him. However, I must voice to you in clear, unvarnished terms the enormous duty we set before him and the conditions under which he must carry it out; and I must secure your solemn commitment to support his decisions amid the bleakest conditions."

Roosevelt listened without expression, and when Churchill had finished, each man sat quietly. "You paint a picture like no one else can," the president said at last. "All right, you have my promise as you've described it, and with that, we'll move ahead. You'll also be happy to know that the combined joint chiefs have bought into your proposal to station six divisions in Ireland. I've given my consent. It's going to happen."

He leaned forward and pointed a finger playfully at Churchill with the hint of a smile. "I mentioned your fatigued appearance when you came in, Winston, because I'm worried about you. You can't keep up this pace."

"You sound like my physician," Churchill groused. "Dr. Wilson."

"Then you should listen to him. Look, the man who heads up my Lend-Lease office, Edward Stettinius, has a house in the Palm Beach area of Florida. It's very private, on the beach, and he's offered it to you for your use. I think you should accept. I've told the press to treat your and my movements like those of our battleships—completely secret, and so far, they've obliged.

"Get away. Rejuvenate. Do some more deep thinking. General Marshall offered to fly you down there and accompany you on the flight. He wants the opportunity for at-length discussion. We'll arrange for you to have unfettered and secure communications with your staff here and in London, and we'll bring you back here before you go home so that you're completely up to date. What do you say?"

Churchill was hesitant. "It's a thought."

"Well think it through. The United Nations Pact is ready for signature. I've convinced the Soviets to include the words 'freedom of religion' in the declaration, and that was no easy task. The Soviet ambassador, Litvinov, was afraid to suggest it to Stalin. I had a private, literal 'come to Jesus' meeting with him where I talked to him about his soul. I don't know how much that affected his spirituality, but the long and short is that he'll have dinner with us in my private dining room to boost his standing. Then the three of us will sign the pact here in a ceremony along with China's ambassador. Beyond that, there's not much for you to do over the next few days while we pull together our Anglo-American accords concerning production volumes and schedules. We've agreed on the priority for each of the major strategic issues, so you might as well go work on your tan on a Florida beach. When you return, we'll go over the proposals, get your modifications and approvals, and then you'll be on your way back home."

Churchill laughed in a way that had become rare for him. "You mean back to the tempest. I see how you were able to persuade a nation, Mr. President. Please tell Mr. Stettinius that I shall be pleased to accept his kind invitation."

13

January 8, 1942
Pompano Beach, Florida

"Nice place," Stephenson said, gazing across an expanse of gleaming sand to where the blue waters of the Atlantic murmured as they rolled ashore in white wavelets. He sat with Winston Churchill and Paul Littlefield under an awning on a wide veranda of the grand beach house owned by Edward Stettinius, Jr.

"I've had enough of it," Churchill huffed. "I appreciate the courtesy, but for all the Secret Service security, on arrival, someone sent me a cartoon from the *Miami Daily News* featuring two corpulent old men sunning themselves on a beach. One was easily recognized as my aide, Tommy Thompson. The caption read, 'Hard work is the thing that will win this war — we must keep at it night and day.'"

"How rude and insulting," Stephenson quipped.

"That's the press, although I must say that they've been good about keeping my whereabouts quiet. That's startling. The people too. Some have recognized me on the beach, but they've been friendly and polite, and no one's made a public proclamation about seeing me. That's quite surprising." He took a deep breath and exhaled noisily. "I appreciate the use of the house. I've used the time to re-write four personal memorandums, but aside from that, I'm impatient with the inactivity during these times."

He stopped and peered at Stephenson. "You're not one to waste time, mine or yours. What do you have for me? And where is your shadow?"

Stephenson chuckled. "You mean Captain Littlefield? He'll be along." The door opened as he spoke, and Paul entered. "Here he is now."

"Good to see you as always, Captain Littlefield," Churchill greeted Paul, and then turned back to Stephenson. "He's been with us through the muck going on a year and a half, including the turbulence and officialdom of the Baltics and Greece, and helping to shape our allies to our own thinking, including meetings at the White House. Shouldn't we be making him a major someday soon? In wartime, promotions come faster, and the rank would be more in keeping with the responsibilities we expect of him."

Paul could hardly suppress a smile from the high praise, but he stood stock still even as his face, neck, and ears turned bright red.

"I'd have no objection," Stephenson said, with a twinkle in his eyes. "People might take him more seriously."

"Good, then I'll have Tommy scribble a message off to London, and we'll consider it done." He turned to Paul once again. "Now, Major, shall we sit and discuss your travels with General Donovan?"

Subduing elation, Paul took his seat with Churchill and Stephenson.

"Sir, before we do that," Stephenson interjected, "I'd like

to get to the main reason for my visit. You were concerned about Brazil tilting toward the Nazis, and I came prepared with a report on what's been done."

"And I want to hear it, but first I have a couple of questions for the major." He turned to Paul. "Did you get the answer to the questions you asked the president?"

"I did, sir. I'm amazed at what's taken place without public awareness on either side of the Atlantic. I'm not sure what I am most taken with, your project with the Liberty ships, the American build-up of its arms factories, the actual production to date, training of crews and repairmen for tanks and planes of all sorts—I had no idea how the president had guided the country for war preparedness—and none too soon."

"The prime minister's bulldog persistence with Mr. Roosevelt is responsible for much of it," Stephenson said.

Churchill brushed aside the comment. "You're not one to flatter," he groused, "and I don't need it. We must win this war. The generations to come will greet us in the afterlife with pitiable, hollowed-out eye sockets if we do not. I cannot live or go to my grave peacefully with that thought."

He turned back to Paul. "Tell me about Camp X. Were you impressed?"

"Very much so. Outwardly, it appears as any other military training facility except that the students were not wearing uniforms. But while General Donovan conducted his inspection, he allowed me to be escorted through each step of training, from the use of Morse code to techniques of hand-to-hand combat, taking down an enemy swiftly, quietly, and with finality.

"I spoke with several chaps going through the school, among them a Brit by the name of Ian Fleming. He's a good sort of chap, though he seems a bit of a lost soul seeking firm terrain. He's been a journalist and wants to write novels after the war. I also met some Czechs. I took particular note of them because they seemed to be preparing for a specific operation. They were nice, but I sensed their tension. They kept mentioning two of their chaps, Jozef Gabčík and Jan Kubiš. They weren't at Camp X, but they had gone through commando training in Scotland. Anyway, the camp is a great school, and I gather it's patterned after those in England."

"Yes, and we've added a few things after seeing the success of our commandos," Churchill said.

Stephenson grunted. "That might be so, but we'll need to beef up security. Paul should never have heard of that operation, and certainly not in such detail."

"Agreed," Churchill said dolefully. "I'll leave that to you to correct." Turning back to Paul, he asked, "What about the Hydra?"

"I saw it in full operation with encrypted transmissions sent, received, and re-transmitted from Europe, South America, and of course, the United States. It's quite mind-boggling and a tremendous asset."

"Good. I'm glad you had a worthwhile trip. All right now, Little Bill," he said, turning to Stephenson, "let's hear about Brazil. It gives a lot of support to the Nazis by disrupting US operations and links between Europe and South American states. And we'll need their northeastern ports when we're ready to invade Africa. Have we managed to edge them away from Hitler?"

"We have, sir." Stephenson took a letter from his inside jacket pocket and handed it to the prime minister. "This was intercepted by Brazilian intelligence and shown to their president, Getulio Vargas. It purports to come from General Aurelio Liotta, the president of Italy's state-owned airline.

Our chaps replicated his stationery and typewriter blips down to the letter, including the straw-pulp paper found only in Europe. They also forged his signature. It's addressed to Commandante Vicenzo Coppola, the airline's regional manager in Brazil."

Churchill took the letter and perused it. It read:

"Dear Friend:

Thank you for your letter and for the report enclosed...I discussed your report immediately with our friends. They regard it as being of the highest importance. They compared it in my presence with certain information that had already been received from the *Prace del Prete*. The two reports coincided almost exactly... It made me feel proud... There can be no doubt that the 'fat little man' is falling into the pocket of the Americans, and that only violent action on the part of the 'green gentlemen' can save the country. I understand such action has been arranged for our respected collaborators in Berlin..."

Churchill studied it for several minutes.

"I suppose President Vargas is the person disparaged as the 'fat little man?'"

"He is, and he was furious and took immediate action."

"Who are the 'green gentlemen?'"

"They're members of a Brazilian political group; essentially, the local flavor of fascists. With the exception of some anti-Semites, they don't buy into the Nazis' racism. They failed at an earlier coup against Vargas."

"I can see why this letter would upset him. He must have found this last line particularly galling." Churchill read aloud, "'The Brazilians may be, as you said, a nation of monkeys, but they are monkeys who will dance for anyone who can pull the string! *Saluti fascisti...*'"

He laid the letter on his lap, blew out a breath, and

peered at Stephenson with mock sternness. "Remind me never to be on the opposite side of you on any matter," he jibed.

"The letter was intended to incite."

"I'm sure it did that. How did you get it into Vargas' hands?"

"One of his sons-in-law is the chief technician for the airline in Brazil. Several other prominent Brazilians have financial interests in the company. We arranged for a micropix of the letter to fall into the hands of some of them and to be blown up to normal size. They circulated the replicas among themselves, and it made its way to Vargas."

"What was the aftermath?"

"As expected, Vargas was infuriated. He canceled the Italian airline's landing rights in Brazil and ordered Coppola's arrest." He laughed. "Coppola had got wind of the letter, deduced the probable outcome, stole five million dollars' worth of Brazilian *réis* from the airline's bank accounts, and tried to flee the country. He didn't make it." He arched his brow. "And now, Brazil is firmly in our camp and will join the fight complete with planes, pilots, and soldiers, and we'll have the ports and bases we need in Brazil when the invasion of North Africa takes place." He smiled, a rare lift to the ends of his lips that an inattentive observer would miss. "There is one sensitivity to be aware of."

"And that is?"

"The FBI's Mr. Hoover is not a fan of ours. He thinks his agents originated the plan and pulled it off on their own. We destroyed the paper, the typewriter, and all the original forgeries to allow him to continue in his belief."

Churchill shrugged. "No harm in that, so long as we get our bases and ports." He turned to take a long look at Paul. "What do you think of all that, Major?"

Taken aback, Paul was slow to respond. "What I think is immaterial, sir."

"Not in the least. You've seen more of the goings-on behind the scenes than most. You must have some opinion on our devious ways."

Paul took two deep breaths and glanced at the ceiling before responding. Then he met Churchill's direct gaze. "Mr. Prime Minister, I've been privileged to witness the war from an unusual perch. I've seen the 'devious ways,' as you call them, and I've even objected to them, strenuously, as I'm sure Mr. Stephenson can attest."

Stephenson chuckled quietly. "No grandstanding, *Major*. Just answer the question."

"Right. I have only one comment, and then I'm done, sir. I've seen the effect of actions taken, and I don't know how we would have achieved crucial objectives otherwise. I fully support what's been done."

Stephenson sat upright in his seat and turned to face Paul. "My word, our young major has grown," he exclaimed.

"We all do that, I should say," Churchill remarked somberly. "People still remind me about Gallipoli."

Quiet descended on the room. Paul alternated his eyes from one man to the other. An impulsive thought entered his mind, and as it developed, his heart thumped loudly in his ears, and his hands grew sweaty.

"Mr. Prime Minister and Mr. Stephenson, I have a request."

Startled, they both peered at him intently. "Is this something you should take up with Little Bill first, and leave it to his discretion about involving me?" Churchill asked.

"Probably, but your approval would be needed." Without waiting for a response, he rushed on. "I'd like to attend one of the spy schools either at Camp X or one of the ones in England, or even the commando course."

The two men stared at him, speechless.

"I mean no disrespect, but I'm sitting out the war in a club box, so to speak, among the spectators. I understand my role as a living archive, but others could do it, probably better. Meanwhile, my brothers, Lance and Jeremy, are in constant danger, and so are my parents. Claire was too, while the battle over London and the *blitz* were going on. Meanwhile I'm leading a rather pampered life. It's not that I crave combat, but I feel like I am shirking my duty by not being in it." He dropped his head forward, and then straightened back up. "Both of you had your time in combat —" He stopped talking abruptly.

Churchill drew a deep breath as if searching for words. Finally, he turned to Stephenson. "What do you think? He's in your charge."

Also taken by surprise, Stephenson did not reply immediately. When he finally did speak, his tone was grave. "We selected him because of what he did during the Battle of Britain. He's done everything we've asked him to do, sometimes leaving him questioning his own and our ethics. But he performed well. He's had this over-vexed sense of having to be in the thick of the fight from the beginning, not quite seeing that he's been there all along. But he's earned the opportunity to serve as he wishes. Having said that, he still carries those state secrets in his head—"

"I carry my suicide pills with me everywhere," Paul interrupted, earning a reproachful glance from Stephenson. "I'm prepared to take them if I must." He produced them from his jacket pocket and held them out.

"As I was saying," Stephenson continued, "I have no problem with allowing him to take whichever course best suits our purposes, but then he returns to me. And that says all that needs to be said about my regard for him and his work. Decisions about what follows can take place then."

Paul sat back, speechless, the impact of what he had just done sinking in. "Thank you." Suddenly, the thought of not seeing his diminutive superior and mentor, Stephenson, for an extended time weighed on him. Separation seemed to have already occurred.

Churchill waved off the gratitude. "Thank us after the war if you still feel the same way. We know where this leads. When you're done with training, you'll want to be in on operations." He turned to Stephenson. "How soon can you release him?"

"Immediately. With winter setting in, we'll have a slow-down. We can cover for him."

"In that case, Major, you may return to Washington with me tomorrow, and when we've completed our affairs there, you'll travel with my party back to London."

14

Bletchley Park, England

Claire Littlefield observed Commander Alastair Denniston seated across from her behind his desk. He had summoned her to his office, but on entry he waved her to a chair and then continued reading a document that had absorbed him before her arrival.

She thought him to be a handsome man with boyish looks despite his more than fifty years, although she had noticed that with the progress of the war, more lines appeared on his face to join his dimples, and the strands of gray hair around his temples increased. Nevertheless, he kept himself trim, and his uniform fit him well.

"So sorry," he said at last, looking up. He flourished the document he had been studying. "We've shared a lot of intelligence with the Americans over the war years, and we expect that the cooperation will become much closer since we're now fighting alongside each other. I'd like for you to be part of the group that prepares for expanded intelligence collaboration, and as such we'll elevate you to a supervisory position—if you don't object."

Caught by surprise, Claire was momentarily speechless. "O-of course, sir," she stammered, "if you think I can do the job."

"I have no doubt, Miss Littlefield. The combination of your ability at cryptology, your fluency in French and German, and your analytical skills have certainly been valuable, and we should make better use of them. The work you did to help find the *Bismarck* was remarkable, as was providing the information from inside the *Wehrmacht* planning headquarters for the invasion of Great Britain. The Americans might have people with similar talents, and if so, we should put you together with them. They are far ahead of us in deciphering Japanese code, and our fight extends to the Pacific too."

"My skills aren't that rare, sir. The opportunities to apply them are scarce."

Denniston chuckled. "Your family couldn't shed its modesty at the point of a gun, could you?"

"My mother taught us to take ourselves with a grain of salt."

"Your mother is a wise woman. How are your parents doing on Sark Island?"

Claire sighed. "She and my father are getting by. That's the best that can be said, or at least that's all I know. They're still alive, but what they can put in a letter that gets past German censors is quite limited." She added grimly, "I suspect that with America entering the war, things could get worse for them."

"I can only imagine." Denniston shook his head and interlocked his fingers in front of his chin. "I keep meaning to ask you about your father. He's American, isn't he?"

Claire nodded. "He's my stepfather, and he was born American, but he took British citizenship after flying for the RAF during the Great War. My birth father died when my siblings and I were quite small."

"I'm sorry. I didn't know."

Claire brushed off the comment. "No need. Jeremy was a baby, and Lance has no memory of him. Mine is vague, and Paul's not much better. We honor him but love our stepfather as well. He adopted us and we took his name."

"It was a matter of curiosity," Denniston said, pursing his lips, "but now as I think of it, we're of course looking to expand contacts in the US, and to do it securely. Do you keep in touch with your stepfather's side of the family?"

Claire arched her eyebrows in surprise and contemplation. "We have relatives in America, mainly around New Jersey where my stepfather was born." She frowned. "If you don't mind, I'll refer to him as my father. That's the way we regard him, and I won't have to keep calling him 'stepfather.'"

"I understand. I recall your mentioning before that he flew for Britain in the First World War. Do you know if any of your extended family is in the military now?"

"I'm afraid we haven't kept up, what with the war and all. He has sisters and a brother. If it will help, I'll see what I can find out. I recall hearing about a family celebration a few years back when one of them graduated from their Naval Academy."

"That's impressive and could be useful, but it was a passing notion. I just thought that if any of your father's family members had similar dedication, we might find good talent among them. Don't go to much trouble. I'm sure your cousin already has his hands full." Denniston handed her the document he had been reading. "This might help in getting ready for our American counterparts, if and when they come. They've had their own code-breaking operation going on for Japanese messaging, and that's a brief summary—very brief. We don't know much about it, but what we do know is in there. Peruse it at your leisure but keep it secure."

"Of course."

Stony Stratford, England

Later that evening at her house a few miles from Bletchley Park, Claire put Timmy, the child that Jeremy had rescued, to bed. He had been orphaned by the bombing of the HTS *Lancastria* at Saint-Nazaire. His late parents, British diplomats, had been ordered to evacuate ahead of the German occupation of Paris. Timmy had been a toddler then and had grown fast in the intervening eighteen months; and he had developed a delightful personality with a mounting vocabulary. However, pronouncing his words in the endearing fashion of a child, he still called his rescuer "Jermy."

After cooing Timmy to sleep, Claire went into the living room and lounged on the sofa to read before retiring. She had just settled in with a favorite book when she heard the sound of tires crunching in the gravel on her driveway.

Her nerves froze and she sat up, hardly daring to part the heavy blackout curtains, relics of the *blitz* but still used in the event of more bombing. On four separate occasions, she had learned of the deaths of close friends when a car on its way to deliver the news made the same crunching sound.

Steeling herself for the worst, she stood and walked to

the window. Pulling back the curtains, she peered through darkness broken only by her own lamp spilling beyond the glass and watched a small sedan with government markings roll to a stop at the end of the garden path. Two men in uniform got out.

With rising dread, she watched them walk toward the house.

Then she recognized the broad shoulders, slender waistline, and confident gait of her youngest brother. Her heart leaped. Rushing to the door, she threw it open, flung her arms around him, and buried her head on his shoulder. "Jeremy," she cried, "is it really you?"

The next morning, Jeremy was already playing on the floor with an overjoyed Timmy and several colorful toy cars and trucks, and Claire was making coffee when Kenyon entered the kitchen. Timmy looked up with big eyes, and then stood, staring at the big sergeant in front of him.

"Sit, sit," Claire told Kenyon. "This is such an unexpected and thrilling surprise. I can't believe I have another one of my brothers' chums in my kitchen. I've heard the stories about you, Lance, and Horton at Saint-Nazaire."

"Thank you for letting me stay here last night. That was kind—"

"Think nothing of it. I've heard so many good things about you."

"She's lying," Jeremy kidded. "There's no way Horton would say anything good about you, and I certainly would not."

Still looking sleepy, Kenyon laughed, took a seat at the

table, and looked about appraisingly. Seeing Timmy still eyeing him, he held his hand out to the little boy, but Timmy remained at a safe distance.

"He'll warm up to you," Jeremy said. "He's quite friendly, even with strangers, but I think you took him by surprise when you came into the kitchen. He wasn't expecting either me or another man in the house, and now, here we are."

Kenyon slid off his chair onto the floor amid the toys. He picked one up, a bright red car, and examined it. Then he held it on the floor and rolled it back and forth a few times, picked it up again, and held it out to Timmy.

The boy, continuing to watch him closely, at first made no response to Kenyon's overtures. Then slowly, hesitantly, he reached out and took the car, and quickly turned and looked to Claire for reassurance. Seeing that she smiled back, he wheeled around, exhaled, and plopped down among the toys. Soon, he was squealing and laughing with Jeremy and Kenyon.

Claire looked on with a wistful smile. "I wish I could take the day off," she said. "I'm afraid the notice is too short. I'll leave for work after the nanny arrives."

No sooner had she spoken than they heard the front door open and close. "We're back here," Claire called, and turned back to pour a cup of coffee.

"Is that for me?" she heard a familiar voice say. She whirled around.

Paul stood there, with his slow, gentle smile.

"Oh, my goodness," she cried, catching her breath, and rushed to him. Happy tears streamed down her face as she hugged her oldest brother. "I can't believe this," she said, her eyes shining through her tears. "Two of my brothers here with me at the same time?" She stood back to look at him, and her eyes widened in even further surprise. "Paul, you're wearing a major's insignia."

Paul nodded, feeling the weariness of his long journey home with the prime minister aboard a seaplane. He thought better of telling her that Winston Churchill himself had pinned the insignia on him and that the plane had drifted off course enough that they nearly flew over enemy anti-aircraft guns off the coast of Brest, France.

Jeremy bounded up from the floor and wrapped his arms around his siblings. "Congratulations, big brother. I'm delighted to see you."

Kenyon also clambered up and stood by in respectful silence. Minutes later, while Jeremy introduced him to Paul, Claire went to make a phone call. When she returned, she announced with her happiest smile, "I've got the day off. My boss said that under the circumstances, there's no way I should be there today. I called the nanny and gave her the day off too."

They took seats around the kitchen table while Timmy played on the floor. "We have lots of catching up to do," Jeremy said.

Claire laughed with a sardonic note. "Some catching up this family will do. Paul, can you tell me where you've been, or what you're doing?"

He shook his head dolefully.

"What about you, Jeremy? Can you tell me where you're going next? Or even where you've been?"

Jeremy mirrored Paul's response, except that he added, "In France."

"Kenyon, can you add anything?"

The sergeant nodded with a chagrinned smile. "We're in training. This is our first break."

"So, there we are," Claire huffed. "And I can't tell you about my work." She shifted her eyes to Jeremy. "Can you tell me about Amélie? I hope the French Resistance isn't sending her out on too many sabotage or spy missions. I loved getting to know her when she came to London for training."

"She's safe," Jeremy replied. "And as beautiful as ever. She doesn't get to play the piano much these days."

"I don't know what she sees in your brother," Kenyon teased. "With all those Frenchmen around—"

Jeremy punched his shoulder.

"They make a cute couple," Kenyon said. "When this war's over, I'll expect an invitation to the wedding."

"And you'll have one," Jeremy declared. He looked around at the others. "I proposed. She said yes. We're engaged to be married."

Once again emotional, Claire leaped to her feet and rushed to Jeremy, beaming. "Little brother is engaged. And Amélie is so sweet, brave, and talented."

After holding him for an extended time, she returned to her seat. "Has anyone heard from Lance?"

"I received a letter from him several months ago," Paul said, "but it made no sense. He mentioned enjoying places he'd never been and visiting relatives we don't have. I thought it must have been written that way to alert us that code was buried in its content. I delivered it over to military intelligence."

"The same happened to me," Claire said, "and I did the same. Now I receive those as well as real letters, but that means I don't get as many that are meant for me." She shook her head. "What a war."

"Paul, does Ryan know you're here?" Jeremy asked. He

turned to Kenyon. "That's his sweetheart," he said playfully. "She's a WAAF."

"She's very pretty, and I'm happy for Paul," Claire remarked archly. "She's the first girl he's ever taken a keen interest in."

"And might be the only one I ever do," Paul muttered.

Claire and Jeremy stared at him. "Are you thinking of marriage too?"

"No, no," Paul said, now flustered. "I can't—I mean I won't—not while the war—"

"The war," Claire said in exasperation. "Always the war." She touched Paul's cheek. "You'll get your chance, you'll see. Have you tried to call her?"

"I have, but she's moved to another assignment, and I haven't yet been able to make contact. I leave London again this afternoon, so I'm afraid I won't be able to see her." Crestfallen, he told Claire, "If you speak with her, tell her..."

He stopped talking as if at a loss for words.

"I'll make a point of seeing her, and I'll tell her you love her and were heartbroken at missing her."

Paul nodded, and his cheeks flushed. "Any word from Mum and Dad?" he asked.

The room became quiet. "They're alive, or they were at the time of their last writing, which was about three weeks ago," Claire said angrily. "I'm sorry to say this, but I'm finding it difficult not to hate Germans at this point."

Gloom descended, but Claire prevented it from dominating. "I have two of my brothers here for the day," she said as she glanced at Kenyon, "and a new friend who was with Lance at Saint-Nazaire." She reached down and patted Timmy on the head. "And we have this sweet little chap to keep smiles on our faces. Let's enjoy our time together, shall we? Things will get better, you'll see."

They spent the morning chatting, reminiscing, telling stories about each other and their parents, learning more about Kenyon, playing with Timmy, and appreciating each other's company. Claire showed them around the gardens of the estate on which she rented the guest house, and then, as lunchtime approached, they reassembled in the kitchen for sandwiches.

"I almost forgot," she said as she laid out the food. "Yesterday, I was thinking about Dad's family in America. Are any of them in the military? I recall that Josh was in the navy, but I've lost track of whether he stayed in or got out. I saw in the newspaper the other day that we are about to be invaded by all the Americans that will be sent over for the war. I thought we might have the opportunity to meet some relatives."

"Ours are mainly around New Jersey, I think, and they must be involved in the war somehow," Jeremy said. "Our cousins should be of military age. If some come over, it'd be nice to see them." He grinned. "Who knows? Maybe we'll get the chance to go over there."

Sitting next to him, Paul froze momentarily, and then relaxed, realizing that Jeremy's comment was an offhand remark and not an indication of having knowledge of Paul's activities. "We should be able to find out. I'd like to renew contact. We haven't spoken with the American side of our family since the Germans occupied Sark Island. That's where they'd send letters, and that's where we'd have their addresses."

All too soon, Paul announced that the time had come for his departure. While Jeremy and Kenyon played with Timmy on the living room floor, Claire walked him out to his car.

"That Kenyon is good-looking and nice. What do you think of him?"

Claire laughed. "Don't start, big brother." She sniffed. "I haven't quite gotten over losing Red before I even had a chance to find out how interested we might have been in each other. I'm not sure I'm open to romance at all before this war is over."

Paul put his arm over her shoulder and squeezed her. "No one deserves to be happy more than you, little sister. You're always trying to cheer up everyone else." He laughed gently. "Things will get better. You'll see."

"Hey, that's my saying," she said, slapping his shoulder. Then she added, "Paul, you know where I work and what I do. If you have the means, would you find out if any of our American relations are in the war and get their contact information to me?"

Paul stopped in mid-stride and pivoted in front of her, staring into her eyes. Then he kissed her forehead and hugged her. "I'll do what I can," he said. Then he released her, opened the car, and slid into the driver's seat.

"Thank you, and please take care of yourself."

While Paul and Claire chatted by the car, and Kenyon and Jeremy played with Timmy in the living room, Kenyon said, "You never told me that your sister is so gorgeous. Her smile is dazzling. And those eyes. I could get lost in them." He chuckled. "Her hair is the same color as yours, but it looks good on her."

"Easy, old boy," Jeremy said, laughing. He added soberly, "She lost a chap that she was interested in last year—to the war. He was a fighter pilot, Red Tobin, one of the American

Eagles. I introduced them. I don't think she's quite over his death, and we lost three other close friends who also flew with me. She used to burst into tears at the drop of a hat. She's toughened up." He paused in thought. "She's as kind and charming as she ever was, but she absorbs the emotional blows with more poise. At least I hope that's what I'm seeing. I worry about her."

Kenyon sighed. "I'm sorry to hear about your friends. That's tough."

Jeremy nodded. "Horton told me about the chum you lost at Saint-Nazaire. He said he had never seen anyone work so hard to save a dying friend."

Kenyon's eyes took on a haunted look, and he swallowed hard.

They heard the car's engine starting and then the crunch of gravel as Paul drove away. Moments later, Claire re-entered the house. She put a grumbling Timmy down for a nap, and shortly after that, Kenyon and Jeremy prepared to depart.

"Thank you for coming," Claire told Kenyon. "You've made a friend forever out of Timmy. You're welcome here anytime to play with his cars and trucks."

"You're most gracious, milady," he replied, and noticed a sudden stricken reaction on her face that quickly disappeared.

She reached up and kissed his cheek lightly. "Take care of my little brother, would you please? I need him back."

"Then I consider that to be my sacred duty," he said gruffly.

She turned to Jeremy. "Come home safely and in one piece. Please." Then she stood smiling and waving as they drove away.

After they rounded the corner onto the main road, she

walked slowly up the garden path. Inside the house, she closed the door and leaned against it. Tears formed in her eyes. She bit her lower lip to stop them, but they kept streaming, and finally she gasped, “Red used to call me ‘milady.’”

15

Oflag IV-C POW Camp, Colditz Castle, Germany

A roar of cheers resounding from the walls of the castle's inner court where high-risk POWs were interned reverberated into the fourth-floor room that Lance Littlefield shared with nineteen fellow British noncoms, alerting them to a commotion below. Along with the others, he sauntered to the barred windows and watched a crowd of prisoners clustering near the arched gates adjacent to a row of low, more recently constructed huts built against the far stone walls. These comprised the "punishment cells," or as the prisoners commonly referred to them, the "cooler."

The portals stood open, and a German *kübelwagen* had driven through and halted. Two guards emerged, escorting two new POWs. Even from this distance, the two prisoners appeared haggard with bowed shoulders, but as they gazed around the towering castle walls and took in the thundering welcome of their new compatriots, they straightened their shoulders and waved.

"I know one of those blokes," a POW standing next to

Lance at the upstairs window exclaimed. "The smaller one with the dark hair. That's Lieutenant Michael Sinclair. I met him at the POW camp at Spangenberg."

Lance strained his eyes to examine the two, but they were too far away to get a clear glimpse of their features. As they gathered their belongings from the *kübelwagen*, a tall POW approached them, and the throng around them gave way.

"SBO has them," Lance muttered. He headed for the door and walked swiftly through cavernous halls, down a flight of stone stairs and up another, checking to see that POWs assigned as security stooges were in place along the way. Arriving at a room inhabited by junior ranking RAF pilots, he knocked and entered.

Flight Lieutenant Pat Reid was there, but otherwise, the room where nine men normally slept had cleared out. Pat was tall and fair-skinned, his hair a shade darker than Lance's.

Like his brothers and sister, Lance had dirty blond hair and the straight Littlefield nose and firm chin. Like Jeremy's, his eyes were green.

As he and Pat greeted each other, the door swung open again, and Lieutenant Colonel Guy German, the senior British officer, entered. He was a big man, with light brown hair and intelligent eyes and a cordial manner masking a rogue nature.

Behind Guy, the newly arrived POWs trailed in. Lieutenant Sinclair was the first one, identified by his height. He had a medium-sized solid build, straight dark hair combed back, and a mustache that Lance judged would probably have been well trimmed but for his adverse circumstances; but it was thick, fully covered his upper lip, and was tapered at each end. His eyes immediately probed the room and took in its occupants with a studious glance.

With him was Lieutenant Grismond Davies-Scourfield, also with dark hair that was thick and combed straight back. He was tall and muscular with friendly eyes and a smile over a square jaw, but he was nonetheless quiet and reserved. When Guy introduced him around, he said, "Call me 'Gris.' All my friends do." Then his eyes landed on Lance, and he hesitated.

Guy noticed. "Don't mind him," he said while the men took their seats. "This is Sergeant Lance Littlefield, and we don't stand on ceremony in this group. You can call him Lance or Sergeant, and he'll answer to either, but probably only the king himself will coax him out of proper military protocol." He grinned at Lance. "Although he might go along with 'Gris.' What do you say, Lance?"

"Whatever the lieutenant prefers, sir," Lance replied blandly.

"I've heard of you," Sinclair said. "You've become quite famous among POWs in other camps for the number of times you've escaped."

Lance grimaced slightly. "No home runs yet, sir," he said, his face deadpan, "but you're the legend, not me."

Sinclair leaned back and rubbed the back of his neck. "As you said, no home runs. Not for me yet either. I'm still a POW in Germany."

Guy gestured toward Pat. "He heads up our escape committee, and Lance assists him. You'll find things are somewhat different from other camps you've been in. This one has become something of an escape academy. That wasn't the German intent, but by bringing here together all those identified as either having attempted or having the propensity to escape, they've assembled the men who've had the most success and can pass their 'craft' on to others —and we do exactly that."

Behind Guy, the door swung open, and another man entered. "Keep your seats," the newcomer said as the more junior officers and Lance started to rise.

Guy glanced over at him. "Oh, hello, David. Glad you could come." He turned to the others. "For those of you who haven't met him yet, this is Lieutenant Colonel David Stayner." After greetings had been exchanged, he continued, "He'll be taking my place as senior British officer."

Amid startled looks, Guy explained, "The *kommandant* accepts that a British officer's duty is to escape, but he thinks that I support such efforts a bit too enthusiastically." He grinned wryly, arched his eyebrows, and exhaled. "He reminded me that our population of POWs was assigned here to prevent escapes. So, they brought David from Spangenberg to replace me, and I'm to be transferred elsewhere."

He turned to Stayner. "I expect they've gone to a lot of bother for little return. What I know of the good lieutenant colonel is that he's as anxious to get out as anyone. He's just more subtle. I'm the bull in the china shop."

As the circle of men broke into laughter, Stayner said, "Right you are, Guy." Then, turning to the others, he added, "I expect no change in plans. When Guy has gone, you should continue with what you've got going on without interruption, and I'll support in any way that I can. Meanwhile, he's still running the show. Like Guy, I don't want to know the plans so that I don't trip up in meetings with the *kommandant*."

The door opened again, and another officer entered. "You called for me, sir?"

Guy looked up at him. "Yes, Dick. Thanks for coming. Take a seat." He turned to the others. "This is Captain

Richard Howe. I've asked him to join us for reasons I'll make clear later."

As Howe perched on the edge of a bunk, Guy continued. "All right then, shall we get down to business?" Then he addressed the two newcomers. "We received coded messages from London about the two of you, and you're known to other POWs here, so we can consider the vetting process complete. This meeting is to debrief you. We need to go over every detail of your escapes and how you were recaptured. Mike, you were loose for weeks at a time between a couple of escapes and recaptures. Tell us where you went, how you stayed free, and what tripped you up."

Sinclair nodded. "I was first captured in Calais during the Dunkirk debacle," he began, "and was taken to POW camp *Oflag* VIIC at Laufen." There, he had escaped for the first time, crossing into Slovakia, Hungary, and Yugoslavia. He had been captured trying to enter Bulgaria. On being returned to Germany, he had escaped again, this time in Czechoslovakia, and was recaptured and held by the Gestapo before being sent to Colditz.

"I'm a slackard compared to what you've done," Lance observed when he had finished.

Sinclair waved away the comment. "This chap should be the legend," he said, gesturing toward Gris. "He's a Sandurst graduate, and he and his platoon were surrounded at Calais and held off the Germans for four days. The only reason they captured him was because he'd been shot four times and was unconscious. They kept bouncing him from prison camp to prison camp and then put him in solitary for several weeks after he was found digging a tunnel at Laufen. He still managed to escape inside a garbage basket last May and stayed loose these seven months until he was recaptured a few days ago."

All eyes swung to Gris. He grimaced, and his cheeks colored. "They caught me on a train to Vienna," he said, shrugging. "My papers weren't good enough, so they sent me here." He chuckled. "Always count on me to be doing something to annoy the Germans."

For the next several hours, the group quizzed the newcomers on their methods and experiences. When they had finished, Sinclair asked, "Have there been any escapes from here?"

Guy blew out a breath and nodded. "No British home runs, but some good efforts. We had four British escapes last year: Lieutenant Allan in May and Lieutenant Boustead in August, but they were recaptured." He indicated Lance and sighed. "He got out twice last year, but as you can see, he's still with us."

"As I said," Lance muttered, "no home runs."

"One Polish officer made it all the way," Guy said. "Lieutenant Kroner. He was sent to the hospital at Königswartha and escaped from there. They've had eight other attempts. Two Dutch officers, Larive and Steinmetz, got out through a manhole in the exercise park below the castle. We assume they succeeded because they've been gone for six months, and we haven't heard otherwise. Another one of theirs, Major Giebel, tried the same way a month later, but he was caught; and they've had nine other failed attempts."

He chuckled. "The French have had the greatest success to date, with nine home runs and three failed attempts. Whatever they're doing, we need to learn from them."

Sinclair listened carefully and fastened his eyes on Guy's. "Why so few British attempts?"

"We're a much smaller contingent," Guy replied evenly. "As of this moment, there are sixty-one of us, including you two. We expect our group to grow rapidly as the campaigns in North Africa continue. The full population of Colditz POWs numbers around six hundred, with the French and the Poles making up most of that. We have a few Dutch and Norwegian officers, one Yugoslav, and a civilian who was caught trying to get to Finland to fight against the Soviets."

He paused and furrowed his brow as he changed subjects. "You need to know that this committee must approve and schedule any escape attempts. We've agreed with the other nationalities to coordinate that way. We had a couple of botched getaways because they crossed with others we didn't know about until they exposed each other by accident. So, we now have a queue, and we discipline anyone who tries to jump ahead by acting independently and without clearing with us." He paused and glanced toward Pat and Lance. "There are only two exceptions, which I'll mention."

"I see," Sinclair said noncommittally. "And how long is that queue?"

"As of now, it's just under a year."

Sinclair straightened in his seat and blew out a rush of air. "A year? That's a long time."

"Yes, it is, but that's the rule. Live by it, and you get our full support, which I'll describe in a bit. Jump the line to go out on your own, and you get no support. If you act independently and you're recaptured and returned, in addition to solitary confinement imposed by the *kommandant*, further disciplinary measures will be meted out by us."

Sinclair took a deep breath and took a moment to consider. "All right," he said slowly, "I'm a team player. But I've got to stay busy. Tell me what to do."

"My sentiments are the same," Gris interjected. "I can't just sit around."

Guy regarded them with a relieved expression. "I'm glad

to hear that, and there's plenty to do. We operate full-time forging and tailoring shops, and of course we always tunnel. When an approved escape attempt occurs, we provide cash, food, travel documents, maps, and as much intelligence as we can gather on the chosen routes.

We also operate a radio in the attic to catch the BBC, and we have reporters who circulate to the various rooms and deliver oral news reports to our compatriots. Beyond that, some inmates are teaching classes, others are taking them, and some are completing university courses via—"

Sinclair sat staring. "Sir," he said, blinking and shaking his head, "you're doing all of that right under the Germans' noses?"

"They have no objection to the classes and the correspondence courses," Guy replied, chuckling, "but I get your point." He waved his hand to indicate the room and the vicinity beyond its walls. "This is a large castle covering more than five acres, and it's ancient. It's six stories high, not including the cellar or attic, with forgotten closed-off rooms, intertwining corridors and staircases, and long-overlooked hidden passages. We have nothing to do but explore." He smiled. "A good thing too. We needed space to house our forging, printing, and tailoring operations, and places to stash our ghosts.

"The Germans have a round-the-clock job maintaining their spotlights, manning their gun towers, keeping up with their miles of barbed wire, and watching us—and they can't do the latter for twenty-four hours a day, despite that they have more guards here than prisoners—and our population contains the best escape artists. You're in good company, and for the most part, our captors treat us with respect. We generally reciprocate, which is *not* to say that we don't voice our displeasure when it suits us—and they discipline us when it suits them. They know our job is to escape. Theirs is to prevent that, and they hope to succeed by keeping us busy and well-guarded."

Sinclair and Gris looked at each other incredulously. "Sir," Gris cut in, "you said you were 'stashing ghosts?'"

Guy laughed. "Ah, yes. You see, we have these POWs who faked escapes. They were sent here because they had attempted elsewhere and were recaptured, but they've had their fill and don't really want to try again. But they're willing to help. So, they fake an escape and hide out within the half of the castle occupied by POWs. We have to take care of them, keep them fed and out of the guards' sight. The strain on them is quite severe, so we watch out for their mental and emotional health as well. Doing that gets complicated."

"I can imagine," Sinclair said. "You mentioned two exceptions to jumping forward in the queue."

"I did." He indicated Pat and Lance, who had listened intently without comment. "Last year, these two chaps agreed to remain here, Pat as my escape officer and Lance as his assistant. By rights, they should have been far forward on the list, but the agreement is that if they made the commitment to stay, and if the opportunity arose, I would release them and move them forward in the line." He indicated Lance. "We have a particular concern about Lance in that he's been identified as a *prominente*—someone with important personal connections. Supposedly they're kept separately for their own safety, but we're sure the intent is to use them as bargaining chips if things go badly for the *führer*. We're concerned that things could go south for the *prominentes* if the bargaining doesn't work out.

"We have one such person in separate confinement now, Giles Romilly, a journalist the Germans apprehended in

Norway during that invasion. He's Winston Churchill's nephew, and he's monitored around the clock, to include a spy hole into his cell through the door so that a guard can see him at all times. He's not even allowed to move his bed out of the line of sight, and he's permitted few outings from his cell. So, his chances of escape are almost nil."

He gestured toward the sergeant. "Lance's mother is the Dame of Sark Island in the Channel Islands, the only British territory that Hitler occupies. As a result, he's been identified as a *prominente*. By a bureaucratic slip, the *kommandant* was not ordered to sequester him as was done with Romilly, and I convinced him that we pose no danger to Lance, so for the time being, we can keep him out of that fate. But who knows what the future holds?"

Sinclair rested his eyes on Lance. "Tough break, old boy."

Lance shrugged but did not speak.

Guy continued. "I've asked Dick Howe to serve as escape officer upon Pat's departure, and he's agreed. I'd like for him to shadow Pat over the next few months, and I'd like the two of you, Gris and Michael, to join the committee and lend your insights into how you both stayed free for so long and any other advice that might be helpful."

"Of course," all three men said in unison.

"Brilliant." Guy turned his attention to Pat and Lance. "Then the two of you are released from your agreements and should start planning your next outing. I don't see it happening for several months, but if you do it together, so much the better."

Lance stared first at Guy and then at Pat. A slow smile crossed his face. "We're going home, chum."

Pat laughed out loud. "That's the first time you've called me anything but 'lieutenant' or 'sir,'" he exclaimed. "The trip is still a ways off, and I'm excited too, but I'm not sure I want to be traveling with you." He reached over and jostled Lance's shoulder. Then he added seriously, "It's time to dispense with that formality anyway. When we're escaping together, that deference could get us recaptured or killed."

Lance took a deep breath. "Good point, Pat." He grinned.

With that, Guy scooted his chair back and stood. "That concludes our business for now. Michael, Gris, welcome." He gestured to the other men. "I'm sure these gentlemen will show you around."

"If there were any gentlemen in the room, I'm sure they would," Pat said, laughing as the group headed toward the door. He elbowed Lance in the ribs. "You and I have business to attend to, Sergeant."

Lance turned to him, beaming. "Yes, sir, we do."

16

January 30, 1942
East Orange, New Jersey, USA

Paul left the British Security Coordination office at Rockefeller Center in Manhattan in the early afternoon, drove through the city's thoroughfares and suburbs for just under an hour, and then turned onto Woodlands Avenue in East Orange. Tall trees lining the street were bare of foliage and strained against a stiff winter wind as he made his way between neat rows of snow-covered houses.

He found the one he was looking for, parked his rented Ford, and took a moment to observe his late uncle's home. It was well kept, projecting warmth against the icy weather, a frame house looking much like the others on the street but with its own arrangements of porches, windows, dormers, and roof to distinguish it. Its light-yellow paint with brown trimming lent an inviting look, and bare vines climbing twin pillars on either side of the front door provided a glimpse of its charm in warmer weather.

Before even reaching the door, it opened, and a frail, bent woman emerged. Her hair was white and gathered behind her head in a bun, and her face was lined, but she smiled broadly with bright eyes. "I was so excited to get your call," she said, extending a hand to guide Paul into the house. "Come in, come in. You'll die of cold out there."

After he entered and she had closed the door behind him, she stood back to take a look. "You're all grown up," she said. "You were a tiny baby the last time I saw you, and you've since had some brothers."

"And a sister."

"Yes, and a sister. Claire, I believe."

"It's good to see you, Aunt Della. I hope I came at a good time." He stooped to embrace her, and she clung to him a moment. Drawing back, she wiped moist eyes with a kerchief.

"You're welcome here. I'm alone now. My children are off to war, and of course, your uncle passed away many years ago, God rest his soul." As she spoke, she led him into the living room. "I laid out both tea and coffee, and I even managed to get some British biscuits."

"You shouldn't have gone to the trouble."

"Nonsense." She sat in an upholstered chair, and he took a seat on a nearby sofa. "It's good to have a visitor of any sort, but especially a nephew, even if by marriage. People are so scarce these days—all the young ones. The men are off training to fight, and the women are taking their places in the factories. Japan attacked not more than two months ago, and already we're rationing." She smiled primly. "But I've still got tea and coffee to tide me over for a while."

She reached a shaky hand toward a tray with china on a coffee table. "Tea?"

"That would be fine. With a little cream and two lumps."

"How very British of you," she said, chuckling as she poured. "Tell me about your family. I wish we had stayed in closer contact over the years. How is Marian?"

"I suppose she's well, though I can't say for certain."

Aunt Della's eyes grew wide with concern. "Of course. I'd forgotten that the Nazis occupied Sark. I hope she and Stephen are okay."

"We receive letters through the Red Cross, but they don't tell us much due to the German censors, but at least we know they're alive. Beyond that..." He shrugged disconsolately. "We keep stiff upper lips."

They conversed for several hours, exchanging what news of family members they could. "Josh was supposed to be in Pearl Harbor the day it was bombed," Aunt Della said. "I was so relieved when he called to let me know he was all right. He's on the *Enterprise*, you know, the aircraft carrier. He was upset before the attack because he had recently been pulled in to work in operations." She hunched her shoulders and leaned toward him, saying in a stage-whisper, "To tell you the truth, I don't really know what that means. I know he'd really rather fly, but I'm glad he's—well, at least he's on a ship and not in the air looking for a place to land."

"Do you know where he is now?"

Aunt Della's face saddened. "I don't, and I worry about him all the time."

Paul patted her hand. "I know how proud you are of him for graduating from Annapolis."

"Yes," she replied tearfully. "He was inspired to a military career by his uncle—your stepfather, Stephen—and what he did with the RAF in the last war. But he wanted to be in the navy and fly off of ships. For the life of me, I don't know why." She wiped her eyes again with the kerchief. "Don't let me get morose on you," she said, laughing through her tears.

"What about the others? Zachary and Sherry?"

Della shook her head and sniffed. "Both in service. Zack is like your brother, Lance, too adventuresome for his own good. He joined the army the day after Pearl Harbor and is training at Fort Jackson, South Carolina. And Sherry had just finished her nursing degree. She went in the army too, commissioned as a captain in the nursing corps." Her voice broke and she wiped her eyes. "I worry about each one of them."

Paul reached over and squeezed her hand. "I know you do."

Regaining composure, Della asked, "How long will you be here?"

"Not long, I'm afraid. I'm on a short assignment for the British Passport Office, auditing files, looking for miscreants, that sort of thing. I'll be off again the day after tomorrow."

Aunt Della regarded him with a crestfallen expression. "I'm sorry to hear that. Your visit was such a welcome event, but you're lucky to be out of the line of fire. I do hope Josh keeps his head low. His father used to say that. He was a veteran of the Great War too, you know. He was a foot soldier in the first big US battle at Cantigny in May and June of 1918." She sighed. "He must have seen some awful things. When he came back from the war, he was not the same man." Her eyes started to tear up, but she caught herself. "He was a great husband and father," she added stoically.

Paul eyed her somberly. Then he took a small notebook out of his jacket, jotted down some notes, and handed it to Aunt Della. "This is my office phone number. If I'm in town, you can reach me there." He indicated the entry.

"I'm going to send a letter to Claire, letting her know

your address. Here's hers." He pointed to it and then the next one on the list. "And you can write to Lance at this address. I'm sure, as a POW, he'd love any mail that comes his way. I don't know how to tell you to contact Jeremy, but if you send something for him to Claire, she'll see that he gets it. And of course, you can still try to get something to Mum and Dad, although I don't know that they'll ever receive it. Just be careful what you say to them in any correspondence." He looked irritated. "German censors, you know."

Aunt Della nodded with wide, serious eyes.

"And please let our cousins know that we're thinking of them and to write to Claire."

Several minutes later, with reluctance, Paul drove off, leaving his aunt standing in the door waving mournfully with a forced smile.

"How was your visit," Stephenson asked when Paul returned to the office in Rockefeller Center.

"Sobering," Paul replied. They sat across from each other at Stephenson's desk. "I'm kicking myself for not having looked her up sooner. My aunt is a widow, living alone, and her children, my cousins, are in the war. She tugs at the heartstrings, and I have no doubt that her situation is repeated millions of times across America." He sighed heavily. "I read somewhere that a soldier more than anyone hates war, and I certainly do, but at least in this case, the alternative is so much worse. We'd be derelict in not fighting. It's not just for the younger generation either. It's for the older generation too. They deserve to live out their lives in dignity, enjoying what they've spent a lifetime building. Unfortunately, as I've learned the hard way, evil zealots exist who would take it all away on a whim."

Stephenson took a long, hard look at Paul, and for several moments, he remained quiet. "You're a gentleman soldier if there ever was one, Paul," he said at last. "I shall miss you. When do you start your training?"

"The day after tomorrow. I leave for Camp X in the morning."

Just then, a secretary knocked on the door and entered without waiting for a response. "Sorry to interrupt, but this might be urgent," she said, and diverted her attention to Paul. "There's a man on the phone for you, a Lieutenant Commander Josh Littlefield." She looked slightly puzzled. "He says he's your cousin, but he's definitely not British. He said he just missed you at his mother's house and hopes the two of you can get together before either of you leaves town."

Nonplussed, Paul stared at her. Then he turned questioning eyes toward Stephenson. "That is my cousin's name. I'd left my office phone number with my aunt. But he's supposed to be aboard a carrier in the Pacific."

"Obviously he's not there now," Stephenson said. "You'd better go speak to him." When Paul hesitated, he added, "Don't worry about goodbyes here. I'll see you when you've finished up at Camp X."

Even before Paul exited the car in front of the house, Josh strode out to greet him. "Cousin Paul," he said, his voice strong. He grabbed Paul in a bear hug. "So many years. You were a baby the last time I saw you. I watched Mom change your dirty diaper." He laughed heartily and stood back to look at Paul. "And you're a major no less."

"And you're a lieutenant commander," Paul rejoined, "and a graduate from Annapolis."

"Mom was thrilled you came by. Come on in. I had suggested that I go meet you downtown, but she insisted that she wanted to see us both here." They started toward the house, and he added, "She's filled me in on what you've told her about your part of the family. What a war we're in."

Aunt Della waited for them by the open door, and she fussed about as they entered and made their way to the living room. "This is so exciting," she exuded, her eyes bright. "My son's home and we get to see a long-lost nephew."

"Tell me again what you're doing here," Josh said as they settled into their seats. "Mom said you're auditing at the British Passport Office, but I'd heard some time back that you were with British military intelligence."

"Well, that's not all it's cracked up to be," Paul replied, thinking fast and recalling an episode in which he and Stephenson had accompanied the FBI in pursuit of a British sailor who was selling shipping schedules to German agents. "I'm an analyst, and that's not as glamorous as flying fighters from carriers, but I suppose someone has to do the job, and I'm lowly enough to have been selected. Essentially, I help track down British subjects in the US who might be lining their pockets by providing shipping schedules to the enemy. It's mostly going through records, looking for irregularities, and working with local law enforcement to try to find traitors."

"Ah, I see," Josh said with a blank expression. "Well, that's important too. The battle in the Atlantic still rages, and the work you do could save the lives of thousands of merchant marines, not to mention the food supplies that don't reach your population in Great Britain when the ships are sunk."

"What about you?" Paul asked. "I thought you were out on the Pacific."

Josh rolled his eyes. "I'm headed down to Norfolk for a conference. I'm really rather irritated about it because Halsey's fleet is heading out to harass the Japanese in the Gilbert and Marshall Islands, and that's where I should be. I'm not divulging any secrets by mentioning that. It'll be in the news very shortly."

Sitting on the sofa next to him, his mother broke in. "I'm glad you're home, even if it's only overnight."

Josh laughed gently and put his arm around her shoulder. "I'm glad to be here, Mom, but I almost had to give up an arm to get leave to detour up here."

The three visited long into the night, and when Paul prepared to leave, he once again took pains to wish his aunt well. As he stooped to embrace her in farewell, visions of his own mother on Sark flashed through his mind, and his throat tightened.

"I'm sure I'll be back in New York at some point, and when I am, I'll stop by," he told her. "And when this war is over, we must all get together on Sark Island."

Josh walked Paul out to the car. "This has been tremendous," he said. "We can't let another two decades go by without visiting again."

"You're right," Paul replied as he opened the car door. Then he stopped and faced Josh in the dim moonlight. "Listen, beyond reacquainting with family, Claire asked me to contact you specifically. She works for the government, and I can't speak about what she does—I'm sure you understand

—but she's anxious that you write to her and let her know how to reach you."

Josh stood stock still, studying Paul's face as best he could in the ambient light. Then he reached forward and grasped Paul's hand. "I'll do it," he said. "Take care of yourself."

17

Four Days Earlier
Aboard the USS *Enterprise*, Pacific Ocean

Josh looked up from his desk in the operations room at the young seaman standing before him. A lurch of the big ship in rough waters knocked the man off balance momentarily, but he quickly recovered. Josh had gripped his desk to steady himself.

"Sir, Bull wants you on the bridge, immediately."

Startled, Josh half-rose from his seat when the force of an ocean swell pushed him back into it. Once more, the seaman fought for firm footing.

"Did he say why?"

"Sir, I've delivered the full message. There was nothing else."

Bewildered, Josh exchanged wondering glances with his colleagues and followed the seaman to the bridge. Captain Browning waited for him there, and immediately ushered him into Admiral Halsey's office.

"I've got a mission for you," Halsey said in his scratchy voice after Josh had reported. Browning stood to one side and looked on. "You'll take the next courier flight back to Pearl Harbor and make your way by the most expeditious means, commercial or military, to the naval air station at Norfolk. There, you'll report to Navy Captain Francis Low. You'll take further direction from him. You're there to observe, and you'll report what you see, personally to me, by secure means. Do you understand?"

"Aye, aye, sir." He hoped his misgivings did not manifest in his expressions.

"Any questions?"

"Sir, you're preparing to raid the Japanese. I should be here."

"Your place is where I tell you it is, Lieutenant Commander."

"May I ask the nature of what I am to observe?"

"No."

Josh pursed his lips and stared into the steely blue eyes now clouded with irritation. "Then I have no more questions, sir."

"Dismissed."

Josh turned to leave, and then stopped. "Come to think of it, Admiral, I do have one question. A request."

Halsey had already turned to study a map on the wall behind his desk, and Browning had joined him. They both glanced at Josh expectantly. "Yes?" Halsey asked.

"Sir, do I have time to make a quick detour to New Jersey?"

Browning smirked, and Halsey's eyes narrowed. "We're at war, boy. Your girlfriend can wait."

"It's my mother, sir. She's a widow and alone, and I haven't seen her in more than a year."

Bemused, Halsey glared at Josh and then at Browning. His expression softened for a split second and then returned to its normal implacability. "Your mother, huh? New Jersey? What part? I'm from New Jersey."

"East Orange, sir."

"I'm from Elizabeth. We're practically neighbors."

Josh stood still at parade rest, hardly daring to breathe while Halsey mulled. Outside, the wind moaned against the steel walls of the ship as it plowed through giant waves.

The admiral glanced at the map, then at Browning, and finally back at Josh. "All right, Commander. You've got one night at home. Just be sure that you're in Norfolk the next day, and in no case later than February 1. Now, unless you have another request, you're dismissed."

Josh hurried out of the office and down to his quarters to pack.

February 3, 1942
Naval Station Norfolk, Virginia

Josh followed Captain Low up the stairs of the island aboard the USS *Hornet*. The captain walked at a fast pace. Though affable, he was short on conversation.

Despite Josh's routinely close proximity on the *Enterprise* to Admiral Halsey, who was already an almost mythical figure to his fellow Americans, Josh was awed by the captain. Low's full title was Assistant Chief of Staff for Anti-submarine Warfare. He was not a large man, and his features were rounded, but he was fit, and his expression brooked no nonsense.

Having flown down two days ago and reported early

yesterday morning, Josh had waited in the reception area of Low's office for more than an hour. At mid-morning, the secretary finally escorted Josh in.

"Thanks for coming, Lieutenant Commander," Low had said brusquely. "I'm sorry I don't have time to spend with you. Be at the dock to board the USS *Hornet* with me tomorrow morning at dawn."

Taken aback, Josh had saluted, departed, and entertained himself for the day. Seeing navy war planes taking off at Chambers Field, one of the navy's major training fields for aviators and where Josh had trained, he made his way over and watched, paying particular attention to a large area of the runway that had been painted over.

Seeing Paul had been an unexpected surprise. After all these years, being with family from afar warmed him. Uncle Stephen, a family hero during the last great war, had taken Paul and his siblings as his own upon marrying Marian, and in a legal and emotional sense, they were truly cousins. He hoped to get to know all of the Sark contingent of the Littlefield family better. News about Lance being a POW at Colditz and his uncle and aunt living under German occupation on Sark was unsettling.

Once again glancing at the big patch painted on the runway, Josh decided to stretch the privileges of his rank and climbed into the control tower. "At ease," he said on entry as air traffic controllers eyed him furtively. "I'm here to observe only."

Moving to the front of the tower, he concentrated on the painted section, done in deep gray, almost black, resembling the color, shape, and dimensions of an aircraft carrier deck. It brought back memories. Here was where he did his initial training for carrier flying. Here was where the arresting cable system was developed that brought a thunderous aircraft landing at velocity to an abrupt halt on every carrier. Although difficult to see at this level, he recalled that from the air, the shape of the painted surface was easy for pilots to recognize.

Josh had continued watching with a sense of nostalgia. He returned to his room at the visiting officers' quarters to refresh himself, and then spent the evening at the officers' club in light conversation with other flyers until retiring for the night.

Before dawn, he made his way through the security checkpoints and then to the dock and stared up at the tall aircraft carrier. Captain Low was already there, waiting for him. "Let's go," he said. "Can't keep the ship waiting."

Within minutes of boarding, they were on the bridge and the ship cast off. It navigated to the confluence of the Elizabeth and James rivers where they poured into the Chesapeake Bay, and then the carrier sailed east into the Atlantic Ocean.

Low had gone to speak with the ship's captain, leaving Josh to his own devices on the observation deck. He chatted with a few of the officers and enlisted crewmen, but although none seemed any better informed on their mission than he was, he sensed no tension that would precede a hostile encounter. He had noticed two large aircraft secured at the back end of the deck that he did not recognize.

At last, Low returned, and curiosity got the better of Josh. "Captain Low, can I please know what's going on? What am I here to observe? I don't believe I'm here on a pleasure cruise."

Low regarded him through squinted eyes. "Admiral Halsey instructed me to tell you nothing," he replied. "He wants your unvarnished reaction to what you see without anyone else's bias. Having said that, look."

He pointed toward the stern of the ship where crews released the restraints on the two large aircraft. As Josh and Low watched, the *Hornet* began a turn into the wind.

"What are those?" Josh asked, straining his eyes to take in the details of the aircraft. "I'm not familiar with them. They look too large to operate from a carrier."

"Here," Low said, and handed him a set of binoculars. "These will help. Those are Army Air Corps B-25 Mitchell twin-engine medium bombers. They've been stripped of all equipment they don't need to fly, and they've been stuffed with the weight of a full bomb load and extra fuel tanks filled to the brim. We're here to see if they can successfully take flight from this aircraft carrier. We get two tries."

Josh gaped as the aircraft squatted on the deck with their wings vibrating, ready to lift into the wind. As he watched, sailors gathered on the permissible areas around the periphery of the flight deck, and others crowded every available perch to witness what they sensed must be a historic event.

Wild cheering erupted as the flight crews emerged and strode toward their aircraft. Behind Josh and Low, members of the bridge staff not involved in running the ship or other crucial tasks crowded together, seeking a glimpse of the two aircraft.

Josh watched the pilot and co-pilot of each plane, now mounted in their cockpits, working through their checklists, testing the flaps, ailerons, and rear stabilizer. Then the propellers rotated, the engines sputtered to life, and the sound rose to a loud roar before settling back to a low idle.

The flight deck crew had already moved into position. The engines of the first bomber rose again to a deafening thunder. The aircraft strained against their final restraints, demanding to be released.

Behind the first bomber, the second one's engines thundered to the pitch of its partner, both planes vibrating in unison, waiting for their respective takeoff signals.

The aircraft handling officer pointed to the pilot of the first B-25, ensured eye contact, and checked around with the other members of the deck crew before glancing one more time at the pilot and waving him into motion.

The bomber leaped forward, gaining velocity as it braced against the headwind, eager to suck lift under the wings. On and on it lumbered, the opposite end of the flight deck careening toward it at increasing speed.

Then the nose and wings were over the edge.

The tail gear cleared, all eyes following as the plane sank below the deck.

All watching held their collective breath.

Then the wind carried the sound of the mighty engines, drawing raucous cheers as the B-25 lifted into view again and climbed into the clouds. Before it disappeared, the second bomber raced the length of the deck and followed.

Barely able to contain his enthusiasm, Josh whirled on Low. "Where are they going?" he yelled above the wind.

"Back to the naval station. This was a test, to prove the concept."

"It's terrific. Who thought of it?"

For the first time, Low smiled. "A lot of people had a hand in it. Someone noticed that the bombers had no problem taking off or landing within the painted area on the runway at Chambers Field." He stepped closer to ensure he could be heard. "Your job now, Lieutenant Commander, is to tell Bull Halsey that the concept works. You saw it with your own eyes."

Realization dawned. Josh studied Low's face. "We're

going to do that on the Pacific side? What are we going to bomb?"

"Yours is not to conjecture, Commander. Yours is but to report to Bull. That's Admiral Halsey to you."

"Aye, aye, sir."

18

February 4, 1942
War Department, Washington, DC

Josh entered the office of United States Army Air Corps chief, General "Hap" Arnold, with some trepidation. In the life of every successful career military officer, a tour here was almost a given, but he had never been in this edifice in Foggy Bottom at 21st and C Streets Northwest and had no inkling why he was ordered to be there by Captain Browning from aboard the *Enterprise*. "You'll attend a meeting there and report the result," was all that Browning had relayed over the phone.

Despite the crowded conditions with makeshift office spaces sprawling into the halls, the flags, wood-paneled walls, and statuary and paintings of heroes and past officials impressed Josh in the way that was intended. He was awed by the trappings of military power and the myriad officers and enlisted personnel from all the services moving busily about.

He had barely sat down in General Arnold's reception area when another officer, a colonel, entered. Josh noticed the secretary's reaction to the newcomer. She was a middle-aged woman with dark, short-cropped hair, perfunctorily courteous but with a standoffish reserve that rebuked just for standing in front of her desk. Yet when she glanced up and took in the colonel's face, her eyes sparkled, and her mouth extended into a broad smile bordering on flirtation.

"Good morning, Lieutenant Colonel," she exclaimed, "the general said to escort you right in." She flashed hooded eyes in Josh's direction. "The lieutenant commander as well, on your arrival."

Startled, Josh stood to attention as the officer turned to regard him. He was at least a decade older than Josh, of medium height, square-jawed with a cleft chin, rugged complexion, high forehead with thinning hair, and he broke an easy smile as he turned and extended his hand. "You must be somebody important to get that kind of reception with Hap," he said as he walked across the foyer to greet Josh. "If I'd been here by myself, he'd've made me wait. At ease. I'm Jimmy Doolittle."

Josh warmed to Doolittle at once, hardly believing that he was meeting this pilot he had heard and read about since high school, and whom he venerated as much as anyone he could think of. As he shook the colonel's hand, everything he knew about the man flooded through his mind.

That for much of his early life from the age of three Doolittle had been raised in a gold-mining town in Alaska was enough to grab attention, but he had been a stunt flyer, a barnstormer, and one of the first to dare wing-walking. He was the first to fly across the United States from Florida to California in a single day, and he was famous for walking away from many spectacular crashes. He ended these stunts only after learning that newsmen aimed their cameras at his wife and two sons to catch their reaction in the event that they witnessed his life terminate in a ball of fire. Somewhere along the way, he had picked up a master's degree and even a PhD from MIT, and he had initiated the design of several avionics instruments, including the attitude indicator.

The secretary opened the door to the inner office and entered to announce the men. As they followed her inside, General Arnold rose to greet them, and once more Josh felt awed to be greeting another man he had admired for many years. He was even more surprised to witness the warm camaraderie shared between the two officers.

"We've got a special mission for you," Arnold told Doolittle when they were seated. "I'll get straight to the point. President Roosevelt wants to hit Japan where it hurts, and we want you to plan the mission and train the crews." He indicated Josh. "Lieutenant Commander Littlefield will be your liaison for the mission with Admiral Halsey."

Doolittle studied Arnold's face wordlessly. If he was surprised, he showed no indication, but his eyes narrowed with keen interest. "Admiral Halsey? I'll tell you plainly that I've never flown navy planes and have no clue about taking off or landing on an aircraft carrier—not that I'm against trying, but I don't know how useful I'd be in training for navy missions. What's the objective?"

"Tokyo."

Both Doolittle and Josh sat forward in their seats, stunned.

Doolittle whistled. "Geez, sir. Y'all sure aren't thinking small. What is it, five thousand miles from San Francisco to Japan? And three thousand miles from Pearl Harbor. Is there a new aircraft I'm not aware of?"

While Arnold shook his head and chuckled over interlocked fingers at his mouth, Josh thought of the B-25s he had seen fly off the *Hornet*. "There's a navy officer in Norfolk," Arnold said. "Captain Low." He turned to Josh. "You met him."

Josh acknowledged with a nod.

"The president directed that a way be found to strike Tokyo as soon as possible. Low found a way. Admiral Halsey is out running raids on Japanese-held islands in the Pacific, but those are gnat stings. For the morale of the American people and to make Japan feel their vulnerability, we need to strike hard and fast at the heart of the so-called Rising Sun, and that's what we're going to do.

"At Norfolk, Captain Low saw the shadow of a plane he was flying on the carrier-pilot-training runway that's painted to look like the deck of an aircraft carrier. It hit him that we might be able to strike Tokyo with bombers flown from carriers. We've already tested the concept. We flew Army B-25s off the *Hornet*. Commander Littlefield observed the experiment. It was successful, and twenty-four of those bombers are on their way to San Francisco on the *Hornet* as we speak. We want you to plan the bombing run and train the pilots. They've already been selected, they've volunteered, and they gather at Eglin Field in Florida at the end of the month."

Doolittle grinned. "You know I'll do it. Am I going to lead the shindig?"

Arnold shook his head. "Just train 'em, and train 'em good, Jimmy. We can't afford to lose you. One of them will lead the raid."

Doolittle's eager face morphed into a frown. "You can't be serious, General. You want me to plan the first strike on Tokyo after Pearl Harbor, get close to the pilots and crews of twenty-four bombers and train them how to do it, and then just watch them fly off the end of a carrier on what is likely to be a suicide mission, and that's it?"

Arnold met his incredulous stare. "That's the way it is, Jimmy. And this isn't a request or a suggestion. You're under orders. There's not another man alive in my judgment who can plan and train this right, and we'll get only one shot. Lieutenant Commander Littlefield is a carrier pilot, selected personally by Admiral Halsey to provide whatever technical help you need regarding carrier operations. But when it's over, we still need you, come hell or high water."

"With all due respect, sir, what you're asking me to do is baloney. Leadership requires that I go with the crews I'm training on a mission like this. None of them are any more expendable than me."

"Leadership also requires following orders," Arnold returned tersely, "and they stand as outlined." He picked up a letter from his desk and held it out. "This letter gives you priority and authority over every other project we have going on and every officer in the Air Corps. With it, you can command whatever you need to carry out the mission and cut through any red tape or other difficulty. If that fails, call me direct." He leaned back and steepled his fingers below his chin. "My operations staff is waiting to get started."

"Sir—" Doolittle's tone indicated that he had not yet acquiesced.

"I've assigned your mission, Lieutenant Colonel Doolittle," Arnold said with an edge to his voice. "Are you going to refuse?"

Doolittle reached over, took the letter, and read it. "When are we shooting for?"

"The middle of April."

"Then I'd better get on it."

As he and Josh passed through the foyer and into the hall after bidding Arnold farewell, Doolittle turned to Josh and grinned. "You watch. I'm going to lead that raid."

19

February 5, 1942
Bletchley Park, England

Claire knocked on Commander Denniston's door, and hearing his call to enter, she did so. He was ending a telephone conversation, so she took a seat in front of his desk.

"You have something for me?" he asked after he hung up.

"Perhaps," she said. "Right now, it's merely a feeling. We've seen a bit less radio traffic between German nightfighters and their ground controllers, yet they've been much more successful at taking down our bombers of late. We know from the agents we've captured and turned that the Nazis didn't put much stock in radar at the beginning of the war, but they had done some preliminary research. By now, they must have discerned that we've made advances in radar that gave us an edge in knowing when and where they were going to strike.

"We know that they've developed technology for intersecting radio waves over targets for the benefit of pilots. One of their first major strikes with that tool was Coventry. Probably Liverpool too, and certainly London. I think the only thing that made them shift their bombs away from us was their need for them in the Soviet invasion.

"Given that they're always working on new technology, why would we not believe that they've come along in radar as well?"

Denniston arched his eyebrows. "Good point, Miss Littlefield, an elementary one really, so obvious that it seems to have been missed. I'll certainly run the notion up higher. What do you suggest we do about it?"

Claire laughed. "That's somewhat beyond my technical ability, sir, but I think relaying on to our pilots and scientists that such a capability might exist could alert them to watch for signs of it. We developed our radar from noticing the reaction of radio signals as airplanes approached their sources—the tall antennas. The Germans might have done something similar. If they are using radar, it must be putting out a signal of some sort. Maybe our pilots could look for it."

"You do come up with weighty matters." He paused. "You've discerned through your own analysis what's become known by other means. It's good to have confirmation. You're correct that the Germans have developed radar. Actually, they've developed two distinct forms. The earlier one, Freya, detects direction, and the most recent one, Wurzburg, establishes height. When the Wurzburg detects our aircraft, it locks onto them and tracks them, and when its data is combined with that of Freya, it makes our aircraft sitting ducks. Paired together on a line along the Atlantic coast, the Kammhuber Line, they've caused our bombers all sorts of problems. That's why you've heard less of their radio traffic despite our increased losses.

"You'll be happy to know that a raid will come off soon

to grab the components of the Wurzburg. One of our RAF chaps, Flight Lieutenant Hill, got a picture of one while on a reconnaissance flight early last December over the coast of France near a place called Bruneval. That was two days before Japan bombed Pearl Harbor.

"In any event, we've laid on a raid to pinch its critical components. For better or worse, it'll be in the news immediately following, and once we have that technology in hand, we'll reverse-engineer it and develop a means of blocking it. If we're successful, it should represent a major element in turning the air war, which, fortunately for us, has now moved over Europe."

"That's sensational, sir, although I pity the Europeans."

"That was impressive work you did, Miss Littlefield, unearthing those clues and piecing them together to arrive at your conclusions. It's good to know that our decryption and analysis sections continue their high quality of work. I'm encouraged that we've developed the means to learn of critical information and confirm it from various sources across our intelligence organizations."

As Claire started to rise, Denniston asked, "How is your family?"

Claire recalled times when he had inquired after them when her emotions had gotten away from her. She steeled herself as she responded. "As always, you're most kind to ask. The truth is, I probably know no more about them now than I did the last time you asked. Ironically, I know more about Lance, the POW, than any of them. The letters from my parents on Sark are censored, so their messages say little; and I don't know where either Paul or Jeremy are, or what they're doing." She took a deep breath and let it out. "Honestly, if I did not have this work here, I think I would have already gone mad."

Denniston chuckled. "I know you too well to believe that. And how's your little Timmy?"

With that, Claire's emotions surged in spite of her composure, and her eyes misted. "When I go home at the end of the day, he makes me forget all the bad that goes on." She paused as her expression turned somber. "I fear that one day, someone with a legal claim to him will show up and take him away."

Denniston remained quiet for a moment. "We're certainly happy to have you here, Miss Littlefield, and any one of us will help in whatever way possible."

"Don't say that, sir," Claire said, forcing a laugh as she took to her feet. "You're going to make me cry again." She glanced at her watch. "With your permission, I must go. I'm meeting a friend for lunch."

"Very good, Miss Littlefield. Thank you for coming. As usual, your insights are appreciated."

Stony Stratford, England

Claire was already seated at her customary table in her favorite pub, The Bull, when the manager guided WAAF Squadron Officer Ryan Northbridge to join her. Seeing Ryan, Claire's eyes brightened over a wide smile, and she extended her hand. "I cannot tell you how delighted I am to see you," she enthused.

"Likewise," Ryan said, stooping to kiss Claire's cheek before sitting down. "It's been too long."

"I've already ordered drinks. They should be here shortly."

"I got your message," Ryan said. "I was so upset to have missed Paul."

"He was equally disappointed." Claire laughed. "Now don't get embarrassed like he did when I promised him that I would tell you he loves you and misses you."

"Stop," Ryan replied with a broken smile. "I'm going to lose my composure, and while in this uniform, that would not be a good thing." She looked around the pub, taking in its polished wooden and brass furniture and fixtures, a piano in one corner, and a view of the cozy town through the windowpanes at the front. "I love this place, but I was surprised when you suggested it—" She stopped herself. "I'm sorry. I know you have painful memories here."

Claire sighed. "I have wonderful memories that became painful when people dear to me were lost to this damnable war. But if I stop going to places because of bad memories, I'll have no place to go." Her voice caught. "I was at my house when Jeremy brought me the news about Red." She took in a deep breath. "Now enough melancholia. Tell me what you've been doing. Can you?"

With a regretful expression, Ryan reached across and squeezed Claire's hand. "I'm sorry, I can't." Then her face brightened. "But I can tell you what I'm *going* to do, and I'm very excited about it. I'm going to fly airplanes."

Speechless, Claire stared at her.

"It's all set. I've been accepted into flight school to become a ferry pilot."

"A ferry pilot. Ryan, that's so dangerous. They fly unarmed and without escort. Several have been killed by enemy fighters still coming over occasionally. Why would you do that? Look at you. You've attained rank. You must be good at your job."

"I am. I can't tell you about my job now, but I met Paul doing it, and he can vouch for my proficiency." She leaned closer to Claire and spoke urgently. "But Claire, I see what goes on as things happen. I know the instant our men are being killed. I'm always in a safe place and observe what they go through.

"I can't do that anymore. If there's danger to be faced, then I need to take my fair share; and to date, I have not.

"The country needs pilots to ferry new and repaired airplanes to where our combat pilots need them, and we don't have enough men. So, many women are doing the job. I can do it too."

The manager brought their drinks, but reading their expressions, he quietly told them to summon him when they were ready to order. Then he departed.

Claire took a deep breath. "Ryan, I don't know what to say. I'm so proud of you, and I'm glad that Paul found you, but now I'm equally afraid for you."

Ryan looked steadily at Claire. "What you're doing is far more important than what I do—taking care of Timmy—and I mean that sincerely. Our children are our future, and they must have a decent country in which to grow up. And you do so much to lift the spirits of those around you. That's as crucial as anything that anyone can do."

Thoughts of her conversation with Commander Denniston less than an hour ago crossed Claire's mind. She took a sip of her drink and brushed her hair back. "Yes, well, I do what I can."

20

February 15, 1942
Marseille, France

Madame Fourcade cast a concerned look at Maurice. They sat alone across the table from one another on the veranda of her villa.

"What's bothering you?" he asked.

"I suppose you heard that Singapore fell to the Japanese yesterday?"

Maurice nodded grimly. "That's bad for the British. That was one of their major holdings and sources of supply in the Far East."

"It's bad for us too," Fourcade replied. "The Japanese didn't attack just Pearl Harbor back in December. They went after a lot of the British colonies in that part of the world. That put the British squarely in the Pacific war, and my guess is that they've had to divert a lot of resources there. We're already noticing that supply-canister drops to us are fewer and lighter."

She sighed. "It's frustrating, but it's the reality. Our wits are our main weapon. We're spread thin, and we've received an urgent, high-priority request for support. It comes from Colonel Rémy, a French Resistance fighter along the northern Atlantic Coast, and it pertains to something called radar—not that I have much knowledge on that subject, I'm not sure I really know what it is. Regardless, although the mission is seemingly simple, I think that it could be most dangerous. His organization, like ours, is functioning at capacity. This is one that we'd assign only to our most trusted agents. The ones I'd consider are all out right now.

"The other thing is the location The last mission we did that far north was a year ago. Since then, other Resistance networks besides Rémy's have activated in the area, the *Wehrmacht* has solidified and increased its presence, and the Gestapo and SS have recruited and coerced infiltrators and informers. The SOE suggested Alliance's help specifically because we've been effective across the country without being overrun by traitors and collaborators."

"Doesn't air reconnaissance give them enough information?"

"Apparently not. They want someone on the ground to get as close as possible and give accurate information on enemy locations, types, and numbers." Fourcade stared across the landscape below as it sank gently to the blue Mediterranean sparkling in the distance. Although too far away to hear the waves, she imagined herself walking barefoot through the gentle surf. For a moment, she savored the illusion of a world at peace.

Maurice broke her reverie. "May I know what the mission is?"

"Of course, and it should be easy, but there are too many unknowns. We don't have direct contact into the area. We don't know how well defended the approaches are to the part of the coast in question. We don't have escape routes or safehouses established—"

Maurice laughed. "Madame, if you'll tell me what the mission is, maybe I can help figure out how to do it."

Fourcade laughed with him. "I'm sorry, my big friend. The information I've received is that there is a villa on an isolated plateau above some cliffs overlooking the Atlantic near this village, Bruneval. On its south side, the land descends as a hillside instead of cliffs. Aerial photography indicates that the beach at the bottom of the hill is secured by German forces, but the photo analysts can't tell which units or how many troops are around or near the area. They want someone to get all the intel possible, and report back. It needs to be delivered within two weeks."

Maurice grunted. "That's a tough one, otherwise I'd say it's perfect for Chantal. She's the best anywhere for surveillance and reconnaissance."

"No," Fourcade said flatly. "She's too young."

"Yes," a female voice said from the door.

Startled, Fourcade and Maurice turned. Chantal stood facing them, her hands on her hips, her mouth set in a determined line.

"Were you eavesdropping?" Fourcade demanded, annoyed.

"No, but as I came out the door, I heard what Maurice said about me. If it's something I can do, I'll do it."

"No," Fourcade said again, adamantly. "You're still a girl. Amélie wouldn't—"

"My sister isn't here, and wherever she is, she's risking her neck too. You know that there are people younger than me active in sabotage and other operations. I'm approaching seventeen, and that's only two years younger than Amélie was when the Germans invaded. Besides that, I've already been on dangerous missions. I killed my father's killer—if you remember."

"I remember," Fourcade said softly. "But on this mission, you'd be alone, or maybe with just one other person. There is no safehouse, and there would be no one to rescue you." She hesitated to continue. "German soldiers would be all around you. What happened to you before could happen—"

"You mean one of them might try to rape me?" Her eyes grew fierce, and she drew a sharp-pointed knife from the folds of her dress. "I have this," she hissed, "and I know how to use it." She flashed a glance at Maurice. "Horton and Kenyon taught me, and I practiced. And I can shoot too." She produced a small pistol in her other hand.

Shifting her glare back to Fourcade, she said, "I'll do the mission. Now tell me what and where it is."

Fourcade and Maurice exchanged glances. He shrugged.

"All right," Fourcade said after a long silence. "We'll plan for it, but if a better alternative comes along, we'll go that route."

"There is no better alternative than me. Where is it?"

"Near Bruneval, a village on the Cherbourg Peninsula coast."

"That's not far from Dinard where we operated last year, and my papers worked then." Chantal turned to Maurice. "They would need to be updated, but otherwise they should be good. Tell me the rest."

Fourcade did, and when she was finished, they discussed how the mission should be carried out. "You shouldn't go in alone," Fourcade said, and when Chantal started to protest, she added, "That's just good tactics. Traveling alone, you'll draw attention, and you won't have anyone to interact with more naturally." She shook her head. "Let me state plainly. You're not going in alone."

"Then who?"

"I could go as her father," Maurice volunteered.

Fourcade shook her head again. "That would be a little strange. A father taking his daughter to a beach that's highly defended with German soldiers?"

"Horton," Chantal said in a low voice.

Fourcade stared at her and then laughed. "Nice try, Chantal. Everyone knows you have a crush on him, but this is serious business."

"Which is why I suggested him," Chantal said, blushing. "I admit that I'm crazy about him, but that's what makes it perfect. Remember, his mother is French, and he speaks the language well with not enough of an accent for the Germans to detect. "We'll go as college students from Paris. He'll be a graduate student doing critical research for the war effort. That'll explain why he's not in the military at his age. I'll be his doting undergraduate assistant." She giggled. "I won't have any difficulty playing the part, and I'm sure he can push away my affections as he always does."

Seeing Fourcade's doubtful expression, she added with a mischievous smile, "Don't worry. I'll be good. I know the seriousness of the mission."

"But he's up in Loire—"

"As temporary liaison to our network there. It has a leader. They can afford to be without him for the time it takes for us to get there and back. I can travel through there and pick him up on the way."

For several minutes, they discussed the issues, and Fourcade gave her consent, with a stipulation. "I don't want you traveling alone for any reason. So, Maurice, you'll travel with her as far as Loire as her father, wait for her return, and bring her back after the mission. She and Horton can travel together to and from Cherbourg." She looked back and forth between the two. "Maurice, can you get the papers forged in time?"

"We'll give it highest priority. Our forgers are true artists and great patriots." He grunted and chuckled. "Despite that in peacetime, they're criminals."

"Chantal and Horton will probably need a car."

"I'll arrange it."

February 23, 1942
Cherbourg Peninsula, France

"I didn't volunteer for this," Horton grumbled late in the afternoon as the train rumbled into its final destination. He and Chantal spoke in low voices in French. He looked disgruntled, and she starstruck. "Do you have to sit so close?"

Chantal laughed and batted her eyes. "I'm your adoring assistant, remember, darling? And you're playing the annoyed graduate student perfectly. Just remember some of those technical terms Fourcade sent along and practice using them in sentences, like, 'I'm here to check the modality of the sensors when they're at full power. We need to know if they'll track the aircraft better if we change the azimuth a few degrees. We just need to take a few precise measurements.' Stuff like that. You need to act pompous and all."

"That's asking a lot. I was never good at school, which is why I'm a sergeant in the army. And who chose those silly codenames? Why do I have to be codenamed Pol, and you get to be Charlemagne?"

Chantal giggled. "Shh. Someone could overhear us, but

good job on acting disgruntled, keep it up." She looped her arm around his and snuggled close to him. He stiffened, rolled his eyes, and looked impatiently tolerant.

At the first security barrier after the train had pulled into the station, they calmly produced their papers and watched as the German guard went through them. The pair had been through sufficient numbers of checkpoints that the anxiety, although present, was low key, and Chantal kept up her exaggerations toward Horton to the amusement of the guards and to Horton's irritation.

Nevertheless, concern arose when one of the sentries suddenly called over to a superior and held up a hand indicating that Horton and Chantal should wait. A *feldwebel* approached, a higher-ranking noncom identified by a silver trapezoidal plate with rounded corners hanging over his chest by a chain around his neck. Stone-faced, he scrutinized Horton and Chantal and then went carefully through their papers.

Throughout the platform bedecked with red and black swastika flags, more soldiers patrolled with submachine guns. Some restrained German Shepherd dogs on short leashes.

"You're a scientist?" the *feldwebel* asked Horton in broken French.

"I'm preparing to be one," Horton replied, "at a university in Paris."

The *feldwebel* grunted while continuing to scrutinize Horton's papers. "You're authorized into the area to do some studies. Can you tell me about them?"

Horton stymied a gulp. He stared at the noncom and then at Chantal.

"He's so shy," Chantal said, grinning, "and he's a lot smarter than he looks."

Horton tossed her a scathing glare and turned to face the noncom, who returned an equally cold expression.

"I'm waiting," the man said. "Tell me about the studies you are to do here."

On impulse, Horton suddenly drew his rugby-player's body upright and stared into the German's eyes. "All right, *Feldwebel*," he replied. "I'll tell you what I'm allowed to. Your *Wehrmacht* contracted with my university to do refinements on some technology in use in this area. If you do not know what it is, I cannot tell you, and suggest you inquire higher. If you do know what system I refer to, I can only say this: I'm here to check the modality of the sensors when they're at full power. We need to know if they'll track aircraft better if we change the azimuth a few degrees. We need to take a few precise measurements."

"You see," Chantal told the *feldwebel*, while hanging onto Horton's arm and giggling. "I told you he was smart."

"And you are his girlfriend?"

"I wish," she said, laughing. She drew her head closer to the German's and whispered conspiratorially, "I'm his assigned assistant, and I have a mad crush on him, but he doesn't like me."

"You study at the university too? A woman?"

"I share your disgust," Horton said with a haughty tone while pulling his arm away from Chantal. "Believe it or not, she is supposed to be highly intelligent and gifted in the sciences. Your government gave special dispensation because they said her talents were too good to waste. And I was unlucky enough to have been assigned as her academic adviser. I've tried to have her reassigned, and I will keep trying on my return to Paris."

The *feldwebel* broke a restrained grin. "Wait here," he said. He strode over to a desk with a telephone and placed a call. Moments later, he was back and allowed them through.

"You used my verbiage verbatim," Chantal chortled as they walked away. "I knew we would be perfect together."

Horton only scowled.

At the exit, they turned right, walked down a block, and waited. Chantal pulled a red scarf from her bag and tied it around her neck. Within a few minutes, a car appeared. The driver alighted and handed Horton the keys.

"Go to the Hotel Beau-Minet," he said. "It's the only one open at this time of year because it has central heating." He gave them directions and instructed them on how to return the car.

Dusk had settled when they arrived. The hotel was small and only a few guests lounged in the foyer. The owner was an amiable man who shot Horton an incredulous look when the sergeant requested two rooms.

"He's not sure he likes me yet," Chantal joked, grinning as she twisted back and forth playfully.

They spent the evening conversing with the owner, learning about the history of the area, and gleaning what he knew of German dispositions in the area. "We'd like to take a walk on the beach, if we can," Chantal said. "I want him there at sunrise. See if that'll soften him up toward me."

"I promised I'd take her there," Horton groused. "I don't know what it is about women, beaches, and sunrises."

"You're a fool," the owner told him. "Look at her. She's beautiful. She likes you, and you're not much to look at." He rolled his eyes as if searching for an explanation for his madness. "Anyway, you can't go down there. The road is blocked by barbed wire, there's a sentry at the top, the area is mined from there to the beach, and there's a unit of soldiers down below. You might have to see your sunrise from the road that goes behind Villa Stella Maris. That's a mansion where about thirty soldiers stay, but it's on the main road past the one to the beach."

Horton and Chantal met in the foyer at dawn. "That was some incredible information the owner gave us last night," Horton said as they headed out the door.

"To say the least," she replied with a mischievous smile. Then she reached for his hand and interlocked her fingers with his.

"Hey, what are you doing?"

"Today, you are my boyfriend," she said, laughing. "That's what's going to get us on that beach. If a unit of soldiers is guarding it, then there must be a path through the minefield.

"Now play the part. We're two young lovers out for an early morning stroll after a night of passion. Haven't you heard? No one can resist young love."

"Aren't you pushing this a little far?"

"And having fun doing it," Chantal said, grinning impishly. "I'm wearing you down, I can see it."

Horton harrumphed but did not object when Chantal moved in close to him and took his hand once more. They reached the end of the driveway and turned onto the road.

"Put your arm around me," Chantal said. "We're supposed to be in love."

Huffing his displeasure, Horton did as instructed. Then together, they strolled in the morning twilight toward a Y-intersection at a bend in the road. Straight ahead, it led downhill, presumably to the beach, not yet visible from their vantage. To the right, it ran behind Villa Stella Maris, which they could now see plainly on the plateau, and beyond it, the Atlantic.

A sentry at a barbed wire barrier for the branch of road leading downhill saw them coming and stood in front of his sentry box. He held his rifle loosely in front of him.

"Leave this to me," Chantal said. She let go of Horton's hand and scurried down the road to the guard.

When Horton caught up, to his amazement, the soldier was grinning and laughing with Chantal. The butt of his weapon now rested on the ground next to his boot, and he glanced at Horton, grinning lasciviously. Meanwhile, he conversed with Chantal in broken French and German as she made him understand that she wanted to be on the beach to watch the sunrise with her boyfriend.

He asked for their identity papers, and when he read Horton's with the permissions to do scientific research, he became slightly more businesslike, leaning toward being obsequious. Stepping aside, he gestured them through a gate, and then led them down the road, while keeping a running commentary with Chantal in their broken French and German.

Horton noted that the sentry paid no particular attention to where he or they stepped. *It's not mined.* He also spotted two machine gun nests on the side of the hill overlooking the beach.

As they neared the water's edge, other soldiers started running toward them, but the sentry called out to them. They all laughed and returned to what they had been doing. Then the sentry left them alone, and waited for them at the bottom of the hill.

Chantal took Horton's hand again. "Now just relax and enjoy the sun coming up. That's what we told the guard we'd do."

They strolled together. Then, Chantal took off her shoes and waded into the water, splashed some up at Horton, and laughed charmingly.

Suddenly, she circled in front of Horton and pressed against him. A wave of shock passed through him from the warmth of her body against his own.

"Kiss me," she said.

"Excuse me? What the bloody hell are you doing?"

"Kiss me. We're in love, remember." She pointed toward the guard. "He's watching, and he'll expect it. So will the others. You don't want to make them suspicious."

Horton leaned his head down and pecked her on the cheek.

"Not like that," she said. Rising on her tiptoes and encircling her arms around his neck, she pressed her lips to his. She held them a moment and then leaned back.

"You've never kissed a girl before, have you? You're trembling."

"What do you expect? I've been in this bloody war for nearly three years. What about you? Have you kissed a boy—"

"You mean a man?" She shook her head and murmured, "Not until now."

February 27, 1942
Marseille, France

"You're grumpy," Fourcade told Chantal. "That was great information you brought. I've sent it off to London. They were very happy with it."

They stood at the rail of the veranda overlooking the city, and Fourcade watched Chantal for a reaction. Seeing none, she inquired, "What's wrong? You did a tremendous job."

Chantal shook her head and turned away. "I can't say. I'm embarrassed."

"Something to do with Horton?"

Chantal brought her hands to her face. "That stupid, stupid man. Why did I ever like him?" She whirled in exasperation, her eyes wide with anger. "I know we were both role-playing for the mission, but he knew I really felt it. And do you know what he did?" Her chest heaved. "When I was leaving Loire to come back here"—her voice rose—"*he shook my hand*."

Fourcade stymied a laugh and reached out to embrace Chantal. "Ahh, the pain of first love," she said. "He'll come around some day, and if not—"

"I know, I know. A lot of fish in the sea," Chantal growled through gritted teeth, "but I want *that* wet fish." She and Fourcade laughed together, and then Chantal added somberly, "If we both live through this war."

March 1, 1942
Bletchley Park, England

"Come in, Miss Littlefield. What do you have for me?"

"Good news, I think, sir," Claire said, taking her seat in front of Commander Denniston's desk. "There is a great deal of gnashing of teeth going on in Berlin right now. The messages coming over Enigma are fast and furious concerning a raid in France at a place called Bruneval. Apparently, a radar station there was taken down by our chaps, and the Germans are concerned that we staged a raid on French soil in the first place, that we did it via paratroopers in the second place, and they're wondering what the implications are for maintaining their radar sites. They're not sure if the components of the Wurzburg were captured or destroyed. Hitler is in a rage."

She laughed. "They've ordered that the ground around all radar sites be closely trimmed for a diameter of twenty feet so that intruders can be spotted easier. I guess they hadn't thought that doing so will also make spotting them easier for our reconnaissance flights."

Denniston chuckled. "You could have started with that statement about Hitler's rage. That would have been enough to make my day. But the rest of your report is also most welcome."

21

Eglin Field, Florida, USA

A hundred and forty members of the US Army Air Corps, pilots and crew, trooped into the operations office and squished together to see and listen to a legend. Soon enough, Jimmy Doolittle appeared before them. With him was a lieutenant commander from the navy, Josh Littlefield.

He began without any fuss, his manner gruff. "If you men have any idea that this isn't the most dangerous thing you've ever done, don't even start this training. Drop out now. There isn't much sense wasting time and money training men who aren't going through with this thing. It's perfectly all right for any of you to bow out now."

"Can you tell us anything about it?" someone called.

Silence descended.

Doolittle shook his head. "Not now. It's top secret, and even your wives and families can't know what you're doing or where you're going until it's over. Don't even conjecture among yourselves. If you arrive at a conclusion, don't mention it—it'll probably be wrong anyway.

"Don't ask me any questions about it, and don't ask our navy friend either. He's here out of curiosity about B-25s and I offered to let him ride in a few. He's a pilot, so if you find him in your aircraft and he wants to pilot it, extend whatever courtesy you see fit. But don't pester him with questions he can't answer.

"Your immediate task is to get in the air and locate all the auxiliary fields around Eglin. You'll be learning a lot of special maneuvers and we need as many of you as possible practicing simultaneously. You should not be spending much time lounging in the operations hut."

When he had finished, the pilots filed out, excited but subdued, their faith in the mission residing in the man who would train them. Josh mingled with them, getting to know as many as he could within a short space of time. Though not unfriendly, most regarded him coolly, but one pilot approached him with a friendly smile.

"Hi, I'm Captain Ted Lawson," he said, extending his hand. "I'll be happy to have you aboard my plane, it you'd like to join me."

Josh accepted the invitation readily, and soon found himself in the co-pilot's seat of a B-25 above Eglin observing the physical layout of the base. "How do you like this aircraft?" he asked above the roar of engines and wind.

"I love it," Ted replied, his voice converted to an electronic sound through the earphones. "It loves to fly as much as I do, and when it lands, it needs very little direction. I had to give a demonstration to the Soviets a few months back before Pearl Harbor, and one of their generals took over the flight controls. He scared me to death, flying low over DC and maneuvering like he was in a fighter, but he's one hell of a pilot. When he was offered his pick of ten plane types to ship to Russia, he chose the B-25.

I've flown them off the California coast in submarine hunts, and I can't ask for a better aircraft."

"I'm impressed," Josh called back. "It's a smooth ride."

"Do you enjoy flying off carriers?"

"For the most part, yes. It has its moments, like all flying."

"I'll say," Ted agreed. "I've lost a couple." He grinned. "But so far, I haven't lost me."

Over the next weeks, Josh took pains to get to know as many of the pilots and crewmembers as he could, but he had formed an affinity with Ted and spent many hours with him. The pilot had set out to be an aeronautical engineer and had joined the Army Air Corps at the urging of a college professor who pointed out that military time could help his career. The service would, after all, teach him to fly.

That had been two years ago, and although the signs of probable US entry into the war were all about, few Americans perceived danger from the east, expecting that they would be fighting German Nazis.

So, Ted had bounced around the country to various training sites. At one point, deciding that he might never have the chance to wed his fiancée, Ellen, if he did not seize the moment, he married her in Coeur d'Alene, Idaho, over a weekend. She flew up with her mother, they went to a justice of the peace, and with two of his buddies serving as Ellen's bridal party, they married. Two days later, she and her mother drove back to Los Angeles, and he transferred to yet another base.

A few days later, after the planes had been reconfigured with broomsticks for machine guns, stripped of their top-secret Norden gunsights and other non-flight required equipment, reconfigured with added long-range rubber fuel cells and a dummy tail gunner, and packed with the weight of a full load of bombs, Ted's curiosity momentarily got the better of him. "You know where we're going, don't you?"

Josh stared at him blankly.

"I can guess," Ted pressed.

"Don't," Josh replied.

They left it at that, and Ted never brought up the subject again. Ellen drove in from Los Angeles, exhausted, but obviously very devoted to her husband. She was petite with a bright smile and mid-length dark hair and prudent enough not to press Ted on what he was doing, taking in stride that her husband had little time to spend with her.

While she was still there, Doolittle called another meeting. As it progressed, two senior officers entered the facility. Doolittle immediately closed down the briefing, an indication of how seriously he took the secrecy surrounding their mission.

After the officers had departed, he told the assembled pilots, "This level of security must be maintained. Leaks would turn to rumors, and mixed with rumors are likely to be elements of truth. If any part of that truth gets out, your lives and those of your crews could be in greater danger, but that's not all that's at stake. A lot of people are working on this operation. One slip could kill it." He chose his next words carefully. "If anyone approaches asking questions, let me know ASAP, and I'll turn him over to the FBI.

"That's the main point of tonight's briefing," he said in conclusion. "But one piece of advice: the most important part of this mission is practicing short, quick takeoffs."

They started that practice at the end of the first week at auxiliary fields to keep them shielded from curiosity. Another navy pilot, Lieutenant Henry Miller, came in to help with improving technique, suggesting that to lift into the air sooner, they lower their landing flaps and rev the engines to maximum power.

More wives showed up and moved in with their husbands. Josh met most of them and enjoyed seeing them, but he worried about security. As time passed and he got to know everyone better, he worried less. The pilots, crews, and their wives took security as seriously as he and Doolittle did. Nonetheless, he kept diligence high.

He was as concerned as the pilots when he discerned that the payloads would be dropped from low altitude. He deduced as much from removal of the top-secret Norden aiming devices to preclude any of them from falling into enemy hands. The Nordens were accurate only for high-altitude bombing. That piece of information had a sobering effect, raising the expectation that some of the pilots and crews might be captured.

Other evidence of the intent for low release were the practice bombing runs themselves. Ted returned to base one evening rubbing his head, and informed Josh that when he had dropped a one-hundred-pound bomb from five hundred feet, the shockwave had bounced him off the ceiling of his cockpit. He and the rest of the pilots and crews were pleased to learn that henceforth and during the mission, the bombs were intended to be dropped at fifteen hundred feet.

"We had a guy quit today," Ted told Josh after a briefing with Doolittle. Josh had been sending a progress report to the *Enterprise*.

"Those low-altitude drops got to him, and so did the short takeoffs. So far, he's the only one to drop off." He sighed. "I can see in Ellen's eyes that she's terrified for me and wishes I would quit, but she won't say so."

Josh had no good response. "It'll soon be over," he said at last. *But at what cost?*

22

March 3, 1942
Ayr, Scotland

Jeremy trooped with the other men of 12 Commando inside the cavernous hangar that served as an auditorium. *At last, we're going to find out what this mission is all about.*

"Any guesses what we're going to do?" Kenyon asked.

"Nothing beyond what we knew when we started training back in January. How was that demolitions course?"

"Intense. By comparison, I had barely been to kindergarten on the subject. We're working with some highly specialized concepts and explosives. With the number of men trained to carry the stuff and detonate it, the target's got to be big, but I also saw hints of something much bigger than indicated by what we were taught."

"How so?"

"It's more of a feeling. There was this Royal Navy chap always there, Lieutenant Nigel Tibbets. He's very smart, and we all liked him despite that he stayed aloof, and he knew demolitions like no one I ever saw. But along with Captain

Pritchard, he taught us what we needed to know in a short time, and after that it was practice, practice, practice. And he was still always there, but not watching us. He was in conferences and talking with scientists—a lot of activity that didn't involve us, but you could tell that it was linked to us somehow."

As they made their way to their seats, a voice at Kenyon's shoulder called his name. Kenyon turned. "Hello," he responded, and made introductions. "Jeremy, this is Corran Purdon. He's the leader of our demolitions team.

"Corran, this is Jeremy. I was with his brother in France after Dunkirk. I met Jeremy in Marseille while he was there on special assignment. Would you like to sit with us?"

Corran nodded. He was a slender man of average height, light-colored hair, and calm, brown eyes. During training, he had impressed Kenyon. Nothing seemed to perturb Corran. He had been inexhaustible during forced marches, climbing mountains, and rappelling; unbeatable at hand-to-hand combat; a quiet leader who rose to the occasion when required but did not push himself to the front; and an unusually nice and courteous individual off the training field. He came from a long line of military figures in British history, his father being Major-General Brooke Purdon, the doctor general.

Clearly, Corran did not need to be in the commandos to realize a successful military career, yet here he was performing among the best regardless of how challenging or menial the task; and only months ago he had participated in the Lofoten raid in Norway. Kenyon counted himself fortunate to be teamed with him.

Almost as soon as the commandos had sat down, Lieutenant Colonel Charles Newman took the stage. "We all know each other," he said, addressing the six-hundred-plus commandos, "so I won't bother with niceties. Let's get right into things.

"You've been training to do a mission, and you'd like to know what it is, but I'm not yet prepared to tell you." He held up his palms to placate a collective groan. "I *can* tell you that we're only weeks away from execution. We've brought together members of multiple groups to form 12 Commando for this mission.

"The reason we organized in this way is that you've trained as specialized teams. Now it's time to put those teams together and rehearse for a unified mission. We've built mockups and scale models, and we're going to rehearse until you can't stand the thought of doing it again, and then we'll rehearse some more."

He dropped his head and strode across the stage as he gathered his thoughts. "We had a bit of bad news early last month, as I'm sure you've heard, concerning Singapore. That was the largest surrender of forces our country has ever known—a national embarrassment, not to mention our loss of access to resources. It was a huge tragedy for our captured brothers and their families with loved ones taken prisoner by the Japanese. Our hearts and prayers go out to them.

"As disheartening as that is, we persevere. The peril to our national existence leaves no choice."

Newman moved to center stage and stood surveying his audience of young men. He was proud of them beyond his ability to express. Each of them had volunteered for the commandos, none knowing what was expected of them for having done so; and every one of those present had proven themselves under the most rigorous physical and mental conditions. And they were here now, offering their very lives to the nation, knowing that the ultimate sacrifice might be made.

"Let me give you a bit of good news," the lieutenant colonel continued. "What I am about to tell you will be released to the public shortly, but not with the amount of detail I'll provide. There was another raid recently, Operation Biting, and I'll tell you up front that it was successful. I'll hold off on how successful it was until the end of my talk.

"Some of you might have heard already. I hope not, because that would represent an unpardonable breach of security."

Grim silence descended.

"This raid was accomplished by the Special Air Service, the SAS, a new part of our military—our parachutists. They fall out of airplanes and float to the ground. This was their first successful mission, and I have to say that my hat is off to them because they had not yet completed their parachute training. But the mission was vital, and the window for completing it spanned only three nights. If not done then, the mission would have been postponed another month, and more Brits would have died as a result.

"This was also only the second raid conducted under Lord Mountbatten's concept of combined arms operations that included all three of our services. The first, of course, was our very successful second commando raid in Norway." At that, a cheer broke out among the crowd. "And I should add that, by the time we depart on our mission, Lord Mountbatten will have been elevated from being an adviser to being the chief of combined operations." The cheering grew louder.

When Newman raised his hand to quiet the men, he saw that they leaned on every word he said. "The SAS mission's objective was on the French coast to seize components of their Wurzburg radar system. The raid relied on very accurate information supplied to British intelligence by a pair of very brave members of the French Resistance who, in advance, reconned the target facility. It was protected by more than ninety German soldiers, yet those Resistance operatives brought out crucial information about enemy bunkers, gun emplacements, and numbers. As an example, they informed us that a supposed mine field was not mined at all. They knew because they had crossed it—and the raiding party would have to traverse the very same area."

At that, Kenyon leaned over to Jeremy and whispered, "I wonder who those poor sods were. They're a lot braver than me."

"And me," Jeremy replied, and returned his attention to Newman.

"Our SAS chaps made mistakes along the way. One group was dropped three and a half kilometers from the target and ran the distance to re-join the mission. There is some question of whether or not the mission leader, Major John Frost, stayed on target long enough or should have stayed longer, but he did his job under heavy gunfire.

"Several men missed being picked up because they arrived at the beach minutes too late. They radioed in, but at that stage, they could not be rescued—presumably they are POWs now—and the whole mission was nearly toppled at the outset when the Royal Navy arrived late to transport the raiding party. The landing craft had been held up by a passing German patrol boat and a submarine, neither of which spotted them.

"Here's the point: the mission could have been a disaster at any of multiple points. At each of those junctures, individuals persevered, and as a result, it was a resounding success. And now I will tell you how successful."

Almost as a single body, the commandos leaned forward in their seats.

"You're all aware of our Chain Home radar that gave us early warning and thus protected us during the Battle of Britain. What you probably don't know is that, since then, Germany built its own radar system along the Atlantic coast. It's called the Kammhuber Line, and each emplacement of it consists of two components, the Freya, and the Wurzburg I mentioned moments ago. When their data are combined, they lock on and give the Germans accurate information on where to engage our bombers. We were losing four out of every one hundred planes and crews sent over because of the Wurzburg and the Kammhuber Line.

"I am happy to tell you now that our SAS brothers succeeded in securing the site long enough for Flight Sergeant Cox, the radar mechanic who went with them, to pinch the Wurzburg's innards. Our lead scientist on this project, Professor Jones, took the unit apart, examined it, and his team is re-engineering it. They tell us that they are confident of developing the technology to jam that radar."

Expectant silence floated like a heavy blanket. When he spoke again, Newman's voice rose to a thunderous volume. "What that means is that our bombers will fly into Europe without giving advance warning. Their system will be neutralized, and we will gain air superiority over Europe."

The commandos jumped to their feet, cheering and whooping until the lieutenant colonel once more indicated for them to take seats. "I have one last thought for you before releasing you to your training. As crucial and far-ranging as the effect of the Bruneval raid was, the mission you will undertake in a matter of weeks is just as crucial, and when you succeed, the effect will be as profound.

"During the Bruneval raid, the SAS suffered only one

casualty not counting the few men who were captured. Our casualty rate is likely to be higher. The danger and difficulty are much greater. Having said that, our brothers in the SAS set an example of perseverance under deadly circumstances that is profound. That same level of perseverance will make our mission successful, and it's why we will win this war. So, I urge each of you to believe in yourself, believe in your comrades, your service, your country, and our new allies. Thank you. Dismissed."

Quiet hovered over the commandos as Newman left the stage and they began to leave the hangar. As they departed, Kenyon went to visit with others he had trained with, while Corran and Jeremy moved slowly with the crowd.

Corran turned to Jeremy. "It always comes down to a nail," he said.

"Excuse me?"

"You must have heard the adage about a war being lost for the want of a nail?"

"Of course. The horse lost a shoe for needing a nail, the messenger lost the horse for its needing a shoe, and the war was lost for needing that message. So, in essence, the war was lost for the need of one nail."

"Exactly. Well, the reverse is also true. The raid was successful because we had the nail."

"Which part do you mean? The colonel said there were many points at which it could have broken down."

"Yes, but only one was in advance of the mission itself, without which the entire operation could have been scrubbed or resulted in disaster. The critical part was the information supplied by the two Resistance members who dared to cross the minefield. Together, they were the nail, and like the horseman in the adage, we'll probably never know who they are."

23

March 22, 1942
Eglin Field, Florida

Ted revved the engines of his B-25 medium bomber. The thunderous reverberations shook the plane as he checked to his right and left, making eye contact with the pilots of the planes next to his own, and then checked the distance to the one ahead. They were packed tightly together in the space of the width of an aircraft carrier at one end of its deck. Today was their interim exam.

Josh sat behind the cockpit in an unofficial role. For him, this was a fun ride, one he found interesting. This was the first time that the entire squadron of twenty-four planes would take off and fly long distances at low level, using dead reckoning for navigation. He had monitored the training closely and deemed the pilots and crews ready for the next phase.

Three rows ahead, the first aircraft started its run. Ted craned his neck to see it, but only the very top of its fuselage was visible, and then that disappeared, the view blocked by the other aircraft in front. Then he saw it again as its nose rose and the plane lifted into the air. Ted let loose a spontaneous cry of celebration, joined by his crew and Josh.

The next plane made its run, and then the next and the next, all climbing to altitude and then departing in a long, single file. Finally, it was Ted's turn. He dropped his landing flaps to full extension and opened the throttle to maximum power. The B-25 rattled and tossed, straining to pounce. Ted watched for the signal flag, and when it waved abruptly, he released the breaks. The bomber leaped forward, rolled down the improvised deck, gained speed, and lumbered into the sky.

Minutes later, the full squadron flew in formation and set its course for Ft. Meyers, four hundred miles across the Gulf of Mexico. There, it changed course, flying back across the Gulf just above the wavetops for more than seven hundred miles to Houston, Texas, and then back to Eglin. The pilots arrived back worn, tired, but pleased at the accomplishment of having flown and navigated more than fifteen hundred miles at low level, non-stop, and had reached the correct checkpoints with the formation intact, on time, and without incident.

March 24, 1942

A loud knock woke Ted from a deep sleep. Ellen sat up, flipped on a lamp, and stared anxiously at her husband as he slipped on a robe and went to see who was at their door at three a.m. Moments later, he returned. His somber look relayed that Ellen's fears were warranted.

"You're leaving?" Tears brimmed.

He nodded. "In a few hours."

"When will you be back."

"I don't know."

The squadron lifted off at eleven that morning. With two other pilots' wives, Ellen had decided to rent a house at Myrtle Beach, South Carolina, for the duration. After stoic goodbyes, pilots and crews waved to their loved ones and climbed aboard their aircraft, headed for an overnight stop in San Antonio, a refueling stop in Phoenix, and March Field in California. Forbidden from communicating with anyone outside their group, on arrival, they engaged themselves in games of cards, sleeping, checking equipment, and doing all the things that warriors do enroute to an engagement. The next morning, they took off early for McClellan Field near Sacramento.

They flew low, at treetop level. Josh, accompanying the flight in Ted's plane, had noticed dark humor overtaking the squadron, one of fatalism. He concluded that, to a man, they expected to ride this mission into their demise. The attitude manifested in almost defiant flying, some banking through an open drawbridge, others swooping low over a river to observe swimmers along a beach. However, on reaching their destination, he noticed a rise in morale from having blown off steam.

Doolittle met them there. He had flown straight from San Antonio, across the Rockies by instruments, a feat that inspired his young charges and lifted their spirits further. "No hell-raising tonight," he told them. "Spend your time checking your crews and your aircraft. Your radios are being taken out. You won't need them where you're going."

Ted cast a sharp glance at Josh and murmured, "We're going to hit the Japanese, aren't we? Where?"

"No comment," Josh whispered, and returned his attention to Doolittle.

"We'll be here a few more days," the lieutenant colonel went on, "practicing short, full-flap takeoffs, low-level navigation, and using our improvised bombing sights—they're pretty much like aiming a rifle, so no big deal. Your propellers are being replaced with very expensive three-bladed ones. Keep them oiled. Scratches will cause them to bubble in sea air."

When he had finished speaking and the pilots were milling about, Josh approached him. Together, they stepped aside from the group. "Sir," he said in a low voice, "have you got your status straightened out yet? Will you be leading this raid?"

Doolittle grinned. "That's why I was late getting here. I just came from a long meeting in DC with Hap. I pressed him again, and he told me I couldn't lead every raid. I kept on him, and finally he said, 'All right, if the chief doesn't object, I'll approve.'

"I figured that was a convenient put-off, so I said okay. As soon as I got outside his office, I hoofed down the hall to his chief of staff's office, that's Major-General Harmon, and relayed the conversation. The chief said, 'If Hap's okay with it, I'm not going to override the boss. Go ahead.'"

Doolittle laughed. "As I was leaving, the phone rang, and the next thing I heard was, 'But General, I just told Jimmy he could do it.'"

Josh laughed with him and pivoted to face him directly. "Sir, I respectfully request to be included on this mission."

Doolittle peered at him, bemused.

Before he could say anything, Josh went on, "Sir, I

listened to the calls from our pilots going down at Pearl Harbor. I saw the destruction. I was there to see the experiment of B-25s flying off the *Hornet* in Norfolk." He gestured around the group of pilots. "I've been with these guys all through their training, their ups, their downs.

"I've met the wives. I've seen the fear for their husbands in their eyes. I belong on this mission. Please let me go."

"Doing what? You know our weight limitations. We have none to spare."

"I don't know. Maybe one of the crew will get sick before the raid. I'm not wishing that, but you've cross-trained every crewmember to navigate, pilot, perform as flight engineers and bombardiers. I trained right along with them and can do any function. Whatever you need doing, I'll do."

The lieutenant colonel blew out a breath and looked past Josh at the rest of the crew. He scratched his head.

"Sir," Josh pressed. "You wangled your way in. Please let me wangle mine."

Doolittle laughed. "How did I know you were going to say that, Josh? The difference is that the raid needs a commander. Someone was going to take up that space, and it might as well be me. I added no weight. If you come along, you will."

"Then just think about it, sir, and if anyone—and I mean anyone on any plane in any crew—if any of them must be substituted, let it be me."

Doolittle stared into Josh's eyes. "You're serious."

Josh nodded.

"Your commander would have to approve."

"He'd love having a navy man on board. I can convince him."

"Convince 'Bull' Halsey?" Doolittle chuckled. "All right. I'll give you this much: if we need a substitute, and if he agrees, you can go. Between now and then, you'll need to stay on top of the training just as you have been."

Josh smiled broadly. "You got it, sir. Thank you."

Doolittle shook his head grimly. "I'm not sure I've done anything deserving your thanks, but we'd be glad to have you, if need be. But there's something you should know that the others will learn at shipside." He looked around to be sure they were out of earshot. "Not all of these guys are going. We can only take sixteen planes. The others were trained in case we needed spares." He sighed as he took a moment to observe the men. "They all came through with flying colors, every one of them. But we're taking just selected crews and a few spares—who, by the way, will have dibs over you. The others will re-join their units." He shrugged. "But you might have a shot."

"I'll take it."

24

Falmouth, England

"Gentlemen," Lieutenant Colonel Newman greeted the men of 12 Commando. Three weeks had passed since he last addressed them, and in the interim they had trained for a mission they still knew nothing about aside from their individual tasks. "I know jolly well you've been wondering what we're up to down here. You'll be delighted to know that we've been selected for a lovely job — a saucy job — easily the biggest thing that's been done yet by commandos. You could say it's the sauciest job since Drake.

"At last, all will be revealed," he intoned to a roar of celebration. Affectionately referred to as "Colonel Charles" by his command but not to his face, he scanned across the faces of six hundred and eleven expectant commandos and a large contingent of coastal defense seamen of the Royal Navy. They had assembled in the theater aboard the HMS *Princess Joséphine Charlotte,* a former passenger ship requisitioned and converted by the navy into a landing ship. It had transported the commandos from Ayr, along Scotland's western coast and around Britain's southern tip, to Falmouth for final mission training, integration, and staging.

Jeremy, Kenyon, and Corran sat with others among the team who had trained with them. All paid close attention.

Newman waited for the cheering to subside. "Look around, commandos. You'll see that I've invited many of our brothers in coastal defense and their leadership to join us in this briefing. I'll explain that later, but first, a little history." He raised his palms to placate expressions of impatience. "Your officers were briefed three days ago, and since then you've rehearsed specific tasks intended to take out twenty-four targets."

He took a deep breath while his audience took in the scale of what he had just told them. "Last year, we sank the battleship, *Bismarck*. She had a sister ship, which was built a little later. It's a little bigger, and just as fast. Hitler planned to unleash them together to rule the Atlantic and starve our people."

Newman paused for effect. "We put a dent in that plan."

Smiling amid more cheering, he waited for it to abate and went on. "That said, the sister ship, the *Tirpitz*, could still tip the balance in the *Kriegsmarine's* favor if she breaches our naval blockade around Iceland. We can't let that happen.

"Recall that our legendary HMS *Hood*, the king's flagship for twenty years and once the mightiest warship ever built, was destroyed with a single round from the *Bismarck* at a distance of thirteen miles. The *Tirpitz* has that same capability, and more. She's currently the largest vessel afloat."

Newman let the sobering thought linger. "The *Tirpitz* is eight hundred and twenty-three feet long and a hundred and eighteen feet across the beam. In more prosaic terms, that's over three regulation football fields that could fit on her deck." His voice elevated as he rattled off the battleship's firepower. "She's equipped with eight 15in main guns; twelve 5.9in smoothbore guns; sixteen 4.1in anti-aircraft guns; sixteen 1.5in anti-aircraft guns; fifty-eight .79in FlaK guns; and eight 21in torpedo tubes. Her steel armor is thirteen inches thick at the belt, fourteen inches thick around the turrets, and nearly five inches thick in some places along the main deck. With her complement of two thousand and sixty-five crewmen, she weighs in, fully loaded, at fifty-two thousand tons. Yet with all that, she plows through the ocean at thirty knots."

He stopped to take a deep breath and arch his eyebrows. "She is the most powerful and fastest war vessel afloat, gentlemen. She can certainly catch and destroy any of our ships. Even without the *Bismarck*, she could defeat us in the Battle of the Atlantic."

"Let's sink her too," someone called, followed by loud acclamation from the audience.

Newman shook his head gravely. "I assure you the prime minister wants nothing more and puts constant pressure on the admiralty to do exactly that. Another group is working toward that end, but that's still in the future. She's hunkered down in Norway, where she threatens our supply convoys to the Soviet Union. Too many ships of our fleet have been sunk to attack her directly, and too many more have been sent to the war against the Japanese in the Pacific on the other side of the planet." He scanned the faces once more, taking in their sober attention. "But." He dropped his voice, and a slow smile spread across his face as his eyes lowered in concentrated cunning. "Her size is her weakness."

Newman paced the stage in his preferred fatherly role. "*This* raid is much more than our normal mission. It is a full military combined-arms operation conceived and pushed by Lord Mountbatten. Furthermore, this mission has occupied the attention of both Prime Minister Churchill and the king himself.

"Lord Mountbatten's been involved in every step of planning, haranguing the joint chiefs for needed resources—" Newman stopped his slow pace across the stage and faced his men. "I met with him just before I briefed your officers three days ago, and he required me to say the following." He pulled a sheet of paper from his jacket pocket and held it up. "I jotted down what he said, so as to relate in his own words."

He opened the paper and read, "'I want you to be quite clear that this is not an ordinary raid; it is an important operation of war. It is also a very hazardous operation.

"'I am quite confident that you will get in and do the job all right, but, frankly, I don't expect any of you to get out again.'"

Newman paused and looked across the mass of now sober faces. Then he resumed reading Mountbatten's message. "'If we lose you all, you will be about equivalent to the loss of one merchant ship; but your success will save many merchant ships. We have got to look at the thing in those terms.'"

Glancing up from his note, Newman paused his reading and said, "When our merchant ships are sunk, our people go hungry, and we find ourselves with fewer weapons to fight this war." He dropped his head, took a step, and straightened to full height. "I was deeply impressed with Lord Mountbatten's care for each of you." He returned his eyes to the paper and continued reading. "'I don't want you to take anyone on the operation who has any serious home ties or worries. No married men. Make that quite clear and give every man the opportunity of standing down if he feels he should. Nobody will think any the worse of him, and we must have that understood, too.'"

Newman stood stock still. No one stirred or made the slightest sound.

Thoughts of Amélie flitted through Jeremy's mind. He forced them aside.

Newman then spoke in a soft voice. "Anyone wishing to depart may do so at any time during this briefing or until we depart the day after tomorrow. No penalty will attach. You will not be RTUed. You'll simply not go on this mission."

When no one moved, he said, "That business taken care of, let's continue with the briefing, reminding that the door to your separating from this raid remains open."

He cleared his throat while he gathered his thoughts, and when he spoke again, his voice took on a strong resonance, his words clipped. "At present, the *Tirpitz* is contained in the North Sea. Hitler knows that if she runs through our blockade, she'll be met with every gun we can make available. We'll suffer heavy losses, but the *Tirpitz* won't break out into the Atlantic unscathed. Chances are, she'll incur damage needing repair. Even if that is not the case, we have our own submarines plowing the oceans, and at some point, she'll be hit hard enough to require the services of a dry dock." Newman's voice dropped again into a conspiratorial tone. "And there is only one in existence in the Atlantic to handle a ship of her size." He dropped his voice again to a piercing stage-whisper. "As I said, her size is her weakness. Destroy that dry dock, and we defeat the *Tirpitz*."

Like his mates, Jeremy listened with rapt attention. Now he turned to Kenyon, who met his glance with shining eyes. "Saint-Nazaire," they exclaimed in whispered unison.

Scuttle had circulated among some commandos that the target would be the dry dock in Brest because that was where the *Bismarck* had tried to go for repairs before she was sunk. Jeremy and Kenyon returned their attention to Newman and absorbed the lieutenant colonel's next comment.

"With the Americans joining us, the Battle of the Atlantic becomes ours to lose." Newman let that thought linger in the air a moment. "But the target is a hard one. The RAF has been bombing her for months with no significant effect.

"Now, let's get to the target and the plan. The day after tomorrow, we'll sail from Falmouth aboard the HMS *Campbeltown*. That's an ancient destroyer formerly known as the USS *Buchanan*, or more familiarly as 'Old Buck.' It's one of fifty ships the Americans were kind enough to let us have during our time of dire need in exchange for the use of a few island bases in the Caribbean." He broke a smile. "The colonials learned too well from us. They drive a hard bargain." A ripple of laughter broke through the commandos but ended abruptly when Newman suddenly became steely-eyed and his voice took on a hard quality.

"Gentlemen, the main target is the *Normandie* dry dock in Saint-Nazaire, and if we can't utterly destroy it, we intend to render it unserviceable for the duration of the war." Once more he smiled, this time with the expression of a sly fox. "That's easier said than done, but we believe we have the resources and the plan to do the job."

He looked across the crowd for a particular face, and when he spotted it, he said, "Commander Ryder, would you please stand and be recognized." As the legendary naval officer took to his feet, Newman introduced him. "This man already wears the Military Cross for gallantry under fire, and when his ship went down, he spent four waterlogged days clinging to a deck chock."

Commander "Red" Ryder stood in a stance that was at once respectful and bordered on nonchalance as he was extolled. In his mid-thirties and of short stature, his hair was dark, his face smooth but tough, his chest deep, and his eyes gleamed with determination and a lack of patience for nonsense.

"He now commands the naval forces that will carry us to rendezvous with a submarine a few miles off the coast of France, and then to the targets. His small fleet consists of the *Campbeltown*; two escort destroyers, the *Tynedale* and the *Atherstone*—"

Newman halted a moment and grinned. "Be nice to those chaps on the *Tynedale* and the *Atherstone*. They're there to rescue us if we need rescuing."

After light laughter, he continued. "We'll also be joined by sixteen B-class Fairmile motor launches with extra gasoline tanks affixed to their aft deck, a motor-torpedo boat, and two machine gun boats." Newman held up a finger to make a point. "Commander Ryder's mission and the men he commands will accomplish much more than just transporting us to our target.

"In fact, let me commend the sailors of the commander's naval forces, most of whom are present in this room," Newman continued. "Each of you commandos was handselected for this mission. That is not the case with our navy brothers. Commander Ryder brought what was available from our coastal defense, which operates primarily in these small, wooden motorboats that will carry many of us to France. Having met these men, I can say unequivocally that there is not one among them I would not have selected if given an option. They are, after all, hand-selected for the jobs they normally perform, which is to attack and harass enemy vessels too near our shores and rescue downed pilots and shipwrecked crewmen.

"Their jobs are round-the-clock, dangerous, demanding, and they complete them superbly." He chuckled. "The one area in which they needed more work was sailing in formation. That is something they don't do in coastal defense, but the good commander exercised them in the maneuvers until they could stand to do them no more." He grinned. "But then he made them do more."

Light laughter permeated. As Ryder started to take his seat, Newman entreated him, "Please, come stand in front of the stage, Commander. I want every man here to know and recognize each member of our leadership."

Newman scanned the room for another particular face and, finding it, introduced another officer. "Captain Bill Pritchard, please stand.

"Some of you might have heard of the good captain," he said. "He's the veteran of countless combat engagements in France. At Dunkirk, he became enamored with what could be accomplished militarily by blowing up bridges." He paused for emphasis. "His task is central to our success. If he fails, we fail."

All eyes turned to the captain. Corran nudged Jeremy. "He's a magnificent chap," he murmured. "I've enjoyed learning from him. He organized the demolitions teams, and I'm glad to be part of them."

"Agreed," Jeremy replied.

Captain Pritchard would have stood out in any crowd for his strong build, but in this one with men of similar physical fitness, his tall height became of note. He had dark hair and complexion, and brown eyes that burned with passion for his current pursuit, but they also glinted with humor.

"I met the captain's father," Newman announced. "He told me that his son lives and loves hard and deems every moment to be important. I have every confidence that we'll succeed because he'll succeed. Those of you who trained under him know him to be a competent instructor in the art of demolitions, having planned for the destruction of Great Britain's ports in the event of a German invasion. Captain Pritchard, please join Commander Ryder at the front."

As Pritchard complied, Newman turned his attention to another man. "With us also is someone I consider to be a pure genius, Lieutenant Nigel Tibbits." The lieutenant took to his feet. In his late twenties, he was of middle height, fair complexion, and had a long face and a slow smile. Intelligence exuded from his eyes.

"Our target is particularly difficult to approach, and once we're on it, the explosive power is massive, so a specialized delivery system and careful timing are imperative. Further, since we are traveling through rough seas, the explosives must be protected against early detonation, and on arrival, they've got to appear to be something other than what they are, in case the Germans should find them before detonation.

"We'll go over how all of that is accomplished a little later, and your troop leaders will provide more detail, but for now, suffice it to say that this lieutenant made the impossible possible. Just as crucially, he will be on the raid with us. Lieutenant, please make your way to the front."

As Tibbits started forward, Newman added, "One final note: the *Campbeltown*, the ship that will carry half of us across to France—*it is the bomb.*"

25

Immediately after his last statement, Newman called for a ten-minute break to allow the commandos to greet the three officers. When they reassembled, he had posted maps and charts on easels on the stage with a scale-model of the target.

"All right, Commandos, let's get right into our mission. Our main objective is to deny the enemy the use of the *Normandie* dry dock at Saint-Nazaire by either destroying it or disabling it. To do that, we'll firstly destroy the two caissons of the *Normandie* dry dock; secondly, we'll destroy the other surrounding dockyard facilities as well; thirdly, we'll demolish the lock gates accessing the submarine basin; and finally, we'll attack any shipping that comes around as targets of opportunity."

As he spoke, he pointed out locations on a large sketch of the harbor. "In all, these targets consist of two caissons, six lock gates, four bridges, six power installations, and six gun positions with thirteen guns between them.

"The caissons, gates, and pumping stations are the demolitions targets and do not include the assault and protection tasks that are sure to draw massive enemy fire." He paused and glanced out over his audience. "Many of you have been training and rehearsing for urban combat. That will be put to good use in this raid. The demolitions teams will be too heavily laden to carry any weapons other than their sidearms, so they'll rely on you, our assault and protection teams, for cover while making their way to their targets and setting the charges."

Seeing exchanges of concerned glances between the commandos as the reality of what they faced settled in, Newman added in a softer voice, "Just a gentle reminder that anyone is free to leave at any time prior to embarkation. And when I say that there will be no adverse action taken against anyone opting out, I mean that."

No one stirred.

"Well then, let's continue. If not for our little escapade," Newman continued, half-smiling, "the main targets, the caissons, would allow the *Tirpitz* access into the dry dock for repair. It was originally constructed for the French passenger ship, *Normandie*, which, until a few days ago, was the largest such vessel afloat. You might have heard that it caught fire in New York Harbor and capsized. Sabotage is suspected, which is a reminder of the need for tight security.

"We have the port's full architectural plans. We also have a man, Captain Pritchard, who has studied exactly how, from an engineer's view, we should go about destroying a facility such as this *Normandie* dry dock.

"Keep in mind that it took four years to build. It's a thousand one-hundred and forty-eight feet long, a hundred and sixty-four feet wide, and it'll handle a ship weighing more than eighty-five thousand tons. It's oriented from north-northwest to south-southeast, and the two giant caissons that are our main targets are stationed at opposite ends to control the flow of water in or out of the dry dock. The caissons are enormous steel gates that slide into giant sockets—that's what distinguishes them from lock gates. Each caisson is a hundred and sixty-seven feet long and fifty-four feet high—"

Newman interrupted himself and took a breath before continuing. "And you are not going to believe what I tell you next." He paused for effect. "Each is thirty-five feet thick. They're built like steel boxes with compartments to be filled with water to withstand various pressures."

Amid amazed gasps, Newman once more paused. "That, gentlemen, is what we intend to destroy. That is the main target. Our objective is to disable that dry dock. The other demolition efforts are to be carried out in case we fail to destroy the southernmost caisson.

"Of course, the enemy will not stand by idly and just let us do it. They have another asset there, a set of nine pens for servicing submarines. Those are covered with steel-reinforced concrete many feet thick, which makes them as impervious to RAF bombing as the docks themselves.

"Further, we've identified two radar stations for early warning and at least thirteen more gun positions stationed along each bank of the Loire that we'll pass on our way in, each equipped with many high-intensity searchlights—and did I mention that there is an underwater steel fence fifty yards in front of the *Normandie* dry dock that we'll have to push through?

"What we know of their defenses is courtesy of the French Resistance and our reconnaissance flights, but I'm sure there's much more we don't know. The *Kriegsmarine's* 280th Naval Artillery Battalion provides close-in defense against naval attack for the port, with twenty-eight guns ranging from 75mm to 240mm railway guns. The latter are stationed less than an hour away at La Baule. There's also the 22nd Naval Flak Brigade, which consists of three battalions with forty-three guns between them, mainly 20mm and 40mm but with a few 37mm cannons. They defend against air attack closer to the estuary and the port itself, and the waterfront is covered with troops with small arms.

"More German reinforcements are readily available. General Ritter von Prager has his headquarters nearby, and his 333rd Infantry Division is garrisoned along this part of the coast."

Newman heaved a large, audible sigh. "Gentlemen, we are going to run a gauntlet." He paced across the stage as he gathered his next thoughts. "We will rely heavily on the element of surprise and use deception to help achieve it, not an easy feat when you consider that we must sail a good part of the distance in daylight and that U-boats prowl the seas between here and there. However, they won't be expecting an attack, and we've taken other precautions beyond our destroyer escorts.

"When Lieutenant Commander Sam Beattie, our carefully selected sea captain, sails the *Campbeltown* into port tomorrow, you'll see that her four exhaust stacks have been replaced with only two, and they've been cut at a slant to the rear to appear German-built. She's been armored and painted to look in every respect like a German torpedo boat, and as we approach the coast of France, we'll hoist the *Kriegsmarine* ensign, as will all of our boats, to further deceive the enemy. The *Campbeltown* and our motorboats are even armed with Oerlikon cannons—and we've gone to a great deal of trouble to scour the country for all available ammunition for those guns.

"Now comes the fun part. When we've sailed far enough out of Falmouth on the day following tomorrow, we'll turn more southwesterly, and then south. When we've drawn even with the longitude that bisects the Loire estuary on the south side of Saint-Nazaire, we'll turn east. After nightfall, and shortly before we sight land, we'll rendezvous with a submarine, the *Sturgeon*, that will be stationed at a designated spot in the ocean for a navigational check.

"That will mark our final run. We'll have to slow to ten knots as we approach land in order to navigate over the shoals in the shallow waters, and we'll cruise six miles up the estuary under German observation and gun batteries lining both shores all the way in, here, here, here, here, here..." He pointed them out on the map as he spoke. "There is a deep-water channel that runs on the north side of the estuary as we approach the port, but it lies immediately below the German guns, so we'll stay in the shallows on the other side.

"Our two destroyer escorts will hold fast outside the harbor to cover our withdrawal at mission completion. On our way in and on our signal, the RAF will begin its first of three light runs over the northern end of the port. Their bombs are intended to attract German attention away from the docks and not inflict much damage because in the first place, bombs don't do much to docks aside from causing a nuisance, and secondly, the town of Saint-Nazaire is immediately past the harbor. We don't wish to harm any French citizens if we can help it.

"No doubt, the Jerries will spot us at some point, and if fortune is with us, our ship's disguise will work. We'll cross under radio silence, and if we're spotted, our radiomen will respond using German signals. If that doesn't work"—he cast a grim glance—"the battle begins early."

He took a deep breath. "When we are within the estuary —the jaws of death, if you like; that's what the shores look like on a map as you enter the Loire—the weight of the mission falls on Captain Beattie. He will navigate the ship up the Loire and maneuver it onto a line along the axis of the *Normandie* dry dock and straight toward those massive south caissons. Only a sea captain highly experienced in destroyers can accomplish that." Newman stopped and peered around the room. "You can guess what comes next," he said quietly. "The ship rams the front gate."

The auditorium remained deadly quiet. "I know what you're thinking. What about the explosives?" He allowed the silence to extend a moment longer. "We expect the momentum of the ship to cause it to ride up and rest its bow on the caisson. At that point, the commandos on the ship will disembark smartly onto the top of the caissons, and go about their tasks, which I will cover momentarily." He gestured toward Lieutenant Tibbits. "If our good demolitions expert has calculated accurately, we'll have roughly four hours to complete our other tasks before the acid detonators set off the explosion aboard the *Campbeltown*." He paused again. "The bomb is an explosive combo of twenty-four Mark VII depth charges, the same ones used to attack submarines. They weigh four hundred pounds each."

Newman peered across the room, making eye contact with as many commandos as he could. "We're talking four and a half tons of explosives. They're encased in a steel tank above the fuel compartments, and they're cemented in. We've used three of the army's 'pencil' fuses, which will detonate eight hours after they're set.

"Everything is connected together with cordtex. We'll set the fuses at about 1100 hours, before the ship enters the estuary, expecting that we'll land around 0300 hours, and the bomb will detonate around 0700 hours. And we'll scuttle the ship after it rams the target." He smiled. "That's so the Jerries don't find the bomb and the ship will be harder to move if it fails to detonate."

Newman pointed to a row of buildings that hovered over the water's edge. "I forgot to mention that the *Kriegsmarine* also services U-boats here. These are their pens, nine of them. Like the docks, their overhead protection makes them impervious to aerial bombardment."

He stopped talking and looked thoughtful. "I also neglected to inform that we have no flexibility of dates because we must go while the spring tides are highest to allow enough water above the shoals for our ship. If we don't go as scheduled, the next opportunity won't come around until the autumn."

He stared at the chart for an extended time while the commandos watched in rapt attention. "I'm going to release you to your troop leaders shortly," Newman said, turning once more to his audience, "but I think it's important for you to know what your comrades are doing while you're carrying out your individual tasks. No one will be idle. Remember, we have twenty-four targets."

He took a deep breath and turned another easel around. "So, this is how we're organized and what your objectives are. You've been training as three groups, each divided into assault, demolition, and protection teams. The assault teams will clear the way ahead for the other two. The demolition teams will carry the explosives and set the charges, and as I mentioned earlier, they'll have only their sidearms. The protection teams will defend the demolitions teams while the explosives are set in place and armed."

He paused and scanned the room again, and then called, "Captain Hodgeson."

When the officer came to his feet at attention, Newman continued. "Your command, Group One, will travel in six motor launches. You'll secure a jetty jutting into the Loire near its harbor entrance on the north side. You can't miss it. It has a lighthouse, Les Morées Tower. We call it Old Mole.

"It's imperative that you take the jetty because that's where we'll rally and make our departure at mission completion. You'll also eliminate anti-aircraft guns on nearby quays.

"When you've met those objectives, you'll maneuver into town and blow up the power station, bridges, and locks for the old entrance into the submarine basin from the Avant port."

He pointed them out on the large sketch map and looked around the theater again. "Captain Burn."

The officer snapped to his feet at attention.

"Your Group Two will also travel in six motor launches and land at the old entrance to the Saint-Nazaire basin, here." He showed the place on the map. "Your objectives are to destroy the anti-aircraft bunkers as well as the German headquarters, destroy the locks and bridges there, and then guard against a counterattack from the submarine base."

Once again, he indicated the positions, and then glanced about for the commander of Group Three. "Major Copland."

As the major rose to his feet, Kenyon nudged Jeremy. "That's us."

Jeremy nodded back.

Newman continued, his eyes roving over the commandos' faces. "You all know the major. He's my second in command for this operation." Then he addressed the major directly. "Your group will travel aboard the *Campbeltown*. As soon as we've rammed the south caisson, you'll secure the immediate area and set the explosives to destroy the dock's water pumps and caisson-opening machinery as well as the underground fuel tanks."

Newman addressed the full audience again. "For those of you who don't know, our demolitions teams will be emplacing their charges in total darkness forty feet below the ground, below the bed of the *Normandie* dry dock."

Leaving the image to linger a moment, Newman struck a lighter tone with a half-smile. "We have one more element to mention. We could call it a special team. Sub-Lieutenant Wynn, where are you?"

"Here, sir," a cheerful voice called out, and its owner popped to attention.

The lieutenant colonel chuckled. He knew Wynn's background. With a reputation for being a daredevil and called "Micky" by most acquaintances and "Popeye" by close friends, he was a young Welshman of Merionethshire and an avid individualist. As a Regular officer in a cavalry regiment, he had found the Army distasteful, resigned as the war was getting underway, and boarded a civilian motorboat to help out during the Dunkirk evacuation. Then he joined the Navy.

Fair-haired with a stocky frame, his normal expression was one of subdued stubbornness. The commandos did not care for him initially. Some had known him at Dartmouth and were put off by comments he made about "pongos"—a derisive term originating from medieval times for soldiers providing security aboard ships. But when his new comrades found him as irreverent regarding admirals, he was forgiven and welcomed into the fold.

"If anyone represents perseverance," Newman told the general audience, "Popeye does. He captains Motor Torpedo Boat 74, which, when he joined our mission, had the peculiar habit of traveling only fast or slow—and not in the speed range of our convoy. So, he would have had to play leapfrog among the waves all the way to France by plying ahead of the rest of us, and then waiting for us to catch up—a rather tedious and dangerous maneuver particularly at night, which is when we'll approach the French shore. The only other alternative was to tow his boat, which was no option at all.

"As a result, we eliminated his participation in the raid. However, he would have none of it, and somehow managed, on his own initiative, to have his boat's entire motor replaced so that now he can do the gentlemanly thing of staying with the pack without making himself a burden."

Chuckling broke out through the gathering.

Newman addressed the officer directly again. "Lieutenant Wynn, your boat will travel with the convoy. On entering the harbor, you'll check to see if the target caisson is open or closed. If open, then you'll go ahead of the *Campbeltown* and fire your torpedoes into the far northeast caisson. If, on the other hand, the ship must ram our target into a closed caisson as anticipated, then you'll have two alternative missions. First, you must ascertain if the *Campbeltown* is sinking, as we intend. If it is, then you'll turn northeast ahead of Group One and torpedo the gates at the old entrance into the Saint-Nazaire basin. On the other hand, if our good ship is *not* sinking, then you'll do us the honors."

Wynn, who had stood with a jaunty grin until Newman's last statement, suddenly straightened and stared at the lieutenant colonel. He coughed when he replied, but his voice was strained, and all he could manage was, "Aye, aye, sir."

Newman moved to the center of the stage and stood quietly a moment, seemingly searching for words. At last, he said, "Well, men, that's it then. You know the long and short, the dangers and the alternatives. Between now and departure, rehearse, rehearse, rehearse. Use the model to get low and see what things look like in the dark at sea level and with a light shining in your face, as the German spotlights most assuredly will do. And get all your questions answered.

"Aside from that, there's nothing more to say except that no words describe how proud I am to serve with you. I hope to see you safely back here, and if not, then the first round is on me in Valhalla!"

Silence ensued. Then, commandos and Royal Navy crewmen alike erupted in loud cheers and leaped to their feet to render an ovation.

"What do you think?" Corran asked when the applause had died down and as he made his way out with Jeremy and Kenyon.

Kenyon laughed and clapped his shoulder. "I think I'm going to be looking up the good Colonel Charles for that drink in Valhalla."

With thoughts of Amélie in Marseille and his parents on Sark Island flitting through his mind, Jeremy said nothing.

26

March 28, 1942
Rendezvous point, off the coast of Saint-Nazaire, France

Jeremy marveled at the technology and skill that brought a tiny blinking light on the dark waters within his field of view. It emanated from the submarine *Sturgeon* that Lieutenant Colonel Newman had mentioned in his briefing, stationed at specific coordinates to provide a navigational checkpoint for Commander Ryder as he commanded his small fleet toward Saint-Nazaire. Jeremy could not actually distinguish the boat, for rough seas and a stormy sky created conditions too dark for that, but he heard the crew aboard the *Sturgeon* as the *Campbeltown* slid past, their voices raised, cheering on the commandos and the men of the coastal defenses, and wishing them well.

He nudged his way to the bridge, hoping to catch a glimpse of Lieutenant Commander Beattie and his navigator, Lieutenant Green, the men who had so ably steered the *Campbeltown* to this precise location on this tossing ocean.

Almost the full weight of the mission now rested on their shoulders, for in a very short time the small fleet would enter the estuary where the waters of the Loire joined with those of the Bay of Biscay. Under German occupation, this body of water had become the veritable "jaws of death."

Jeremy managed to edge into the bridge and stood a moment in the darkness illuminated only dimly by ambient light emanating from instruments. Nevertheless, he made out the figure of Lieutenant Tibbits leaning against the opposite wall in conversation with another officer whom Jeremy presumed to be Beattie. He saw no indication of Lieutenant Green.

What he knew of Beattie came only from bits and pieces gleaned from other commandos. The son of a parson, the lieutenant commander was known to remain unruffled under the most disturbing circumstances and to be highly competent, with notable good looks and a charming personality. He had married very young and already had three children at home. He sounded like someone Jeremy would have enjoyed knowing under better circumstances, but in the darkness, he could make out none of the officer's features.

Jeremy left the bridge and made his way to rejoin Corran, Kenyon, and their troop, one deck below, immediately under the bridge. "I saw Beattie," he told the others. "At least I saw someone who might be Beattie, but in this darkness I could not be sure. I didn't see Green. How much longer?"

"Since we've just passed the *Sturgeon*, we should be within sight of land soon," Corran replied. "I saw Tibbits head below a little while ago. He was supposed to set the charges around 2300 hours, so I'd say we're less than two hours out. When Popeye's torpedo boat moves out front flanked by the machine gun boats in a diamond formation ahead of us, you'll know we're drawing near; and when you hear the RAF fly over, our attack is imminent. By that time, you should already have found a spot to brace yourself against the collision."

The passage to this point had not been without incident. Early yesterday morning, while sailing south still under the Royal Navy's white ensign, the fleet had been spotted by a German U-boat. The *Tynedale* had pursued her, openly firing on her and then dropping depth charges when the submarine dove, but it escaped. Unknown was whether or not she had sounded the alarm.

A short time later, they encountered a whole fleet of French fishing boats. Murmurs of suspicion circulated because they had appeared so soon after the German U-boat had disappeared. Two of the fishing vessels were separated from the others by distance, and Jeremy had watched with interest as first the *Tynedale* and then the *Atherstone* had sunk one each. Two of the gunboats rescued the French fishermen who seemed more than happy to have been captured and would be transported to England.

No other incident of concern had occurred during the crossing. When going out on deck, the commandos had been required to wear navy overcoats in case they were spotted unawares. The ship's store had been well provisioned with rum, chocolates, and assorted snacks, and the commandos availed themselves, dutifully paying with cash until someone noted that all the merchandise and the cash box would be blown to smithereens with the rest of the ship in a few short hours. So, the men passed their time as fighting men do enroute to an engagement: sleeping, playing cards, checking equipment, exaggerating war stories, laughing uproariously, thinking quietly of home, chattering about nothing...

The *Campbeltown* plowed on through the waves while the commandos continued at their various activities to fill the void of merciless waiting. At one point, they sensed more than saw that they had entered the estuary. Trivial activity wound down as they became alert to imminent danger. Then, overhead, they heard the thunder of engines droning eastward through the clouds.

Jeremy and Kenyon moved to the front of the ship. Noticeable only from foaming white wakes against dark waters, the machine gun boats were already in position. And then, a brilliant searchlight bathed the ship in a ghostly aura juxtaposed against its own deep shadows.

On the bridge, Beattie whirled to Signalman FC Pike. He was a man of special skill in that he had been trained in a secret department of the admiralty to be able to intercept, decipher, and send messages in German code.

"We're ordered to halt," Pike called. "I'll signal back our pre-planned message."

"Let's hope the subterfuge works," Beattie muttered.

Minutes passed. Popeye's torpedo boat continued deeper into the estuary. Slightly behind and to the left and right of him, the two machine gun boats kept pace, followed by the *Campbeltown*, which had now increased its speed to twenty knots. The other twelve motorboats flanked the ship on both sides.

On the deck, the men had stirred and moved into crouched positions, most of them facing toward the ship's bow. Each of them braced against a wall or other piece of equipment to protect themselves from the jarring that would occur when the ship rammed the caisson. Overhead, the rumble of bombers continued with sporadic explosions from occasional bombs. Apparently, the clouds were too thick for heavy bombing for fear of causing civilian casualties in the town.

Suddenly, the night was ablaze with searchlights probing from every angle, and tracers arced from both shores onto the ship and its accompanying boats. With surprise blown, Commander Ryder radioed off orders to the fleet to return fire, and immediately, the coastal defense forces manning the Oerlikon cannons and the machine guns opened up.

The commandos held their fire. Their job was still ahead.

On the bridge, tracers crisscrossed in front of and through the glass windshield, now with blinding light washing through and reflecting off its surface. Inside, Beattie held a steady hand on the wheel as he followed the estuary around a gentle curve to the right and slid past Old Mole. And then, two hundred yards ahead, he saw the entrance to the *Normandie* dry dock.

It was closed.

Aboard the torpedo boat, Popeye Wynn maneuvered his boat behind the fleet, sought the shadows to watch, and awaited Ryder's orders.

Within the harbor, German guns found their marks, sinking several of the motorboats.

Meanwhile, the *Campbeltown* plowed on through the dark of night, unstoppable now from sheer momentum, needing only the fine hand of Captain Beattie to steer it on its final course. After passing the Old Mole jetty, Beattie almost turned into the canal leading to the new submarine basin gates, but at the last moment, he caught and corrected his error. Then all hands felt the grating of the steel anti-torpedo net scraping along the bottom of the ship as it closed the final distance.

A sudden jolt tossed Beattie from his station by the wheel. Tibbits immediately stepped in for him.

"Port twenty," Beattie called. Tibbits made the correction, intending to swerve the stern to starboard while ramming the caisson without blocking the old entrance.

From atop the massive gate, machine gun fire erupted as the German defenders fought desperately against a massive, brightly lit apparition they could not stop.

All weapons on the *Campbeltown's* front deck, including the Oerlikons, returned fire on the Germans, now only yards away.

On the deck below, the commandos braced themselves.

The *Campbeltown* struck the caisson at 01:34 hours.

"Bring hell down on them," Kenyon yelled to Jeremy. "I'll see you when it's over, hopefully not in Valhalla."

Then the sound of gnashing steel against steel erupted simultaneously with an abrupt thump, and another one, but not quite a halt. The bow of the ship lifted into the air and then continued forward as the metallic grinding rose to high decibels and the warship's mighty engines thrashed the waters at full power, forcing the bow farther forward and higher on the caissons even as the lower part of the bow crumpled against the caisson. And still the mighty engines pushed until the *Campbeltown* had seared a gash in the huge portal and extended the ship's fo'c'sle across the caisson a foot over its far edge. Only then did the camouflaged destroyer, surrounded by gunfire and small explosions, its bow shrouded in searchlight-drenched black smoke with tracers arcing all about, settle onto the rent structure of the enormous gate, and stop.

In the wheelhouse, Beattie looked at his watch and muttered, "Four minutes late."

Below, with a quick last glance at Corran and Kenyon, Jeremy leaped to his feet and headed out in front of them to the ship's starboard side. He was part of the assault force that would run ahead of Corran's and Kenyon's demolitions team.

Jeremy's job was to clear the way for them. Led by Lieutenant Roderick, his team scrambled over the side, intent on destroying four gun positions immediately east of the caisson that the *Campbeltown* had just breached. Another team under Lieutenant Stutchbury set out to destroy any guards in the area. Then the combined teams would form a protective block around an adjacent hut for winding the huge cables that opened and closed the massive gate. There, Corran, Kenyon, and their team would set their charges. Another team led by Lieutenant Etches would follow behind the demolitions team to provide rear guard and further protection while the explosives were emplaced. As they assaulted the blazing German positions, their Tommy guns spitting fire and lead, they would also seek out opportunities to drop incendiaries down ventilators of oil tanks.

However, Group Three's numbers were already diminished. Corporal O'Donnell and Private Mattison took bullets to their legs before reaching the side of the ship.

Jeremy landed hard on the caisson's steel surface after scrambling down a shaky ladder put there by the first teams over the side, and he barely had time to notice a jab of pain in his leg from the force of landing as the roar of battle surrounded him. Searchlight beams swayed over the melee, illuminating attacking British commandos and retreating German soldiers while machine gun fire cackled, mortars exploded, men fell amid gushing blood, some already dead, others wounded and struggling, and still the shriek of metal on metal resounded through the freakish night.

Jeremy scanned his front. There, just as it had appeared on the model, stood the winding hut, a small building resembling a turret that housed the cable and winching mechanism for opening and closing the caisson. He needed no further guidance. Each commando knew his job. His was to clear the path for Corran and Kenyon to the winding hut. Jeremy glanced back to check their progress. They were over the side of the ship, they landed very hard under the weight of the explosives they carried, and now they struggled to their feet even as comrades were cut down by merciless gunfire.

Watching them a fleeting moment, Jeremy thought about what must be happening on the other side of the ship. The scene had to be the same, with teams spreading out under fire to their individual targets, and casualties already taken.

And still in shadows aboard his torpedo boat, Popeye waited for Ryder's instruction to either blow the gates at the old entrance or unleash his torpedoes on the *Campbeltown*.

Two crewmen, Howard and Reay, had been stationed inside the bottom of the ship to open the valves and scuttle it. Another sailor, Torpedo Gunner Hargreaves, would detonate charges for further assurance that the rear of the ship would sink. Captain Beattie along with a subordinate officer, Lieutenant Gough, went through to ensure that no one was left behind.

Meanwhile, behind Jeremy, Corran and Kenyon, with

another team member, Chung, set out at a trot for their winding hut target at the far end of the dry dock. They arrived streaming sweat, out of breath, and feeling fortunate that they had survived the blistering gunfire that had followed them for the full one thousand one-hundred and forty-eight feet of its length. While Jeremy went ahead to take up security, Corran encountered a steel gate at the hut's entrance. When shooting the lock with his pistol failed to break it, Chung and Kenyon wielded sledgehammers until it gave way. Then, working swiftly, Corran's demolition team laid their charges on their motors and between the spokes of the huge driving wheels, and then smashed junction boxes and cut electrical lines with specially insulated axes. Another team worked to perform the same task at the south end of the dry dock where the *Campbeltown* lay wedged atop the torn caisson.

Watching the ship from his bridge, Popeye saw that its stern had sunk deeper. Then Ryder swung by and gave his final instruction. Accordingly, Popeye turned his boat into the channel heading toward the outer locks of the old entrance to the submarine basin, fired his two torpedoes, and watched their wakes as they sped toward their targets and struck.

Nothing happened.

When Corran's team had completed its task, connecting their explosives to the ring main with attached safety fuses and igniters, he sent Chung to inform his higher, Lieutenant Gerard Brett, that he was ready to detonate. However, Chung returned shortly, wounded from a curtain of enemy lead that bounced in all directions from the steel surface of the northern caisson.

Inside both caissons, north and south, the teams moved in darkness, descending forty feet from memory of the scale models. At the north end, German troops counterattacked the entrance into the bowels of the caisson, twice wounding Lieutenant Brett. Using pistols, his demolition commandos quickly dispatched two German guards inside the caisson and dragged him to safety against a wall, where he continued to direct his operation from a sitting position.

In deep darkness, Brett's team found that the actual structure did not match the blueprints they had used in training, but they continued to emplace their deadly plastic. Inside the south caisson, similar challenges and firefights ensued, but at last, all the explosives were in place.

The plan called for the two caissons to be blown first, and then the winding huts and pumping stations. Sergeant Carr of the Royal Engineers, seeing no one else in charge, coolly walked the length of the northern caisson and back to the western side, clearing everyone away as he returned. Then he withdrew the safety pins on the igniters and withdrew to a safe position.

Sixty seconds passed. Then the ground shook and a deep boom reverberated through the night. When it abated, not much had changed in the way the caisson looked, but when Carr went to check, he found water trickling through at the seam and knew that this part of the mission had succeeded—the enormous portal had been damaged to the extent that months of repair would be required to put it back into operation.

In his position at the northeastern winding hut, Corran received word from Brett's second-in-command to detonate, also informing him of the lieutenant's wound, and that he was being carried out. In completing his mission inside the northern caisson, Brett had lost seven men.

As Corran took in the scene around him, he heard the underwater boom and felt the ground tremors caused by the explosion at the north caisson, followed by the flash and disintegration of the corresponding winding hut on the opposite side. He heard the subdued sound of commandos' receding footfalls as they began their withdrawal, and from those signs, he took his cue.

Corran pulled the safety pins, and immediately the winding hut lifted several feet in the air in a blinding flash and disintegrated. On the other side of it, Jeremy, Lieutenant Roderick, and the rest of the assault team were in a running gunfight with German troops who, having been initially driven back, now pressed toward them with reinforcements. Simultaneously, Group Three at the north end of the dry dock began their withdrawal to their rally point on the jetty of Old Mole, nearly a kilometer away. With them, they carried or aided their wounded, and somewhere along the way, Corran took a bullet to his left leg.

With Roderick in the lead, the small group reached the no-man's land at the site of the *Campbeltown* lying languidly across the southern caisson. A breathless courier, Lance Corporal Harrington, met them with the news that the signal flares to order retreat to the rally point had gone down in one of the boats. Therefore, Newman had sent him to orally give the order.

At last, the remaining men of Group Three, exhausted but otherwise sensing success, joined the remnants of 12 Commando gathered on the jetty of Old Mole. Each member of Group Three had fought to their objectives, completed their missions, and then fought through the port, across the docks, and onto this pier where rescue was anticipated.

Arriving there, Corran and his group found Newman with the commandos who had already arrived. The lieutenant colonel, cheerful as ever, stood against a girder on the pier looking across the water. When Corran limped up to him, Newman said with no recrimination, "Same as in training, transportation has let us down. I don't see any coming." His face took on an expression of concern. "How's that leg?"

"It'll have to do, sir, until I can get it seen to properly."

"Yes, well, see that you do." Newman chuckled and added, "My comment regarding our coastal defense chaps is meant only in jest. They had their own challenges to contend with, beginning with securing this jetty, and they fought as well as could be expected of anyone. Unfortunately, Captain Hodgeson's Group One was shot up in the water. At last count, we'd lost seven boats, their crews, and the commandos who were on them. Very few made it to shore. I'm afraid we'll have to fight our own way back out. We'll wait for the others to gather."

Corran turned away and sought shelter within the shadows with his team. There he encountered Jeremy, who first stared at him and then looked around.

"Kenyon?" Jeremy asked.

Corran shook his head. "He went down fighting. That's all I know. I didn't see it."

Jeremy sought deeper shadows, needing a fleeting moment to be alone with his anguish. He had worked closely with Kenyon in Madame Fourcade's Alliance Resistance group in France. Along with Sergeant Horton, Kenyon had been the last person to see Jeremy's brother before Lance had been captured. Kenyon had played with Timmy on the kitchen floor in Claire's house and had even tugged at her heartstrings. And now, like so many other great fighters, he was gone.

He subdued his grief and went to help with the wounded. Corran was already there. He had dressed his own injury and now aided others. Jeremy joined in.

27

Saint-Nazaire, France

"There's nothing for it," Newman told the assembled commandos on the Old Mole jetty. Daytime was still hours away. "No rescue is coming. We must forge our own." Despite the desperate circumstances, he maintained an upbeat countenance.

He estimated that more than five hundred of his commando force of six hundred and eleven had been killed or captured. Of those remaining, about a third were armed with only pistols, having been the group protected in order to accomplish their explosives-setting missions. Also, roughly the same proportion of men were wounded, some seriously enough that they must be carried.

Around their inland perimeter, German reinforcements built, flames shot up from various structures, and gunfire rained on them from every direction. Down alleyways and behind edifices, wounded British and *Wehrmacht* soldiers screamed for help.

Newman sought out Major Copland. "If we're going to

have a chance of escape, we'll have to break out of here. What do you think? Is it time to call it a day?"

Copland was a veteran of the Great War and known to be cool under fire. "Certainly not, sir. We'll fight our way out."

"Good," Newman responded with a gleam in his eye. "Just checking my sanity. Organize what's here into groups of twenty and divide those into three subgroups. Put the commandos who were in the assault and protection teams in the front group under Roderick, Watson, and Denison, and put Roy overall in charge of them. I'll have Sergeant-Major Haines compose and lead the rearguard. Put the wounded in the middle with the demolition teams around them—recall that they only have pistols. However, if a larger weapon becomes available, give it to an able-bodied demolitions chap and move him to the assault and protection group."

Copland saluted and moved out smartly. Fifteen minutes later, he reported back to Newman that preparations were complete and the men were ready to move. He had appointed leaders of the subgroups and brought them to the colonel for orders. Among them was Jeremy.

"As usual, we'll have to find our own transport to get home," Newman told them with a jovial air.

They grinned back at him.

Then, noticing Jeremy, Newman peered at him. "Glad you made it, Littlefield. This is where you earn your keep." Broadening his attention to the larger gathering, he told the young leaders, "We'll have to break out of the town into the surrounding countryside, and from there determine how to get home. Fortunately, we have with us someone who's done it before—from Dunkirk. Littlefield can give us an idea of where to go once we're outside the town."

Amid a muted cheer, Newman said to Jeremy, "Where's your mate, Kenyon? He should be useful at this too."

Jeremy stared into Newman's eyes. "He won't be coming with us, sir. We lost him somewhere in the vicinity of the northeast winding hut."

"Oh," Newman said grimly. "I'm sorry to hear that." He turned to Copland. "Have you charted a route and briefed it."

"I have, sir. The shortest way is down a main street and through the old town square and across Bridge D. That's a distance of about two hundred yards from here, but the enemy's got it pinned down with automatic weapons. It would be a suicide run.

"Instead, I propose to take a more circuitous route behind sheds and warehouses north of here, and back along the quays next to the submarine basin to the old town square. The distance is somewhat over half a kilometer. Either way, we'll have to cross that square and that bridge. We're prepared to move on your order."

"We'll follow your recommendation. Let's depart in five minutes."

Jeremy marveled at the spirit of the commandos he had joined barely three months ago. Battered, some wounded, all exhausted, they roused themselves and prepared for an impossible run through town where their enemy might be only yards away when they passed by. Yet they formed up as Copland had instructed and prepared to run that gauntlet rather than surrender.

At the appointed time, Newman appeared before them. He signaled to Copland, who relayed orders to proceed, and the motley formation, channeled by the narrow streets and alleys, set out, one group of twenty after the other.

Gunfire from every window, doorway, and rooftop erupted almost immediately. Commandos with weapons returned fire. More were wounded, and their mates helped them along, but the column proceeded at a swift and steady pace, alternating their movements so that one group maneuvered while another provided covering fire. As some of the wounded found keeping up to be impossible, they volunteered to move to the side and await their fate, in keeping with a commando philosophy that the lame should never impede an operation.

That included Lieutenant Gerard Brett, who had led the team into the northeastern caisson. Too shot up to move more than the first twenty paces, he gave his pistol to another commando and sank into a doorway to await capture. The others kept moving.

They proceeded through the dark streets, illuminated now only by firelight of burning buildings, the searchlights having been doused and in any event were useless in the urban setting. The commandos fought their way forward, reinforcing when need be, hunkering in shadows for intermittent respite, ducking behind walls, and always refusing to accept defeat.

They turned through the back street, covering the distance as rapidly as they could, and soon came to the old town square. As Copland had predicted, rapid fire blazed at them as they sprinted through and then came within sight of Bridge D.

In the dark, they could not discern how the bridge was defended but knew it must be. Their movements were most certainly tracked, and now all firepower would be aimed at the bridge.

Newman, Copland, and Haines conferred. They saw no indirect approach, no cover, no room to maneuver.

"I have a Sten gun," Haines said. "It's the best I can do for covering fire."

Newman stared at him, extended his hand, and grasped Haines'. "I'll see you soon," he muttered. Then, tossing his head toward the waiting commandos, he called, "'Away you go, lads!"

With that, he bolted to his feet and set out at a trot with Copland next to him. The surviving commandos soon caught up in a makeshift formation as they headed toward Bridge D and the way out of Saint-Nazaire.

Gunfire erupted immediately, with tracers breaking through darkness in streaks of light. The bullets hammered against the bridge girders, resounding as lead bounced off steel. They ricocheted from walls and tore through glass and skins of close-by vehicles, sending sharp particles flying through the air, but the commandos proceeded at their steady double-time pace.

For reasons they could not fathom, the Germans seemed to be firing high and wide, their rounds piercing the air with spitting sounds as the commandos took to the middle of the road across the bridge with Newman and Roy in the lead. Enemy soldiers at the other end, seeing the formation coming in unrelenting strides, leaped from their positions spanning the road and retreated to better cover.

As had occurred since they began their run, the commando group grew steadily smaller, the way they had come marked by their dead, dying, and wounded. Among them were students, bakers, bankers, plumbers, carpenters, wealthy, poor—all manner of British citizenry who answered their country's call for men who would leap at the throats of her enemies. Steadily they ran, never breaking formation, intent on driving through and past those who would stop them.

Trotting at the front of his group of twenty, Jeremy wondered how many remained. He also worried for Corran, who had begun this final run on a wounded leg. Was he still in the formation?

A bullet struck the center of his Tommy gun just above the trigger. Jeremy saw at a glance that it had been rendered useless. Grateful that it had probably saved his life, he tossed it to lighten his load.

When the column reached the other end of the bridge, Copland suddenly broke ranks and went straight for a pillbox spewing hot lead from machine guns at his comrades. Reaching it, he pointed his weapon inside the slit and emptied it while sweeping the muzzle back and forth. Other commandos, seeing his action, joined him.

Near Jeremy's group, a grenade exploded. A commando went down. Jeremy rushed to him and found Corran struggling back to his feet. His leg bled profusely, but he waved away the pain and rejoined his group.

Enraged, Jeremy whirled to see Copland hurl a hand grenade at a German soldier escaping from the pillbox. The soldier went down. Then Jeremy joined Dennison and Haines in a headlong attack against a machine gun firing from a window of a nearby house. The gun went silent.

A motorcycle of sorts with a sidecar and mounted gun sped into the area. It was quickly dispatched by every commando shooting at it.

Newman glanced around. The way to the left was blocked by an armored vehicle streaming machine gun fire. More armed motorcycles appeared.

Newman turned right and led his surviving commandos in

the opposite direction. The formation, held so tightly till now, broke apart into small groups as the commandos sought shelter from the withering fire. And then the gunfire ceased, the sound of it replaced by the rumble of engines as the Germans brought in reinforcements and established a perimeter.

Observing the Germans rushing through town shooting anything that moved, including each other, the commandos moved off the streets. They clambered over fences, hurtled through yards, and even hurried through houses, their goal being to disappear.

Jeremy estimated that dawn was two hours away. He had lost track of Corran but had managed to keep Newman in sight and followed as best he could, seeing that several others also followed the commando leader. He imagined that, by now, the Germans were already rounding up the wounded and the unfortunate. Later, they would round up the dead.

Newman entered a building. The loose group behind him followed, as did Jeremy. Inside, they descended stairs into a cellar and found that they were in an air raid shelter, lit dimly by a single bare bulb hanging by a wire from the ceiling, and complete with straw mattresses. More commandos found their way there, and soon fifteen had gathered. Among them, to Jeremy's relief, was Corran.

Corran was pale and shaking. Jeremy guided him to one of the palliasses. His leg caked in damp blood, Corran eased down but chose to sit rather than lie down.

"I think this is the end of the road for me," he croaked to Jeremy. "I've lost too much blood and my leg is stiffening." He looked through bleary eyes around the room. "Honestly, this might be the end of the run for all of us. Look at us, we're out of ammo, out of food, and we're in a dead end. If the Germans come through the front, we have nowhere to go."

Sitting next to him, Jeremy put an arm over Corran's shoulder. "Having you for a chum is an honor," he said. "You didn't have to be here. You had alternatives that would have been easier."

Through his pain, Corran chuckled. "I know who you are, Jeremy Littlefield. I read the newspapers. I remember when you rescued that little boy from a bombed-out troopship right out there in that same Bay of Biscay at the mouth of the Loire by Saint-Nazaire. I've read about your family on Sark Island. Your brother's a POW. Shall I go on? You didn't have to be here either. Frankly, I was dumbfounded when you accepted me as your leader. It should have been the other way around."

Jeremy sighed and smiled tiredly. "Get some sleep. Regardless of what tomorrow brings, you'll need it."

Corran nodded and accepted Jeremy's assistance to stretch out. As Jeremy straightened up, Newman approached him. "How is he?" the colonel asked, gesturing toward Corran.

"I think he could be fine, sir, but he's lost a lot of blood, and I worry that without attention, infection will set in."

Newman breathed in and out deeply. "And he isn't alone. I've decided that if we're discovered, we'll surrender. Steele is pulling security and will warn us of a German approach if it happens, as I suspect it will. But we're in no position to fight, and we can't take proper care of our wounded."

Jeremy regarded him somberly. "I'm sorry, sir." He held out his hand. "If I may be so forward, serving with you has been a privilege."

Newman grunted and shook the extended hand. "Hmph. The honor is mine."

Shortly after dawn, as anticipated, the group in the cellar heard noises indicating a methodical search. Steele reported to Newman that German troops were preparing to enter the building. On his straw mattress, Corran struggled to a sitting position.

Minutes later, the door at the top of the cellar stairs swung open. A German soldier entered cautiously, swinging his submachine gun from side to side.

At the base of the stairs, Lieutenant Colonel Newman stood at attention. He had grasped his pistol by the barrel and now held it out to the soldier. Moments later, a *Wehrmacht* officer entered with several more soldiers. He accepted Newman's pistol and then motioned for his new POWs to assemble in the center of the room.

Ordering his soldiers to surround and disarm the commandos, he glanced around the cellar with disdain at the squalid conditions and the smears of blood all about. Already, the wounds had started to smell.

He barked another order, mounted the stairs, and vacated the room, leaving a sergeant in charge to escort the prisoners to headquarters. The noncom remained businesslike but was not unduly harsh. He issued orders to his subordinates and supervised them, stationing his men along the way that the commandos would traverse to leave the cellar and the building. When most of them had climbed the stairs, he went ahead to ensure that they were gathered and secure, leaving a guard to watch and close the door behind the last one up the stairs.

The POWs filed out in a line. Once outside, they marched straight across the street to the *Wehrmacht* headquarters, much to Newman's amusement. Medics had been brought to render first aid, and ambulances stood by to carry the wounded to German military hospitals. Corran welcomed the sedative that eased his pain.

Back in the cellar, all was quiet. Jeremy almost dared not breathe. From his flimsy hiding place against the floor and the wall covered by an edge of Corran's straw mattress, he had watched and listened without stirring.

When the group had first heard the Germans approach, on impulse, Jeremy had slid off the straw and under it, against the wall. With no time to say anything to Corran or Newman, he could only hope that they would not look around for him or do anything that might give him away.

Neither did.

28

As a dull gray horizon outlined dark clouds in the eastern sky, signaling the approach of a dismal dawn, Captain Beattie was dragged aboard a German rescue boat from the chilly waters of the Bay of Biscay. Stripped of his soaked clothing, he was thrown only a blanket by one of the *Wehrmacht* soldiers who surrounded him, but otherwise he stood among them with other rescued Brits, barefoot and naked. He held the blanket close as he rode through the frigid morning air until, nearly an hour later, he stumbled onto the dock at Saint-Nazaire, disappointed to see the *Campbeltown* still resting where he had last seen her.

The time for the ship to have blasted itself into millions of shrapnel pieces was well past.

Welcomed by fellow prisoners, Beattie walked between two lines of guards and climbed onto the canvas-covered bed of a truck where his companions gathered around to make him warm.

The captain was a tall, slender man who, but for his current circumstances, carried a commanding presence. He sported a dark beard and a full head of hair, and now his blue eyes regarded his captors with sharp interest, but he put up no resistance.

Since shortly after laying his ship on the altar of the southern caisson, he had treaded the dark waters of the Biscay Bay, and was eventually forced to take off his footwear and uniform for fear of sinking under their weight. Earlier, while the battle still raged, Commander Ryder directed Lieutenant Mark Rodier in Motor Launch 77 to steer his boat alongside the stairs on the *Campbeltown's* starboard side to rescue Captain Beattie and the remaining crew as the ship's stern settled deeper and deeper into the murky, oil-slicked brine.

On boarding the small boat, Beattie had joined Rodier on the tiny bridge. The lieutenant had just delivered Sergeant-Major Haines with his troop of commandos to their target at the old gates into the submarine basin and was on his way back out to sea. The boat had been filled to capacity with wounded who were being treated by the *Campbeltown's* physician, Dr. Winthrop.

Feeling good about having completed their respective missions, Rodier and Beattie made light conversation about families, schools attended, and other topics of mutual interest. Suddenly, they had been bathed in searchlights and peppered with machine gun fire from the riverbank.

Rodier pushed his boat's five engines to full power, maneuvered an irregular course, and was soon out of range of light weapons. However, within minutes, the searchlights farther out along the estuary's banks had reacquired ML 77, and heavier weapons were brought to bear, including 75mm and 6.6in guns.

Beattie had just left the bridge when it took a direct hit. He found himself in the water far from shore, floating among many dead companions. When pulled into the

German rescue boat, he made a mental note that Rodier was not among those rescued.

Now, as he settled into the back of the truck, he counted himself fortunate to be among the living. "Lieutenant Tibbits?" he asked, as he took his seat.

The commandos regarded him mournfully, and one shook his head.

The truck started moving, and Beattie stared out its rear as it drove away from the docks. The *Campbeltown*, now swarming with people, was visible.

Suddenly, Beattie sat up straight and stared, not believing his eyes. At the point where the ship's deck met the caisson, allowing people access to board, two German officers flanked a British commando officer: Captain Pritchard.

Beattie looked at his watch, grunting at the irony that it was still on his wrist. Then he sat back, breathed out heavily, and closed his eyes. *Ten o'clock.* The explosion was three hours overdue and outside the time range that Tibbits had said it could occur. But it could still go off, and Pritchard knew that, and as Beattie watched, the captain calmly followed his captors aboard the broken *Campbeltown. He didn't betray the mission.*

Marveling at the courage and dedication of the man, Beattie closed his eyes. "At least we delayed the *Tirpitz* for a few months," he muttered to no one in particular.

Monsieur Grimaud, assistant mayor of Saint-Nazaire, surveyed the horrific scene before him, his mind numbed at the sight of dead soldiers, British and German, scattered across the old square and the streets of his town as well as along the docks. Spatters of blood on bullet-pocked buildings and gooey blotches outlining where wide-eyed corpses sprawled in unnatural reposes appeared in every direction. German soldiers hurried across the docks, their faces revealing uncharacteristic anxiety, intermixed with curious townspeople who whispered to each other that the attack to re-take the European continent had begun.

More worrisome was that men and women wore the khaki that had been common at the beginning of the war when the French citizenry still believed they could fight the Germans off. From far in the distance, he heard sporadic gunfire. That could only mean that Frenchmen had taken up arms and were shooting at Germans in hopes of aiding an Allied invasion.

But the British raid had obviously been defeated.

That no Allied invasion was underway was indicated by the empty ocean spread beyond the mouth of the estuary. The most dramatic evidence, however, lay just beyond the old town square at the far end of the *Normandie* dry dock, where the bow of a British warship jutted into the air above the seared caisson.

The ship was alive with officers, their girlfriends, and tourists who flocked to see the strange scene, and to walk the steep decks of the destroyer, itself stained with blood, its guns mangled and ripped from their bases, and its steel wall riddled with bullet indentations. A cordon established by the *gendarmes* was ignored. Word spread that mounds of chocolates, candy, and other snacks as well as stores of rum and even sherry had been discovered on the lower decks, and people lucky enough to have grabbed some emerged with big smiles and bright eyes.

Grimaud watched a group of German senior officers with their technical specialists in deep discussion on the front deck. They had been there early and had clambered all over the ship. Among them was the admiral-superintendent of the dockyard. He had suspected that a bomb might be aboard and ordered a search, but when it came back negative, he reported the result to Grimaud by way of informing Saint-Nazairians that Germany was firmly in control. With a sneer, he said, "The British must be very stupid to think this is a problem." He laughed contemptuously. "Removing this destroyed destroyer from the caisson is no difficult engineering task."

Grimaud had nodded grimly, and the admiral had departed, but the other senior officers still remained on the ship's forward deck, apparently discussing alternative courses of action to repair the damage in the least amount of time. As Grimaud watched, he saw two German officers escort a British commando back aboard the ship.

Still wearing nothing aside from the blanket draped over his shoulders and covering his body, Captain Beattie sat in a chair across from his interrogator. His guards had noticed that the commandos deferred to him, and he had provided his identity information as required by the Geneva Convention. Possibly because he was the only man among the British POWs with a beard, his captors had concluded that he must be the ship's captain.

"Earlier this morning, I interviewed Lieutenant Colonel Newman, your commando leader," the interrogator said in excellent English. He was a slight fellow, pleasant, and made plain that he had been less than successful at gaining useful information from the colonel or anyone else, and said he hoped for better cooperation from Beattie.

He gestured out the window in the direction of the dry dock. "Your people obviously did not know what a hefty thing that lock gate is. Did you really think that small boat could destroy it?"

The second he finished speaking, the window shattered, and a booming explosion shook the building where Beattie was held. Through the window, he saw a roiling cloud of dark, multi-colored smoke and debris rise up over the port. In the adjacent room where other commandos were held, a loud, sustained cheer arose.

Assistant Mayor Grimaud felt the ground shake before he heard the explosion, and seemingly, so did everyone else in the vicinity, for movement and talking ceased. Then a flash of towering flame leaped skyward, water from the Loire gushed upward in violent sprays, and metallic shrapnel chunks and fragments flew through the air, slicing indiscriminately through people, cars, windows, anything in their paths. The group of officers conferring on the ship's front deck disappeared in the flash and smoke, as did the tourists and German officers' lady friends who seconds earlier had been enjoying their chocolates, candy, and glasses of sherry.

The force of the explosion rolled through the ground, dislodging cobblestones, cracking walls, shattering glass; and it did not immediately subside, the reverberations causing even those who had not been victims of flying debris to be unsteady on their feet. And when finally, it abated, anguished voices cried out all around. The horrific desolation was unimaginable.

"That," Captain Beattie told the erstwhile pleasant interrogator now staring in abject horror at this bearded apparition before him covered with only a blanket, "is proof that we did not underestimate the strength of the gate."

When, an hour later, having been put among the other captured commandos for safekeeping while the German command sorted things out, Beattie heard another, smaller explosion from the direction of the locks and smiled to himself. *That would be one of Popeye's torpedoes.*

When he heard a similar one five minutes later, he smiled again. *And that would be the other one.*

Then he contemplated what he had seen of Pritchard boarding the *Campbeltown* under escort. *Did he reset the fuses?* The thought both saddened him and filled him with pride. *Regardless, he didn't divulge the bomb. He had known his life was forfeit.*

Even in the cellar where Jeremy had remained since the capture of Newman, Corran, and the others, the thunderous boom of detonation reverberated, and its tremors rocked the room. Slamming a fist into an open palm, he grinned despite his grim situation. *The mission succeeded!*

He listened as the explosion subsided, keeping a close watch on the door at the top of the stairs. It was his only way out. He had pondered what he might do if someone entered. The possibilities were too numerous with too few options to handle, but recalling that his odds of escaping Dunkirk had also been bleak, he refused to dismiss any eventuality. He still had his pistol but no ammo, and his only other weapon was his commando knife strapped to his leg inside his trousers.

Having entered the building in pre-dawn hours, he had no idea of whether it was a home, an office building, or what other structure it might be. As the hours had passed, he heard no movement in the floor above and conjectured that he might be in a storage facility of sorts.

Hunger had set in hours ago, but he had determined to stay put at least until nightfall, and then to venture a glimpse of his surroundings. The thought had led him to think about finding clothes to replace his uniform and boots. Searching about the cellar, he found nothing of help. The only provisions for comfort were the straw mats. He pulled one on top of another and crawled between them for warmth and to remain hidden in the event that someone entered.

Late in the afternoon, famished, sore, and exhausted, Jeremy woke with a start, sat up, and peered around the room by the dim light of the bare bulb. He listened for a sound, but hearing none, he started to lie back down, but thought better of the notion, deciding that he needed to prepare for his escape. And he recognized what had awakened him so suddenly: a rush of adrenaline in a mind bent on escape.

His first order of business had to be to alter his appearance, move to a safer place, and find food. Rising from the straw, he searched every part of the room without making a sound, looking for something that might aid his escape.

Finding nothing, he took inventory of what he already had: his uniform, his empty pistol, and his commando knife. He propped one foot over his opposite knee to examine his boot. Brown and just covering his ankles, the boots were dirty enough to pass for farmer's boots, but his trousers and blouse would give him away.

He continued thinking his way through alternative solutions to his predicament, and when he was certain that darkness had fallen, he climbed the stairs.

Jeremy had rolled his trousers to look like shorts, untucked his blouse, opened the collar, and mussed his hair, hoping that, if spotted in the dark, his silhouette would not immediately identify him as being military. The mission planners had preferred a full moon to assist in bomb targeting. Now, Jeremy hoped for a cloudy sky to help him evade capture.

Reaching the door at the top of the stairs, he opened it a crack and peered out. Hearing no sound, he stepped into the pitch-black hall.

29

April 1, 1942
Sacramento, California, USA

Lieutenant Ted Lawson stood at the rail of the *Hornet* looking out to sea, impressed at the support warships that materialized out of the mist as it proceeded into the Pacific to rejoin the carrier group. It had cast off a few hours earlier. He heard his name called and turned to see Lieutenant Commander Josh Littlefield sidle up next to him.

"Are you settled in?" Josh asked.

Ted laughed. "As well as could be expected. The two ensigns in my room weren't particularly impressed by the fact that I'm wearing silver bars and they're wearing gold. They kept their nice comfy beds and consigned me to a cot. I slept well enough, though, and spent today wandering the ship, getting my bearings. Some of your fliers were curious about our bombers, so me and some of the guys took them through, bragging about speed and agility. Pilot stuff." He laughed. "And they took us below and showed off their dive bombers, torpedo planes, and fighters. It was all very interesting, with the folded wings and the planes jammed together to make room for us."

Josh chuckled. "You haven't lost your sense of humor. C'mon. Doolittle is about to hold a briefing. I think all is about to be revealed."

The squadron had flown singly or by ones and twos out of McClellan early the previous morning, winging above the Diablo Mountain Range and descending over its face to Alameda Naval Air Station. After passing the Golden Gate Bridge, Ted and his crew had spotted the *Hornet* with three planes already loaded, exclaiming in wonder at how small it looked from the air. Within minutes, standing next to it while watching a giant crane hoist their B-25 slowly from the edge of the wharf where the aircraft carrier was docked, they were as awed by its immense size.

Navy seamen had taken charge of the plane when Ted parked it, drained fuel from its tank, leaving only a fraction of its capacity, and an army "donkey" had towed it the rest of the way onto the pier below the crane. Sixteen B-25s were now tied down to the deck with chock-blocks preventing them from rolling.

Eight of the crews had been informed that their aircraft would not be going on the mission. Ted had been with them for lunch before boarding the *Hornet*, and they were sick with disappointment to the point of not wanting to eat. Some of the crewmen were taken as spares and felt somewhat better. Ted felt sorry for those left behind.

Now he followed Josh to a briefing room where the other pilots gathered. A few other naval officers also attended. When all were assembled and seated, Doolittle stood before them. "If you haven't guessed yet, we're headed for Japan, to bomb Tokyo, Yokohama, Osaka, Kobe, and Nagoya. This ship will take us as close as possible, and then we're going to take off from its deck."

A loud and spontaneous whoop arose from the pilots, their eyes bright, their smiles broad amid much backslapping, shoulder-punching, and fists pumping the air. Doolittle continued, "It's going to be a tight squeeze, but it's all been worked out. After we've made our bomb runs, and with the cooperation of the Chinese government, we'll land at small fields inland a short distance on China's soil. We'll fuel up there and fly on to Chungking."

Listening to the colonel and watching his fellow pilots, Ted's chest welled with pride and relief. The weeks of training, sometimes inexplicable, had provided hints about the objective, and he had guessed correctly. He and this small group of pilots, co-pilots, navigators, flight engineers, and bombardiers would strike at the heart of the enemy that had so mercilessly struck, unprovoked, at their country. The notion was both exhilarating and terrifying.

He thought of Ellen. *Will I ever see her again?*

"One final thing." Doolittle cleared his throat and exhaled. "Anyone wanting to bow out of this mission is free to do so."

No one moved or spoke until Doolittle dismissed them and they filed out. Then Josh nudged Ted. "The show's on."

Word spread rapidly. Ted could see it in the way the sailors looked at him and jumped to comply with any request. And that night, on retiring to his stateroom, the two ensigns had rearranged their things to accommodate him in the most comfortable of the three beds.

April 15, 1942

"What's this meeting about, and why out on the flight deck?" Ted asked Josh.

"You'll see. Bull Halsey joined us last night."

"I know the main part of his task force, including the *Enterprise*, joined us north of Hawaii a few days ago—"

"No, I mean he's on the *Hornet* now. The news reporters are gathering, so there's going to be some kind of stunt. I heard that all the naval officers who received Japanese medals during peacetime had turned them in. Someone got hold of them and shipped them out here. They came in on that blimp that rendezvoused with us."

Ted had seen the blimp approach with interest, and had watched as items had been lowered to the deck of the ship and others hauled aloft to the lighter-than-air vessel. He had heard that the capability existed, but until then, he had not seen it.

They arrived outside the ship's island, where many of its crew who were not currently occupied and most of the pilots and flight crews had gathered. A five-hundred-pound bomb with its rounded front, stubby body, and tail fins had been positioned on a lorry across from a group of newsmen and a bank of cameras. Then the door at the island's base opened, and Bull Halsey walked out.

He peered pugnaciously at the cameras and then around at the crowd of navy men and army pilots. Then he strode to the nose of the fat bomb and patted the top of it. Another officer opened a box that contained a jumble of all the medals that had been gathered from navy officers. Halsey took one at random, interlaced it with string, and tied it to the nose cone. Then he turned and addressed the B-25 pilots.

"Boys," he commanded while speaking into the cameras, "return these medals with interest. Good hunting."

Josh and Ted joined in with the loud cheers.

30

April 18, 1942
Aboard the USS *Hornet*, Pacific Ocean

The ship vibrated. A muffled noise spread and increased to a resounding roar. Guns from the escort ships were firing. Then, over the PA system, a clear, calm voice announced, "General quarters! Man your battle stations!"

The effect was instantaneous. The announcement set off a sequence of actions that the men aboard the *Hornet* had practiced every morning and evening. Men scrambled at full speed up ladders and through passageways to their appointed places under combat conditions, swerving and dodging to avoid colliding with each other.

For Ted and his fellow pilots and their crews, their duty station during these drills was in their B-25s, ready for immediate takeoff if attacked from the air, so that the fighters, torpedo planes, and dive bombers could be brought up to establish air cover over the carrier group. With that in mind, the Army pilots and crews kept themselves informed at all times of the direction and distance to the nearest friendly shore. If attacked by surface ships, the pilots would remain in place and rely on the big guns of the escorting destroyers to stave off the enemy.

But this was no drill. That had already taken place earlier in the morning. And the raid was scheduled for the next day.

When the guns erupted, Ted was in his room deciding what to pack. He looked up, startled, at Lieutenant Tom White, the gunner for B-25 Crew 15. White was also a physician. He stared back with equal consternation.

Then they both ran, scrambling up three decks, encountering other members of their crews as they mounted the stairs, firing questions as they went and not waiting for answers. Meanwhile, the *Hornet* continued to reverberate with the sounds of its own guns in rapid-fire.

When Ted and Tom reached the flight deck, a cruiser off to port, one of their own, fired a broadside, with flames leaping over the turbulent waves. Across the waters, a ship, low on the horizon, spewed black smoke into the air as dive bombers from the *Enterprise* plunged on it, dropping their deadly loads and pulling out to climb back into the sky.

Josh caught up with Ted on the way to the aircraft.

"What is it?" Ted yelled between more salvos from the cruiser aimed at the plume of smoke.

"A Japanese patrol boat."

Ted stared only a moment. "It could have radioed a warning to Japan," he shouted above the wind and the guns. "Surprise is blown. We'll have to take off now. That's the contingency plan."

Josh nodded, a beseeching expression on his face.

Ted read the unspoken plea. "Sorry, sir. We're still eight hundred miles out. Every drop of fuel is precious now, and every ounce of weight depletes it." He glanced around at the

Army's bombers as the *Hornet* surged to full power into the wind, its turbines thumping a powerful, rhythmic vibration throughout its hull. "Besides, you guys are likely to have your hands full with Zeroes here shortly. You'll need this deck cleared so you can bring up your own fighters."

"I know," Josh accepted grimly. He grasped Ted's hand. "Good luck."

Ted held his grip a moment. "Thank you, sir, and all you Navy guys. You did everything you could for us. We appreciate it. Tell your crew." With that, he sprinted the remaining distance to his plane.

Meanwhile, the clear, calm voice over the PA system directed, "Army pilots, man your planes. Army pilots, man your planes."

As Ted climbed into the cockpit, he glanced at the bridge high up on the island. There, unmistakably silhouetted against the gray sky, Admiral Bull Halsey watched deck operations, his tough chin jutting against the wind.

Josh hurried to the entrance at the base of the island. As he entered, he encountered Doolittle hurrying out to his own plane. Josh shot him a questioning glance.

"Not this ride," Doolittle shouted above the din, anticipating Josh's query. "We're full up. Bull's ordered mission-go from here. He's got to get his own aircraft in the air and turn the fleet around. If that patrol boat got a message through to Tokyo, the Japs' long-range bombers are already on their way."

Stoking disappointment, Josh acquiesced and headed for the operations room.

Ted reviewed the squadron's situation grimly. They had hoped to sail to within four hundred miles of Japan before launching. Even flying from there was pushing fuel to the extreme of the bombers' range, and now they would cover twice that distance before engaging their targets. As it was, their fuel had been expected to get them to their landing sites in China, but just barely. And they would consume forty precious gallons just revving up and getting into the air. On top of that, the crews had not eaten breakfast yet. He kicked himself for not having thought to pack sandwiches and water aboard his aircraft. A quick query among the crew revealed a single thermos to share between them, and they faced hours of non-stop flying before reaching China.

Suddenly the deck was alive, deck crews yanking chock-blocks from beneath the bombers while others steered "donkeys"to them, latched on, and pulled them into takeoff position. Then lorries appeared with their five-hundred-pound bombs, and crews loaded three each onto the planes, plus an incendiary that would be released at low level after the other three had been dropped. Next came the fuel tenders, topping off the tanks against evaporation and rocking the planes to break up bubbles to allow taking as much gas as possible. In addition, they lifted five additional five-gallon gas cans onto each plane, a small compensation for the added distance they would travel.

Ted glanced at the tower again. Large cards now displayed compass headings and windspeed. He swallowed on seeing that the latter had reached gale-force strength.

He watched as Doolittle made his way to his plane and disappeared into it. His co-pilot, Lt. Richard Cole, had already prepared the bomber for takeoff.

After the pre-flight checks were completed, Ted looked across at his own co-pilot, Lt. Dean Davenport. "You know what's scared me the most about this raid?"

Dean shook his head.

"It's the cables on those barrage balloons. They could slice off a wing, and we were going in at night. In the dark. At least now we'll be able to avoid them."

Dean grinned wryly. "Yeah, well there is that."

Ted glanced forward through the windshield again. His throat tightened and he took a deep breath. Doolittle's plane was being pulled into final position. As soon as it was there, the propellers began to turn. All around Ted, the other pilots cranked their engines, and he did likewise. Within moments, the spinning propellers and deep, throaty engines added to the thunderous noise of wind, waves, ships, and guns.

An aircraft handling officer stood to the left of the ship's bow with a checkered flag. He swung it in a circle, faster and faster, signaling to Doolittle to rev up his engines.

Ted and Dean watched, riveted. They had listened to procedures in a classroom, and they had practiced them on an airfield, but this was their first attempt at sea.

This was their final exam.

They heard Doolittle's powerful engines rise to a scream.

A wave broke over the bow. The officer with the checkered flag watched, and Ted realized that he was timing the waves so that Doolittle would start his run as the bow began to rise. As it did, he gave a different signal, and sailors stationed at Doolittle's plane pulled the blocks away from the wheels. The aircraft handling officer waved his flag again, this time in a downward flourish that ended toward the open sea.

Doolittle's engines roared at full throttle. He pulled the

flaps full down and released the brakes. His B-25 leapt into motion. With barely half the flight deck available to taxi, his right wing nearly touching the island, and only a white line to guide where his left wheel should go, he gained speed, and strongarmed the bomber into the gale-force winds blowing the length of the deck from bow to stern.

The waves lifted the front of the *Hornet* high. As they did, and with yards to spare, Doolittle's plane launched into the air and continued to rise. He circled around the carrier and flew low and straight over the *Hornet's* painted line. Admiral Halsey had pointed it directly at Tokyo.

Behind Ted, the crew cheered, and as he looked out at the men watching from every safe vantage, he saw the Navy men cavort and throw their fists up in celebration as Doolittle's plane continued low over the ocean, soon to disappear in the dark clouds.

Lt. Travis Hoover and his crew went next, followed by the B-25s of Lieutenants Brick Holstrom, Bob Gray, and Davey Jones. Each in turn circled the ship, flew low the length of her deck over the white line to gain their bearing, and set out for Japan.

None waited to organize into a formation; doing so would burn too much fuel. Each had its individual targets, and each pilot set his aircraft's nose on its own particular azimuth.

Then it was Ted's turn.

The donkey pulled him to the line and got out of the way. Blocks were set in front of his wheels.

On signal, Ted dropped his flaps, but then, fearing that the force of the wind combined with that of the propellers might cause them to blow off, he lifted them. The aircraft handling officer made no objection, waving the checkered flag in faster circles, instructing Ted to power up to full throttle.

He did so.

And waited, for what seemed like an interminable time.

Long after Ted was satisfied with the pitch of the engine, the aircraft handling officer held him in place. In that thirty-second span, Ted's mind raced through what he would do if he scraped a wing, blew a tire, an engine failed, or he experienced any other myriad things that could halt this very precarious takeoff. His instructions were explicit. Stop the plane, douse the engines, get the crew off, and help push the bomber overboard.

There were still nine more planes to go. The loss of one could not be allowed to stop the mission.

At last, the officer with the checkered flag gave Ted the final signal; the blocks were pulled from in front of his wheels.

The wind caught his wing and blew him to his left.

He jammed on the brakes.

Maneuvering his left wheel back on the white line, Ted took a deep breath and started his roll down the deck again, gaining speed. Then he crossed the *Hornet's* bow, dipped, and rose into the air.

He swung back around the ship, barely taking note of the other eight planes still awaiting their turns, took his bearing from the white line on the deck, and set his course.

Next stop: Choo Chow Lishui, China.

Next critical checkpoint: Tokyo.

But he had twenty-two hundred miles to traverse at twenty feet above the waves, an unknown quantity of enemy ship's guns, anti-aircraft fire, and barrage balloons to avoid, and Zeroes to outmaneuver. And he had already burned forty gallons of fuel.

31

April 19, 1942
South Coast of Japan

Low on the horizon, barely discernible in a haze, land appeared. The weather had cleared and turned into a spectacularly beautiful day, not conducive to surprise bombing operations over a forewarned and heavily armed country.

"That's got to be Japan," Ted shouted at Dean, his heart suddenly pounding. They had been sharing the controls, and at the moment, Ted had them.

Dean squinted, stared, and nodded. "I see it." Half turning in his seat, he called over the intercom, mimicking a pirate. "Look sharp, mateys. Land ho!"

"It's not like I expected," Ted said. "I thought it would be mountainous. We hardly need to gain any altitude at all, and we're at, what—" He glanced at his altimeter. "Twenty-eight feet."

They flew over a beach, staying low to avoid spotters and radar, bracing against expected gunfire from the myriad small boats anchored there, but none came. To Ted's surprise, the vessels were modern, with motors, and they were well-kept. He was not sure what he had expected, but this evidence of modernity and prosperity was not it, and as he flew over them, the people on them waved and smiled.

"It's the emblems on our planes," Dean remarked. "We've got the old ones with a red ball in the middle of a white star inside a blue circle. The red ball could look to them like their 'rising sun.' They probably think we're theirs."

They were surprised to see the lushness of the land, so well cultivated and manicured, the farms laid out in geometric symmetry with their crops and fruit orchards. And as they flew over, the farmers stopped what they were doing and waved.

Ahead of them, a building appeared on the horizon, requiring Ted to raise the nose of his aircraft and climb until he was past it. It had a bright red roof and appeared to be a temple, and as they went by and took in the peaceful scenery around them, they lost their sense of danger for a few minutes, particularly when they flew by what must have been a school building complete with playground, where hundreds of children waved at them.

They were brought up short when, flying over the other side, they were suddenly confronted with a flagpole flying the rising sun symbol on a white background—the Japanese flag.

Arresting his mental lapse, Ted diverted his attention back to his airplane and the sound of its engines. "Keep your eyes open," he called back to Thatcher, the bombardier.

They followed a valley slanted toward Tokyo and flew below its ridges until McClure, the navigator, informed that it led off course. Increasing altitude, they spotted another valley and followed it until it too led astray, and they found another. In this way, they approached closer and closer to Tokyo, always keeping low.

"Six bandits at twelve-o'clock high," Dean suddenly blurted. "Zeroes."

Ted and the bombardier, Lt. Bob Clever, had seen them too.

"I've got 'em," Thatcher said. "One's breaking loose from the formation and making like he might dive on us."

"Let me know when to switch on the turret," Ted called back. He had turned it off to save power.

The twin V-formations swept over and past them.

"Thatcher? Where's the lone Zero?"

"He disappeared. He must have gone back to the formation."

Ted continued on, skimming the treetops of evergreen forests and the roofs of villages, and beginning to worry because they saw no sign of the city, and they had already been over Japan for ten minutes longer than they should have taken to reach Tokyo. Spotting a larger town, he registered it in his mind as a target of opportunity in case they did not manage to locate Japan's capital. But just then, they climbed to avoid another temple, and there before them was Tokyo Bay, the mid-afternoon sun reflecting spectacularly from its waters.

As they gazed in awe at the beauty of the landscape where it met the ocean, almost as one, the entire crew spotted a huge aircraft carrier. It looked serene and unprotected, and the temptation to hit such a target was almost overwhelming, but the strength of their training prevailed, and they flew on, very slow, to conserve fuel, and now at only fifteen feet.

"You know," Ted called over to Dean, "it looks like we

were not expected. We've got surprise working for us. That Jap patrol ship didn't get a message out."

"I think you're right."

Thoughts of the fast-flying Zero fighters crossed their minds, but they saw none at the moment despite scanning the sky in every direction. Then they spotted one of their own bombers climbing hard into dark smoke clouds that suddenly appeared and spread from below his plane. Within five minutes, they had crossed the bay and encountered the dreaded barrage balloons anchored between Tokyo and a town across the river, Yokohama.

Flying above graceful yachts among crowded wharves, they passed dredgers and heavy ships, and then were back over rooftops. Ted was surprised at how spread out and modern the city was, having expected it to be crowded together, but his view was limited by the necessity to stay low and out of reach of anti-aircraft guns, which would now be on alert from the bombing done by the B-25s ahead of Ted's.

Then, the first objective appeared right in front of them.

"Dean, there it is." Ted throttled up to full power while Dean adjusted the pitch in the propellers, and they climbed rapidly to fifteen hundred feet.

In the rear, Bob opened the bomb bays.

Ted made a short run, a red light blinked on his instrument panel, and Bob released the first five-hundred-pound bomb over its target. Seconds later, they heard a boom, and Thatcher called over the intercom, "Direct hit. Smoke shooting into the sky."

The plane gained velocity, and the red light blinked again. Bob dropped the second bomb, but now shock waves from anti-aircraft explosions rocked the plane. Its height had been accurately estimated, and shortly the Japanese flak lead would narrow.

They flew over the southern part of the city, and Bob released the third bomb and then almost immediately, the incendiary. It would split into dozens of small firebombs as soon as it hit the wind, which would descend and ignite fires over a wide area.

Both releases registered as flickering red lights on Ted's instrument panel. He pushed his stick, dropping the bomber's nose into a steep dive and banking slightly to see the effect of the third big bomb on its target, a steel-smelter. At first the walls seemed to billow outward, and then they collapsed into clouds of black and red smoke.

The dive had driven their speed to three hundred and fifty miles an hour, but miraculously, no Japanese guns seemed aimed at them or in front of them. Ted stayed low over rooftops once more, and while not discounting the continued danger, at last he could breathe easily. Mission accomplished. From start to finish, the bomb run over Tokyo had taken thirty seconds.

Ahead of them was the long and uncertain flight to China.

32

April 19, 1942
London, England

Lieutenant Colonel Crockatt greeted the two young commandos warmly. "Thank you for stopping by," he said. "That was some operation the lot of you pulled off there in Saint-Nazaire. Operation Chariot, was it? It certainly tipped the battle in the Atlantic, not to mention how it raised the country's morale. People are still buzzing about it. And you got away and made it home safely."

"Thank you, sir. We arrived two nights ago," Corporal Douglas replied while Private Harding nodded. "We were happy to do our bit." They had been comrades in 2 Commando before being selected to join 12 Commando for the raid.

Having by now met a few of their number, Crockatt scrutinized these two as if searching for a visible quality that set them apart to perform their heroic deeds, already becoming legendary. He was struck by how ordinary they seemed, very young, any mother's sons, courteous, quiet, and respectful. And they had just arrived back on British shores after traversing across both the occupied and Vichy sectors of France from the cauldron that they had helped ignite in the French port city.

French Resistance cells reported panicked activity among the *Wehrmacht* ranks and increased sabotage operations by partisans in and around Saint-Nazaire in the immediate aftermath of Operation Chariot; and Bletchley Park's decoders discerned that Hitler had sent his own interpreter to interrogate the captured commandos and coastal defense POWs. Further, word was that the *Tirpitz* had been berthed at Trondheim, Norway, and the *Kriegsmarine* would not venture her out again until victory in the Atlantic was achieved, not even to attack resupply ships for the Soviet Union bound for Murmansk.

"Well, once again, thank you for coming," Crockatt said. "We interview all successful escapees. MI-9's mission is to assist escape activity, and these interviews provide insights into methods, contacts, perils, and the like. We feed that information back to the Resistance through our trained agents in the field and to the POW camps."

"We know one of your agents," Harding said. "He was on the Saint-Nazaire raid and escaped with us." The private could not be over nineteen years old, but the confidence emanating from his light blue eyes bespoke a person experienced beyond the years credited to someone with his straight blond hair and ruddy face.

Crockatt glanced at him in surprise, and then realization dawned. "Would you be speaking of Captain Jeremy Littlefield?"

"Maybe he was a captain before he came to the

commandos, but he wasn't during this raid," Douglas interjected, "though I'm sure he would have attained that rank soon enough. He had just joined 12 Commando. But yes, that's him, and we were jolly lucky to meet up with him. He spoke French like a native and is fluent in German, and he knew the countryside."

"He asked us to give you a message," Harding added.

Crockatt looked at them askance. "And what would that be?"

The two soldiers exchanged glances. "He was not sure how pleased you'd be," Douglas replied, "but he said he would await your orders in Marseille."

Crockatt chuckled and shook his head. "The cheek of that young captain," he said, restraining laughter. "I suppose he intends to return to my fold."

He pressed a button on his desk, and shortly, Vivian appeared. After explaining the situation, he told her, "Would you please call over to the commandos and inform them that we've located another of the lost souls from Saint-Nazaire, and per my agreement with Lieutenant Colonel Newman, Captain Littlefield is returned to my command. Tell them I've already assigned him another mission and he's in France."

Vivian took notes, and when Crockatt had finished, she smiled. "Well, sir, it's nice to know that he's all right. We have been rather anxious."

"Yes, there is that, after all." As Vivian left and closed the door, Crockatt turned back to Douglas and Harding. "Now please tell me your stories. How did you get away?"

Douglas spoke first. "Captain Littlefield wasn't with us at first, but we came up with the same idea for how to dress until we could get some civilian clothes." He explained how they had rolled up their trousers and opened their collars. "Surprisingly, it worked, and we went right through the *Wehrmacht's* street barriers at the edge of town even though I had my corporal stripes on. Littlefield saw us go through and caught up with us on the other side."

"After that, we traveled mostly at night," Harding chimed in, "until we got to La Roche Bernard. That's only twenty miles from Saint-Nazaire but took a few days because we had to be so careful."

"And we had a close one there," Douglas said. "A flak battery nearly caught us, but a butcher saw us, figured out what was going on, and took us off the streets."

Harding nodded enthusiastically. "Not everyone was helpful, but most of the people knew about what had happened in Saint-Nazaire, and that lifted their spirits—the idea that help was coming to liberate them."

"The butcher took us to an American lady. She provided us food, money, clothes, and bicycles, and sent us to a lawyer in Loches."

"That was a long ride," Harding interjected, rolling his eyes. "Nearly two hundred miles."

"No more difficult than some of our hikes in the Scottish Highlands," Douglas countered, and returned his attention to Crockatt. "The French lawyer and his wife put us up in his house while he had identification and travel papers forged, and then they took all three of us to Marseille. Captain Littlefield knew what to do there. He led us to a villa to see a woman, Madame Fourcade, who arranged our passage back here."

"We came by a Lysander flight and arrived the night before last."

"Yes, well, she sent a message to expect you," Crockatt

muttered, arching his brows, "but she said nothing about Littlefield. I suppose you also met Amélie?"

The two commandos exchanged troubled glances and shook their heads. "No, sir," Douglas replied. He was barely older than Harding, with brown hair and fair skin darkened by the sun and weather. "She was out on a mission, and the captain was quite distraught when he learned that she was gone."

"We did hear parts of their stories, though," Harding said. "I can understand why he would be upset. She saved his life."

Crockatt nodded somberly. "Yes, she did, and her family has contributed to the war in more ways than most."

"We met the younger sister, Chantal," Douglas volunteered. He laughed and added, "Harding here was quite taken with her."

"Oh stop. She's pining after some bloke called Horton up in the Loire Valley, and I'll probably never see her again." Harding turned back to Crockatt. "Apparently she was one of the observers who supplied the ground information at Bruneval for that airborne raid to get the Wurzburg radar."

Stunned, Crockatt's eyes opened wide, and then he shook his head. "She's only sixteen—"

"Nearly seventeen," Harding interrupted a little too quickly. "Sir."

Crockatt noticed but disregarded the comment other than to allow a slight smile. "Yes, well, as I said, that family has done more than most." He stood to end the meeting. "Thank you again for coming. I assume Madame Fourcade knows how to contact the lawyer and his wife in Loches? They could be useful in future operations."

After assuring the lieutenant colonel that such was the case, the two commandos departed. Vivian ushered them out, and then Crockatt called her into his office. "Please get a message to Madame Fourcade. Something is going on with Amélie. We don't know what it is, and she's one of ours, not SOE's. If she's on an operation, we need to know what it is. And find out what Jeremy is up to."

33

April 19, 1942
Marseille, France

Jeremy noticed the strain showing in Madame Fourcade's eyes, in the dark half-circles that had formed under them, and in the lines that had begun to appear at their corners. She had pulled her normally dark, lustrous hair into a tight bun at the back of her head.

He marveled at the skill this small, beautiful woman who, though dressed in a way to disappear unnoticed into any crowd, somehow commanded respect on entering any room. Currently, she ran the largest and most effective intelligence gathering organization in the Resistance.

The two sat together on the veranda of her villa. Spring had brought a profusion of growth, but without the usual gardening, the villa presented a desolate atmosphere. Besides the single servant girl to prepare food, the two of them were the only current occupants of the great house.

"Did your friends arrive safely in England?" she asked.

Jeremy nodded. "They planned to meet with Major Crockatt today."

"I'm sorry Amélie is not here to see you. She'll be disappointed to have missed you."

"Can't you tell me anything about what she's doing now?"

Fourcade shook her head. "It's too dangerous for either of you to know what the other is doing, especially given your next assignment."

"Which is?"

"It's complicated," Fourcade said with a sigh. "The mission itself is not difficult, but it is dangerous, and you need to understand the background.

"I'll tell you honestly, Jeremy, I'm uncomfortable with a new request from MI-6. We're supposed to be SOE intelligence gatherers, and we also get involved in sabotage. But I'm being asked to do something far outside our usual function."

Jeremy watched her face, perceiving the mental activity spinning behind her intelligent eyes. She had been one of the few people to correctly discern Hitler's intentions long before the war. With a former intelligence officer holding similar ideas, she had begun preparing, as a civilian, to build Alliance, the vast network now numbering over three thousand operatives. Many of them were former senior military officers who helped recruit, organize, and execute missions. Her adeptness had garnered British financial, logistics, training, and communications support to the extent that military intelligence now relied on her, which was why the unusual request that troubled her had come her way.

"Just tell me," he said.

She nodded. "Two days ago, a man escaped from

German imprisonment. General Henri Giraud. He's a French hero from the last war and commanded troops in Belgium during the *blitzkrieg*. He had taken up a blocking position in the Ardennes and was with a reconnaissance mission at the front when he was captured.

"His escape was rather spectacular. Word spread all over France. The man is sixty-three years old, and he scaled down a hundred-foot cliff from Königstein Fortress on the Elbe River near Dresden. He used a rope of sheets and copper wire that he and other prisoners had made."

"He sounds like an incredible man," Jeremy broke in. "What's the problem?"

"We're getting into the realm of politics, Jeremy, and I don't like it. We are primarily intelligence gatherers, not even war fighters, and certainly not equipped for internecine power struggles."

"That's a big word, 'internecine.' I'm not following you."

"Sorry. I imagine every war has its strange relationships at the top, which leaves the poor soldiers at the bottom for cannon fodder. Even my own uncle is a highly placed officer in Vichy intelligence. We've always been close, but I know he keeps an eye on me. 'Internecine' simply refers to infighting, and between Germany and France, we seem to have created the most impossible instances of it.

"The long and short of the situation is that Hitler is furious about the escape and wants Giraud back. He was the highest-ranking French officer captured during the Battle for France.

"Pierre Laval, the Vichy version of prime minister, has had a long history of involvement in the French government. He was previously the head of government, serving under a president, which is now Marshal Pétain. Laval acceded to the role at the beginning of last month.

"Laval told Giraud that he must surrender himself to the Germans. But Pétain stood in the way. Laval doesn't dare to arrest Giraud because doing so would cause a revolt among the French forces we have left here in France and those in North Africa. So, Giraud is in hiding, we believe around Lyon."

"Then what's the issue?"

Fourcade took a deep breath. "We, Alliance, helped him escape. We smuggled the materials to him to make the rope he used, we had our operatives waiting when he came out to get him into hiding, and we got him across the border into Switzerland and then into Vichy France. Others in our organization think that because we helped him, we are allied with him. The fact is that we did it because he was a POW with a plan of escape. He needed our help, and we provided it. Simple as that."

"And now he wants you to do more? Who in Alliance wants to support him, and to do what?"

"Those are three questions, Jeremy." Fourcade chuckled. "Give a girl a chance to get her thoughts together." She shook her head. "Giraud asked for nothing more. It's Léon Faye, among others, who's pushing for us to support him."

Jeremy whistled. "Léon? I see why that would present a problem."

"Yes," Fourcade said, blushing slightly. "I've grown very fond of him—"

"And he likes you too," Jeremy teased, grinning. "Anyone can see that."

"I know. He is handsome, isn't he?" Fourcade smiled and took another deep breath.

Léon Faye, the former French fighter pilot, had been the French Air Force's deputy chief of staff in North Africa at the time of the French capitulation. His unusual good looks, courteous manner, and roguish humor had captured Fourcade instantly, and he had been equally charmed by her, though for the sake of the war, they kept their affection in check.

"But there's very little chance for us while this war goes on—" Fourcade murmured.

Jeremy interrupted, "I certainly identify with that dilemma."

Fourcade reached over and squeezed Jeremy's hand. "I know you do," she said. "Your day with Amélie will come. I'm sure of it."

Jeremy grunted, and Fourcade continued. "Léon carries a lot of influence within Alliance and within the Vichy army in North Africa. I'm not even sure yet that I have a problem, but to give you a sense of it, Giraud has sworn his loyalty to Pétain, and if you'll recall—"

"Léon came here originally looking for your support to depose Pétain," Jeremy interrupted. He stared into the distance at the blue Mediterranean. "What does he want you to do now?"

Fourcade shook her head. "He hasn't asked for anything. There's this." She held out a note. "It comes from MI-6."

Jeremy took it and read it out loud, a single line. "Find out if Giraud will serve his country again." He read it again, and then again, and finally looked up. "I must be dense. I'm not seeing the issue."

"I wouldn't expect you to without more background." She took a deep breath, retrieved the note from Jeremy, and held it up. "This came from Major Eddie Keyser, my handler at MI-6. He reports to the head of MI-6, Director Menzies. So, that's a request from on high. It's the British government asking the question.

"At some point, there will be an invasion of Europe by

the Allies. The Germans expect it; we know it. That's the only way that Germany will ever leave the countries they've conquered. De Gaulle calls for it, and when it happens, our people in the Alliance will be heavily involved.

"Until now, at least, the Brits have always supported General Charles de Gaulle and his Free French. Giraud and de Gaulle are rivals. De Gaulle is known to be difficult to work with, but he's electrified the French people.

"Alliance succeeds because we stay out of politics. We have communists working for us who do it because of their ideological differences with Naziism; we have Free French supporters and even some Pétain followers who cannot bear to believe that France will become a German vassal. They hold onto hope that, in the end, the great war hero Pétain will somehow win against Hitler. Then there are the military members who cannot believe that France capitulated so quickly. Some still support Pétain, but most hate him. And, we have ordinary citizens who just hope to return to the way they lived before the Germans came, and they willingly put their lives at risk for that purpose. And, of course, we have the thrill seekers. My point is that keeping an organization fighting together on the lethal battlefield that is France is difficult with purposes as diverse as those of our members. We cannot be seen as supporting one side or the other of French internecine squabbling—there's that big word again."

Jeremy bobbed his head and chuckled. "I understand it this time."

Fourcade sat quietly a moment. "I might be jousting at windmills, but given where the question came from and the stature of Giraud, I suspect that the British might be contemplating a shift of their support from de Gaulle to

Giraud. From my point of view, there can be only one reason why they'd do that."

When she did not immediately continue, Jeremy prodded. "Are you going to tell me what that is?"

"Sorry. I'm still trying to put things together in my head. Look, I've met de Gaulle several times at cocktail parties in Paris before the war. He's an arrogant know-it-all who thinks his way is always right, but he was the only French officer to escape to Great Britain and mount the cause of re-taking France. And since those dark days of mid-1940, he's recruited an army of hundreds of thousands; he has ships and planes and pilots. Hundreds of our volunteers came to the cause right here in France, because they heard his call."

Fourcade paused in thought and then continued. "But now, we must think about how to win this war." She sighed. "What do you suppose would happen to this organization and to the one de Gaulle built if we suddenly tried to impose on our fighters and operators a new leader selected by the Brits—and I have to ask myself why would that happen? Why would your people in British intelligence suddenly want to replace him?" She posed the question rhetorically. "They've never shown displeasure with him."

Jeremy pursed his lips. "I can't think of a reason, but then your view of things is at a higher level than mine. Have you come to any conclusions?"

Fourcade nodded. "I think it's the Americans. At this point, that's just a hunch, but I've tried to think through all the possibilities, and that's the only one that makes sense. Word is leaking out that the Americans don't want anything to do with the Free French, and I think their opposition stems from their perceptions of de Gaulle; besides which, the US recognized Pétain and his Vichy regime as the legitimate government of France.

"I think they're worried that the resentment is too great against the British because they destroyed our fleet in Algeria and killed thirteen hundred of our men in the process. That's who de Gaulle aligned with, and he went to London to do it. I expect that the Americans think the Vichy French troops in North Africa can never be brought around to support him.

"The Americans will have to fight in North Africa. I don't see any way around that. Either that or they'll expose their flanks to an armed and capable enemy when they invade France. But if the US does invade there, I'm sure they don't want to fight the Vichy troops. So, they estimate that if they can bring in an anti-Gaullist general untainted by having surrendered to Germany, the Vichy troops might be convinced to support the Allies rather than fight them."

"That's a little above my head," Jeremy said, but nodded in agreement. "What do you want me to do?"

"Léon is still my chief of staff. I've agreed with him to send Duke MacMahon to speak with Giraud and find out what the general is thinking about his future and that of France." She chuckled. "The duke is more than a fancy name and title. He's an accomplished fighter pilot, from a long line of aristocrats both here and in Ireland. His grandfather was head of the French government under Napoleon III. His background and influence can be useful."

She paused again, distraught. "I want you to go along. You'll be introduced as an aide, and it's understood that you'll attend their meetings. But—"

She took a deep breath. "I need to know the nuances that pass between Giraud and the duke, and I'm not sure I can get them if Léon is in the mix. His bias will come through. I've told him that, and that I want you to accompany the duke and report back your observations. Léon is angry with me over the issue, but the stakes are too high. Personal considerations cannot interfere."

Jeremy stared. "I-I'm not sure I understand what you're asking," he stuttered.

"It's not as complicated as it sounds. Léon is pro-Giraud and anti-Pétain. Giraud is sworn to Pétain—"

"Explain something to me," Jeremy interrupted. "I'm not understanding all these French senior officers' devotion to Pétain. He capitulated to the Germans almost immediately."

"Yes, but the armistice he negotiated with the Germans kept them from taking the rest of France and our colonial holdings in Africa. Part of the agreement was that the senior officers would swear an oath of allegiance to Pétain—in that way, the Germans didn't have to worry about the French army participating in Resistance against them. French army officers take their oaths very seriously, but as you know, many of them refused the oath and work with us.

"Giraud took an oath of loyalty to Pétain. If he were to now renounce it, declare his opposition to Petain, and support a plan to displace de Gaulle, he would profoundly influence the loyalties of French officers. If these things are going to happen, I need to know sooner rather than later. I'd also like to know if Giraud would be acting of his own accord or taking the duke's lead. We can't have Giraud acting under perceived pressure from Alliance, communicated by Léon through the duke, to disrupt de Gaulle's efforts.

"Whichever way it goes, we'll need to prepare our people and hope the tensions don't tear Alliance apart. If Alliance is disrupted or destroyed, the ripple effect on Britain's intelligence apparatus in France will go far and wide. Do you understand?"

Jeremy nodded, and the two sat in silence for a few

minutes. He broke it. "You said the mission could be dangerous, but I'll just be attending some conversations. It doesn't sound dangerous."

"It shouldn't be," Fourcade agreed. "But the Germans are looking for Giraud, and Pétain has allowed the Gestapo to operate with almost a free hand in the unoccupied zone. Giraud will have his own protection around too. Obviously, we have the means to reach him, but you could find yourself exposed and even captured by the Germans. You most certainly would be interrogated, probably tortured, and you could be executed."

Jeremy chuckled. "I'll try not to let any of that happen."

Fourcade winced. "Amélie would never forgive me."

34

April 29, 1942
Marseille, France

"It's good to see you safely back," Fourcade greeted Jeremy. "I've read Duke Maurice's report. I'm anxious to hear your observations."

Jeremy returned the greeting and cast an uneasy look toward Léon.

"Don't worry about me," Léon said, stepping forward and grasping Jeremy's hand. "We have no secrets here. I spoke with the duke. The meeting with General Giraud sounds like it was a bust—he's letting visions of grandeur get in the way of his patriotic duty."

"That's the way I see it," Jeremy agreed as the three sat down at the table on the veranda. "He essentially wants the central position of authority over all French military actions and the Resistance movements across all of Europe."

Léon harrumphed and Fourcade scoffed. "Walk us through the particulars. What is he asking for?"

Jeremy let out a small laugh. "For starters, he would

condescend—my word—to lead the French forces in North Africa once the invasion starts on the condition that the Allies also execute a simultaneous invasion of France."

"So, he wants to dictate military strategy to the Allies who actually have armies and tanks and bullets," Léon interjected skeptically. "Amazing. I thought better of him. Go on."

"He demands that the Free French be excluded from any military operations."

Léon arched his eyebrows. "He's delusional. The Free French are good people who want and will fight for exactly what their name implies: a free France. Alienate them, and you alienate much of France."

"Anything else?" Fourcade asked.

Jeremy nodded. "As mentioned in the report, he wants control of all Resistance organizations across Europe. He's very pro-American but anti-British, so while he's willing to accept British aid, he is not willing to go to London. He said that if the US and the British supply him with sufficient arms and equipment, he could lead armies to victory all across Europe."

Fourcade scoffed again. "I'm astounded at the arrogance. Resistance organizations would have nothing to do with him. Why would they? He's shown no interest in helping them. And now he wants to lead them? He has no clue about how difficult it is to recruit volunteers, organize them, maintain security, plan missions, ferret out infiltrators, and recover from their actions. He's accustomed to leading with the clout of the government to back up his orders. Our authority comes from our right and determination to be free, and we fight in shadows under threat from tyrants who will shoot us on the spot." She tossed her head and took a breath. "Tell me, Jeremy, what was his demeanor? How did he look and sound?"

"He carries himself well. Dignified. He wore his full uniform and he's mentally sharp. I kept my thoughts to myself, but I sensed that he was a bit over the top in his expectations. He had newspaper clippings lying on a table. They came from around the world, with headlines about his escape. They might have gone to his head."

"Sounds like it," Léon remarked. "He's not our man." He glanced at Fourcade. "You were right to doubt him."

She dismissed the comment. "It wasn't him so much as all the infighting he could cause. But now he *is* the issue.

"We're in a ticklish situation, though. The Brits want him, and my guess still holds that they're reacting to American pressure."

"So, what do we do?" Léon said.

Fourcade's smile expressed a shade of cunning. "I'm going to send off a very short message to Major Keyser at MI-6. All it will say is that the general prefers to stay in France for the time being to work with the French Resistance."

"I'll make a prediction," Léon said with a sigh. "This won't be the last we'll see of General Giraud."

"I suppose you still won't tell me where Amélie is or what she's doing?" Jeremy asked later, after Léon had left.

Fourcade shook her head as she regarded him with compassion. "You know I can't. We've had to modify the way we operate to maintain security. Last year we had a scare, during the *blitz* over Britain. We were infiltrated and nearly destroyed."

"I remember," Jeremy said. "I worry about Amélie. Chantal too."

"And they worry about you. I'm not sure you're aware, but we even had to shut down operations here and leave Marseille. Maurice got word to us shortly before the Gestapo arrived. We fled to Pau and stayed there for a while until it was safe to come back. Fortunately, we have some *gendarme* friends who watch out for us."

Surprised, Jeremy drew himself up in consternation. "I didn't know. I'm sorry."

"Seriously? You were flying night-fighters then, during the *blitz*. How could you have known and what could you have done? You were already risking your life. Apology not accepted. None is owed."

Jeremy shrugged. "What about Chantal?"

"She's out at Maurice's farm. He still does his vegetable runs and she still helps him, and they're both as heavily involved with the Resistance as ever. He's done a magnificent job of running security around the villa and operating the local arm of Alliance, but he and Chantal come here less frequently. We've decentralized so that if we're infiltrated again, the whole organization doesn't collapse."

"And Horton's done a good job up in Loire?"

"He has. They like him, but his official job is still to be my liaison with London. We can bring him back here so you can take over back there again." She chuckled. "Chantal would like that."

Jeremy laughed slightly, and then shook his head. "If he's being effective and he likes what he's doing, I see no reason to change. Is he really needed here as liaison?"

"Not so much anymore. With the Lysander flights, our ground crews well-trained, and our radios and operators in place, communications with London are frequent. They have finally understood that our operators cannot stay on the air a long time, either broadcasting or receiving long messages. The Germans were tracing our radio signals, and our operators were getting killed that way. Their life expectancy for a while, once they got into position, was about two weeks. So now, the communications mandate is: be punctual, reduce messages to bare essentials, and send the longer ones by Lysander—or submarine if the occasion arises."

"Progress," Jeremy muttered absently. "Always good to see progress."

Fourcade detected a stressed note in his tone. "What's on your mind, Jeremy?"

"Well, I seem to be out of a job at the moment. I've left the commandos—"

"That was quite spectacular what your group pulled off at Saint-Nazaire. I'm sure you don't know that Chantal and Horton did the surveillance at Bruneval."

Jeremy stared at her in astonishment. Then, reflecting on what Corran had observed about horsemen and messages in battle, he breathed, "They were the nail."

He related what Corran had said.

Fourcade nodded. "Yes. They put themselves at great risk." Then she laughed. "The tension between those two is amusing. She thinks she's in love with him, he knows it, and I think he likes her too, but he still sees her as a little girl and fights it."

Jeremy chuckled. "I hope they get a chance to get that all sorted out one day." Then he sighed and added seriously, "You know I stayed here without orders—"

"I've taken care of that with Crockatt. He knows of your assignment with Giraud."

"That's good." Jeremy sat picking at his fingers and then

looked up. "You said you helped General Giraud escape from the Königstein Fortress. How did you do that?"

Fourcade gazed at Jeremy fondly. "You're thinking of your brother, Lance, in Colditz, aren't you?" When Jeremy nodded, she continued, "The general's plan took two years. He learned German while in there, and we smuggled in bits and pieces of material he needed over a long time. He had established a simple code with his family and forwarded instructions through them. Then, when he was ready, we stationed men to guide him out of Germany through Switzerland and then into Vichy."

"My brother's already been a POW for nearly two years. I must try to help him." He dropped his arms on the table and faced Fourcade. "He's worked out some kind of code with military intelligence. I know because he sends letters that are meaningless. I turn them over to MI."

"What did you have in mind?" Fourcade asked softly.

"I should go there. I speak German and French. I could cut through Switzerland. That would shorten the distance and exposure to being discovered. Giraud did it, and he was high profile. I could come out the other side disguised as Swiss, visiting relatives or something."

"Or something." Fourcade eyed him skeptically. "Don't invite capture."

"I wouldn't. But right now, I have no mission, and when I first came back to France after Dunkirk, one of the reasons was to find a way to help Lance."

Fourcade smiled teasingly. "You mean besides coming back to see Amélie."

Jeremy grinned back. "Yes. Guilty." Then he asked somberly, "Will you help me?"

Fourcade heaved a sigh. "That's asking a lot, Jeremy. I

can't risk irritating Crockatt or my real masters at MI-6. We need their support."

"And they need your organization. If France is lost, Britain is lost. It's that simple."

Fourcade raised a hand in protest. "It's still a great risk."

Jeremy persisted. "Look, we'll call it a reconnaissance mission. I'll need some forged documents, some train tickets, and some guides along the way. You've already operated inside Germany, so you can arrange that. That's all I'm asking."

Fourcade laughed. "That's all, huh?"

Nonplussed, Jeremy added, "Well, I'd need a little money for food and a place to stay—I'd pay for the trip myself if I had access to my funds. In France, I don't, but I'll repay it when I get back to England." He beseeched her with pleading eyes. "Please."

"You look pathetic," Fourcade jibed, and then added seriously, "Your country owes you a lot, Jeremy, and so does mine. But we can't throw caution to the wind out of gratitude—not to mention risking your life and those of others who would help you."

Jeremy gazed back at Fourcade without speaking. Finally, she said, "I want to see a good, solid plan."

35

May 2, 1942
Manhattan, New York, USA

Stephenson stood and greeted Paul warmly. "You're back. I take it things went well. What's it been, three months since you left?"

"Yes, sir. That's about right. It was quite educational. Camp X gives a very different perspective on many things."

"Welcome to the world of pragmatic freedom lovers," Stephenson said jovially while gesturing toward a seating area in front of his desk. "Let's catch up." He regarded Paul with a rueful smile. "You're alive, so that's evidence enough that you made it through Bill Fairbairn's close-combat course."

"You mean 'Dangerous Dan's' tactics," Paul said, taking his seat. "I wake up at night with his voice in my head yelling, 'Get down in the gutter, and win at all costs ... no more playing fair...to kill or be killed.'" He sighed. "For good or bad, I shed a lot of naïvetés at Camp X."

"That'll keep you alive, and that's a good thing because

you'll keep others alive—innocents, still strapped to their own naïvetés." He peered at Paul. "You even look more rugged. Not that you didn't before, what with growing up climbing the cliffs of Sark and all. But that Camp X course is close to what the commandos go through, with specialties thrown in for the clandestine work our graduates do. Now you look like you really could take a man's throat out with your bare hands."

"And the frightful truth is that I can. I'd better stymie the look, though. I don't want to be terrifying people around me all my life."

"That journalist you mentioned the last time you were here, Ian Fleming. He's here now and has a mission you could help with. I'll let him fill you in."

Paul shrugged. "I'll help if I can. He was a bit of a strange duck, kept to himself a lot. I gather he came from a family that sent him to boarding school far away because he was unmanageable."

"I recruited him myself. He'll make significant contributions to our intelligence effort along the way."

Paul glanced around the office. "What's been happening here? Keeping up with the news was not easy."

"There've been some changes," Stephenson replied, appearing less than pleased. "The Americans have moved in with us. Our good friend, Wild Bill Donovan, recruited Allen Dulles for that billet, and I suppose that's a good thing, although I don't yet see how we benefit. Wild Bill is busy setting up his Office of Strategic Services in DC patterned after what we do here, and I'm afraid it'll move us into the sphere of politics.

"I'm also hearing that US academics are snooping about the country lanes around Bletchley Park." He shook his head. "Things are going to get complicated. They were much easier when it was just Churchill, Roosevelt, Wild Bill, and me." He bestowed one of his hints of a smile on Paul. "And of course, you."

Paul accepted the approbation with a steady gaze but no comment.

Stephenson contemplated. "You went up to Camp X right after New Year's. Our General Auchinleck was winning in North Africa at the time, but he's since been outfoxed by the Desert Fox—Rommel, that is—and he's lost the ground he gained. I think his days in command might be numbered. One bright spot in that regard is that a few weeks ago, the Roosevelt administration approved full production of the M4 Sherman tank. It's being shipped out to US divisions now and I expect that when they've reached their fill, more will be sent to British troops in Africa. At this point, the Germans have nothing to match it. When those troops get them, that should offset things in our favor."

"That's good," Paul broke in. "I remember Wild Bill mentioning that when we visited the production plant last December."

Stephenson nodded. "The Germans started their spring offensive. It's not going to work. Everyone knows that but Hitler. The Soviets are dug in, and they've had nearly a year of supply and equipment from America. Meanwhile, Adolf is draining his industrial capacity. I'm sure somewhere deep inside his torso, he knows his only hope is that Japan will somehow throw things back in his favor."

His face brightened. "You must know of the spectacular raids the Allies just pulled off: one by the Brits at Saint-Nazaire, and one by the US over Tokyo."

"We heard about them both. Quite remarkable. And Admiral Halsey's been giving it to the Japanese in the Gilbert and Marshall Islands too. I see in the streets how all of this has raised morale, at least in the US. I imagine the same to be true in Britain."

"Spirits are lifted, but I think the sense there now is one of relief for not being bombed nightly and having more food in the shops and on the dinner tables. That comes from turning the tide in the Atlantic. With the *Tirpitz* no longer a threat—at least for the time being—and with better anti-submarine technology and equipment, courtesy of the US, our convoys are getting through."

"Things are still bad in the Far East, though."

"They're still bad all over. Most of the fighting is ahead of us, but at least we're having more say about the makeup of the battlefield. The Allies have not yet settled over whether to go straight into Europe or to defeat the German forces in North Africa first. The Americans are quite keen on invading France as soon as possible, but Churchill thinks we're not ready yet, and I agree with him. I imagine another summit will have to take place between him and Roosevelt to iron that out."

A pause settled over the two of them. "What about you, Paul. What do you want to do now?"

"Sir? I thought it was understood that I'd come back to work with you. Am I being given a choice?"

Stephenson laughed spontaneously and heartily, an event that Paul had not witnessed before. "You make that prospect sound like a fate worse than death."

"I certainly didn't mean it that way."

"It's all right, Paul. You've earned your stripes. Welcome to the club. You've made yourself into a valuable asset, one that's probably wasted in just being my constant companion. Your intelligence, discipline, and now your increased capabilities learned at Camp X all say that you can make greater contributions, and those opportunities should be made available to you. So, tell me what you'd like to do."

Dumbfounded, Paul at first could only stare. Then he chuckled. "Am I still confined to quarters, so to speak? Or can I travel the world like a grown man?"

"You know the constraint."

Paul tapped his shirt pocket. "I keep my suicide pills close at all times."

Stephenson inhaled deeply and let his breath out slowly. "Let's talk about that. The last time we did, you took your time telling me whether or not—"

"I no longer have such reluctance, sir. If I am about to be captured, I'll pop them into my mouth and bite down faster than an assailant can whop me over the head."

Stephenson remained serious. "It's important that you mean that. With what you know about Bletchley, Camp X, Hydra, and some of the operations we've been involved in, you could be a treasure trove of intelligence to the enemy."

"I understand that sir." Paul gathered his thoughts quickly.

Stephenson wrinkled his brow and took a moment before speaking again. "There's a project I need you to be part of as my eyes and ears. It's one you know about, and I can identify it in one word: Czechoslovakia."

Paul's breath caught, and he felt the hair on the back of his neck rising as heat inflamed his face. "I recall the project," he said. "The one I was not supposed to know about. I had mentioned some students at Camp X who were involved in it on my visit there before I went there for training."

"Yes, that's the one. And it's about to execute." Stephenson took a breath. "I need a trusted agent on the ground to see what goes on, but I must tell you that we expect no survivors."

Paul swallowed hard. "I'll go where I'm needed. Do you think I'm ready?"

Stepheson scoffed. "As ready as anyone will ever be. Aside from the few military regulars, this whole war and our covert activity has been conducted by amateurs learning as they go, and they've done a jolly good job. The men who will carry it out will be on their own first outing too. We need to know from you firsthand what goes right and what goes wrong.

"This is a mission that finally confronts the face of evil directly. Other operatives will be there to record what takes place and capture the event on film. But you must understand that you'll be there to watch and get out. If things go wrong, you are not to step in to help. Do you understand?"

Stephenson's eyes narrowed and he leaned forward. "I want to be sure your head is in the right place before you go —make sure you're mentally steeled to it. Let's do this. Fleming's mission is local and messy. The preliminary work is done. If after it's done you've performed your part competently, you'll be on your way."

Paul stopped pacing and faced him. "What do you want me to do?"

"I'll call Fleming in. He'll fill you in."

36

May 27, 1942
Prague, Czechoslovakia

Paul ambled along a cobblestone street in Libeň, a picturesque district in Prague, a block from where the main thoroughfare of Kirchmayerova třída made a tight turn to his left at the bottom of a long hill, crossing in front of him into V Holešovičkách. From this vantage, he had a clear view of the intersection and a tram stop on the opposite side. Two men waited there, one with an overcoat hung over his arm, the other carrying a briefcase.

Although Paul had never met either man, he knew of them and revered their courage. Both had been hand-picked for the assassination they were about to carry out, their mission having been approved by the Czech government-in-exile in London.

Unlike the other countries that had fallen under Nazi rule, the occupation of Czechoslovakia had been peaceful, the German army having moved in without objection by western powers. The *Reichsprotektor*, a German official who ruled this far western region known as the Sudetenland and containing Bohemia and Moravia, had raised the wages of factory and farm workers such that little resistance to Nazi rule was encountered. As a result, the area produced much in the way of supplies and equipment needed by the voracious *Wehrmacht*.

In London, the government-in-exile's president, Edvard Beneš, was pressed by the British government as well as those banished governments of other German-occupied countries—Free France, Poland, Belgium, Greece, Luxembourg, the Netherlands, Yugoslavia, and Norway—to develop a resistance movement within his country. Beneš' intelligence officer, František Moravec, had sought a mission that would express to their allies that Czechoslovakia was in the war with them, to win.

The man with the raincoat whom Paul now watched was Jozef Gabčík, and the other was Jan Kubiš. They were there to carry out Moravec's mission.

Jozef was light-skinned, an ordinary-looking man whose deadly serious eyes, even at this distance, belied the warm-hearted craftsman and farrier that he had been. That was before the British and French had agreed to allow Hitler to occupy this area as part of the Munich Agreement in an ill-fated effort to stave off a war.

It was where Jozef had been born and raised and learned to love life until the Nazis had arrived and turned it into a dark night. Now he wore a business suit, and his light brown hair was combed back closely to his scalp. Under his overcoat, Jozef carried a Sten MKII British 9mm sub-machine gun, a weapon inexpensive to produce, making them readily available to resistance and insurgency groups. A notable weakness was that they often jammed.

Despite the danger of the mission, Jozef's companion,

Jan, bore an expression of hope and humor as he greeted passersby in a friendly manner. He was dark-skinned with big eyes and thick dark hair, close-cropped on the sides and brushed back on top. Inside Jan's briefcase, he carried a specially designed grenade, one that was light but with enough explosive power to penetrate an armored Mercedes limousine.

Both men had been part of a group of twenty Czechoslovakians to attend the commando school in Scotland, and they had emerged as the best operatives to carry out this mission. They were supported by seven other Czech commandos who had parachuted into the country with them three days before New Year's Eve. They were led by Jiri Potucek, who was responsible for setting up the support group in observation posts around the target and establishing radio communications with SOE in London. He had set up his headquarters in a rented house in the area, and it was to him that Paul had been directed upon arriving via parachute inside Czechoslovakia.

"This is an in-and-out mission for you," Stephenson had told Paul. "You are to observe only and not attempt to speak to either Jozef or Jan, or any of the other commandos besides Potucek. Given the probable repercussions, the Czechs are likely to be cold to your presence. Only under extreme conditions should you become involved. When it's over, get out of the area fast.

"Your cover and documents show you to be a mid-level German bureaucrat doing inspections in the arms factories on orders from Berlin. That should give you enough clout to make demands and get you across the country by train, but you can't linger anywhere long enough to be checked out. You can use the same ruse at the French border, and once inside France, we'll have Resistance members to guide you south to Vichy for a Lysander flight to Britain."

Stephenson had paused in deep thought, and when he spoke again, his voice carried an element of reluctance. "A man traveling alone draws more attention. If one of the commandos manages to escape after the attack, you might think of traveling with him. The Czech commandos have their own cover stories and forged papers." He paused again and sighed. "However, in all likelihood, none will survive to travel with you."

On parachuting onto a moonlit field outside of Prague and making contact, Potucek had tersely reinforced the notion that Paul was to have no contact with the other members of the commando team. "What do your bosses think," he said in good but thickly accented English, "that we can't handle this without a babysitter?"

"No," Paul had replied evenly. "We've seen the *Reichsprotektor's* plans. He must be stopped, his ideas exposed, and I'm to make an eyewitness account. I'll stay out of your way. Just put me where I have the best vantage."

Potucek had acquiesced, and within a day, he had warmed up to Paul. He revealed that his group had already abandoned two concepts for engaging the target. The first was to attack the *Reichsprotektor* on his train, but that proved impractical because of the heavy security surrounding it. The commandos would be executing a suicide mission with a low probability of success.

They tried the second idea, which was to ambush the target on a forest road he was known to frequent. However, when hours passed and he did not show up, they abandoned the plan, and went to the third option.

Potucek explained it. Each time he said the *Reichsprotektor's* name, his lips curled with visceral hatred. "This Reinhard Heydrich," he snarled, "this protégé of the devil, Hitler—he is the worst of the two. The people here have names for him: the Butcher of Prague, the Blond Beast, and the Hangman. Take your pick. They all apply."

Paul had studied *Reichsprotektor* Heydrich. The man had taken over in an 'acting' capacity when he and the *führer* agreed that his predecessor, Konstantin von Neurath, was not aggressive enough in pushing the populace to meet Nazi production quotas, and that was harming the war effort. Furthermore, when Germany had invaded the Soviet Union a year ago, local communists had begun a campaign of sabotage, which had spurred Hitler to make the change. Heydrich's steel-fisted rule had quickly corrected the issues, his actions earning his monikers as he terrorized the local population with threats, tortures, hangings, and firing squads—and no one doubted that he would stay in position as long as he liked.

Ensconced in an opulent villa in Panenské Břežany, his daily drive to his office at the magnificent Prague Castle was only nine miles through scenic forests and countryside. So confident was he of his hold over the people that he rode in the back of his armored Mercedes convertible and read documents while his chauffeur drove him with the car's top down.

As the hours advanced into the evening of Paul's second day in-country, he sat with Potucek on a forest bench far from the listening ears of others. Potucek had brought along a bottle of *slivovitze*, a version of local moonshine. He took a swig and handed it to Paul, who downed an equal amount and held back a cough as the liquid burned down his throat.

Potucek noticed and smiled. "Don't drink too much. It's strong stuff." Nevertheless, he took multiple deep swigs, and when his eyes had begun to swim, he turned to Paul, hung his arm around his neck, and leaned toward him. He held up a finger to hold Paul's attention.

"Listen to me, my friend," he said. "The Czech Resistance does not want this operation. They begged our president in London, Edvard Beneš, not to do it. They told him that the retribution would be a blood bath, that hundreds of people would be slaughtered."

Potucek's head swayed, and his speech slurred. "They are correct. The Germans will kill anyone who crosses their path. The families too; women, children, old people—and they will laugh."

His chest heaved with a deep breath as he took another swig. "But Beneš got on the radio to Resistance fighters personally and ordered the mission to go forward." He grunted. "Politics and politicians. They muck up everything. Beneš was concerned that his government-in-exile had not been recognized by the British, and so we must make a grand gesture to show our commitment to winning the war to be sure that Czechoslovakia can be re-formed as a country after the war."

He leaned his head back, dropped his arm from Paul's shoulder, and sighed. "But, as Machiavellian as his thinking was, he made the right decision, because if we do not do this thing, many more thousands of people will die." He laughed, a pitiable, disconsolate guffaw. "You know we call this mission Operation Anthropoid. Do you know what anthropoid means?"

"I'm afraid I don't."

Potucek chuckled. “It’s Greek for ‘having the form of a human.’ This man is not human. He only looks like one with his tall frame, blond hair, narrow face, and the eyes of a serpent.” He stood suddenly and whirled to face Paul. “He had thirty-three thousand people shot and killed in just two days.” Potucek’s face contorted with rage. “But when we do this mission, Hitler and all his generals will know they are vulnerable to the wrath and might of the people. We can and will strike them down and take our country back.”

He spat and then handed the bottle to Paul once more. “Have another swallow, friend. It’ll help you sleep. You’ll need it. Heydrich is reported to be leaving for Berlin, and we want to hit him before he departs. So, tomorrow we strike.”

Paul sat in the dark staring out a bedroom window in Potucek’s rented house. In the silence, he recalled his last hours in New York before leaving for Czechoslovakia: his conversation with Stephenson about the operation, as well as his initiation into the gruesome art of assassination.

“It’s interesting that you should mention the Czech operation,” Stephenson had said as he stood and rounded his desk. He pulled a key from his pocket and opened a desk safe. “I obtained this document back in February while you were in training. It’s the secret minutes to a conference that Reinhard Heydrich chaired at a villa in Wannsee, Berlin. Thirty copies were made. They were to have been burned. I got one. Pay attention to the parts I underlined.”

He handed it to Paul. It was stamped Top Secret and titled, “Wannsee Protocol.” Paul read the first line and froze, reading over and over a portion of the sentence that Stephenson had emphasized: “The following persons took part in the discussion about *the final solution of the Jewish question* which took place in Berlin, am Grossen Wannsee No. 56/58 on 20 January 1942."

Below the sentence were listed the attendees. Aside from Heydrich's, Paul did not recognize the names, but their titles indicated the high-level importance of the conference:

Reich Minister for the Occupied Eastern Territories

Secretary of State, Reich Ministry for the Interior

Secretary of State, Plenipotentiary for the Four-Year Plan

Secretary of State, Reich Ministry of Justice

Secretary of State, Office of the Government General

Under Secretary of State Foreign Office

Party Chancellery

Ministerialdirektor, Reich Chancellery

Race and Settlement Main Office

Reich Main Security Office

SD Commander of the Security Police

Paul looked up at Stephenson in disbelief. "Are they serious?"

Stephenson nodded. "Given who chaired the conference and who attended, I'd say they're very serious. That is their plan for ridding any territory they occupy of Jews, and we've had multiple reports of mass executions. And of course, their aim is world domination."

"I'm looking at this one sentence in particular," Paul said, pointing to the passage and quoting, "'The Reichsfuhrer-SS and the Chief of the German Police...was entrusted with the official central handling of the *final solution of the Jewish question without regard to geographic borders.*'" He looked up again. "That's Heydrich."

"Correct. He chaired the conference, he developed the plan, and he is in charge of carrying it out."

"Look at the list of countries and the numbers," Paul exclaimed, his astonishment unabated. "He's identified the size of the Jewish population in well over thirty countries, and he states clearly that he intends to evacuate them at their own expense. That's eleven million people."

"Exactly. He needs to go."

A soft knock on the door had preceded Stephenson's secretary announcing the arrival of Ian Fleming wearing a British navy uniform that fit him well. Roughly six feet tall with a high forehead, wavy hair, and penetrating eyes, he had a narrow face that bore little expression.

"Good to see you again, Littlefield," he said to Paul, extending his hand in a manner slightly beyond perfunctory warmth. "Glad you made it through at Camp X. Congratulations." He turned to Stephenson. "You sent for me?"

Stephenson nodded. "I want Paul to go with you on your mission tomorrow. You told me that the other operator took ill. You've just enough time to get on a range, zero his weapon, and work out your details."

Fleming regarded Paul with a deadpan face. "Does he know the objective?"

"You can tell him."

"We're going to kill a man."

Paul regarded Fleming somberly and then shifted his eyes to look at Stephenson. "May I ask why?"

"Does it matter? Fleming has his orders. He's prepared to carry them out."

"Does he know why?"

Stephenson nodded.

"Then I think I should be afforded the same courtesy."

"Do you recall that shortly after you came here last year, the FBI picked us up and took us to an apartment belonging to a British merchant marine sailor who was selling convoy schedules to the Germans. Those convoys carried weapons for our military and food for our people, and the Germans were sinking our ships."

"I recall."

"This is a similar situation. This time, we've located a Japanese agent in this very building. He's cracked our codes, and he's preparing to deliver them and messages he's already deciphered. Do I need to explain the implications?"

Paul shook his head. "I get the picture. What is my role?"

Fleming broke in. "We've rented a room on the fortieth floor in the RCA building across the street. It has a direct view into his room. The windows on these skyscrapers are thick and designed to withstand high winds and block noise. A shot fired through them will deflect. You'll shoot out the window glass. I'll take the kill shot."

The mission had gone as planned. Paul and Fleming had both changed into civilian clothes and entered the rented room with a pair of Remington 30-30 rifles equipped with scopes and silencers. Within minutes they had set up.

Paul had quelled nervousness on the way up, and as he sighted the scope, he wondered whether he could help deliberately snuff out the life of a stranger whom he had never met and would barely be able to see. Then, as he looped the tip of his index finger over the trigger and adjusted his sight, he recalled the horrors he had witnessed during the Battle of Britain, with people he knew shot out of the sky and his own brother's life endangered; the burned-out hulks and numerous funerals during the *blitz* in London; the destruction he had seen in the Baltics from the Italian invasion; and images of Pearl Harbor captured in photographs.

They did not have to wait long. Fleming knew the

target's schedule. Across the expanse of empty air many stories up in the building, Paul saw the man enter his room.

Paul's task was easy: aim at the window and fire on order.

A light flipped on inside the target room. A blurred figure appeared behind the thick glass.

Fleming signaled to Paul and peered through his scope.

Paul did likewise, controlling his breathing and putting light pressure on the trigger.

"Now," Fleming called.

Paul squeezed off a round, feeling the rifle recoil against his shoulder. Instantly the glass across the way shattered, and then he heard Fleming's shot.

"I caught him in the mouth when he turned," Fleming said.

Paul had fought down nausea that lingered as the two of them made their steady way out of the building.

Noticing his slight green coloration, Fleming asked, "Are you all right?"

Paul nodded. "I don't know if I could ever get used to that."

"You won't, unless you're no longer human."

Memories of that night intruded as Potucek stationed Paul where he could be unobtrusive but with a full view of the target area. At odd moments, he wondered about Fleming's last comment about no longer being human. *Has that already happened to me? I volunteered for this. I wanted to see it.*

Potucek broke into his thoughts. "We observed Heydrich's pattern for going to work for several days," he said. "His car will drive down the broad street on that hill."

He pointed it out. “We have a man stationed across the intersection with clear sight both up the hill and in the direction of the road after it curves away from him at the bottom. Heydrich is so arrogant that he rides around without a security escort. When our man sees his car, he’ll flash a signal to Jozef and Jan at the tram stop to prepare them. You’ll be able to see the entire operation.”

He grinned morosely and shook Paul’s hand. “Good luck getting home, my friend. Look for me when you get to Paradise.”

The time that the car was expected came and went. Paul calmed himself so as not to appear anxious or reckless. He was also mindful of remaining in place too long, but he saw no cafés where he could linger without drawing attention or raising suspicion.

Finding a park bench along the street, he took a seat, opened a local newspaper he had acquired along the way, and feigned perusing it while occasionally checking his watch as if waiting for someone. Passing pedestrians paid him little mind.

At the tram stop, which was nothing more than a designated place for picking up fares, with neither shelter nor seating, Jozef and Jan waited, appearing as commuters not acquainted with each other. They stood casually looking in various directions, as waiting passengers would.

Paul kept an eye on the street coming almost straight in his direction from the top of the hill. Then he saw the unmistakable vehicle—a large aqua-colored 1938 Mercedes-Benz 320 Cabriolet B with the top down, its two prominent chrome headlamps gleaming in the sunlight on either side of its rectangular grill, the Mercedes emblem affixed to the front edge. Paul could not see who was inside because the windshield blocked his view and reflected the sun from his angle. But despite no other security being around the sedan, he knew it was the target vehicle from the small, triangular red flag with a black swastika flying over the left fender.

He glanced at Jozef and Jan. They must have received their signal; both stepped to the curb, no longer pretending to be waiting passengers. Jozef dropped his jacket, exposing his Sten gun.

The driver slowed the Mercedes to take the curve to his right.

Jozef stepped into the street and aimed his weapon as the sedan rolled into view.

Nothing happened. Jozef jerked his weapon. It must have jammed.

The car screeched to a halt. Heydrich, easily recognizable now, stood, drew a pistol, and fired.

He missed.

Jozef dropped the Sten and ran to his bicycle.

Meanwhile, Jan threw his explosive briefcase, intending it to land in the back seat. It flew through the air, bounced off the right rear door, and fell against the tire immediately below where Heydrich stood.

A massive explosion erupted with billowing smoke and an enormous roar.

Heydrich slumped to the floor. Unbelievably, he stood back up, holding his side with one hand and his pistol with the other, and staggered from the car, shooting at Jozef, who stood paralyzed momentarily before trying to reach his bicycle. Heydrich's continued shooting forced Jozef to abandon the bike and seek cover behind a tree, from which he returned fire with a pistol.

A tram stalled in the roadway. Heydrich sought cover behind it.

Meanwhile, the driver leaped from the car and started to

pursue Jan, who fled headlong on his bicycle down the street toward Paul, firing a Colt M1903 pistol in the air to scatter the crowd.

Vehicular traffic pulled to either side of the street and halted. Pedestrians, at first frozen in place, rushed in all directions seeking shelter.

The driver, still dazed from the explosion, took aim at Jan, but when he tried to pull the trigger, he mashed the magazine release, jamming his weapon and allowing Jan to escape.

Turning, the driver saw Jozef still taking cover behind the tree.

Seized with pain, Heydrich emerged from behind the tram and staggered to a rail at the side of the road. He croaked to the driver, "Get that bastard," and then collapsed against the rail.

A woman rushed to Heydrich and put pressure against his massive abdominal wound to stop the bleeding. A delivery vehicle stopped in the street, and a man, with the woman's help, supported the Nazi officer into it, and it roared off to a nearby hospital.

The driver ran at Jozef, who shot at him and then sprinted down the street toward Paul, who had remained on the park bench. As Jozef and the driver exchanged shots in a running gun battle, Paul took cover behind a tree. The pursuit moved to the other side of the street where Jozef darted into a butcher shop, seeking shelter. Moments later, the butcher ran shouting into the street with a terrified face and dirty apron, pointing wildly into his shop.

The driver closed the distance, but Jozef emerged, seeking escape, and the two collided in the door. Jozef pushed off the driver, who fell but immediately struggled to his feet. Jozef shot at the driver again, wounding the man's leg. He then disappeared down the street and around a corner.

Police sirens blared, German troop trucks roared, and at the intersection, barricades were already being erected. Paul moved with the crowd of confused pedestrians putting distance between themselves and the site of the attempted assassination.

37

June 2, 1942
USS *Enterprise,* Pacific Ocean, North of Midway Atoll

Josh hurried from the operations room to the upper reaches of the carrier's island. Going straight to the adjoining observation deck and finding it empty, he called across the bridge, "Anyone know where to find Admiral Spruance?"

Admiral Halsey had been hospitalized with a rare form of psoriasis and to recover from extreme fatigue on return of his task force to Pearl Harbor following his attacks on Japanese positions in the Gilbert and Marshall Islands and the raid on Tokyo. Meanwhile, in the Coral Sea, Admiral Frank Fletcher, leading a two-carrier task force, had also engaged the Japanese in the Coral Sea. The battle had been a tactical defeat but a strategic victory in that Fletcher had scuttled Japanese plans to attack and occupy and expand its presence from Port Moresby, the capital of Papua New Guinea.

If the Japanese had succeeded, they would have cut Allied supply lines and threatened the northeastern coast of

Australia from only two hundred miles away. But the cost of success had been steep: during the battle, the carrier *Lexington* took a pounding and was later scuttled.

Combat had raged for four days and had been the first engagement between capital ships at sea during which they never came in sight of one another. Throughout the battle, American F4F Wildcats and Japanese Zeroes buzzed around their respective carriers protectively, engaged in dogfights, and provided escort for the torpedo planes and dive bombers that attacked relentlessly.

Concussive waves rolled over the ocean. Dark clouds spewed into the sky among black anti-aircraft puffs. Giant columns of water erupted into the air from the force of high-explosive main-gun rounds firing into the ocean to down low-flying fighters.

As damaged aircraft spiraled out of control, the fading whine of their engines signaled their doom against the turbulent ocean surface. And then came the deep, throaty booms as torpedoes or dive bombs hit their targets on carriers and destroyers, detonating ammunition magazines and spreading giant fires.

The battle had been costly for both combatants. On the US side, in addition to the loss of the *Lexington*, the carrier *Yorktown* incurred severe damage and limped back to Pearl Harbor for repair; a destroyer and an oiler were sunk; sixty-nine aircraft were destroyed; and, worst of all, six hundred and fifty-six pilots and crewmen were killed.

Admiral Chester Nimitz commanded the Pacific Fleet and all Allied forces in the Pacific Ocean Areas, which included most of the Pacific except the waters around the islands in the southwest of the ocean. It was he who had ordered Halsey to see a medical doctor who, in turn, ordered Halsey hospitalized. Nimitz then appointed

Admiral Raymond Spruance, Halsey's trusted subordinate, to take command of the task force during the ailing admiral's absence.

"Admiral Spruance took Captain Browning for a walk," a crewman on the bridge told Josh.

"Can you page him to let us know where he is? I've got a priority signal from Admiral Nimitz."

Slender with dark hair, average height, and no-nonsense eyes, Spruance was known to be always on his feet, often roaming whatever ship he was on and engaging with the men under his command. He regularly conducted business with senior subordinates while on these walks.

Moments later, a deep-throated voice announced over the PA system throughout the ship, "Bridge to Admiral." Within seconds, a phone on a control panel lit up and a crewman answered it. He listened a moment, hung up, and turned to Josh. "He's down below, inspecting aircraft."

Josh found the admiral in the cavernous hangar in deep conversation with Captain Browning. They were surrounded by Douglas Dauntless dive bombers, Grumman F4F Wildcat fighters, and Vindicator torpedo planes, their wings folded over their canopies. The bindings that held them in place groaned with the rhythmic rise and fall of the ship amid the waves. The two men looked up as Josh approached.

"What is it?" Browning inquired.

Josh grinned. "We've got 'em, sir." He handed over the message.

Browning scanned it rapidly, and then handed it to the admiral. "Midway it is," he said.

Spruance read the message. It stated simply, "'AF' is Midway."

"The Japanese took Nimitz' bait and confirmed his suspicions," he murmured. "They thought they'd flank us. Two can play at cat-and-mouse." He smiled slightly. "It's easier when we have their code book."

He turned to Browning. "Nimitz guessed right. We won't be going any farther north today." He took a deep breath and pushed it out. "We've got our work cut out. Our orders are to engage the Japs by attrition and not to unduly risk our carriers and cruisers." He chuckled. "As if we'd 'unduly' risk anything.

"Do this," he told Browning. "When we get back upstairs, prepare a directive for my signature telling our ships' captains to apply a principle of calculated risk. That means they should not expose themselves to a superior force without a strong probability of inflicting severe damage on the enemy. That goes for any landing force and our air forces too. Let me see the message before it goes out. Meanwhile, let's continue our rounds."

"Aye, aye, sir."

Making his way back to the operations room, and despite the enormous implications of the message he had just delivered, Josh could not help being amused at the chain of events leading to them. Some months ago, a brilliant cryptologist, Lieutenant Commander Joe Rochefort, with his team in a top-secret set of rooms known as Station Hypo below the 11th Naval District Headquarters on Oahu, had broken the Japanese code by long hours of tedious work, piecing together bits of information that finally made the encryptions plain.

In recent weeks, the Japanese had changed their code, but not the settings. US cryptologists were therefore able to update their Japanese codebooks by watching for clues coming across in the new code and matching them against Japanese actions. Enemy radio traffic from the Battle of the Coral Sea had been so voluminous that, within days, US cryptologists had reconstructed almost the entire new Japanese codebook. The cryptologists' success led Nimitz's staff to conclude that Japan's next move would be on the Aleutian Islands.

Japanese naval doctrine had been built around the primacy of battleships and its main guns, similar to the doctrine of most other world powers. Japan's senior admirals had wargamed the United States as their chief foe and planned to lure the US Pacific Fleet into sea battles in the western Pacific, close to Japan. There, they envisioned, Japanese battleships would outflank and destroy their American counterparts.

The US, on the other hand, had built a navy balanced between battleships and aircraft carriers. Given the destruction inflicted on Pearl Harbor, its current strategy was simple. By agreement with Winston Churchill, as of March 17, the US took responsibility for the war in the east. In particular, it would engage Japanese forces in the western Pacific, deny their ability to advance east, and prevent them from invading the US mainland.

The strategy derived from studying recent history. US naval theoreticians were impressed by the near destruction of the Italian fleet by obsolete biplanes launched from an aircraft carrier at Taranto. Similarly, they appreciated the role of those same biplanes in hastening the destruction of the *Bismarck*. Those events, along with wargames at the Naval War College, pointed to the growing obsolescence of battleships as the primary naval weapon. The carriers could deliver destruction far deeper into enemy territory with greater precision than the main guns of battleships.

That notion had been driven home with the attack on Pearl Harbor by aircraft launched from carriers many miles away in almost the same way that Britain had attacked Taranto. The saving grace for the US had been that her carriers had been out to sea and had avoided the Japanese onslaught. Thus, although Japan enjoyed overall naval superiority in the Pacific, its battleships, sliding into obsolescence, were a large measure of that strength.

"And they forgot to keep up with communications security," Josh muttered with a slight thrill, thinking through the situation as he continued toward the operations room. In after-action analysis, the group in which he worked had estimated that Japan's intent in the Coral Sea had been to extend its defensive positions along a twenty-eight-hundred-mile southeastward line extending to Samoa that incorporated the Solomons, New Caledonia, and Fiji.

Admiral Fletcher had disrupted those plans in the Coral Sea, denying the Japanese use of those islands and Port Moresby and costing them heavily. Intelligence on the extent of damage inflicted still filtered in, but what was certain was that Fletcher's forces had destroyed two enemy fleet carriers, a light carrier, nine cruisers, fifteen destroyers, a number of lighter vessels, and well over a hundred aircraft. Nevertheless, with the loss of the *Lexington* and supporting ships and the damage to the *Yorktown*, the engagement had been considered a tactical defeat—but a strategic victory. No longer could the Japanese hope to expand their reach farther west and south.

"And they don't know that we know their plans and positions," Josh breathed.

In May, the Hypo team had informed Nimitz that the Imperial Japanese Navy, the IJN, had divided into five task forces with plans to expand their defensive perimeter to the north, south, and east. The main force would be composed of a four-aircraft carrier group, but its target was not identified. Nimitz's staff had reached a conclusion that Japan would attack in the Aleutians because, prior to the battle in the Coral Sea, Japan had intended to take those northern islands arcing southwest from Alaska, as well as Midway Island in the center of the Pacific and nearly three thousand miles due north of Samoa.

Despite that the results of the Coral Sea battle had been disappointing to Japan, it had not been a complete failure in that the IJN had succeeded in securing Japanese oil supply lines from the East Indies, a major objective. And they still had New Guinea and the Solomon Islands to protect the southern flank.

The rest of the plan remained to be executed.

The Hypo team intercepted and deciphered the IJN order to proceed east, but US analysts could not determine for certain whether the main objective was Midway or the Aleutians. One of those locations would meet the full force of the Japanese four-carrier group. Therein lay the question: which direction to send Spruance's fleet?

A Japanese victory in Midway would deny the US navy the Pacific west of the island and cut its communications lines to Australia. Japan would then be in position to attack the US directly once again at Pearl Harbor.

The Aleutians, on the other hand, were an easier target which, once seized, would have a similar effect farther north. Further, it placed Japanese soldiers on US territory, positioning them to attack farther into the United States. Beyond those advantages and the psychological blow on the US similar to that of the Doolittle raid on Japanese citizens, taking the Aleutians would also force US approaches to the Japanese homeland to sail farther south, straight across the full seven-thousand-mile breadth of the Pacific.

Regardless, one element of the Japanese plan became clear: attacks on the Aleutians or Midway were bait to draw out the US fleet.

The real objective was the carriers themselves.

A month before the IJN set sail, Hypo intercepts revealed Japanese intent to mount another attack to the east, without further specifics. They further revealed that Admiral Isoroku Yamamoto, the Japanese commander in chief of the Imperial Japanese Navy's combined fleet who had formulated and commanded the attack on Pearl Harbor, feared that the damage done to the US Pacific fleet was only temporary and that US industrial might would replenish and expand its naval forces in the Pacific in short order.

Once Japan's capital ships had been destroyed, they could not be replaced quickly. Without natural resources, Japan had built its fleet with scrap metal from other nations.

As a remedy, Yamamoto intended to destroy all American Pacific Fleet carriers at one time. The rest of the US fleet would be ineffective against Japan, thus perhaps drawing the US to the negotiating table.

Further Hypo messages revealed the Japanese admiral's belief that the US had kept its fleet at Pearl Harbor in a defensive posture and thus would not expect or detect his fleet's approach east. After attacking either the Aleutians or Midway, he could lie in wait for US carriers to rush to defend US territory. Yamamoto could then attack from the flank with four carriers and all his aircraft and pick off the rest of the US fleet at his leisure anywhere in the Pacific.

US naval analysts in Washington argued to Nimitz that, given America's losses in the Coral Sea, the IJN would opt for the easier target in the Aleutians. The still formidable IJN presence in New Guinea and the Solomons, they argued, would be enough to inhibit US supply lines in the south. For that reason, Yamamoto was likely to move against targets in the north Pacific, specifically in the Aleutians.

Nimitz disagreed. Relying on intelligence from Rochefort and Station Hypo, he believed the main attack would target Midway in the early days of June. Still, he acknowledged the possibility of an attack against the Aleutians, so he deployed Spruance's Task Force 16 to a position three hundred and fifty miles northeast of Midway and twenty-two hundred miles south of the Aleutians, to lie in wait.

Task Force 17, under Admiral Fletcher, was also designated for the anticipated battle, but *Yorktown* needed extensive repairs from its mauling in the Battle of the Coral Sea. Amazingly, the repair crews, working around the clock and against all odds, had put her in seaworthy shape within seventy-two hours.

Yorktown set sail with her carrier group to catch up with Task Force 16, bringing the composition of the two task forces under the overall command of Admiral Fletcher to three carriers with eight cruisers, fifteen destroyers, sixteen submarines, and three hundred and thirty-three aircraft. Furthermore, a hundred and fifty land-based heavy bombers were stationed on Midway.

Rochefort's team at Hypo estimated that the main Japanese force, commanded by Vice Admiral Nagumo, consisted of four aircraft carriers, two battleships, seven cruisers, fourteen destroyers, and two hundred and seventy-six aircraft. An IJN amphibious transport group carrying assault troops also sailed farther south.

The Japanese had coded their main target with the encrypted letters AF.

Although Rochefort's team readily decrypted the letters, they had found nothing that identified which target—Midway or the Aleutians—they represented. Twenty-six hundred miles of ocean spanned between them.

The decision of where Nimitz should send his three-carrier group rode on determining precisely which objective those two letters, "AF," referred to.

Josh shook his head at the thought of what would happen if Nimitz guessed wrong. *Disaster.*

He grinned at the simple ruse that Nimitz had run to resolve the issue. Several days earlier, Rochefort instructed the signal intelligence operators on Midway Island to send out a distress message in the clear, stating that their desalinization plant had malfunctioned, and the troops were without water. Shortly, the cryptologists at Pearl Harbor intercepted a message from the Japanese to their higher headquarters relaying the news of a water shortage on "AF." *It's Midway.*

Josh entered the operations room, stopped for a cup of coffee, and took it to his desk where he sat down, stretched back in his chair, and breathed a contented sigh.

"You look happy, sir."

Josh smirked and shook his head. "Who could be happy in this war? We got our shorts handed to us at Pearl Harbor, but then we stung the Japs with our raids in Gilbert and the Marshalls, surprised them in Tokyo, knocked them on their heels in the Coral Sea, and they won't be ready for what we're bringing at Midway."

Just then, the door swung open, and Captain Browning held it for Admiral Spruance. Everyone in the room popped to attention.

"As you were," the admiral said with a subdued smile. "I came to review plans and make sure we're ready. We'll make enemy contact tomorrow."

At first no one moved or spoke, but as duties required actions, crewmembers returned to what they had been doing, albeit in a more somber atmosphere. The admiral moved about the room with Browning as the two studied maps, reviewed documents, and asked questions. Several minutes later, they headed for the door.

On impulse, Josh lunged to his feet. "Admiral, if I may?"

Spruance and Browning stopped and turned, regarding him questioningly.

"Yes, Commander?" the admiral said.

Josh took a deep breath while looking back and forth between them. "Sir, I should be flying."

Browning regarded him with reproachful amusement. "Commander, we need you here."

"Sir, you need pilots. That's what I am. Operations is a sideline I didn't ask for. When the first plane launches, all plans go out the window." He gestured around the room at the other men. "This is a competent team. They don't need me."

Spruance regarded Josh without expression. "You heard the chief." He turned to leave.

"Captain Browning, plcasc," Josh persisted, addressing the chief of staff. "I'm a pilot. I did what you asked. I went with the Doolittle fliers, liaised, and trained with them, watched them fly off the *Hornet* bound for Tokyo, but I couldn't go with them. We still don't know the status of some of them, including Captain Ted Lawson, who became a close friend.

"The team here did fine without me during the Gilbert and Marshall raids, and I manned this office during the Coral Sea action where I lost more friends—please don't leave me in a position to lose even more while I sit in a chair—"

Spruance regarded him sternly. "You know this ship is a prime target? None of us 'sitting in chairs' during the battle will think of ourselves as being in a safe place."

Josh's face turned scarlet. "Yes, sir. I mean, no sir." He became slightly flustered. "What I mean, sir, is that my place is defending your ship—from up there." He jabbed a finger in the air.

Spruance peered at him a moment longer and then turned to Browning. "What's he talking about with the Doolittle raiders?"

"We sent him to watch the B-25 trials in Norfolk off the *Hornet*, and then we had him stay with the pilots while they trained. He volunteered to replace any crewmember on the raid if needed, but the occasion didn't arise."

"I see." He looked back at Josh again, studying him. "I'll talk to your boss. No promises."

38

June 4, 1942

Horrified, Josh stared at the map in the operations room. Behind him, a radio streamed disturbing commo from pilots engaged in battle. Early that morning, the *Enterprise* had received frantic reports that Dutch Harbor on the island of Unalaska was under attack, as were Attu and Kiska, two islands four hundred miles farther west along the Aleutian chain. The attacking force consisted of two small carriers with fewer than a hundred planes. Intelligence analysts pored over communications to learn if the contact was a feint, an operation independent of that taking place west of Midway, or the front end of the main attack.

Nimitz still believed that the Japanese main force was aimed at Midway and therefore had chosen not to commit heavy forces to the Aleutians. Regardless, he was unwilling to relinquish a single American island to the Japanese. In response to enemy actions there, he ordered Task Force 8, commanded by Spruance's Annapolis classmate Rear Admiral "Fuzzy" Theobald, to "inflict maximum attrition on the enemy." Task Force 8 was equipped with two heavy cruisers, three light cruisers, and four destroyers.

At 0900 hours yesterday, a PBY Catalina scout plane spotted the Japanese transport fleet mentioned in Hypo's intelligence reports. It was headed toward Midway. The scout shadowed the ships until a second one joined to confirm and take a closer look. Then a flight of B-17 Flying Fortresses flew over and dropped bombs, sinking an oiler but otherwise doing no damage.

At 0300 hours today, Josh received word that more Catalinas had taken to the skies from Midway in a wide fan to the west to search for the IJN's four-carrier group. Then at 0545 hours, one of the scouts reported sighting a carrier. Seven minutes later, two more Catalinas separately reported seeing two more carriers.

Within minutes, an urgent message from Midway's radar station reported a large formation of inbound aircraft ninety-three miles to the northeast at an altitude of eleven thousand feet. Crewmen in the *Enterprise's* operations room moved markers on a wall map to represent the estimated one-hundred-plus enemy aircraft, and then different symbols for the Marine Buffalo and Wildcat fighters launched from the island to meet them. Sixteen Dauntless and eleven Vindicator dive bombers followed, and then six Avenger torpedo bombers and four B-26 Marauders, all headed to intercept the Japanese fleet.

Realizing the scale of what was about to happen, Josh shook his head. Most of the American aircraft were considered no match for the Japanese Zeroes sent up to protect their carriers. He was further dismayed when, shortly afterward, thirty-seven Flying Fortresses flew to encounter the carriers without fighter escort.

The Marines burst into the sky, and by the time aerial combat started at 0616 hours, they had gained height advantage. Escorted by fighters, the torpedo planes and dive bombers dove on the formation of Japanese bombers, but the Zeroes quickly demolished their numbers, spinning around them, outmaneuvering them, and knocking thirteen Buffaloes and two Wildcats from the sky.

Continuing on to Midway almost without disruption, but with no aircraft on the ground to attack, the Japanese flew through massive anti-aircraft fire. They dropped bombs on a field of fuel storage tanks, igniting them, and sending black smoke and billowing flames leaping into the air while their dive bombers attacked hangars and other support facilities.

The phone rang in the operations room where Josh watched the carnage play out on the wall map. A crewman took the call and then crossed the room to him. "Sir, Captain Browning wants to see you on the bridge."

Josh bolted out the door and hurried along the decks and up the ladders of the pitching ship, arriving on the observation deck by the bridge within minutes. There he encountered Spruance and Browning in conversation. "Sir, you wanted to see me?"

Browning caught his eye, nodded, and motioned him closer. Spruance moved away to the rail and looked out across the ocean.

"Admiral Fletcher ordered an early launch," Browning said. "Our guys spotted three Japanese carriers, and we know there's a fourth. The enemy aircraft from the first strike on Midway are heading back to their carriers to refuel and re-arm—and that's when to hit them. I've notified flight operations to move up their timetables. I need you to make sure everything is coordinated and goes smoothly."

"Aye, aye, sir," Josh replied without expression, and started to hurry away.

"Commander," Browning called after him, "this is why I wouldn't approve your going back to flight. We need someone to make sure this gets done right. For what it's worth, your boss was reluctantly in favor of letting you fly."

"Aye, aye, sir. I follow orders."

As combat continued past 0930 hours, Josh's spirits plunged. The few Marine planes that made it past the Zeroes' gauntlet were mauled on reaching the Japanese carrier group. Only two Flying Fortresses arrived safely back on Midway, and Josh continued to see the entire battle unfold on the map. Already, among the names of pilots known to have gone down were several close friends.

He received word that the Japanese had spotted Task Forces 16 and 17. Amazingly, however, their scout had reported only ten surface ships with no mention of the three American carriers. *They'll figure out their mistake soon enough, but that one'll cost 'em.*

As the aircraft from the *Enterprise* and the *Hornet* launched, he monitored their progress. Instead of organizing into formations, most of the planes headed straight toward the Japanese carriers, and were joined by those of the *Yorktown*, a hundred and fifty-six aircraft spread in a line astern at irregular intervals stretched across a hundred and thirty-five miles above the ocean. They included forty-six Devastator torpedo bombers, eighty-nine Dauntless dive bombers, and twenty-six Wildcat fighters.

Then, about the time that Josh expected to hear news of contact, the radio crackled from the lead planes. "Be advised, we do not see the carriers. I say again, we do not see them. They must have changed course."

Josh inhaled and let his breath out slowly, wondering which was worse, hearing the terrifying radio chatter of ongoing combat and screams of wounded and burned pilots plunging to their deaths or that the enemy had disappeared.

The IJN still lurked somewhere, preparing to pounce. Meanwhile, brave men used up precious fuel in search.

The US planes dispersed to scout, the lead Dauntless dive bombers from the *Enterprise* continuing straight while fifteen of *Hornet's* slow-moving torpedo Devastators turned north, and after some minutes, reported spotting the carrier group. Flying low and slow to drop their torpedoes in the water on their trajectories without breaking them, and unescorted by protective fighters, the Vindicators closed the distance and attacked.

The radio sizzled with strained voices, screams, grunts, the sounds of gunfire, explosions, and bullets slamming into the small planes. Plainly, the Zeroes had struck back, and then, within minutes, all was silent from that quarter of the ocean.

Josh's head drooped, and he hid his face. The only plausible conclusion was that the entire squadron had sacrificed itself to delay the Japanese task force.

Minutes later, the scene repeated. As Josh and the operations crew monitored in horror, fourteen Vindicators from the *Enterprise* began their run, also without fighter protection, and quickly met the same fate as their predecessors.

Adding to the tragedy, not a single torpedo reached a target.

"The Japanese are celebrating an easy victory," Josh muttered under his breath.

Struggling to maintain his spirits, he watched the tragic

situation on the map. *If there's a silver lining, it's that we've forced them to use up fuel and ammo, and we've delayed their second strike.*

And then, yet another wave of twelve Vindicators, this time from *Yorktown,* flew into the same fate, with two of them managing to escape back to their ship, but no targets hit. Then, a decrypted message came through that another Japanese scout had correctly identified that the group of ten American warships spotted earlier included three aircraft carriers.

Suddenly, a crewman called to Josh from across the room as others rushed to change the configuration of symbols on the map. "Sir, Captain McClusky's group of dive bombers, the ones that continued straight on? They turned north and conducted a box recon. They've spotted all four carriers, and they're converging on them from their left rear. The Zeroes are flying low to engage our torpedo bombers and apparently haven't seen the dive bombers—they're coming in high, forty-seven of them, in formation."

"Put them on the speaker," Josh ordered.

"That's the *Kaga,*" a disembodied voice called over the speaker. "Spread out or we'll collide on our dives. Spread out."

"Pulling away." Josh recognized the voice of one of his best friends. "Going after *Soryu.*"

Then, the first voice. "Diving now. Keep your intervals. Follow me."

Someone flew with an open mic, and Josh was glad of it for sharing in the next exhilarating moments. The roar of wind and aircraft resounded through the operations room, and then the unmistakable rat-tat-tat of anti-aircraft weapons.

"A direct hit on *Kaga*!" another voice called, followed by the far-off booms of multiple explosions.

"Diving on *Soryu*," McClusky called. Moments later, "Three direct hits!" More explosions reverberated. A cheer erupted across the operations room.

"Sir," a crewman called across to Josh. "A formation of dive bombers from the *Yorktown* is converging on *Akagi*. That's the flagship."

"Patch us in."

The crewman nodded. Another voice sounded over the crackling radio speaker. "Two carriers burning out of control," a pilot yelled in elation. "Diving on *Akagi*."

Everyone in the operations room stopped to listen. And then, "Direct hit! Magazines detonating."

Another cheer erupted, but a radio operator held up a hand. "Sir, the *Yorktown's* been hit by a flight of bombers. She's on fire and listing. Her planes are being diverted to land here on the *Enterprise*."

Silence descended.

"All right," Josh said. He turned to another crewman. "Make sure we know the type of each plane as it lands and keep a running count of the total. They'll want to know that upstairs." He looked across at the bank of radio operators. "Any word on that fourth carrier, the *Hiryu*?"

Negative responses came in shakes of heads or murmured comments.

Captain Browning entered and stood next to Josh, staring at the map. He observed the small markers showing the estimate of current dispositions of friendly and enemy ships and planes and the names of downed pilots.

"Your buddies kept the enemy at bay until we could mount a counter-attack," he muttered to Josh. "They didn't die in vain."

Josh nodded somberly. "I suppose you heard about a group of planes from the *Hornet* that flew west to nowhere."

Browning frowned. "That was an honest mistake. Admiral Fletcher believed that two of the Japanese carriers were operating up to a hundred and fifty miles behind the first two. Recall that our first reports mentioned only one carrier. That's the fog of war, and their ships took advantage of the real mist hovering over the ocean this morning. The good news is that we'll get those fliers and planes back intact."

He was quiet a moment, started to speak again, hesitated, and then said, "We're cobbling together a group to go after the *Hiryu*. She's like a wounded wolf now, with the younger, smaller members of the pack still following her, and she'll seek revenge. If we don't kill her, we'll meet the fate of the three carriers in her group. She's cruising toward the *Yorktown* and has already launched an attack of Nakajima B5N torpedo bombers and escort fighters. We don't know how many, but that leaves her with a thin air cover to defend her right now.

"I'm not sure I'm doing you a favor, but we're pulling every pilot aboard this ship. We've got forty-two dive bombers to launch, and we've got one without a pilot. Your senior operations noncom can take over—"

Josh's head swung around. "I'll take her."

"Have you ever flown a dive bomber?"

"No, sir, but I know the basics. Start the dive at twenty thousand feet. Seventy-degree angle to the target. Lift the perforated dive-flaps located on the upper rear surface of the wings. Release at fifteen hundred to two thousand feet, and pull out. A piece o' cake."

"Don't forget those flaps. They'll stabilize your dive."

"I'll be sure to remember that." Josh took a final glance

at the map. Then he grabbed his flight gear stashed below his desk and rushed for the door. "Thank you, sir. I'll see you on my return."

Browning watched him go. "I hope so," he muttered.

Josh hurried through the passageways, passing the ready rooms of Scouting Six and Bombing Six squadrons along the way. Only nine pilots were in Scouting Six's room where seventeen of them had prepared for battle that morning. For Bombing Six, the losses were even greater, having lost ten of fifteen planes and their pilots.

Josh had hardly dared to look inside, expecting to see disconsolate survivors of the morning's fight. They looked exhausted with deep lines and eye sockets, but he saw only alacrity and determination as they prepared for yet another sortie.

Emerging onto the flight deck, the sweep of wind nearly bowled him over with an overwhelming stench of smoke, but as he steadied his legs and gazed about, the look and feel of battle was nearly as overpowering. On the opposite side, a crew struggled with a Dauntless so blackened by fire and riddled with bullets that it could not be repaired. They pushed it overboard while Josh wondered how it had managed to fly back to the carrier, and then what had happened to its crew. Here and there along the deck, medics worked on pilots and gunners writhing in pain, some burned, others shot up, and still more rescued from the ocean, half-drowned.

Then in the direction of the *Yorktown*, tiny black dots zoomed across the skies, climbing, diving, spewing streams of fire and smoke, some circling in such close proximity to each other that they appeared to be dancing a minuet between the clouds. And then, one would plunge to the ocean's surface, leaving a trail of black smoke.

Josh watched only a moment, and then a voice blared over the PA system, "Pilots, man your planes."

He suddenly realized that he had not asked where he should report. He searched across the backend of the ship where a mass of Dauntless dive bombers had gathered in takeoff formation, the propellers already whipping the wind on the ones out front. Recognizing pilots from Scouting Six, Bombing Six, and Bombing Three, Josh sprinted toward them, worked his way around to the rear of the formation, and grabbed a deckhand.

"Which one's empty?" he yelled.

The deckhand pointed. "It has a gunner. Just needs a driver."

As Josh glanced toward where the man pointed, he gasped. The plane was blackened with soot and bullet ridden. A dark reddish smear trailed from the cockpit on the left side down to the wing. Dried blood. "Are you sure it'll fly?"

The deckhand grimaced. "The mechanics went over it. Everything works and the engine sounded good. They patched as many holes as they could and released it for operations."

"Where's the pilot?"

"Below getting repaired. The medics took him."

39

Amid the rumble of the SBD-2 Dauntless' 1200 hp Wright R-1820-60 Cyclone 9-cylinder air-cooled radial piston engine and the pitching of the massive *Enterprise* riding the waves, Josh peered around his cockpit at the instrument panel, ensuring he knew where the perforated flaps and the bomb release levers were, taking time to check out the aiming device, and taking note of dents and quickly-patched-over bullet holes. The space was comparable in size to the Wildcat fighter he usually flew. All the torpedo planes had been lost and the fighters were in the air providing cover.

Just before strapping in, a deck crewman had explained the bomb-release lever on the left side of the aircraft. "Yank this hard when you're ready," the man had yelled above the wind and the roar of engines of many dive bombers.

"And then pull up immediately," the crewman continued. "Control your breathing, or you'll black out. You'll be pulling about nine Gs. Your flight leader, Lieutenant Gallagher, will let you know when to dive. Your aiming device might fog up as you get to lower altitude. You'll have to work through it. Dive to the center of mass, but keep watch left and right. It's gonna get crowded with this many planes diving for the same ship."

Josh had acknowledged, and on signal, he started his engines. He flipped a switch and called over the intercom to his rear-facing gunner behind him, "Are you ready for this?"

"I expect so, sir. This is my second outing today."

"What happened to your pilot?"

"He took one in his right leg, and maybe his shoulder too. I'm not sure. The aircraft's fine, but getting back on the carrier was touch and go."

Josh glanced down and to his right, noting another smear where blood had been wiped away. "And what about you? How are you doing?"

"Ask me again later, sir. When we're down for good."

"Got it. What's your name?"

"Radioman Ben Crenshaw, sir. I'm your gunner."

"Pleased to meet you, Ben. Since we might be the last humans either of us ever speaks to, we might as well be on a first-name basis. Call me Josh."

Ben chuckled audibly over the intercom. "That'd be difficult for me, sir. Habits don't break easy, and I come from a long line of navy noncoms."

"Suit yourself, Ben. Which carrier did you fly from?"

"The *Yorktown*. I came over when the *Lexington* went down in the Coral Sea. And by the way, I had this same plane on Ford Island when the Japs attacked Pearl Harbor; and she attacked the *Akagi* this morning. It made a direct hit."

"I saw that. Three bullseyes. When did your pilot get hit?"

"On the way out of the target area. The Zeroes were flying low, going after our torpedo guys. By the time they saw us, it was too late to stop the bombs. They chased us after we dropped. Good thing that they were about out of gas and ammo."

"Did you get any of them?"

Ben laughed. "One came up behind us so fast and close that I could see the pilot's face. I had to be careful, so I didn't shoot out our stabilizer. I think the Jap's magazines were empty—he didn't shoot—he intended to ram us from the rear. My pilot dove so that the Zero flew over us, and I blew him out of the sky. I shot at some others too, but I can't claim any more damage."

"Good job. We'll make a great team, and we'll get back together."

Ben laughed again. "The only thing I know for sure, sir, is that I won't get back here without you."

With images flitting across his mind of fellow pilots now gone, Josh swallowed hard. Then, watching the deck crew, he called back, "Hunker down. Here we go."

Minutes later, taking his turn, he revved the mighty engine, and with a wave from the launch officer, he sped the length of the deck and lifted into the wind behind multiple aircraft that had taken off ahead of him.

High noon came and went as the flight of Dauntless dive bombers droned west. Although the distance between the three US carriers and what was left of the Japanese force had closed, at least an hour was required to reach the *Hiryu*. Most of the time was uneventful and might have turned boring but for the fury anticipated ahead and Josh's need to further familiarize himself with the cockpit. He took pains to reach for the bomb release and the perforated upper flaps repeatedly until they became natural motions, and he pictured the dive, imagining the stresses and the actions he would have to take.

Flying at twenty thousand feet, they expected and saw no engagements. "I'm playing follow the leader," Josh called back to Ben, "and trusting that Gallagher knows how to spot the target."

"I've flown with him a few times," Ben replied. "He knows what he's doing."

"Glad to hear it. By the way, I've never honchoed a Dauntless before. When we're in the dive, if I forget to raise those flaps, give me a holler."

Ben snickered. "Sir, I can't see the wings the way I'm sittin', and I'll be hard-pressed to turn my head that far around; besides which, Zeroes are known for following the dive bombers down. I might be kinda busy. But I'll keep your request in mind. I suggest you don't forget. And make sure you leave enough room to pull out after you drop them bad boys."

Josh grunted. "Point taken. At least try to let me know if one of ours is wandering too close."

"Roger that."

Sooner than he could believe, Gallagher waggled his wings. Josh quickly searched the ocean below but saw nothing to indicate a vessel, much less a large aircraft carrier. Then his peripheral vision picked up motion and, turning his concentration to that point, he saw a slight form moving across the sky far below, and then recognized the shape of a Japanese Zero. As he watched, it climbed to meet them, joined by several others.

Then a short distance ahead on the ocean's surface, Josh saw the white line of a wake on the ocean, tiny from this distance. Searching along it, he spotted the *Hiryu*, looking the size of a small bug.

Gallagher dropped his nose. In succession, those behind followed.

"Here we go," Josh called to Ben. His heart raced as he pushed his stick forward, lined up on the small spot at the end of the wake, and throttled up.

The formation of Dauntless bombers screamed toward the ocean, accelerating to greater and greater velocity, pulled by gravity and their twelve hundred horsepower engines. Exhilaration spread through Josh's arms and legs at the thrill of such speed, with the ocean hurtling toward them, and the outlines of the aircraft carrier becoming distinct and growing.

The wind buffeted the Dauntless. Maintaining control became difficult, and then he remembered to set the dive flaps. The pummeling turbulence subsided but holding to his flight path took all his concentration and strength.

Josh had enjoyed many hours of flying fighters, but always in practice. Being sent to Norfolk and then to train with the Doolittle raiders, and subsequently confined to the operations room, the thought suddenly struck that he had never flown in combat.

He had practiced many maneuvers including diving and taking tight turns, and he knew to tuck his chest into his knees when he pulled out of the dive to force oxygen into his upper body and brain, but he had never done that at the speeds he now reached. And he had never experienced gravitational forces of nine Gs. *Can I do it?*

The ship grew larger in the aiming device, and then, just as the deckhand had predicted, the lens fogged up. Momentarily panicked, Josh sat up in his seat, centering his view over the top of it, holding the sight of the *Hiryu* steady as it continued to enlarge before his eyes.

Then a loud, repetitive, pounding sound mixed with the

rising whine of the aircraft through buffeting, condensed air, and he realized that Ben had fired his twin, flexible-mounted Browning M1919 machine guns out the rear. *Zeroes are on us.*

He registered that the interval between the screaming dive bombers of his squadron converged as they dove on the same point. Glancing at his altimeter, he was astounded to see that he had plunged to four thousand feet.

His breath came in short gasps as adrenaline surged through his body and beads of sweat dripped from under his helmet onto the instrument panel.

He grasped the bomb release lever and held it, glancing once again at the altimeter. The indicator spun past twenty-five hundred feet.

The ship appeared of immense size now, shimmering alternately between clear and blurred vision. Plumes of water rose high into the air where dive bombers ahead of Josh had dropped and missed; and peripherally, he saw them pull up sharply and rise back into the air.

Glancing down again, he saw that he had plummeted below two thousand feet, and the altimeter arm spun. Jerking hard on the release lever, he felt a bump as the bomb cradle on the underside center-line station of the aircraft pushed the bomb below the radius of the propellers and dropped its lethal projectile.

With no time to see where his bomb had struck, Josh inhaled to capacity, leaned his torso hard against his upper legs, pulled the stick back with all his might, and mashed his pedal.

The steel-gray ship and the turbulent waves careened toward him. Pulling, pulling, pulling on the stick, darkness closed around his mind, obscuring his vision.

He breathed deeply and shook off the brain fog.

The aircraft shuddered as it leveled out only a few dozen feet above the frothing water and began to climb.

Then the engine sputtered and died.

Josh looked about rapidly. He was well away from the *Hiryu* but not out of the battle area. He attempted to restart the engine. He was too low.

"We're going in," he called back to Ben. "Get ready."

He heard no response.

Josh pushed his regular flaps down. He wondered fleetingly if he should also lower the dive flaps on the top surface, but he had no time to think the action through. The aircraft glided silently, the only sound being the rush of wind against the canopy and far-off booms.

Then, a few feet above the water, having slowed the aircraft as much as he could, Josh flared it, and it hit the waves. It bounced across the crests and fell lower among the wavetops. Its nose dropped, it spun around, and then settled upright.

Barely conscious, Josh tried to call back to Ben, but found he could not finger the mic. Darkness closed in, and he vaguely thought that strange for being too early in the day despite the overcast sky.

And then in the distance, he heard a thunderous explosion that reverberated across water, shocked him to greater consciousness briefly, repeated several times, and then died away. Distantly understanding its import, Josh broke into a pained smile.

The *Hiryu* was no more. The Imperial Japanese Navy main force was defeated.

40

June 19, 1942
Hyde Park, New York

"You needn't have picked me up," Churchill told Roosevelt, climbing into the front seat of the president's 1936 Ford Phaeton convertible at a nearby airfield. "I'm sure someone would have given me a lift."

"Nonsense. I love driving this car and showing it off. It gives me a sense of freedom." He indicated a set of levers on the stem of the steering wheel. "Since polio precluded the use of my legs, a mechanic in Poughkeepsie, Fred Relyea, modified the clutch and brakes so I could operate them with my hands."

With the top down and a security detail keeping a respectful distance in another vehicle, they drove out of Airhaven Airport and turned onto North Quaker Lane, heading south on a plateau that descended gently on their right. On either side, wide farmland divided by stone walls and framed by huge old-growth trees spread out, and the fragrance of June wildflowers filled the air. Both men reveled in the wind against their faces.

"This is magnificent," Churchill called, "and refreshing. Doing this often enough, I could feel young again."

Roosevelt beamed. "My ol' stomping grounds. I want to show you around where I grew up. Our family home is right on the Hudson with lots of views. How was your trip?"

"Much more pleasant than the voyage on the battleship last December. I came by one of Boeing's flying boats. Hard to believe we made it in thirteen hours instead of eight days, and I got to sit in the co-pilot's seat for a couple of hours. That's great fun—one of the few advantages of my position during a world war."

Roosevelt's eyes gleamed. He nodded as the road stretched straight ahead of them, and he pressed the accelerator. "Hold onto your hat! We've got to enjoy life's small pleasures where we find them." He reached across and clapped Churchill's shoulder. "We'll use this drive to catch up. Privately."

Roosevelt slowed the sedan as they neared an intersection with Crum Elbow Road, and then he turned right onto it. It curved gently downhill, turned hard right, and took them to New York State Route 9G, which then curved west, became Andrews Road, and traversed through thick forest.

"The last time you visited, you predicted that things would be rough this year," Roosevelt said. "You were right."

"But not without success. You had your Doolittle raid over Tokyo, and we had ours at Saint-Nazaire. Something tells me your victory at Midway was even more significant than was apparent at first blush. Then again, we lost Singapore." Churchill's tone turned somber. "That was a bitter pill. The worst defeat of British forces in history along with our other losses in the Far East. I feel we did General Wavell a grave injustice."

"Ah, but we fight on. No sooner did Admiral Spruance's task force finish up at Midway than he was ordered to prepare for our first major land offensive in the Pacific at a place called Guadalcanal. It's a small island in the Solomons. The Japanese are building an airfield there to interdict the supply line between Hawaii and Australia. We can't let that happen. The operation will commence in early August."

Churchill sighed. "Fighting on is a noble sentiment, but it's not always embraced. The Australians and New Zealanders are good fighters, but their national 'leadership,' if you can call it that, now feels the war on their doorsteps. No longer are they just sending aid across the world to the Mother Country. They jump at the slightest setback, pressuring us to safeguard their soldiers regardless of strategic or tactical issues. Their own neglect of defense budgets before the war left them vulnerable, and now they vacillate between providing barely adequate support or not nearly enough. We had to pull the Australians off the line in Malaya at the worst possible time to allay the concerns of their prime minister, Mr. Curtin. And they keep changing governments."

Roosevelt nodded. "Curtin didn't do himself any favors with that article he published in the *Melbourne Herald*. In effect, he told you that Australia would cozy up to America at Britain's expense. The Canadians saw the situation that way too, and they were not impressed. Fortunately, Australia's old prime minister from the Great War put the situation in context when he called Curtin's notion suicidal."

"Yes, he did. Billy Hughes is a good man, and he was a great PM, but we've had other setbacks. The situation in

North Africa goes back and forth. At present we're winning, and of course, our chaps have held out heroically against all odds at Tobruk."

They came to a T-intersection and the president steered to the right onto Albany Post Road. "We're almost there," he said, and then asked, "Your soldiers at Tobruk were under siege for how long?"

"Seven months, with much hardship and bloodshed," Churchill replied. To his left between the trees, he caught glimpses of the mighty Hudson River. "But General Auchinleck managed to push Rommel back three hundred miles. I'm hoping that continues. We must hold Tobruk at all costs. It's key to a supply base for offensive operations, and without it, we'll lose Egypt and the Suez. Losing Tobruk would threaten our access to the Far East, seriously threatening support from Australia and New Zealand. India as well, not to mention our oil supplies in Iraq and Iran. Hitler is already trying to push down through the Caucuses to get at them. Those oil fields must be defended, and we're stretched thin."

They came to a set of ornate wrought iron gates on their left. Guards opened it, and Roosevelt turned in and drove down a long lane shaded with tall oak trees. Grassy fields stretched away on either side of the car.

"You survived a vote of confidence in the parliament," Roosevelt observed.

Taking in the magnificent view, Churchill scoffed. "That's a perfectly acceptable constitutional process, but it's little understood in America. I called for the vote. It's a way of measuring real support for actions taken and anticipated. In this case, the result showed that the people are firmly behind me, and that's something the Loyal Opposition needed to see, which was why I did it."

The president threw his head back and laughed. "You're crazy like a fox, Winston." His tone turned serious. "We're going to have our differences, you know that. While our main objectives of defeating Germany and Japan are the same, our subordinate objectives might differ, and our concepts of how we meet our common objectives might sometimes be at odds."

"I understand your subtext, Franklin, but as you know, I'm an unapologetic defender of the British Empire. I've seen the good that it's brought to many parts of the world."

"And I'm an anti-imperialist. I think it impudent to ask for support from India to save the Mother Land when you don't allow them self-governance."

Churchill shrugged impatiently. "Those are larger issues more complex than the simple formulations we just uttered which won't be solved here, now. Joseph Stalin is antithetical to anything either of us stands for and he's as bad as Hitler. You know he engineered that famine in Ukraine that starved eighteen million people, yet we are now allied with him. Thankfully, he's not currently threatening the world. But give him time."

Roosevelt frowned. "I agree, which is why we must adhere closely with the war objectives we hold in common."

"Are you thinking of any issues in particular."

Roosevelt shook his head. "Just rumblings. Your raids in Norway and at Saint-Nazaire were tremendous morale boosters for Britain, and the raids we pulled off in the Marshalls along with the success we had in Tokyo, the Coral Sea, and at Midway lifted the spirits of our people; but the war is far from decided despite our rising confidence. Couple that with the threat Japan still poses to our west coast, and it's easy to see why a push to defeat them now is a strong sentiment among the citizenry and the military."

Churchill studied the president's face. "What are *your* thoughts in that regard."

Roosevelt blew out a breath of air. He reached a Y-intersection and steered the car to the left. A short distance off to their right was a beautiful red carriage house set back among some trees. Continuing past it, they arrived at a two-story brown-brick mansion, white-trimmed with a semi-circular portico, and green shutters on many windows.

"This is Springwood," the president announced. "This is home. Welcome."

Churchill gazed about at the elegant beauty of the grand house and the surrounding gardens and trees. They were on a plateau above scenic bluffs overlooking the river. "It's beautiful," he murmured, and started to get out.

"Wait," Roosevelt urged. "I'll show you around the whole estate, but let's finish this discussion. You asked for my thoughts on the question of Germany or Japan first."

The prime minister nodded and turned to listen.

"The Pacific is a big ocean," the president said, "and the Japanese have no replacement capability for their capital ships. That could change, but they won't be able to do it at the speed or in the numbers that we will. Meanwhile, German U-boats are right off our eastern shore, sinking our Atlantic supply convoys." He paused and cast a searching glance at the prime minister. "I don't think Hitler's given up on invading your island. I think he intends to do it once he's defeated the Soviets." After a pause he said grimly, "While you're here, we'll need to talk more in depth about 'Tube Alloys.'"

"Yes." Churchill matched Roosevelt's grave tone. "The situation remains as it was when we first started discussing the matter back in 1939, except that our scientists now believe that an atomic bomb is possible. Our atomic research facilities are still the most advanced in the world, but Hitler still occupies Norway, the only source of heavy water in quantities sufficient to develop an atomic bomb."

Roosevelt contemplated the thought. "So, Britain must not be allowed to fall. That dictates a Europe first strategy."

Churchill's eyes narrowed. "For those very pragmatic reasons, that is correct. Obviously, my motivation extends far beyond them."

"Of course. I didn't intend to imply otherwise, but the subject of Tube Alloys is something we can't yet divulge to either of our peoples, so we are left with bringing along their support by other rationale. This dilemma affects the military, too. Some of my advisors want to either take the fight to the Nazis now or cut bait and go after the Japanese. They're calling for either an immediate invasion of Europe or to shift attention to the Pacific."

Churchill scoffed lightly, barely containing his impatience. "Is your army trained up enough? Only a few months ago, it numbered in the low hundreds of thousands, and we agreed then that we'll need millions to make an effective cross-Channel invasion and carry out our other military objectives. Do you have the shipping capacity to transport an army of millions across the Atlantic? Do you yet have those millions of soldiers? Two years are needed to develop a seasoned soldier, and you have only a few combat veterans from the last war to train and lead the new recruits. And we'll need air superiority over Europe. Despite the arrival of your Eighth Air Force, we have not achieved that, and I don't see it happening soon."

Roosevelt chuckled. "Winston, you don't mince words." He turned serious again. "But neither of our populations is aware of the danger out of Norway with its heavy water. We might have to do something about that without waiting for decisive action in either Europe or the Pacific. But I'll tell you this." Roosevelt's voice lowered with matter-of-fact resonance. "America had better be in combat in the European theater this year, 1942, or the public clamor to shift priority to Japan will force my hand."

The two sat in silence for a few minutes. Then Churchill said firmly, "We've spoken about North Africa before, the belly of the crocodile. That's your point of entry into the European theater. That's where your army gets blooded. That's where we end the legend of the Desert Fox, and hand the *führer* his first major defeat."

The president exhaled. "Stalin would argue that he's already done the latter on the outskirts of Moscow last winter."

"And I would argue that the *winter* delivered that defeat just as it did to Napoleon. Hitler's soldiers were frozen in the snow by the thousands, within sight of the Kremlin, and yet he pushes another offensive toward Stalingrad as we speak." Churchill turned to face the president. "It's North Africa, sir. That's where we strike first."

Silence once again descended, and once again, Churchill broke it. "Getting back to the matter of Tube Alloys and Norway: for a number of months, we've been preparing for action there. Operation Gunnerside. It'll come off early next year." He cast a sidelong glance at Roosevelt. "We tried bombing the heavy water plant without success. It's quite inaccessible, ensconced as it is on the side of a steep mountain with thick forest all about. It's well defended, hardened, and only a very lucky bomb strike has a chance of penetrating the facility and doing much damage from the air."

Roosevelt took a long look at the prime minister. "Another commando raid?"

Churchill nodded. "Norwegians. We're training them."

"Will you keep me apprised?"

"Of course."

Roosevelt grunted. "The North Africa matter must be resolved at once. We'll hash it out among our staffs when we go to DC. We'll need to speak more about Tube Alloys and bring them in on that as well. Our scientists owe me information on the subject. Harry Hopkins is bringing it with him tomorrow so that we can discuss the matter authoritatively, but to my mind now, it's time for a joint effort." He was quiet a moment, and then mused, "Maybe we'll build our own atomic bomb."

The three men met the next afternoon in Roosevelt's favorite study where he could look out through the glass doors, past a veranda under an arched roof, and across the grounds. "I feel at peace here," the president told Churchill and Hopkins. "I can think."

Bill Stephenson joined them, having driven up from Rockefeller Center that morning at the prime minister's request. "Good to see you, Little Bill," the president said. "Where's your protégé, Major Littlefield?"

"He should be making his way out of Germany soon, if he hasn't done it already. He went to observe the operation against Heydrich."

Roosevelt's head swung around, and he arched his eyebrows. "You don't say. I wouldn't mind hearing his recount of that, not to mention how he managed his escape."

"I'd like that as well," Churchill chimed in. "Have Paul stop by to see me in London before returning to New York."

"Of course, sir."

Roosevelt then addressed Churchill. "I briefed Harry on yesterday's conversation. I imagine you've done the same with Little Bill?"

When the prime minister affirmed, Roosevelt held up the papers Hopkins had brought him. "The senior staff is not yet read in on the Tube Alloys matter, so we'll hold that close and delay discussion regarding an invasion of North Africa until we're together with them. Right now, we need to reach a decision about atomic research and building a bomb."

Hopkins, a dapper, balding, thin-faced man, was taken aback. "That's a long stride," he said flatly. As Roosevelt's closest advisor on foreign affairs, he had worked closely with the president on developing his New Deal and subsequently in administrative positions, including Secretary of Commerce. He had crossed the Atlantic several times on various missions as a personal emissary and had met with Churchill in that capacity in London.

"We have no choice." Roosevelt pointed to an entry on one of the pages Hopkins had brought and then summarized the content. "This man, Dr. Niels Bohr. He's in German-occupied Denmark, only a thousand miles from the heavy water plant in Norway, and he's one of the leading atomic researchers. He seems like a good enough man, but naïve, not believing that evil exists. His attitude is that all scientific discovery should be shared—and he doesn't exclude the Nazis.

"The only thing I see holding Hitler back from possessing the weapon is his own disinterest. He's more bent on his final Jewish solution and conquering more territory. But some of his staff follow Bohr's work closely, and the degree of security around that plant is a powerful statement about how important it is deemed to be."

Roosevelt's anger rose as he spoke. "Sooner or later, Hitler will come around to understanding what he has, and if he ever grasps the value of the research facilities in Great Britain, conquering that island will once more top his priority list in his drive for world hegemony. And he'll have technology that could level New York City in a flash." He grunted. "The Japanese might find themselves rethinking their new alliance."

He turned to Churchill. "Could Bohr be whisked out of Denmark under the Nazis' noses and brought here to work with us?"

Stephenson spoke up. "It would have to be a British operation. He's a pacifist and doesn't believe his work will benefit the *Wehrmacht*. He's unlikely to join an effort with the objective of building a bomb. But he keeps correspondence with professional colleagues in Great Britain whose work he respects."

Roosevelt listened intently and then stared at Churchill without saying a word.

"We'll put it on our agenda and keep you informed," the prime minister said. He glanced at Stephenson, who nodded.

The president took a deep breath and exhaled as he stared out his window across the verdant landscape. Then he chuckled. "It's ironic that we're discussing these things here in my peace sanctuary. Forever seared into my mind will be the memory that we made these momentous decisions here, in my study."

He turned to Hopkins. "Look, Harry, if the Nazis get this weapon before we do, that would be an incalculable calamity." He gestured to Churchill. "My friend, Winston, offered to provide all of their research and bring their own scientists and any others among the refugees of the war-torn countries to work with ours. Obviously, the project cannot be housed in Britain as it's still being bombed—less frequently lately, but the bombing continues, nevertheless. I've spoken with the Canadians. They'll participate." He glanced at Stephenson. "We can organize the project at your offices in Manhattan?"

Stephenson shifted his eyes to Churchill, who nodded. "We'll be happy to oblige."

"Good. Later we can move it to wherever makes sense." He held the prime minister's steady gaze. "Does that Manhattan project suit you? Have I left out anything?"

Churchill eyed the president gravely. "You've covered the essentials. I'm gratified, and I would say even enthralled were it not for the unknown destructive power we now proceed to introduce to an unsuspecting world. I wish there was another way. But evil begets evil and necessitates the ability to strike harder than its wielders."

Roosevelt stared at him, and then laughed gently. "What a very Churchillian thing to say." Gazing out the window again, he muttered, "But true."

He looked around at the other three men. "Are we done?"

"We're not, I'm sorry to say," Churchill remarked. He produced a document from his jacket pocket and handed it to the president. "I prepared this for your perusal. It's a summary of the strategic questions we see at the moment. I can tell you what they are briefly, and you can study that paper at your leisure."

Roosevelt leaned back in his chair. "Please do."

"These matters came up in communication with my staff after our conversations yesterday, and they arise because of the continued sinkings of our convoys in the Atlantic. We must develop further measures to end those attacks.

"Secondly, Operation Bolero, the build-up of US forces in Britain, will hopefully start this year, but certainly next year. In conjunction with that, we're hearing talk of landing six to eight divisions in Northern France early in September. That's only three months away, and our view is that such an action would lead to disaster for reasons you and I have already discussed. Until we are ready to invade with all forces at our disposal with an aim to stay on the Continent, such a move courts disaster and does not help the Russians, who are clamoring for the landings along with your military. We are simply not ready for such an expedition this year. It would waste manpower and equipment, and the Nazis would surely seek retribution against the French population.

"Further, we've seen no plan for how the landings would meet the objective, or even what the objective is. We'd welcome, support, and participate in an operation that has a chance for success, but there is no mention of landing points, landing craft, or any of the rudiments. Success would rely on a demoralized German force, and they seem in no shortage of spirit at present.

"We agree that action needs to proceed this year, including planning for Bolero, exclusive of this ill-conceived notion of launching divisions onto the coast of Northern France in three months, and we urge you to look to French Northwest Africa."

The room remained quiet when Churchill finished speaking. The president sat with his hands steepled in front of his face, staring at the horizon of the waning day. Finally, he turned to the prime minister. "You're an open book, Winston, and a good one. I'll read your paper." He looked at his watch. "Now, unless I've miscalculated the time, we should be leaving soon for the train back to Washington."

41

June 21, 1942
Washington, DC

Churchill sat with his chief military assistant, General Ismay, in the president's private study. Roosevelt sat at his desk.

The overnight presidential train had arrived at eight o'clock that morning. When the two statesmen and their staffs had reached the White House, they had gone to check in with their respective advisers with an agreement to meet again later in the morning. After completing other tasks, Churchill and Ismay stopped in the hall outside the study to chat with Hopkins, and then entered.

The president was in a pleasant mood. The three of them, Churchill, Roosevelt, and Ismay, conversed on light subjects, passing time until a scheduled meeting with the combined chiefs of staff.

An aide entered. Without speaking, she crossed to the president and placed a note in his hand. He read it and fixed a stare on Churchill's face. Without a word, he handed the note across.

Churchill took it and blanched. The message read, "Tobruk has surrendered, with twenty-five thousand men taken prisoner."

He passed the message to Ismay and instructed, "Call London immediately. Find out if this is true."

As Ismay departed, the prime minister stood and paced. "I'm in shock. I can't recall a heavier blow during this war. At Singapore, eighty-five thousand of our soldiers surrendered to inferior numbers, but they were new to battle. Those in Tobruk were seasoned." He hung his head. "This is a bitter moment. Defeat is one thing. Disgrace is another."

Roosevelt pulled his wheelchair away from his desk and steered around it, approaching his friend. "What can we do to help?" he asked firmly.

Churchill swung around, his hand rubbing his chin, his eyes introspective. At first, he seemed not to have heard the president. Then he focused on Roosevelt's face. "Give us as many Sherman tanks as you can spare and ship them to the Middle East as quickly as possible."

Just then, Ismay re-entered the study and handed Churchill a telegram from Admiral Harwood in Egypt. The prime minister read it and handed it to Roosevelt. It read, "Tobruk has fallen, and situation deteriorated so much that there is a possibility of heavy air attack on Alexandria in near future...I am sending all Eastern Fleet units south of Canal to await events."

The president wheeled back around his desk and picked up his phone. "Get General Marshall here. Urgent."

Marshall arrived minutes later and was quickly apprised of the Tobruk defeat and Churchill's request. He told the president, "The M4s are just coming off the production line and are being distributed to our own line divisions. The ones they replace are obsolete. Taking weapons away from our soldiers is a terrible thing, but if the British need is so great, we'll do it. I can scare up three hundred Shermans, and we can also let them have a hundred 105 mm self-propelled guns."

Overcome, his head slightly bowed, Churchill scratched the back of his neck. "I can never express my personal gratitude sufficiently," he murmured. "Thank you."

Making his way back to his quarters with Ismay after leaving the president, Churchill once again encountered Harry Hopkins. "I heard the bad news. I'm sorry."

"The Opposition will have a field day with this in London. No doubt they will call for a vote of no-confidence or censure, but I daresay they won't get more than twenty votes among all the parties in Parliament."

"Let's hope so. Our two countries need you."

Churchill grunted. "That's nice of you to say, but I'm certain we can find contrary opinion."

Hopkins replied, laughing, "It's good to see that you haven't lost your sense of humor. I came to tell you that two major generals are coming here this afternoon. They are highly regarded within the army, and the president thinks well of them. If you have time, he'd like you to meet them. They'll be here around five this evening."

At the appointed time, Churchill heard a knock on his door. When he opened it, two army officers with twin stars pinned on each shoulder stood there, their service caps held under their arms.

The senior of the two held out his hand. "Good evening, Mr. Prime Minister. I'm Major-General Mark Clark, and—" He gestured toward his companion. "This is Major-General Dwight Eisenhower."

"I enjoyed visiting with the two generals you sent my way this afternoon," Churchill told Roosevelt when they met again late in the evening. "They're both well informed and asked pertinent questions. I suppose I'll be seeing more of them in the future?"

"Could be. They're both bright stars. Dwight has never been battle-tested." Then Roosevelt laughed. "Let me rephrase. He endured ten years of working directly for Douglas MacArthur. They started out as friends and ended as professional associates. That's all I'll say about that, but if you know Douglas, you could call that combat duty.

"Douglas said one time that Dwight was the best officer he'd ever known. Other senior officers share that assessment, and of course, Mark is also terrific. I've known of them by reputation, but I met them for the first time myself this afternoon. I wanted you to be acquainted with them in case we consider them for major combat commands."

"I was impressed with both and gave them each a copy of my paper outlining my thoughts about a cross-Channel invasion. I had prepared it for our own chiefs of staff."

"Good. Do you remember that the other day, you asked me rather pointedly about the readiness of our army? I've arranged a demonstration for you. There's a train ready to take you down to Fort Jackson, South Carolina. That's where we produce divisions. Rapidly. You're going to see how we do it, and you're going to watch a mass drop of our paratroopers."

Churchill beamed. "I'm ready."

"And you can inform General Auchinleck that he will soon receive reinforcements in the Middle East in the form of the 2nd Armored Division. They've been specially trained in desert warfare."

Churchill smiled broadly. "I'm much obliged."

Roosevelt regarded him with a steady gaze. "There's something else you should know. My staff wishes to proceed with the idea for a cross-Channel operation as soon as possible. We feel that invading Northern France, the Netherlands, or Belgium offers the greatest political and strategic gains."

"We?" The prime minister's face showed his misgivings. "Not North Africa? I thought we agreed in January that until German forces are sufficiently weakened, our efforts in Europe would be limited to strategic bombing, assisting the Soviets, maintaining a naval blockade, and aiding European Resistance groups."

The president jutted his jaw forward. "General Marshall and our chief of naval operations, Admiral King, believe we should hit Germany with a knock-out blow as soon as possible so that we can then turn all attention to defeating Japan." He glanced away momentarily. "We intend to pursue Bolero fully, to move our troops to Britain soon, and to be in combat this year. And we've committed to a thorough study of invading the French North African coast."

Churchill met his steady gaze. "A study?" He held his frustration and nodded noncommittally. "Well, I shall look forward to the demonstration in South Carolina."

The president watched the prime minister's face closely.

A ghost of a smile crossed Churchill's lips. "Are you familiar with a planned operation we have for next month called 'Rutter?'"

Looking perplexed, the president hesitated. "I've heard of it, but I can't say I'm familiar with it."

"It's another raid on the French coast. It's large, ten thousand men, but hardly the scale needed to re-take Europe. One of the objectives is to test German shore defenses. Another is to learn what it takes to execute a successful landing. And I hope to allay some of Stalin's angst about opening another front in Europe.

"I suggest we see what the results are before we commit to a full-scale invasion of Europe. Most of the raiding force will be Canadian, at Ottawa's insistence, to give their troops combat experience. I believe some of your Rangers are to be involved as well, about fifty of them."

Roosevelt's eyes narrowed. "I'll get Marshall to arrange a full briefing for me."

42

July 1, 1942
London, England

Paul approached 10 Downing Street with some trepidation. This most famous of British street addresses looked unassuming in pictures, but the security checkpoints and guards just outside of news camera view gave the prime minister's official residence an imposing atmosphere.

As he approached, the door opened, and a butler ushered him through. "You can go right in, sir. The prime minister is expecting you." He showed Paul into a sitting room where Churchill rose from a sofa to greet him.

"Sorry to put you through all the fuss of getting in here," Churchill said after initial greetings. "Bill Stephenson should be here shortly, and I'm seeing two other guests in official capacity soon. I've been meeting with them weekly over the last month, and the atmosphere here is much more conducive to developing relations than at Whitehall."

"I'm at your service, sir." Paul gazed around the well-appointed room. “I’ve never been here. It’s rather grand and looks much larger from the inside. Lots of history.”

“Sit, sit. I’m anxious to hear about your adventures in Germany and Czechoslovakia.” They took seats in facing overstuffed chairs. “Tell me about the Heydrich operation. How did our Czechoslovakian commandos perform?”

At that moment, the door opened, and Stephenson entered. After greetings, the three took seats, and Churchill told Stephenson, “I was just asking the major about his foray into Czechoslovakia.”

“Ah, yes. I’m anxious to hear his report too. We haven’t had a chance to meet since his return. I just arrived from New York myself this morning.” He turned to Paul. “Go on.”

“The team in Prague was professional, sir,” Paul began. “There were some slipups and some learning of local conditions once they parachuted in, but their courage and dedication to the mission was remarkable. They might have got clean away if that Sten had not jammed. Did you know about that?”

Churchill nodded. “The German press blared the news about that malfunction. Sad situation, but I doubt the team would have escaped in any event. I’m sure the members knew that.” He regarded Paul with a questioning expression. “I don’t suppose you’ve heard anything about the aftermath.”

“Not much, sir. I had to keep moving. I made it to England only this morning. Progress was slow. I couldn’t be, or look like, I was in a hurry anywhere along the way.”

“You came by Lysander?”

Paul nodded.

“You might know that only one of the commandos survived,” the prime minister interjected. “We received reports from the Czech Resistance. Hitler threatened horrific repercussions for anyone harboring them. The people turned them in.

"Meanwhile the Gestapo shipped three thousand Jews from the Terezín ghetto to death camps in Poland on special trains marked 'Assassination of Heydrich.'"

Churchill paused and shook his head sadly. "But that wasn't enough for Hitler. He selected a small village in Bohemia, Lidice, for annihilation. On the day they buried Heydrich, policemen from his hometown shot every male there, fifteen years and older.

"The massacres were carried out very orderly, in groups of ten, and they took all night and most of the next day. The women were sent to a concentration camp in Ravensbrück in Northern Germany. Over a hundred children were given to German families to be 'raised properly.' We still don't know the fate of many of them."

He sniffed and wiped his eyes. "The SS torched the town, blew up its homes, the school, and a small church. They dug up the local cemetery and diverted the course of a stream that had run through it. Nothing is there now to indicate the town ever existed."

Churchill paused a moment and breathed heavily. "Aside from the one commando, they were all caught and executed. The survivor turned himself in and gave up the others under pressure from his family in return for amnesty and a bounty of a million *Reichsmarks*." He peered steadily at Paul. "That is the nature of the beast we must slay."

Stung, at first Paul could only stare as his mind coped with conjured images of the slaughter. The room seemed to spin around him. Barely able to speak, he rasped, "Was it worth it, sir, the operation?"

Churchill took a moment to respond. "History will have to judge. Heydrich had already put thousands to death. He had in mind doing the same to millions more, using industrial methods. In the final analysis, your question will be asked for decades, and the answer will be contained in whatever the balance of deaths turns out to be. Were more lives saved or lost by Heydrich's departure? We might never know. Certainly, we now have a better measure of the savagery of that regime."

Stephenson watched as Paul recovered his equanimity. "How were the people as you traveled back to England?" he interjected. "You came through Czechoslovakia and Germany?"

"Yes, sir. Switzerland and Vichy France too."

"So, you were able to meet up with your Resistance contacts? Did you have any trouble?"

Paul shook his head. "I didn't, but I saw some of those trains heading into northern Germany and Poland carrying Jews, I suppose. They were ghastly. Cattle cars. People herded onto them. I saw the terror in their eyes. Children and babies, all hungry and thirsty. Pregnant women barely able to walk. Old men and women, shoved along at the points of rifles with growling dogs grabbing at their heels. I heard that gypsies, Poles, and other 'undesirables' were packed in as well."

His voice trembled and faded off. He stopped to take a deep breath. "The only danger to me was getting out of the area of the Heydrich operation after it occurred. As you can imagine, the German military and security services were everywhere. But the best forgers prepared my papers, and my cover as a mid-level arms bureaucrat served me well across the occupied countries. My German was fluent enough for the situations I faced. Linking with my guides through France was uneventful."

"What about the attitudes of the citizens in those countries? Can you categorize them in a general sense?"

Paul nodded. "Easily. In Czechoslovakia, they are angry and morose, but also terrified. They've heard of the trains and the treatment of Poles, so they wear blank stares as they go about their business, hardly daring to look at each other. Those who work in the arms factories are well paid and their hours are reasonable, but happiness is not a part of their lives."

A knock on the door sounded, it opened, and the butler peered through. "Sir, your next guests are here."

"Give us a few more minutes," Churchill replied. "We're almost finished. I want to hear the end of this." As the butler closed the door, he turned to Paul. "Go on."

"In Germany, the people are proud, haughty even. I'm sure there are many who are wonderful. My mother spent years among Germans and loved them, but honestly, I didn't see anyone among them objecting to the trains or the treatment of the people herded onto them. Then again, maybe they dare not protest."

For a few moments, no one spoke. Then Churchill momentarily redirected the conversation. "Your mother, she would be the Dame of Sark?"

"Yes, sir."

Churchill sighed. "I'm sorry about what's been done with our Channel Islands, or rather what's not been done."

"Britain was attacked, sir, and stood alone. We understand that."

"You're generous. Go on with your report."

"As I was saying, only a few years ago Germany was poverty-stricken, and now its people see themselves at the top of the heap, so to speak. And they thank Hitler. They're awed by his successes; and his setbacks hardly faze them. Our raid on Saint-Nazaire comes to mind. They see him as sublimely capable of overcoming any such obstacle and expect that the Atlantic Wall, when complete, will preclude such situations.

"Switzerland is interesting because, although the country is neutral and the citizens enjoy personal freedom, they know that war and tyranny is only a few miles away. So, they are cautious in their expressions. Should the axe fall on their country, individuals do not wish to be pointed out as having opposed the Nazi regime.

"And Vichy is mixed. There are Nazi sympathizers among the population as well as active Resistance fighters and people who want to be left alone. Distrust and fear are hallmarks there now. It's sad to see."

Churchill sighed. "Yes, well, welcome back." He started to rise. Stephenson kept his seat, but Paul stood to leave. "Stay," the prime minister entreated him. "I'd like you to meet my next guests. I've invited them for lunch. Stephenson will dine with us too. I'd love for you to join us."

Doing his best to hide his astonishment, Paul glanced at Stephenson, who nodded approval with a slight smile. "As you wish, sir."

Churchill ambled to the door, opened it, waved, and returned to his seat, although he remained standing. Soon the door swung open, and the butler ushered in two American officers. One wore three stars on his shoulders, the other two stars.

"Lieutenant General Eisenhower," Churchill enthused, extending his hand in greeting. "Congratulations on your promotion."

For a fleeting moment, Paul saw a look of dismay cross the other general's face. He liked both men immediately. Of average height, Eisenhower wore a kindly expression with a quick if crooked smile on his round face. He bore himself with quiet, friendly dignity despite his thinning light-colored hair and blue eyes.

By contrast, Major General Clark towered above the men in the room, and Paul suspected that the same would be true in almost any setting. Thin-faced and blessed with a full head of dark hair, he was professionally courteous but reserved, and his brown eyes darted around, landing on Paul and studying him while Eisenhower and Churchill spoke.

"And Major General Clark," Churchill greeted him. "I believe you've met Bill Stephenson," he said as the two men shook hands. Then he turned to introduce Paul. "This is Major Paul Littlefield. He's Bill's protégé of sorts." He gave a brief rundown of Paul's background and activities, ending with, "He was among our earliest graduates from Camp X in Canada and just returned from Czechoslovakia where he observed the operation to take down Reinhardt Heydrich."

The two generals regarded Paul with subdued surprise. "You do get around," Clark remarked, extending his hand.

"Pleasure to meet you, sir," Paul said. In spite of himself, he let out a small laugh as he shook hands first with Clark and then with Eisenhower. "When the prime minister describes my activities like that, it does sound grand." He turned to Churchill. "My contributions seemed small at the time, and in all honesty, they still do."

"I'm sure you'll do more." Churchill raised his arms and swept them toward the dining room. "Shall we continue over lunch?"

As they ambled along, Churchill teased Paul. "How's that WAAF you're interested in? Is she still around?" He turned to the other three men. They smiled benevolently as Churchill said, "Young love. We can't let the war kill it too."

Paul felt his face burning. "I hope she's still around, sir; but honestly, I don't know. With all my moving around, I've lost touch with just about everyone."

Churchill looked at him sharply. "Including your sister?"

Paul nodded.

The prime minister swung around to Stephenson. "He's not to leave London again until he's been to see his sister." Turning back to Paul, he said, "That's an order, and we'll see what we can do about—"

Paul's heart skipped a beat. "Flight Officer Ryan Northbridge, sir."

Weighty matters set aside for the interim, conversation was light at the noon meal, the men taking time to become acquainted on a personal level. Paul listened and replied to questions, but Churchill seemed most eager to learn the backgrounds of the two generals, so Paul absorbed what to him was a surreal experience.

He had received the summons to be at the Downing Street address that morning, delivered at RAF Tangmere on landing there aboard the Lysander that transported him from France, and he had to rush around to find a suitable uniform. Although he had never heard of either American general before, he was sure that Churchill anticipated that both would play major roles in the conduct of the war.

After lunch, the group retired to the sitting room. Sensing that matters beyond his level were about to be discussed, Paul excused himself.

"Stay," Churchill said and, turning to the generals, added, "the major is a trusted agent. He has more secrets in his head than either Little Bill or I do. Speak freely in front of him." Then, chuckling, he turned back to Paul. "Do you still keep those pills close by?"

"Right here, sir," Paul responded, nudging his shirt pocket.

When they were seated, Eisenhower said, "Mr. Prime Minister, you survived Parliament's censure. That was good news."

"It had to be done. The loss of Tobruk was a blow. It hit the morale of the country quite hard. A few in the loyal opposition were dismayed that the issue raised concerns worldwide. We either had to unite behind the national direction I've pursued or find a better one. I feel now that we can go forward with the full support of Parliament.

"On another topic, General Marshall visited here in April and presented three plans. Can you go over them again? The details can be difficult to keep straight. Start with Bolero."

Eisenhower and Clark exchanged glances. "That one essentially is the operation to build up forces in Great Britain for an invasion of the Continent. It foresees about a million men coming over by April 1943. The idea is to deliver a knock-out punch to Germany with thirty American and eighteen British divisions and nearly six thousand plus aircraft from the RAF and US Army Air Corps. Then we'd turn our attention to Japan. Admiral King supports Marshall's position."

"That would be in keeping with the decision made in DC back in January to defeat Germany first—"

The two generals nodded.

"Except that it would not get US troops fighting the Germans in this year as President Roosevelt said he wished to do," Churchill continued. "To date, roughly thirty-six thousand soldiers have arrived in the European theater while a hundred and eighty-four thousand have been deployed to the Pacific theater and elsewhere. That's out of balance with the agreed-upon objective of defeating Germany first.

"As I understand things, Operation Sledgehammer is a subset of Bolero, and it raises a couple of questions: can America manufacture the equipment for a million soldiers in this calendar year? We're past the mid-year mark already. And what about the ships to bring them here? We don't have enough merchant ships between us to move all the men, equipment, and supplies we'll need, and we're still building the cargo fleet—those Liberty ships."

Clark stirred restlessly while Eisenhower leaned toward Churchill. "I was under the impression that you approved of Bolero."

"Of course, I do. I'm for getting on with the war and ridding the world of Hitler's menace as soon as possible. But we have to deal with the practical difficulties, and what I see is that we can't yet muster sufficient mass to confront a veteran army in France. Not only would we go in undermanned and underequipped, but our troops would be green. Britain's battle-hardened troops are in North Africa.

"We're in July already, and the weather dictates that the operation would have to be completed before the end of August, and you couldn't even field one division over here in time." Churchill shifted his eyes between the two American generals. "I see a bloodbath in France if we go in prematurely, and I won't have another Dunkirk."

Silence descended. The men regarded each other somberly, each with his own thoughts. Then Churchill said, "I have the highest regard for both General Marshall and Admiral King, but they're not on the ground here, so please extend my expressions of support for any final decisions with a request that they give serious consideration to my reservations. I'll also communicate my thoughts to the president. Now, tell me about Sledgehammer."

Eisenhower gestured to Clark. "You explain this one, Mark."

"That's really a contingency plan that falls under Bolero," Clark began. "Its purpose is to be ready for an opportunity to go in earlier if the *Wehrmacht* pulls troops from the French coast to reinforce at the eastern front with the Soviet Union, or if Stalin has such success that the Germans become demoralized.

"Sledgehammer foresees going into France in the autumn at Cherbourg with five divisions to take control of the port there and on the Cotentin Peninsula and keeping them. We'd keep our forces supplied through the winter in anticipation of a spring break out."

Churchill contemplated before asking his next question. "And if German morale remains high and Stalin doesn't turn them in 1942?"

"Sledgehammer goes by the wayside."

"Hmm. That would get the troops fighting in this calendar year but relies on the Russians to demoralize the enemy. I doubt that Stalin has yet sufficient offensive capability to drive the Germans to despondency, and under that plan, we're not seizing the initiative. Further, if successful, the plan creates a complicated cross-Channel supply requirement. What's the next one to discuss?"

"Bear with me," Clark said. "This can get confusing. The third proposed operation is Roundup, also a cross-Channel invasion. If Sledgehammer is executed, Roundup could exploit its success. On the other hand, if Sledgehammer doesn't occur, Roundup can go forward independently after completing the buildup under Bolero. Either way, it's seen as taking place in 1943. We'd first establish air superiority over our initial area of operations with six thousand aircraft. Then, we'd establish a front from Le Havre to Boulogne and reinforce it with a hundred-thousand troops per week to drive inland and spread north along the coast to Antwerp, which, as you know, is a main supply point for Germany. When we capture that city, we'll put a major stranglehold on *Wehrmacht* supplies."

"Sir," Eisenhower broke in, "if I may be frank, you must know that our combined chiefs of staff determined that meeting Bolero is logistically not in the cards *this year*. That obviates both Sledgehammer and Roundup in the near term.

"As you well know, General Clark and I were sent here to plan a cross-Channel invasion based on Bolero. Nothing is concrete yet, so you can lay your cards on the table. What is your real concern?"

Paul's heart skipped a beat. He took a breath while glancing between Stephenson and Churchill. Both of their gazes had locked on Eisenhower.

Churchill smiled. "This isn't a poker game, General. I think I've stated my concerns. But let me go over a few more points. Those Higgins boat landing craft were ingeniously designed, but we have only half as many as we'd need. Even if we could get sufficient numbers, they're no match for rough seas. We'd suffer many casualties of our own making before we ever encountered enemy fire from onshore. I understand that to resolve that issue, priority has now gone to building landing ships for tanks, but construction of carriers and destroyers comes ahead of them."

"Mr. Prime Minister, meaning no disrespect, can you get to the point."

Churchill chuckled. "Do I sense grit behind that charming smile?" He leaned toward Eisenhower. "Your president wants US action against Hitler in this calendar year. Neither of us wants combat for its own sake. We want to strike a blow and make it count. We want victories." He paused for breath. "So, can we talk about Operation Gymnast?"

Barely audibly, Clark sucked in his breath. "The soft underbelly," he muttered.

Churchill shifted his eyes and they froze on Clark. "Yes, the soft underbelly. Look, Bolero has really only been postponed, with notions of completing it later in 1943. That means no joint US/British action against Germany this year unless we execute Gymnast by attacking in North Africa.

"When I was in DC last month, we agreed that an invasion of the Continent should take place this year only under two conditions: that once we land, we plan to stay in France until victory is secured—it won't be a quick hit-and-run raid. The second condition is that the Germans have been demoralized from losses against the Soviet Union. We're not prepared for the first condition, and I don't see the *Wehrmacht* being sufficiently changed by the end of next year either. Even if we gained ground on the French coast, we would be hard-pressed to support the troops there, and the Germans could easily mount a counterattack to push us back into the Atlantic.

"A letter I'm developing to Roosevelt will say that no responsible British officer in any of our services would recommend such a cross-Channel action until we've fully built up our forces. Last month, I discussed with him, and at times he seemed to agree, that our safest and most fruitful strike this year lies along the North African coast. With a full invasion there by US and British troops, Hitler will be forced to move men and equipment out of the eastern front to buttress Rommel, and we'd protect our Far East access through the Suez as well. That's the second front of 1942 and is the way that we can best ease German pressure on the Soviet Union."

He leaned back thoughtfully. "An invasion of North Africa is not without problems. There's been some talk of Vichy forces in North Africa joining us. We can't count on that. They're still angry with me for my attack on their navy at Mers-el-Kébir, so they could even shoot at us. Even so, the fight they'd mount can't compare to the ferocity of the German soldiers we'd face around Calais.

"And by the way, the *Kriegsmarine* causes us immeasurable difficulty along our shipping lanes north of Norway. We're taking action there to keep those lanes open for our convoys to Murmansk."

Both generals listened intently as Churchill spoke. When he had finished, Clark took a deep breath and glanced at Eisenhower. "Since you broached the subject of Vichy troops in North Africa, has any thought been given to installing a respected former French military leader there who might bring them to our side? If we could make that happen and we invade there, we might avoid needless bloodshed."

Churchill nodded. "We made overtures to General Giraud. He was the French general who caused a worldwide sensation when he pulled off that spectacular escape from the Königstein Fortress. We queried him through Alliance, a Resistance organization in Marseille, on taking a lead position. A French fighter pilot with an aristocratic Irish ancestry, Duke MacMahon, was our envoy. The reply we received said that Giraud preferred to remain in France at present and work with the Resistance."

"Maybe he could be convinced."

"What about de Gaulle?" Eisenhower interjected.

Churchill chuckled. "That would be an obvious choice, but for whatever reason, your president detests him on a personal level. I don't think the two have ever met, but de Gaulle's managed to develop a reputation that precedes him wherever he goes.

"He's arrogant, self-righteous, and self-centered, seeing himself as a modern-day male Joan of Arc. I can attest to that personally. His advisers keep having to remind him that Germany is the enemy, not Great Britain. But he's captured the hearts of his people in France. That said, despite how he's loved at home, the military in Vichy's North African colonies remember the British naval bombardment at Mers-el-Kébir and resent that de Gaulle set up shop in London. We'll have to deal with him more as the war continues but perhaps not for the operations under discussion."

Conversation paused as the three men mulled their separate thoughts. Then Eisenhower asked Churchill, "Would you mind if I forwarded to General Marshall a copy of your paper regarding a cross-Channel invasion?"

"Not at all. I understand his rationale for a quick blow against Germany, but I don't think he's getting a clear picture. Perhaps you can help."

Eisenhower smiled gently. "It's not just our senior military leaders who think we should be delivering a punishing blow to Japan immediately. The public feels that way too. But I can certainly put your document in General Marshall's hands and relate the points discussed today. Would you go over your concept for Gymnast?"

"You're a diplomat," Churchill said, chuckling. "Well, diplomacy is needed too."

"Before you go into it, sir, I know the plan from the paper you gave to Mark and me. The general outline is known at the War Department, and I must tell you how Gymnast is perceived among my colleagues there—"

"I know how it's perceived," Churchill interrupted sharply. "As a means of preserving the British Empire. Your president informed me of that himself."

He took to his feet and paced. "I make no apologies for my hope to see the empire emerge intact; the final disposition will eventually have to be worked out after the war—but let me remind you that Britain has already evolved into a commonwealth where the members are there by choice. The question of India remains, but that will sort out, and note that they send soldiers to our common fight. What's at stake right now is civilization as we know it, and we either defeat our mutual enemy or we perish. Citizens of our nation have been killed by this war every day since Dunkirk."

He whirled around and threw his hands up in the air, his face trembling with fury. "Think of it! This bloody Berlin monster sends people to their deaths by the trainload." He pointed at Paul. "And Major Littlefield there witnessed the disgusting persecution with his own eyes."

The prime minister's chest heaved, and he reached for a handkerchief to wipe his forehead. "Whatever my motives, and I assure you they are not the ones ascribed to me, only Germany's and Japan's unconditional surrender will stop the carnage. My aim is to get to victory by the swiftest possible means, all other considerations be damned."

Eisenhower stood. "Sir, I—"

Churchill waved him off. "And so you know, my own military chiefs are not keen on Gymnast either. They'd prefer that we send your resources to buttress them in Egypt. General Brooke believes that in no event should we invade anywhere until the Soviet position is clear: will Hitler defeat Stalin or not?

"My simple point is that when we secure North Africa, not only will we have destroyed much of Germany's fighting ability, but we will also have deprived them of Libyan oil and defanged their Desert Fox." He took a deep breath. "Then we will also have gained a launching point to invade Europe from the south."

Reaching into his jacket, he pulled a cigar from a pocket and thrust it into his mouth. As if catching himself, he glanced at the others. "Anyone else?"

None accepted, but as Churchill lit the cigar, he muttered, "You can jolly well have a drink, though, can't you?"

He strode to the door, opened it, and called to a servant, who brought in and poured a round of brandy. Then the servant retreated.

"You asked about Gymnast," Churchill told Eisenhower while the others sipped their drinks. "Very simply, the idea is to invade at Casablanca, Morocco, and at two places in Algeria: Oran and Algiers. If we can get Vichy forces to join us, so much the better, but otherwise, I don't expect stiff resistance from them. We sweep east while our forces in Egypt push west, and we catch them in the middle. US weaponry is superior, and your supply capability is better. The Allies will gain air dominance. The British army is battle-hardened and will fight tenaciously. Yours will be blooded in North Africa, where it will gain the experience and confidence to take back the Continent. That, gentlemen, is my plan.

"Without Gymnast, we risk losing Egypt to Mussolini, who will then drive up through Iraq and Iran, taking their oilfields and linking up with the Germans in the Caucasus. Gymnast obviates that scenario."

After the two American generals had departed, Churchill, Stephenson, and Paul once again gathered in the sitting room. "Thanks for coming by," the prime minister said, and then directed a question to Stephenson. "What are your plans for Paul back in Manhattan?"

Stephenson looked at the prime minister sharply. "Are you thinking of taking him from me?" He chuckled. "He's not very bright, you know. He didn't utter a word during that entire meeting."

"Exactly. Nor did you. I'd say he's probably as mentally endowed as you."

"Ah, sir, you're taking liberties with me." The signature slight smile appeared on his lips, and then he shook his head. "Things are changing at BSC since Donovan started up his OSS. We're not the small group we were to start with. Paul's been off on larks for most of the past six months anyway..."

While they conversed, Paul sat quietly, his heart beating in his ears, hardly believing what he was hearing. He maintained a neutral façade.

"Then take him back to New York with you," Churchill said. "Let him finish up whatever he needs to do there, then he can gather his things and come back to work on my personal staff here. I could use a younger perspective that is informed at high levels and knows when not to speak."

Stephenson let loose rare spontaneous laughter. "Good luck with that, sir." Then he added, "I'd hate to lose him, but if you need him, he's yours."

Churchill shot a sideways glance at Paul. "Go on, then. Go see your sister and Flight Officer Northbridge." He turned back to Stephenson. "When should he rendezvous with you?"

"I'll call in a day or two, when I'm ready to go."

Paul held the grin off his face until he was well past the security station of 10 Downing Street. Then he bounded through London's streets until he waved down a taxi.

43

Stony Stratford, England

Claire had dozed off while lying on her sofa reading a book when she was awakened by soft rapping on her door. She sat up with a jab of consternation for having slept so hard that she had heard no sound of an automobile approaching in her driveway. Through a crack in her blackout curtains, she saw that night had fallen.

She had put Timmy to bed more than an hour ago and had slipped into a nightgown. Pulling it tightly around her, she went to the door. "Who is it?"

"I'll never tell."

Recognizing Paul's voice, Claire jerked the door open and lunged at him, throwing her arms around his neck. "Paul? Is it really you?"

She grabbed his hand, dragging him into the light. "I can't believe it. So many months have passed—what? Since January? And now here we are in July. Timmy will be so happy to see you."

Paul laughed and squeezed his sister. "It's wonderful to

see you too, Claire. And don't wake Timmy. I'll just have a peek in on him."

A few minutes later, he entered the living room where Claire had already poured drinks. "He looks so peaceful," he said. "And he's grown so much."

"Not a toddler anymore. He's into everything and so curious."

"And still nothing from his birth family."

"Not a peep. I keep having nightmares that someone wonderful will show up with absolutely no reason why a claim on him would be denied by the courts." She sighed. "I'm past thinking that would be best for him. I'd fight for him like a banshee. He belongs with me now."

Paul smiled, stretched an arm around her shoulder, and pulled her head close. "My sister the mother. It's heart-warming." He straightened and faced her with a somber expression. "Have you seen or heard anything from Ryan."

Claire pursed her lips and shook her head. "Not in a while. I saw her shortly after the last time I saw you. Hasn't she written you?"

Paul shrugged. "I don't know. I've been—" He stopped himself. "Too many places." Suddenly, an image of the assassination he had taken part in with Ian Fleming in Manhattan loomed before his eyes, the window of the apartment across the way in the RCA building appearing real enough to touch. The image morphed into the street in Czechoslovakia where he had observed Heydrich's assassination.

He shook off the apparitions and found that his forehead had moistened and he was almost panting.

If Claire noticed, she did not let on. "Ah, big brother. Sometimes I wish I knew what you were up to, and then I think maybe not. I'm glad you're safe."

"What about Lance and Jeremy? Anything from them?"

"I hear from Lance more than anyone, but the German censors don't let much through. He also sends those nonsensical letters that I deliver to military intelligence. Who knows what's in them? It's enough for now to know that he's alive and seemingly healthy. Mum and Dad too, given what letters still arrive. Jeremy is all but lost to me. Like you, he couldn't say where he was going back in January, and I haven't heard from him since."

The telephone rang in the kitchen, and she went to answer it. Paul sipped his drink, thinking of home on Sark Island, his mother and father, and his siblings. He pictured the craggy cliffs with the plateau above them, and running in the wide green fields, and sighed. *How long has it been since we were all together at home?*

Claire called from the kitchen, "Paul, can you come here?"

When he entered, he found Claire, her eyes shining, holding the phone receiver out to him. "It's for you."

Reading her look, he grabbed it, holding down a surge of excitement. "Hello?"

"Can't you call your girlfriend on your own?" Ryan's musical voice rang out. "You've got to get the prime minister's staff to do it for you?" She laughed. "I'm glad to know you're alive."

"Yes, I'm alive. And you, you're alive too." He rolled his eyes at how ridiculous he sounded, suddenly for all the world shy and tongue-tied. "It's good to hear your voice. Where are you?"

"In Glasgow. I'm sorry not to be nearby. Did you get any of my letters?"

"Sorry, no. I wish I had. I've been—well, traveling." He glanced around the kitchen. Claire had moved off into the living room to leave him alone. "I've never stopped thinking about you. What are you doing now? Can you say?"

"Didn't Claire tell you. I'm a ferry pilot now. I get planes of all sorts to where our pilots need them. New ones, repaired ones. If they need them, I get them there." Her voice lowered. "And I love you too."

Paul caught his breath. "I had barely arrived when you called. I'm sure Claire would have told me about your— ferry flying? That's dangerous. Those pilots get shot down sometimes. Can't you go back to what you were doing when we met?"

"What you do is dangerous. Are you going to stop?"

"I can't. There's a war on, you know?"

"Exactly." Ryan chuckled. "You sound inconsolable. How long will you be there?"

Paul's head popped up straight. "A couple of days."

A resolute tone entered Ryan's voice. "I'll be there tomorrow. I don't know how yet, but I'm coming to see you. Don't go anywhere."

"I'll do my best."

When Paul hung up and re-entered the living room, Claire looked up and laughed. "I don't think I've ever seen a wider smile on your face."

"Stop it," Paul snapped in mock exasperation. He could not keep the excitement from his voice when he added, "She's coming tomorrow."

"That's wonderful," Claire exclaimed. "I'm so glad you'll get to see her."

"She said she's ferrying planes now."

"That's right. I forgot to mention that." She sighed. "This war has so many people doing so many strange things, and keeping up with them is impossible, especially when no one can talk about what he or she is doing." She looked up at him. "Well, I get to have you here for at least one night—maybe two?"

He chuckled. "Maybe two. I'll get a call when it's time for me to leave."

Ryan grinned as she turned into Claire's driveway and sped up the remaining distance over the gravel road. She tingled with excitement, already seeing Paul's face in her mind's eye. Pulling in front of the house, she slid the car to a halt amidst flying dust, alighted, and hurried up the garden path.

Claire opened the door and met her before she reached the landing.

Ryan grinned broadly. "Where is he?" Then she laughed at herself. "Sorry. I'm acting like a schoolgirl. It's wonderful to see you. How are you? It's just that I hadn't seen or heard from him in months. I thought he'd forgotten—"

The look on Claire's face stopped her. Crestfallen, she said, "He's not here, is he? What happened?"

"He so wanted to see you. About an hour ago, he received a call. He couldn't tell me anything about it, but shortly afterward, a government car came to pick him up. He tried to reach you, but you must have been well on your way to come here."

Ryan nodded in dismay. "I hate this war, I really do."

"Come along inside. I'll get you a drink. I could use one too. This is all so frustrating."

A few minutes later, Ryan cupped a tumbler in her hand and took a seat on the sofa while Claire sat across from her. "Do you know he all but proposed to me that night he took me back into London during the *blitz*. But then he said he wouldn't because, with the uncertainties of the future, he would not like to leave me a widow. Words to that effect.

"Like a fool, I told him I wouldn't accept anyway because, with whatever secret thing he's doing, he could disappear, and I'd never know what happened to him. I've regretted saying that ever since. He was thinking of me, and I was thinking of myself." Her lips trembled. "He was so close and now he's gone again—"

She grasped her tumbler tighter.

Claire put a soothing hand on her arm. "He'll be back. I'm sure of it, and things will get better. You'll see."

Ryan wiped her eyes and broke into a slight, involuntary laugh. "'You'll see'—that's your phrase, isn't it?"

Claire smiled. "I suppose it is." She sipped her drink. "I'll tell you one bit about Paul. He's changed a tad."

"In what way?"

"It's hard to define. Last night, before you called, he suddenly went into a momentary, trance-like state, but then he pulled himself right out of it. He's still the stalwart, loving brother we always knew, but he's toughened. Physically, I've never seen him in better shape. He's lean, not an ounce of fat, and his muscles are hard. But he seems always on alert and not quite as willing to share his thoughts. His eyes give a sense of hiding things he never wants to mention, almost a haunted expression."

Ryan sighed. "I hate to think of how this war might change people. I only hope that we emerge as a still decent and caring nation."

"Agreed. And have no fear, Paul is still the deeply caring person I've known all my life. Now, tell me about your flying, if you don't mind. What's it like?"

Ryan took a deep breath. "It's fun with such a sense of freedom in a three-dimensional world. I would do it for the rest of my life if allowed, but my guess is that once the war is over, female pilots will be relegated to private aviation only. That would be such a shame, because those of us doing it are very good, and we love it."

"But it's dangerous."

"What isn't, these days? If I'm going to be under attack, I'd rather go with a fighting chance to escape and retaliate than get hit while sleeping in my bed."

"Good point. Which planes do you fly? Do you go in only certain ones?"

Ryan shook her head. "We fly whichever ones need delivering to wherever they need to go. I'll get a call directing me to an airfield, and when I arrive, I find out which aircraft it is. A mechanic gives me a briefing on the peculiarities of the plane and what difficulties to expect. Then I study the manual, get in, and it's 'off we go.'"

"Just like that?"

Ryan pursed her lips. "Just like that. I even had to fly a bomber by myself once, and it usually takes a seven-man crew. Now, that was a challenge. We all have our favorites, of course, but what we fly is dictated by who's available when an aircraft is ready to go. Personally, I like the Spitfire, but who doesn't?"

"Have you gotten into any sticky situations?"

"Do you mean besides the bomber?" Ryan laughed and took another sip of her drink. "I could have used one of these then," she said, holding up the tumbler. "Another time, I was taking a Spitfire down to RAF Tangmere. Of course, this was after the Battle of Britain and the *blitz*, but we still get German fighters and bombers coming over once in a while. I flew low as we usually do, and a flight of *Luftwaffe* bombers came in several thousand feet above me. I don't know what their target was—they were flying on past in the opposite direction, and one of their escort fighters spotted me and must have thought my plane posed a threat to them.

"It didn't. We never fly armed.

"Anyway, the German came after me in an Me-109, and of course we're only trained in how to get from here to there, not in fighter tactics. I stepped on the gas, so to speak, and went into a tight turn. I remembered your brother, Jeremy, saying that German planes could not hold the turns and their pilots avoid going into one behind a Spitfire for fear of finding it behind them. By that time, the bombers had flown on by, and I guess the Nazi decided that I was no longer a threat because he left.

"I was near Tangmere, so I landed a few minutes later, but I have to tell you that I was shaking when I finally stopped the plane. I had to sit still a while to calm my nerves. Honestly, I don't know how our combat pilots face that day in and day out."

"I don't either," Claire murmured, thinking of Jeremy and those of his friends who had lost their lives in aerial combat. Then she said brightly, "As long as you're here, you might as well spend the night. Timmy will love it."

"Where is Timmy? I haven't seen him."

"He's in the back garden with the nanny. I asked her to keep him out there while I explained to you about Paul."

"I'd love to see him, but I'm afraid I can't stay overnight. I wasn't going to be able to anyway. I have an early flight tomorrow morning." She looked around the sitting room and then out the window across the front garden. "Ah, I do envy your tranquility here."

Claire took a hard swallow of her drink. "Yes, it is nice." She stood up. "Let's go see Timmy."

On a Transport Plane Over the North Atlantic

"Sorry to pull you away with short notice," Stephenson said. After some minutes, he asked, "Did you see your sister?"

"I did, sir. Thank you."

Stephenson grunted. "Don't thank me. You had to stay somewhere. And what about that WAAF, Flight Officer Northbridge."

"We spoke on the phone last evening. Thank you for arranging that."

"That was the prime minister's doing." Stephenson cast him a piercing glance. "I mucked up your reunion, didn't I?" He grunted. "When you get back to town, we'll have to make sure you get to see her."

Paul grimaced. "You have bigger concerns. The trip was a bit sudden, though. Is anything the matter?"

Stephenson pursed his lips and nodded. "A bit of bother. General Marshall did not receive the prime minister's paper kindly, and neither did Admiral King. They thought Churchill was on board with an invasion into France now. They're very much opposed to Gymnast. We're headed to Washington to help sort things out."

44

August 2, 1942
RAF Lyneham, Wiltshire, England

"Strap in," Churchill told Paul as their plane started its roll to the runway. "This will be a long flight." Minutes later, it lifted into the midnight sky. Paul looked about the small cabin that had been prepared for the prime minister in the cavernous aircraft he had dubbed "Commando," a Consolidated B-24 Liberator heavy bomber that had been modified for passenger transport. Paul sat facing him across a small tabletop fixed to the wall between two square windows.

"We don't have the creature comforts in here of the Boeing flying boat I like so much," Churchill remarked. "The seats are barely tolerable and there's no heat, so when we get to altitude, we'll have to stay warm the best way we can. But this plane will get us there. It's built for distance."

Paul strained to hear above the roar of the aircraft and the wind against its skin.

"The pilot, William Vanderkloot, is very good," Churchill went on. "He's somewhat of a free-spirited American civilian ferrying our planes. Most of the crew is Canadian. We'll fly straight to Gibraltar over Vichy and Spain to save fuel and avoid flying through the Mediterranean, where we would have been exposed to Germans on both sides." He laughed. "Heavens! That could be a calamity. We'll spend the day on the Rock, and then tomorrow night we'll fly on to Cairo, but we'll have to detour around some known combat areas. I'll get to the purpose of our trip in a bit.

"I'm pleased to have you join us. Stephenson was not happy to let you go, but I think his original reason for recruiting you has been overcome by events. Others will have to build his archive."

Paul nodded but regarded the prime minister with a questioning expression. "Sir, I'm honored that you brought me along, but what am I supposed to do on this trip? What is my function?"

"I want you to do the same thing for me that you did for Stephenson: be there, listen, and provide me with your observations, analysis, and conclusions when I ask for them. If I have anything in particular for you to do, I'll let you know."

He paused as he pulled his thoughts together. "I found your observations about your trip to Czechoslovakia and your insights into the citizens of those various countries enlightening, not to mention your report on what you saw regarding the cattle-car trains of Jewish detainees." He tossed his head with disgust.

"Do we know at all what's happening with the Jews?"

Churchill shook his head. "We've heard rumors too ghastly to fathom without yet having hard proof. I fear that when we get to the end of this war, what we find will be beyond the public's ability to comprehend or accept."

Paul took a moment to let the somber statement sink in. Then he asked, "Are we the only passengers?"

"My physician, Dr. Wilson, flies with me. That's his seat—"

"Oh, sorry, sir." Paul started to rise. "Where should I—"

Churchill gestured with his palms. "Stay. The doctor is in the cockpit with the crew. I do that too. I'll sit in the co-pilot's seat at dawn. Vanderkloot pretends to let me fly the plane. I love doing that while watching the sun come up. It's all silvery and gold, reflecting off the water or bringing the landscape to life."

He pulled a cigar from his jacket pocket, lit it, and took a puff, savoring the flavor. Then he eyed Paul and held it toward him. "One of life's pleasures, if you like."

Paul studied it without speaking.

"Ahh. You don't smoke."

Paul shook his head but, sensing the prime minister's disappointment, grinned. "But I could be ordered to, if you like."

Churchill laughed. "You should go far, Major, but today, you become a man."

He offered the cigar again, and Paul took it. A minute later, he was coughing helplessly while Churchill looked on in amusement. When Paul finally settled down, both men had tears in their eyes: Paul from his ordeal, and Churchill from laughing.

"Thank you for that," Churchill said, his body shaking from contained mirth. "I have few opportunities for unbridled hilarity."

Paul regained his composure and found himself enjoying his cigar, albeit with eyes that still watered.

"I must handle a few difficulties in Egypt," Churchill said, becoming serious once more. "Our Eighth Army is not performing well. Rommel has once more pushed us back. I'll need to make some changes in command. We cannot lose Egypt. The Suez Canal is critical, as you know, and it straddles the path leading north through the oilfields in Iraq and Iran to a possible linkup with other German divisions in the Caucasus." He sighed. "When we're done in Cairo, we'll be on to Moscow for a meeting with Comrade Joseph Stalin."

"Oh," Paul exclaimed in surprise. "I had no idea."

Churchill chuckled. "Winning this war also relies on diplomacy—which, loosely translated, means holding one's nose and placating undesirables in the name of abiding friendship in which neither side believes. The Americans in Appalachia would call the relationship a shotgun wedding."

He drew on his cigar and let the smoke out slowly in rings. "All my life, I've detested Bolshevism, and I still do. Stalin knows that. He knows full well that we would not lift a finger to rescue his regime but for the threat that the Nazis impose on the world, now joined by the Japanese form of fanaticism."

He studied the end of the cigar and tamped it into an ashtray. "We've finally got the president and senior staff on the same page with us regarding an invasion of North Africa, but I'll tell you, General Marshall and Admiral King are none too happy about it." He glanced at Paul and laughed. "Would you believe they snubbed me when the president sent them over to work things out in London? That was after you and Stephenson went to confer with them in DC? I invited them to spend a weekend at Chequers, and they declined.

"I heard through backchannels that when General Brooke and I refused whole-hearted support of Sledge-hammer three times, the two of them urged the president to vacate the European theater altogether, leaving it to us to sort out. And they recommended that America concentrate all its energies against Japan instead."

Paul sucked in his breath. "That would have been terrible."

Churchill cocked his head to one side. "To say the least. Roosevelt ordered Marshall and King to support the invasion in North Africa, which, by the way, has been renamed from Gymnast to 'Operation Torch.'"

"I'd heard that, and the name has a nice ring to it, more indicative of what we expect to do with the operation."

"I'd say so."

"So, if I may ask, what's the issue with Stalin?"

"He still pushes for a second European front. He's going to take some handholding." Churchill leaned toward Paul. "Tell me your observations of the two American generals you met at Downing Street at the beginning of July, Eisenhower and Clark. This is a good time to talk about that."

Paul leaned back in his seat just as the plane bumped in a pocket of turbulence. "They're both very courteous and professional. General Eisenhower was quite congenial. He listened carefully, and his responses to you always began with a reference in one way or another to demonstrating that he understood what you had just said. Sometimes, he might have disagreed, but he caged his comments in such a way as to avoid offense while making his point.

"General Clark seemed somewhat less approachable. I saw him react when you congratulated General Eisenhower on his promotion—"

"That's because Eisenhower was promoted over him. When I first met the two, Clark was senior. Now he's junior. Furthermore, with the final decision to go ahead with Torch,

Eisenhower is the commander-in-chief for the operation, and Clark is his deputy."

Paul raised his eyebrows. "I can see how that could cause some competition and certainly explains the expression I saw. Perhaps Clark should get points for taking the situation in stride. His pride must be wounded a bit, I should think."

"Agreed," Churchill said, nodding. "They're both very capable and handling the situation well, and I think the personality difference you detected swung the decision in Eisenhower's favor."

He moved the blackout curtain aside a bit and stared into the inky sky. "We have several issues of command coming up. The operation to build up US forces in Britain, Operation Bolero, is a huge undertaking. All land operations in the European theater will fall within its purview. The Americans and Russians will push to invade Europe in 1943. For that to happen, we must see victory in North Africa this year. So, we need an overall commander for Bolero to do the planning and be ready to execute, and he must subordinate command of Torch. I've suggested General Marshall for the job, with Eisenhower as his deputy to handle Torch. That leaves intact the current command relationship between the two."

"Marshall is very calm and deliberate," Paul interjected. "I met him in Washington in June when I was there with Stephenson for the Sledgehammer discussions."

"Which is now defunct," Churchill interjected. "My military chief of staff, General Brooke, says Marshall is more interested in preparing for the fight than in fighting, or words to that effect."

"Begging your pardon, sir, that's beyond my level."

Once again, the prime minister chuckled. "I see why

Stephenson and Donovan like having you around. They said you're a stickler for toeing the line."

Paul smirked. "I have to say that between the two of them, along with you and the president, I've been disabused of that principle."

"Not altogether, you haven't," Churchill said, peering at him, "and that's a good thing. This war is being fought to preserve principle, not stamp it out. Unfortunately, we have to do unpleasant things that would be unthinkable during peaceful times."

"Which is itself a worthwhile principle, is it not, sir? Doing what must be done."

"Good point, so long as those actions support the public good." Churchill leaned close to Paul. "At the end of this war, principled leaders must emerge."

Relaxing back into his comfortable posture, he continued, "As a ground soldier going into combat, which of those two men would inspire the most confidence from many levels above you, Eisenhower or Clark?"

"I'd hardly call myself a ground soldier, sir, though I admire both men greatly."

"You had your brush with ground warfare in Albania on your fact-finding tour with General Donovan. Tell me what you think."

Paul took his time to mull before hazarding a response. "I think I cannot fairly answer the question because I've seen neither of those generals in action. That said, I can tell you what I observed."

"And that is?"

"They both asked a lot of questions, but during the discussion, I could not figure out General Clark's opinion about your concern over invading France now rather than North Africa first. Given his suggestion about General

Giraud, I think he sees the sense of your position, but he did not necessarily support it. Not then."

"And Eisenhower?"

"He knew that Marshall firmly believed we should go into France first, but at the end of the discussion, he brought up that paper you wrote and requested permission to forward it to Marshall. That paper seemed to have fomented the brouhaha, bringing about the president's order to Marshall and King to support Torch.

"In London, Eisenhower appeared to support your position but couldn't say so explicitly, so he found a way of communicating his support subtly. I doubt that he felt compelled to get your permission before showing it to Marshall. He must have known Marshall's likely reaction, which is why he hadn't shown it to him before."

Churchill peered at Paul. "So, you're suggesting that Eisenhower is both a diplomat and a politician, in addition to being an army general. We'll need those skills to hold this Grand Alliance together."

He leaned back and sat in reflection for a time, and then told Paul, "Relax and feel free to move about and get to know the crew. And get some sleep. This will be a long journey. There are a couple of benches at the back where you can lie down. We'll have to rotate with the good Dr. Wilson, though."

45

August 10, 1942
Cairo, Egypt

"Next stop, Moscow," Churchill told Paul as the Commando winged into the night sky. "Now that we've got our command issues sorted out in this part of the world with General Montgomery replacing General Auchinleck, we can get on with the rest of our mission. We'll need to refuel in Tehran, so we'll be there a few hours. This time, the passenger list also includes President Roosevelt's envoy, Averell Harriman. Two more planeloads of our entourage are also in flight."

"Shouldn't Mr. Harriman be in here with you instead of me?"

Churchill waved away the question, his cigar leaving a thin trail of smoke in the air. "We'll have plenty of time that I can spend with him, and I enjoy my conversations with you." He chuckled. "Please be sure to treat me kindly in whatever books you write, which I encourage you to do for the benefit of future generations. Like all others that have gone before, they are likely to ignore the lessons of history, but we should at least leave them an accurate record to use if they so choose. I'll be writing my own history as well."

"I'm not much of a writer, sir."

"And you haven't much vanity either, but you have a good mind and your heart's in the right place. I'll predict that you'll tell the story out of a sense of duty, if for no other reason."

"You give me more credit than I deserve, but may I ask what you hope to accomplish in Moscow?"

Churchill harrumphed. "I suspect a good many people are asking that question."

He took a puff on his cigar while he gathered his thoughts. "Stalin is between a rock and hard place." He arched his eyebrows. "Then again, aren't we all? But he's produced his own predicament, which started long before Hitler betrayed him."

"How so?"

Churchill contemplated before responding. "Despite that strong jaw, his piercing eyes, and thick hair and mustache that photographers love to show as a 'man of steel'—which is what his name, 'Stalin,' means—he's only five feet five inches tall, and he has a club foot and a withered arm. And that's not even his real name. He was born 'Visarrianovich Dzhugashvili.'"

The prime minister cocked his head as if in surprise. "I hadn't thought about it before, but perhaps he's owed some credit for overcoming his physical disabilities and becoming this towering figure that the public perceives. He has a sharp mind, and an incredible memory, and he gets to the heart of any matter quickly. Facts matter to him. Plans and theories don't.

"In any event, he mastered the art of being underestimated, getting himself appointed as Party Secretary—the keeper of records—in the Bolshevik Revolution's early days. There he learned the best-kept Party secrets and used them to grow his power."

He took another puff on his cigar and watched the smoke swirl. "Do you recall that, through German messages intercepted and decoded at Bletchley Park, we learned and tried to warn Stalin of Hitler's intention to break their neutrality agreement and attack the Soviet Union? That was Operation Barbarossa."

Paul nodded.

"Those messages informed us of an intelligence operation that the Germans ran on him, the brainchild of Hitler's propaganda minister, Joseph Goebbels. Essentially, Goebbels had sensed Stalin's underlying insecurity and fed it by dripping false information into the Soviet Union that made its way to Stalin. His insecurity evolved into roaring paranoia, and Stalin ended up persecuting seventy-five thousand people whom he considered to be personal threats. Among those, he had executed thirty thousand Red Army members, including more than eighty of his hundred and nine generals. Some of them were many of his closest advisers."

Paul listened with a neutral expression, containing his sense of being appalled.

Churchill grunted. "That 'Great Purge' weakened Stalin's own defenses. He lost centuries' worth of military experience and had to rely on inexperienced underlings driven by fear. But he believed that we, Great Britain, were intent on plunging him into our war and that Hitler would not be so stupid as to attack the Soviets. When Germany did invade, Stalin was so taken by surprise that he froze into inaction. A whole week passed with no response. After Minsk fell and the Germans were on the march toward Moscow, the politburo went looking for him at his *dacha* to mobilize a defense. He thought they'd come to arrest him."

Churchill shook his head and chuckled. "He's a realist if nothing else. He at least gave the appearance of softening toward his people. In his next speech to the nation, he addressed the citizens as 'brothers, sisters, and dear friends,' and admitted candidly that western Russian had been lost.

"One other point, and then I'll get back to your question about what we hope to accomplish in Moscow. The man is not without courage. Last October, on the 16th, I think, he was at the train station. His staff had recommended an evacuation of the government to a town five hundred miles east, Tbilisi. All had been prepared and he had given the order. And then suddenly, he told his staff, 'No! We stay here until victory has been achieved.'

"So, Stalin, this son of a shoemaker from Georgia, seems as determined to beat the Nazis as we are, but he needs to understand the Allies' abilities and constraints. He keeps pushing for a second front in France, apparently believing that we are holding resources back from him. The opposite is true. Great Britain has shipped thousands of tons of supplies and equipment provided to us over and above what the US has already sent him, and we've done it at the expense of our own soldiers in the field. But it was necessary to prevent Germany from overwhelming Stalin and seizing control of his army and weapons factories, which Hitler would most assuredly have turned on us.

"As you know, despite German failure against Moscow last winter, they've renewed their offensive, and now they're headed toward Stalingrad, hoping to seize its factories and publicly humiliate Stalin. Three months ago, Stalin overrode his generals and ordered a counterstrike against the

Germans to regain territory around Charkow. The initiative failed terribly, and I sense that Comrade Joseph is in a panic.

"Believing that Hitler's true objective was still Moscow, he misplaced his forces, and now the *Wehrmacht* approaches Stalingrad with greater ease than they did Moscow last year. Stalin's military blunder could cost us dearly, and it's causing him to rethink his entire strategy, including his relations with the west. He's dropped his post-war territorial claims on Eastern Poland and the Baltic states.

"But frankly, the situation causes me great concern. Perhaps Stalin will negotiate with Hitler again. That would be catastrophic, so we must keep him with the Allies.

"There is potential fallout from Stalin's blunders regardless of whether he enters into a new pact with Germany. If the Wehrmacht continues its push through the Caucasus, Hitler might be able to pressure Turkey into joining the Nazis and providing a path on the western side of the Black Sea to link up with Rommel in the Middle East. Or the Germans could turn south on the eastern side of the Black Sea, seize the oil fields in Iraq and Iran, overrun us in Egypt, and link up with Rommel that way. With control of the Suez, Germany would cut off our supply line there and threaten India. In that scenario, Hitler would no doubt see the possibility of linking up with the Japanese in the far North Pacific of the Soviet Union. And then all bets are off."

Churchill sat quietly a moment in deep contemplation. Then he sighed. "You can see that the stakes are astronomically high for this trip. Last year, Hitler directly threatened the British Isles. The potential I just described to you directly threatens the entire British Empire."

"It would certainly be a bleak picture, sir," Paul agreed.

"So, very simply, we must meet face-to-face. That will

give me a chance to take the measure of Stalin. I intend to establish a personal relationship, one in which he understands our plans, rationale, and limitations, as well as the sacrifices we're making on his country's behalf. Meetings to handle such momentous affairs must be done in person."

"But you don't personally like him?"

"Like him? He's a street thug, a bank robber. At one of his heists, he left forty people dead. Remember the *Holodomor*, when he starved millions of Ukrainians between '32 and '33 with a forced famine? How could I possibly like him? But the immediate threat to Britain is Hitler, so I swallow my pride and personal preferences and do what must be done to save our country. And right now, we need Stalin as much as he needs us."

46

August 12, 1942
Moscow, Russia, USSR

Paul stood stock still, careful not to make a sound, controlling his expression so as not to show his utter shock. A few feet away, General Alan Brooke seemed to also be struggling to contain his own astonishment. Dr. Wilson had already vacated the common area of State Villa No. 7, the guest *dacha* assigned to the British delegation. Harriman had gone on to stay at the American Embassy.

In the center of the well-appointed sitting room, Churchill stared up at a chandelier over a round table. He bellowed an insult, and then stalked away and disappeared into his bedroom.

The day had gone well by Paul's measure, and the prime minister had been effusive. They had arrived that morning, were met at the airport by Foreign Minister Vyacheslav Molotov, and after some pomp and ceremony including a short Churchill speech about the tight bonds between the

Allies, the delegation had been driven to a lavish *dacha* put at their disposal.

That evening, they drove to meet their host at the Kremlin. The stately white cathedral with its gleaming golden spires within the famous red walls encircling the seat of Soviet power had captured Paul, and he wondered about the genius and craftsmanship that had fashioned them. The sight was far removed from the ruins of the war-ravaged city with bombed-out buildings he saw as they rode through Moscow.

Stalin received the delegation in his office that evening. Harriman had already arrived. Stalin was dressed in a green tunic buttoned around his neck and hanging loosely over matching baggy trousers thrust inside knee-high, dark-leather boots. He was just as Churchill had described him, diminutive with a square jaw, thick hair and mustache, and piercing eyes. Greeting them with perfunctory courtesy, he showed the prime minister and Harriman to a row of chairs set up for formal photos. Curiously, he seated his foreign minister, Molotov, to his left, Harriman to his right, and Churchill at the far right.

Paul wondered if the arrangement was done deliberately to unsettle the prime minister. Whatever the reason, the first two hours of discussion had been testy. Churchill went over all the points that he had used with Roosevelt, Marshall, Eisenhower, Clark, and the members of the combined chiefs regarding why an amphibious assault could not be carried out in 1942. Stalin remained unconvinced, telling Churchill that a man who was not prepared to take risks could not win a war.

"Why do you think Hitler did not invade Great Britain when he was at his height of military power, and we were at our weakest?" Churchill retorted. "It was because crossing the Channel is very difficult."

"It's not the same as what I propose," Stalin replied. "Your people would have fought a German invasion. If you mounted an amphibious assault in France, you would be liberators. The French people would welcome you and join the fight."

"Which is all the more reason why we should do it only when we are fully equipped and ready. The worst thing we could do is expose French citizens to a bloodbath, get ourselves tossed off at the beach, and then leave them to the retaliation of Hitler. He would consolidate his position, and we would lose."

As the discussion continued, Paul's ears perked up when Stalin suggested a smaller invasion. "You could take back the Channel Isles."

Paul's thoughts immediately went to his mother and stepfather, Marian and Stephen, but he had been present at sufficient numbers of discussions to know Churchill's response. "That would be a useless waste of resources that would accomplish nothing toward winning the war."

Watching both men as the discussion continued through interpreters, Paul was struck by how emotional they could be. Stalin's disposition sank into sullenness with sparks of anger, particularly when Churchill told him that, in consultation with their American allies, a decision had been reached that no invasion of France would be attempted this year.

"May I have a pencil and paper?" Churchill asked.

Surprised, Stalin ordered that the items be brought, and Churchill then sketched a crocodile, telling him, "This is France," and indicated the head. "And the Mediterranean is the soft underbelly." He tapped the spot with his pencil. "You kill a crocodile by attacking the soft underbelly."

Stalin had leaned in, and Churchill revealed the concepts of Rutter and Torch. "We are preparing to launch these operations this year, and when we do, they are certain to draw some of Hitler's resources from the Caucasus. That will relieve pressure on Stalingrad, and we will kill German soldiers. If we are successful in these operations in 1942," Churchill said emphatically, "we will launch a deadly attack against Hitler next year."

Stalin was visibly elated, fully engaged, and asked many questions. When finally, the meeting ended, he and Churchill were smiling and agreeing with each other's comments. Shortly afterward, the British delegation bid the Soviets goodnight.

Churchill was in high spirits when they reached the *dacha*. "My strategy was sound. First, I gave him the bad news. Then glad tidings. Stalin was enthusiastic when we left." He laughed out loud. "Stalin is a peasant. I knew exactly how to handle him."

That was the point at which Paul froze. General Brooke shook off his own surprise, strode over to the prime minister, whispered in his ear, and pointed at the chandelier, a likely place for a bug.

Churchill swung around, looking wide-eyed about the room. Then his eyes narrowed, he stepped closer to the table, and glared up at the chandelier. "The Russians, I am told," he shouted, "are not human beings at all. They are lower on the scale of nature than the orangutangs." He started to walk away, but then added, "Now, let them take that down and translate it into Russian."

When the parties rejoined discussion the next morning, the *bonhomie* of the night before had disappeared. Stalin did not rise to greet Churchill. He leaned back in his chair, smoking a pipe.

"Your crocodile's underbelly is irrelevant," he growled, close to a sneer. "You promised an invasion into France this year. Your broke your promise." He turned slowly to face Churchill, who had taken his seat. "If the British army had fought the German army as hard as the Russians have, you wouldn't be so frightened of them."

Furiously, Churchill took to his feet and retorted loudly, "Obviously, you know nothing of fighting a war to win. You took no action to defend your own country for a full week after being attacked. You signed a non-aggression pact, leaving us to fight alone when you could have helped. We sank the *Bismarck* and the Italian navy, and we all but grounded the *Tirpitz* by destroying the only dry dock that could handle her *on French soil.* And we sent you supplies and equipment that we needed as much as you did. You've got problems and you look to us to bail you out when Britain's got its own problems to deal with."

Paul watched in disbelief, his gut wrenching at the thought of the ramifications that seemed almost certain to result from the tumultuous meeting. The confab lasted not much longer.

The next morning, cigar in hand, Churchill took Paul into the garden outside the *dacha* and away from the bugs. "That man insulted me," he fumed. "From now on, he'll have to fight his battles alone. I represent a great country, and I am not submissive by nature."

Paul remained silent.

"Aren't you going to say anything, Major?"

"I take my role now as one of listening," Paul said. "I'll

listen all day long if you like, but I am hardly anyone to advise you on matters as weighty as how to handle Stalin."

Churchill stopped walking and stared at him. Then he laughed. "That must have been some spectacle to watch," he said. "Good thing the press wasn't there. I can see the headlines now, 'British PM and Russian Dictator in Shouting Match.'"

He lowered his head. "The fact is that we need each other, and our countries need us to get along."

Another man approached, and Paul recognized Sir Archibald Clark Kerr, the British ambassador to Moscow. His expression was that of contained anger.

He glanced at Paul. "Please leave us."

"He can stay," Churchill said gruffly. "Speak your mind."

"As you like, Mr. Prime Minister," Kerr replied while tossing an impatient glare at Paul. "I have to ask, are you going to flounce off home, all because you're offended by a peasant who didn't know any better?" He paused for breath. "You are an aristocrat. These Soviets are rough and inexperienced, straight from the plow and the lathe. Don't let your pride blur your judgment." He pivoted in front of Churchill. "You've got to unbend, sir. You must ask Stalin for another talk."

Churchill took a long puff on his cigar and watched the smoke swirl as he let it out. "You're right, of course," he said at last. "But what if Stalin isn't receptive? What if he won't 'unbend,' to use your word."

"I think he might," the ambassador replied. "He's received bad news from the front. The *Wehrmacht* just routed the Red Army along the Don River. Stalingrad is in their sights."

Churchill's head popped up. "You don't say."

"I do say, sir. Stalin needs us. And we need him."

They met in Stalin's office again that evening in a pervasive atmosphere of allies-of-necessity doing their duty. They reviewed matters and points already covered, and then Churchill rose to leave.

He was surprised when Stalin suddenly stood with him, extended his hand, and said, with a broad smile, "Please come to my apartment in the Kremlin and have a drink with me. I'd like you to meet my family."

Somewhat bewildered, Churchill accepted, and discovered a side of the dictator he had not seen before. He turned to regard the others of his party. "What about them?"

"Bring them," Stalin said, laughing. "If we're to be allies, we should get to know one another."

Churchill looked peaked at the airfield the next morning as they prepared for a return journey to Cairo. He stood dutifully between Molotov and Ambassador Kerr and was surrounded by the delegation as bands played renditions of the US National Anthem, "God Save the King," and the Communist "Internationale." As he was about to board the plane, Kerr approached and whispered something in his ear. Once aboard, Churchill went straight to one of the benches at the back and lay down.

Mid-flight, he called for Paul to join him in his makeshift cabin. "That was a night to remember," he said. "Years have passed since I drank as much. Stalin brought his young daughter, Svetlana, to meet me, and he was as proud as any father I've known. You could see the pride in his eyes. It was as if he wanted to convey, 'See, we Bolsheviks love our families too.'

"But he's a cheeky bastard. When I started telling him about my ancestor, the Duke of Marlborough, he laughed and told me that he preferred the Duke of Wellington because Napoleon had presented the greatest danger in the history of the world, and the duke had defeated him."

Churchill grunted. "He should study history better," he muttered. "He'd find that it was a sixty-seven-year-old Russian, General Mikhail Kutuzov, who set the stage for the Corsican corporal's defeat."

"Do you mean by setting fire to Moscow and luring the French army to chase him into the Ural Mountains in winter and then decimating it?"

Churchill nodded. "It's good that you know history. The Russian winter defeated Napoleon, it held the *Wehrmacht* at bay last winter, and it'll do the same at Stalingrad. To cause that particular defeat we must hold the Allies together." He took a deep breath and exhaled. "I think our alliance is cemented. Stalin and I can do business together."

"That's good news, sir. So, the trip was a success?"

"I believe so. Time will tell. I believe our alliance will hold because, as unsatisfactory as he might consider what equipment and supplies we've sent, at least we're not taking away territory—whole gobs of it—and we haven't broken any treaties. From Stalin's viewpoint, we are less untrustworthy than Hitler."

"That's a mite cynical."

"Perhaps. But true, I think." He looked out the window at the blue sky. "Our ambassador relayed a piece of news just as we were leaving. Eisenhower received a directive from the combined chiefs to proceed with Torch. That means Roosevelt gave his approval. I'd already given mine.

Sledgehammer is dead. The invasion of North Africa is on —at least the next stage."

He paused pensively. "You know, I've a mind to send you to Gibraltar to be my envoy on Eisenhower's staff. That's where he'll set up his headquarters to run Torch."

"Am I to spy there?"

Churchill chuckled. "My, my. You have descended into your own miasma of cynicism, haven't you? No, no. It'll all be aboveboard. I know your sense of ethics would never allow you to lurk in the shadows within our own camp— and Eisenhower would figure out the lay of the land if we attempted anyway. I need an unvarnished view of the goings-on from someone who is not involved in decision making. You've performed in that role for some time."

"I see, sir." Paul mulled that a moment. "I'm at your service. And if I may ask, why are we going back to Egypt now?"

Churchill took his time to respond. "This war is multi-faceted, as you well know. German U-boats and the combined German and Italian air forces had successfully blockaded our access to Malta with hundreds of submarines and an ungodly number of aircraft. That island is a critical supply point and refueling station for our ships in the Mediterranean, not to mention that it's a wonderful plat-form for long-range guns and a base for aircraft. If we lose it, the Mediterranean becomes an Axis lake. The island was critically short of supplies, going months without the arrival of a single supply ship."

He blew out a long breath between pursed lips. "While we were in Moscow, the Italians and the Germans attacked a convoy we'd sent to rescue the island.

"But the Axis couldn't seem to coordinate their assaults. The Italian and German submarines attacked seemingly independent of each other, and apparently with no coordination with the *Luftwaffe's* bombardment. The long and short is that a remnant of our convoy broke through the blockade and reached Malta, but the price was high on both sides. We would have deemed the operation a success if only a single merchant ship had reached Grand Harbor at Malta. The situation there was that desperate.

"We ran the largest and most protected convoy of the war to date. It included two battleships, four aircraft carriers, seven cruisers, thirty-two destroyers, and myriad tankers and supply ships. The convoy had both British and American ships with aircraft cover from the carriers, and thirty-six Spitfires to be delivered to Malta.

"Earlier this year, we supplied fifty-two Spitfires there, and the *Luftwaffe* bombed and destroyed all of them before we could turn them around and put them in the fight."

He pulled a paper from his jacket and drew long on his cigar. "I promise you, we did not make that mistake this time. We downed fifty-two enemy aircraft, but we lost the carrier *Eagle* and nine merchant ships. Two cruisers, the *Manchester* and *Cairo*, were hit and had to turn back to Gibraltar. And our destroyer, *Foresight,* was sunk. The carrier *Indomitable* was also crippled. It didn't go down, but it couldn't support air operations. And we lost the ships that carried our main radio capability, so coordinating air cover for the last two days was next to impossible."

Churchill looked up with a pleased expression. "But our chaps never quit. One of our destroyers, the *Ithurial*, rammed an Italian submarine to keep it from firing its torpedoes, and special mention must be made of the American tanker, *Ohio*. It was hit by a torpedo three days out from Malta. That tanker carried enough petroleum for thirteen weeks of operations. Can you imagine the explosion if it had ignited? But those Americans fought the flames and kept the ship afloat. It was stranded for a while, but three of our destroyers latched onto her and towed her all the way into Grand Harbor."

He jabbed the air with his cigar again. "I'll tell you, not enough credit can ever be given to the merchant seamen in this war. They sail bravely where they're told to go delivering food, ammunition, and supplies to where they're needed." He indicated the paper again. "Vice Admiral Seyfret commanded the convoy, Operation Pedestal, and he included this in his dispatch to me." He read the message. "'...both officers and men will desire to give first place to the conduct, courage, and determination of the masters, officers, and men of the merchant ships.'"

Churchill sighed and muttered in a low voice, "He says further down that after being attacked by Stuka dive bombers all day, he watched seamen pushing a fully fueled, armed, and burning Hurricane off the flight deck, and they did it while covered in the blood and entrails of their mates."

He tossed his head in slight obstinacy. "My senior military advisers had thought the island to be indefensible and wanted to abandon it. Our Mediterranean Fleet headquarters had been located there for decades, but we moved it to Alexandria two years ago. Now we can see more than ever that Malta is crucial to both sides because it's halfway between Gibraltar and Alexandria. Whoever controls that island controls that sea and wins North Africa. If we had lost it, Torch would be a bloody useless exercise."

Churchill stood suddenly with a triumphant air. "But our men arrived in Malta with fifty-five thousand tons of supplies, the *Ohio's* oil, and thirty-six Spitfires. It's in the fight."

The prime minister re-took his seat as the bomber rumbled on through the air. "And there's another operation going on at present, on the other side of the planet. The Americans are engaged in the Pacific in a fierce battle at that island called Guadalcanal. It's already raged for more than a week."

He sighed. "And then there's India to contend with."

"Is it serious, sir?"

Churchill grimaced. "It's all serious, and of course I'll be accused of imperial tendencies again. While we've been basking in Cairo's sun and feasting on stuffed pig at Stalin's apartment at the Kremlin, the Congress Party in India has gone violent with its "Quit India" movement, sabotaging railways and fomenting riots. Mobs are running wild over large segments of the country demanding an end to British rule. The Viceroy's Council proposed unanimously to arrest Mahatma Gandhi and Jawaharlal Nehru, two of the Party's leaders—and by the way, only one Englishman sits on that council, and our War Cabinet endorsed the plan. And then of all things, Generalissimo Chiang Kai-shek in China read the published reports of the events in India and tried to influence things by protesting to President Roosevelt. Seems that Chiang views himself as freedom's champion in Asia."

"Fortunately, the president backed him off, the plan of arrests in India was executed, and the Congress Party's influence appears to be fizzling."

Churchill took a deep breath. "Meanwhile, Operation Rutter has been renamed Operation Jubilee and is about to launch. We're on the verge of a large raid into France at Dieppe."

Paul barely contained his surprise. "Then why are we going back to Cairo?"

"Two reasons, I want an extended visit with Lord Gort.

He took over as governor in Malta only four months ago, in April. He'll be arriving in Cairo with his aide, Lord Munster. I want to congratulate them for their courage under fire in sticking it out through that awful siege, and I want to hear from Gort personally about conditions at Malta." He paused. "And there's one other reason."

Paul waited.

"We won't make it back to England before Jubilee launches. I need to be in a secure location to monitor that operation. Moscow is not the place, and neither is Tehran."

Paul cast the prime minister a skeptical glance. "But Cairo is?"

Churchill chuckled, took a puff from his cigar, and blew out a series of smoke circles. "It's the safest place we can get to in the time allotted."

"What's the objective at Dieppe?"

"Quite simple. Seize a major French port and hold it for one day. This was one of Lord Mountbatten's combined operations ideas, to show Hitler that the Atlantic coast is vulnerable, requiring him to shift troops from the east for the western defense. That should alleviate some pressure on Stalin. Next is to gather intelligence about coastal fortifications and destroy critical elements in the vicinity, to include some artillery batteries, a radar station, and an airfield. And third, to get out. This raid is not intended to be the main thrust into Europe, and of course, we'd seek to limit the number of French civilian casualties.

"The 2nd Canadian Division will provide the bulk of the raiding force with five thousand men. Canadian senior leaders are concerned that their men have been training in the UK for two years, but they've seen no action. They want their troops blooded before the main invasion. Fifty American Rangers and fifteen Free French will be in the mix too.

Our commandos, who will have about a thousand in the operation, trained them on the grounds at Achnacarry Castle in Scotland.

"Hmm. Come to think of it, this will be the first time Americans are in ground combat against Germans in this war."

47

August 19, 1942
Dieppe, France

Lieutenant Colonel Simon Fraser, commander of No. 4 Commando and otherwise known as Lord Lovat, 25th Chief of Clan Fraser of Lovat and 4th Baron Lovat in the Peerage of the United Kingdom, squinted through inky darkness at an even darker mass of land rising against the horizon. The landing crafts carrying two hundred and fifty-two commandos and twenty US Army Rangers under his command broke through the waves, driven by twin sixty-five-horsepower Ford engines. His command, on the right flank of Operation Jubilee, was one of six elements on this first raid-in-force spread along twelve miles of the French coast at Dieppe and its vicinity.

Lovat was a slender man, unpretentious despite his pedigree, and dark-haired with a downward-curving mustache. He turned and scanned the sea all about, imagining the two hundred ships and landing craft carrying six thousand men deployed and spread out over twelve miles to the left of and behind his own small craft.

Operation Jubilee, the first major Allied operation on European soil of this war, was about to execute.

Lovat groaned. At the back of his mind was the comment the overall raid commander, Canadian MG John Roberts, made aboard one of the ships while addressing troops just before sending them into battle. "Don't worry, men, it'll be a piece of cake!"

Lord Mountbatten also addressed the commandos and Canadian soldiers. He was hugely popular with the men for the success of the raids in Norway and at Saint-Nazaire, and he had planned Operation Jubilee, though Lovat had heard that he had misgivings about it that were overridden. Namely, Mountbatten thought a heavy aerial bombardment should precede the raid, and he was against a frontal assault on Dieppe itself because it was heavily fortified. Lovat agreed with both sentiments.

Also present at the sendoff was a senior American officer Lovat had become aware of only recently, Lieutenant General Eisenhower. The general had gathered the fifty rangers together to address them. One of them had related to Lovat the gist of the general's remarks: that the recently formed and not quite fully trained 1st Ranger Battalion was the first test of rangers in battle and the first Americans to fight on European soil since the last war. Eisenhower was sure that they would conduct themselves well. "You're the first of thousands."

The rangers, Lovat had observed, were a spirited lot, all volunteers who had surprised their training cadre in Scotland with their wit, determination, and tenacity. His concerns were not with their fighting ability but with the mission itself.

In addition to Lovat's unease over the lack of a preliminary aerial bombardment, he also retained lingering concern that no battleships were among the flotillas. With the loss last December of the battleship, *Prince of Wales*, and the cruiser, *Repulse*, off the coast of Malaya at the hands of the Japanese in the Pacific, Royal Navy authorities had been averse to risking yet more capital ships close to shore where land-based batteries and aircraft could potentially sink the vessels. They had instead sent in several destroyers, but the ordnance on these smaller ships would hardly be as effective as a battleship's heavy guns for a pre-assault bombardment of onshore defenses.

Seventy-four squadrons of aircraft, including sixty-six fighter squadrons, would fly air cover after fighting started. Perhaps, in a ground-support role, they could pinpoint and subdue stubborn gun positions. He arched his eyebrows as the thought flitted by. *That assumes less than heavy Luftwaffe opposition.*

The element Lovat commanded for the raid, No. 4 Commando, would proceed to Varengeville-sur-Mer, a village six miles west of Dieppe. Their objective was to destroy a battery of six 150mm guns, stopping it from firing on friendly naval forces and the Canadian troops conducting the assault on Green Beach at Pourville, a village nearly halfway between the battery and Dieppe.

Ninety minutes after landing, he was to be in position when a flight of Hurricanes was due to strafe the battery. Immediately afterward, Group 2 would overrun the site while Group 1 penetrated from Varengeville, east of the battery.

As dawn's first light illuminated the landscape, Lovat sucked in his breath. Pre-mission aerial reconnaissance had been poor, and most of what anyone among the six thousand men on this raid knew about the terrain came from tourism posters of the area. The cliffs that rose along the beach to his left now seemed steeper and taller than anyone had been able to discern from maps and photos. Fortunately for the commandos and rangers under his command, their landing point was protected from view from the east by a curve in the coastline.

Speed and surprise were the elements on which Operation Jubilee depended, but as he sped to his objective at Orange Beach on the right flank, he wondered how long that surprise could last. He set his jaw, seeing that once his objective was secured, his men would be in relative safety, but he saw nothing to indicate that the same would be true for those elements farther east. No. 3 Commando was to secure the left flank, Yellow Beach at Berneval, where another coastal gun battery was located, and Lovat could only hope that those comrades would find cover similar to this bend in the shoreline.

Lovat's plan was to send Group 1 of No. 4 Commando to a position on the east side of the objective to pin down the Germans defending the guns at Varengeville. Major Derek Mills-Roberts would lead the group to a landing where, according to the map, two gullies might allow him to approach the battery from below its seaward flank.

Mills-Roberts had been a friend for years, a loyal subordinate, and completely competent. Light complected with dirty-blond hair and mustache, he was a formidable foe, though this would be his first test under fire. He would attack his objective with Troops B and C. His Troop A had been attached to Lovat's group.

The other five raiding parties of Operation Jubilee had no similar protection, coming ashore at Beaches Green, White, Red, Blue, and Yellow, along the rough shore.

Meeting Lovat's objective would eliminate a major threat at the right flank; but the cliffs, in particular those that the troops at adjacent Green Beach would encounter to the east and west of Pourville, appeared to be impenetrable. If caught on the beach in either of those places, the raiding party there would have no cover or concealment.

Observing down the coast to the east, Lovat saw no other break in the cliffs before the town of Dieppe itself, where they appeared to taper down to the water where White and Red Beaches were located in close proximity to each other. From this distance, he could not see beyond Dieppe's tiny harbor at the end of a narrow estuary, but he recalled that, in the mission briefs, cliffs had been mentioned along the full length of the assault area except at Pourville and Dieppe. No one had anticipated their being so high. They portended calamity.

Fortunately, on his end, the cliffs descended westward along the Quiberville-St. Marguerite Road where the Saane River emptied into the English Channel. Lovat had pinpointed this low ground on the map and intended to use it to reach his objective.

Captain Patrick Porteous came to stand next to him. "Things look a mite bleak down that way," he said, gesturing to their left toward Dieppe.

"They do," Lovat said, turning to signal his boat's pilot to speed up. "Let the other crafts know to go full speed. We'll need to hit our objective fast and hard or the enemy will rain hell on our mates east of us."

He watched the captain move to the rear of the vessel. Lovat liked Porteous, a good-looking, tough, and jovial light-haired Scot, born in Abbottabad, India, and bearing bright eyes and a sharp nose that looked like it had been twisted by too much rugby. Porteous had volunteered to take on the dangerous job of liaison between Lovat's two groups. In the event of a radio outage, he would relay messages back and forth, exposing himself to enemy fire.

The land mass, the white cliffs, and the strip of beach seemed to rush to meet the landing craft, and sooner than he could believe, Lovat felt the crunch of sand against the bottom of the landing craft's thin wooden floor. Leaping into the shallow water, he waded ashore and glanced down to where Major Mills-Roberts' boats also came to a halt and disgorged their commandos and rangers.

Far off to the left, the unmistakable booms of heavy guns rolled across the waters. Flashes of light lit up the sky in that direction. Almost simultaneously, a lighthouse at the end of the promontory in Lovat's sector went dark.

The raid had been detected. Surprise was blown.

Mortar rounds peppered around the soldiers. Then, swift hisses through the air and small eruptions in the sand preceded the rat-tat-tat of machine guns. Four commandos dropped into the sand, lifeless.

Lovat had time only to glance down the beach where Mills-Roberts' group came to shore a hundred and fifty yards away. The men immediately sought the limited shelter of the gullies, but to get there, the soldiers had to contend with barbed wire strung over tank obstacles. Under withering fire, some immediately flopped on the barbed wire, lifeless, their blood staining the sand. Others called for medics.

Lovat's own Group 2 commandos encountered obstacles and thick barbed wire. They threw rabbit netting across the barriers, using it to cross, and sprinted to the mouth of the Saane River, taking more casualties as they went. Then, the enemy fire redirected to the retreating landing craft, and the men reached limited cover.

The sound of many aircraft reverberated across the water. Hawker Hurricanes overflew, drawing fire from the machine guns, and in that interval, Group 2 escaped to Quiberville-St. Marguerite Road. Crossing it, soldiers skirted along the eastern bank of the Saane. It had overflowed, impeding their progress, and already, they sweated, their lungs heaving with the exertion, some of them nursing wounds.

Full daylight now exposed them, but the steep riverbank protected them from fire from St. Marguerite, and they prepared smoke to conceal their movement from the enemy at Quiberville. At a bend in the river, they continued east, staying below a ridge of low hills, and continuing to where the terrain opened up with less cover and concealment. The formation spread out, sections of it maneuvering in alternating bounds across open areas. As his group approached the rear of the German battery, Lovat heard the sounds of a firefight. Group 1 was already engaged.

Group 2 reached a wooded area, and there split into F Troop and B Troop.

B Troop continued east, followed the southern edge of the woods, and then split again into sections. There, they engaged the enemy, using fire and maneuver to advance through an orchard, destroy a machine gun position, and enter the village. Only five minutes late, they prepared to attack the main objective, the German battery of six 150mm guns.

Meanwhile, F Troop maneuvered to the northeast. Laying a smoke cover, they advanced and penetrated the wire surrounding the German position and surprised an enemy patrol preparing to counter-attack Group 1. When the ensuing brief battle ended, no enemy remained alive.

F Troop commandos continued on, intent on securing

their objective, and swiftly dispatched inferior German resistance. Nevertheless, the troop sustained additional casualties but persevered, finally reaching their planned position from which to launch the final assault. There, they waited.

Lovat, with Porteous and his headquarters group, moved up between the B and F Troops' positions, attracting friendly fire from F Troop. Urgent radio calls quickly doused it.

While the troops positioned themselves, another section crept behind the lighthouse to cut telephone cables connecting German observers to their gun battery, and yet another section worked forward to the edge of the facing woods. The final section took up a flanking position among the houses in the village. An hour and forty minutes after landing, all Group 2 elements were in position for the assault.

Meanwhile, the powerful German guns pounded rounds along the shore east toward Dieppe, raining steel onto the thousands of Allied soldiers assaulting the beach.

While Group 2 maneuvered into position behind the battery, Mills-Roberts led his men to their position. Immediately on debarkation under fire, a quick reconnaissance had found the left gully to be impassable. A check revealed the right gorge to be blocked by wire and obstacles. Mills-Roberts' men blew the impediments with explosives and continued up the steep ravine, perspiring and lugging light mortars and other weaponry. Equipment they carried broke free from bindings intended to muffle noise, threatening to reveal their position.

On reaching the top of the gully, they found that the terrain broke into a wide, verdant field and to one side was a barn. A section of C Troop led the way, scouting into the woods on the north side of Varengeville, clearing houses as they proceeded. They set up a mortar position a short distance from the village on the battery's flank and settled to wait. Almost immediately, they were spotted, fired upon, and took wounded.

One of Mills-Roberts' men, Corporal Franklin Coons, an American Ranger, grabbed an injured man and dragged him to the barn, returning for others. When all were out of the line of fire, Coons searched inside the barn. Seeing a chink in the wall, he used a manger below it as a steady support for sniper fire and picked off enemy combatants on the near side of the objective. Outside, the remainder of Group 1 cut loose with M1 Garand rifles, Bren light machine guns, Boys anti-tank rifles, and mortars.

Then from above came the sound of more aircraft, the promised flight of Hurricanes. They flew in from the north-west and descended in fury, strafing the battery, hitting magazines; and suddenly explosions boomed, the overcast sky lit up, black smoke rose into the air, and the thunderous roar of lethal weapons of all sorts spewed fire, smoke, lead, and the threat of death in every direction.

Then, just as suddenly, a new sound added to the cacophony. A flight of FW-190 Fokker-Wulf fighters interrupted the Hurricanes' strafing runs, the aircraft wheeling, turning, diving, and shooting high above the battlefield.

Seeing the British aircraft otherwise engaged, Lovat whirled about seeking Porteous. Grabbing the captain's shoulder, he yelled above the din, "We're out of commo with Group 1. Get over to Mills-Roberts and tell him air support is out of the question now. We'll wait ten minutes, and then assault. Go."

Porteous took off at a fast trot, skirting the battle area, sprinting through open places, ducking behind cover and concealment when available. He had barely cleared Group 2's area when he stumbled onto a road and nearly collided with a German officer. The two stared at each other, and the German, with his pistol already in hand, raised it and pulled the trigger.

Porteous felt the impact through his hand and arm before he heard the report. Furiously, he charged. The officer had heard another sound, turned, and was about to shoot a British sergeant. The road was littered with dead bodies and war equipment, including a rifle with affixed bayonet in the hands of a German in death's grip. Porteous grabbed the rifle with his good hand, slashed the enemy's arm with it, and then stabbed him. The man fell without a sound, and the British sergeant cast him a grateful stare.

Looking wildly about but seeing no immediate danger, Porteous took off at a run again. Crashing through brush, he surprised two German soldiers hiding in a slit trench. On instinct, he grabbed a grenade from his belt, pulled the pin, tossed it into the pit, and hit the ground.

After the explosion had cleared, and seeing that no threat existed in close proximity, Porteous leaped to his feet and continued on, arriving a few minutes later at Mills-Roberts' headquarters near the barn. Corporal Coons saw him coming, intercepted him, and led him to the major.

Hunched over, unable to speak at first for lack of breath, and dripping blood, Porteous looked up and pointed at his watch. "Five minutes," he gasped. "Attack."

"We're ready," the major replied. He glanced at Porteous' hand and arm. "Get a medic on that."

Still panting, Porteous shook his head and stumbled back in the direction he had come. "When this is over," he said.

"Tell Lovat that the US is fully engaged in this theater," Mills-Roberts called after him. He clapped Coons' shoulder. "This corporal gets honors as the first American to fire at German soldiers on European soil in this war."

Porteous nodded between breaths, raised a hand to wave his good wishes, and took off again at a trot. On arriving back at Group 2 headquarters, he found that Lovat had been wounded and was unconscious.

Whirling on the Troop B leader, he ordered, "Clear all the buildings in the village." Then moving swiftly to Troop F's area and finding its leader, he yelled, "Time for the assault. Follow me."

At that moment, a giant explosion erupted inside the German battery perimeter. Apparently, one of Mills-Roberts' mortars struck the ammunition dump. Porteous held his men back, and when the smoke had cleared, they charged in.

Fifteen minutes later, twenty-six minutes after reaching their assault position, and having destroyed and entered the battery and finding no enemy survivors, Porteous collapsed from loss of blood.

48

Lieutenant Colonel Charles Merritt, Commander of the South Saskatchewan Regiment, Canadian Army, stared with incredulity. He was a big, broad-shouldered man, in his mid-thirties with dark brown hair. He sometimes wore a mustache, but he was currently clean-shaven, his strong, rounded chin and stern expression belying his normal jocular demeanor.

His astonishment resulted from the situation in which he found himself. While still on his landing craft, he had heard explosions to the north and east of Dieppe signaling that surprise had been lost and he should expect hurried actions and subsequent confusion. Such was to be expected in war. But he had not anticipated having his unit so scattered before reaching the beach that landing craft carrying his regiment's main force, including himself, would arrive on the wrong side of a bridge, with his remaining elements on the other side. "Then again," he muttered, "dawn has barely broken. No one can see anything with any certainty of what they're looking at."

Bodies lay bleeding on the shore where they had landed,

and the beach was steep, the sand of a shale type, exhausting soldiers' legs before even reaching the seawall. "Like climbing a mountain of acorn shells."

His first worry was getting his men off the beach from under blistering gunfire, but his biggest concern was that his objective lay on the other side of the bridge spanning the River La Scie. And once across, he had to get a particular member of his command to the top of the cliffs on the east side of town. Failing that, the Dieppe operation could well be for naught.

He glanced around to ensure that he had eyes on this special man, Private Jack with no last name. At this point, Merritt was glad he did not know it.

When they had first met, and when asked his name, the private had responded with the utmost courtesy and humility, "I'm not allowed to tell you, sir. You could be captured too. Perhaps you should just call me Jack."

After being briefed on the nature of the mission, Merritt had accepted it and had assigned Jack to Captain Murray Osten, commander of Company A. Osten, in turn, had summoned his own sergeant major, Ed Dunkerley, to discuss the matter in Merritt's presence. Jack was not there.

"He's an RAF canary," Osten said to Dunkerley's amusement.

Merritt arched his eyebrows. "You mean a coward? I'd hardly call him that. He knows what he's in for. He's certainly not too yellow to shoot."

"Sorry, sir," Osten replied. "That comment was disparaging." He turned to Dunkerley. "Make him look and act like a soldier. Jack's going to Dieppe with us, but he cannot be captured. Recruit the best of our command to be his bodyguards. If he's wounded during the raid and cannot be recovered, or if he is about to be captured—" He stopped talking and made direct eye contact. "Do you grasp my meaning?"

The sergeant major sucked in his breath and shifted his eyes between Osten and Merritt. "I need to understand my orders clearly, sir. Under no circumstances is he to fall into enemy hands alive. Is that correct?"

Osten nodded.

"May I know why?"

"Not now. Put two teams together to protect him. Ensure that the leaders of both teams are crack shots. They'll escort him to do his task."

"He knows?"

Osten grimaced. "That he might be executed by his own mates? Yes. He'll also carry a cyanide pill in his escape kit."

Dunkerley blew out a quick breath. "Then he really is not a canary, sir."

Osten and Merritt had agreed somberly.

Now, here on the beach, amid machine gun rattle, the hiss and pop of bullets, and explosions all around, the probability of Jack being killed before completing his mission was great; but even if he succeeded, the threat grew of having to end the man's life to prevent capture. And while the main element of the South Saskatchewans remained on this side of the river, no chance existed for Jack to complete his mission.

As his men sought cover and returned fire and gradually worked their way off the beach, Merritt urged them on while keeping an eye on the small group surrounding Jack. So far, it was intact, but that might not be the case if Merritt completed what he had in mind to do next.

The lieutenant colonel was proud of the men in his command. They came from the prairies of Canada, from Buffalo Gap, Swift River, Moose Mountain Creek, Old Wives Lake, and other quaintly named towns where streets were made wide so that men rode their horses abreast to avoid the others' dust. They were drawn from law offices, blacksmith's shops, farm and ranch fields, banks, schools, and all manner of common and obscure occupations to fight for an island country thousands of miles away that none had ever seen but to which they felt bound by ancestry and tradition. And after training for a year, they had sailed aboard filthy ships to Halifax to endure yet two more years of training to commando level.

And they were guileless. Merritt had many times smiled at the memory of accosting a private at whose feet rested a still-smoldering cigarette. "Is that yours?"

"That's all right, sir," had come the sincere reply. "You saw it first. You take it."

They were hard, they were brave, good-humored, and determined, yet this was their first battle, and they were being churned under merciless enemy fire like glass bottles on a shooting range wall. And he had to move them.

RAF Flight Sergeant Jack Nissenthall, Number 916592, known to his combat mates as Private Jack with no last name, moved lithely with his protective squad. One of the qualifications for the task he had been recruited to do was to be in superb physical condition, so he had no trouble keeping up with his mates. But his mission-specific training had lasted barely two weeks, not months, and beyond his sessions with Flight Sergeant Cox and memorizing the technical details of the Freya radar system, it had mainly consisted of adjusting his behavior to blend in with soldiers.

He had spent hours with Cox, the technician who had accompanied the paratroopers on the raid at Bruneval to capture the Wurzburg radar. Cox had volunteered for the Dieppe mission, but his superiors told him that he would not be sent to risk his life that way again; besides, Jack was more technically qualified. And the Dieppe raid was deemed to be considerably more dangerous because of the intent to assault a fortified port along the Atlantic Wall.

Jack was a highly gifted radar specialist with an interest going back to childhood in all things electronic. His knowledge had been developed formally at Regent Street Polytechnic and informally through keen interest, hours of personal research and tinkering, and unpaid experimental work at the Bawdsey radar station. At Bawdsey, he had shinnied up towers two hundred and forty feet high amidst gale-force storms to repair and operate relays. His skill was such that RAF crews often requested that he fly with them to resolve issues that baffled other technicians.

Having volunteered for flight crew at the beginning of the war, he was instead assigned to RAF Yatesbury to help establish the first top secret radar school. Since then, he had worked at radar stations across the country, from North Scotland to South Devon, and he had even volunteered for commando training.

Jack was also an avid athlete, spending many hours outdoors hiking, climbing, and riding bicycles. Recognizing the nature of the war, he had months earlier volunteered for any special operations that came along involving radar. Having been turned down, he was surprised to have received a recruiting call for this raid, and his only regret during the interview process was a remark made by an administrative officer to another worker, neither of whom knew anything of his mission, "You'd think they could find someone better than a Jew for a special job, wouldn't you, whatever it is?"

Jack shook off a sick reaction to the comment. Certainly, he had heard news about Jews being rounded up in France, even in Vichy, but no one knew definitively what happened to them. Rumors abounded of death and labor camps, but they were too horrific to be believed. No civilized nation could possibly indulge in such evil.

Dr. Reginald Jones, the top radar scientist of Air Intelligence, had described the mission to Jack. Since the raid on Bruneval, British radar development technologists had become increasingly worried that not only had the Germans improved security around their radar sites, but that they had also improved the technology itself. The team thought the *Luftwaffe* might have developed an anti-jamming capability as well. They also worried that a backup radar system in the 250-megahertz range might have been devised to be employed immediately if the *Luftwaffe* detected RAF jamming.

The British team had deduced that a broad radar band that Germany had been using in Freya had been narrowed, which allowed them to identify objects more precisely. They needed an experienced scientist, Jones explained, to gain access to a Freya system, physically examine it, calculate the accuracy of the system, determine if significant modifications had been made and, if so, how effective they were. And finally, they needed to know if the Freya included anti-jamming technology.

"What we know already," Jones said, "is that the Freya has been improved to see out to a hundred and twenty-five miles. Coupled with its Wurzburg close-in system, its ability to identify targets is incredible, and deadly to us."

He stopped talking for a moment and rubbed his eyes, his stress and fatigue evident. "If we can't counter their system, there will be no successful invasion of Europe without an exorbitant cost in blood."

Dr. Jones let the thought sink in, and then went on, stressing that few people possessed Jack's technical expertise. Of those who did, he said, Jack was the only one capable of handling the physical demands. "The risk is that you know the secrets of the cavity magnetron, our most closely guarded radar secret."

As he spoke, he pulled from his desk drawer a small, round piece of metal. It was painted black, and around its rim, four cooling fins had been cut. Eight small holes surrounded a larger one in its center. They were linked by narrow passages to a center cavity.

Jones twirled the metal object absently in his hand. "This small device is what gives our radar incredible accuracy and lets us reduce our stations to a size that can fit in our bombers and fighters." He locked eyes with Jack. "But you know that."

Jack nodded, not sure where this conversation was going.

"If the Germans get this, they'll win the war. We will lose."

Jack stared, gravely. "I know, sir. Say what you have to say."

Jones sighed. "You're our top candidate for this mission, but the knowledge of this device cannot be allowed to fall into enemy hands. If you accept, you cannot be captured under any circumstances. Do you understand?"

Jack had gazed back somberly, certain that he understood the implication. After some moments, he nodded.

The mission consisted of joining an assault force on one of the most heavily fortified segments of the Atlantic Wall, a town called Pourville, near Dieppe on the French coast. He might have to scale the front of sheer cliffs, scurry across open uphill ground to the heavily defended radar facility, break in, examine the radar equipment, carry away critical parts, and return with them to the beach to be evacuated. "You'll probably be under fire the entire time."

Jack had left the meeting without immediately accepting the assignment, but while mulling that evening, he went to see a movie with his mother and his girlfriend. An old newsclip had shown a naval officer briefing volunteer boatmen of the dangers of sailing their small boats to rescue the British army from the German onslaught at Dunkirk near the beginning of the war. The officer had told his listeners that anyone who wished to back down could do so with no shame. None did.

The next morning, Jack had accepted the mission.

Lieutenant Colonel Merritt stood just outside the line of fire by a house that must have been beautiful up to the predawn hours of today, but now was marred with bullet holes and pockmarked from the strikes of larger caliber weapons. Its windows were shattered, its roof caved in, and even now, it offered only tentative cover.

Around the corner was the bridge, and across it the rest of his unit. The bridge was heavily defended, the sounds of battle as loud and angry as on this side of the river where the adjacent unit, the Cameron Highlanders of Canada, maneuvered around Merritt's main force to continue their mission farther inland to take out a *Luftwaffe* airfield at St. Aubin.

His own mission, to get Jack to the radar station, was stalled. Observing the open, grassy, steep slope inland of the cliffs on the other side of the bridge, he saw the facility within his regiment's reach—if they had just landed where they were supposed to. Meanwhile, in rapid succession, live soldiers were reduced to blood-soaked, horrifically sprawled corpses.

Jack viewed across the bridge the same green slope, noticing cows munching peacefully higher up toward the ridge away from the battle. There, silhouetted against the sky, the roofs of the blockhouses with protruding guns raked the town with deadly precision.

Some members of the South Saskatchewan Regiment had swum across the muddy stream and now maneuvered on the other side to join the rest of their force, but too few to increase the effectiveness of the comrades on that side. Others had attempted to sprint across the bridge. Already their bodies lined its surface, running with their blood, and still the pillboxes rained down fusillades of hot lead.

Then Jack witnessed a remarkable event.

During a break in firing, Merritt stepped out into the road. Helmet in hand, he turned, waved it, and called to a loosely organized section of his men, "Come on, boys. Come on, let's go get 'em."

Then he turned and sprinted toward the bridge. Behind him, his men hesitated. He ran back to them and urged them again with his helmet, calling to them and running back to the bridge. And they followed.

Bullets splattered all about, striking steel and concrete, splintering into shrapnel fragments, and flying within inches of Merritt. He reached the other side unscathed, and men who had taken shelter in doorways and behind fences joined and ran with him.

Some made it all the way across, some were wounded, some died, but those who reached the other side flung themselves to the ground to avoid sniper fire and to provide covering fire for those who followed.

Merritt shouted orders, waited for the next break in gunfire, and returned across the bridge. There, he organized another group, and waited.

Once more, shooting died down, and once more, Merritt stepped into the road, swinging his helmet by its strap, inspiring others to follow. "We must get ahead, lads," he yelled. "We need more men up front as quickly as possible. Who's coming with me?"

A sergeant called back, "We're all going with you."

"Then let's go!"

Jack turned to his bodyguards. "At the next lull, I'm going."

Two more times, Merritt returned across the bridge, and two more times brought more Canadian soldiers with him. And when those still alive and able were on the side required by their mission, they added to the covering fire of those already there.

On Merritt's third crossing, Captain Osten, Jack, and Jack's bodyguards ran with the lieutenant colonel. A bullet caught Osten's shoulder and knocked him over the bridge and into the muddy water. Jack leaned over the edge to see him.

Down below, the cold water shocked Osten into awareness even as his blood swirled in the muddy water. Struggling to shore, he clambered up the bank.

"Let's go," Merritt shouted down to him. "Up and at 'em."

When finally on the other side, Jack and his bodyguards raced through volleys of bullets to a storm ditch and dove in, grateful for the shelter, scant as it was. Looking uphill over its edge, they saw a pillbox, its guns aimed toward their position, and the gunners methodically adjusting their leaden barrages at them.

After his fourth run, Merritt maneuvered his soldiers along a road going east for roughly three hundred yards to the base of the hill where the pillboxes sat. Jack and his bodyguards slipped out of the storm ditch and followed.

Bullets flew, explosions erupted erratically, and smoke blotted the sky in patches. Wounded men screamed and called for help. Among the dead, some wore Canadian khaki, and some wore German gray. Scattered about them were rifles, smoke cannisters, unexploded grenades, spent cartridges, backpacks, rifles, Tommy guns...

The Canadians headed uphill, closing on the pillboxes. Jack and his bodyguards crossed through a farm where an English-speaking farmer called good luck wishes to them from a trench he had dug, away from the farmhouse, to shelter his wife and two daughters.

A German soldier crossed in front of the group near a pillbox. A Canadian rose to shoot him and promptly took a bullet to his forehead. A sergeant called for mortars and received a shouted response that the ammunition had run dry.

Jack heard a voice say, "They've got a blindside."

Merritt appeared out of the dust and smoke. He maneuvered to one side of a pillbox and, during a lull, walked up beside it, pulled the pin on a grenade, tossed it through the firing port, and dropped to the ground. When the explosion subsided, the gunners inside were still. Across the side of the hill, one by one, Merritt's troops silenced the three remaining pillboxes.

Jack watched, holding back any emotional response to the carnage he had so far lived through. His task lay ahead, and the tall, rectangular, spindly frame of the Freya radar antenna was in sight. Previously seen only in the half-light of dawn from the ocean, it turned in full view now, less than two hundred yards away.

"It's still turning," Jack called, peering up at the Freya. He lay in the grass that had looked so trimmed and smooth from below but now offered cover within its tall blades; and the rough ground underneath provided greater shelter in depressions and natural ditches.

The stench of gunpowder, smoke grenades, and explosives filled the air, but a breeze from the ocean occasionally blew it away, allowing the scent of wildflowers and freshly mown hay to pass over him. Overhead, fighters circled, spun, climbed, and dived, their exhaust trails tracing white designs against the blue sky. And the big German guns on the cliffs above Green Beach had gone silent.

From a few yards away, Captain Osten called back, "That's your target. Go get it if you really want it."

Jack laughed in spite of himself. "I'll do my best." Turning toward Osten, he noticed a pallor to the captain's skin color. The scarlet stain around his wound had grown. "How's your shoulder."

"Passable. Look, we don't have enough men to do a frontal assault. I've tried to get a naval bombardment on the facility, but so far, no dice. My radio antenna was shot up, so sending and receiving is sporadic at best. I'll keep trying to get you some field artillery, but that's about the best I can offer. We're hitting the bottom of the barrel for resources."

Jack nodded and glanced up at the radar antenna. He recalled what Dr. Jones had said about the cost in blood of an invasion to re-take Europe from the Nazis if the information he needed about the Freya was not obtained. And he reflected fleetingly on the consequences of his own capture and the danger of revealing the secret of the small black object Jones had toyed with in his hand, the cavity magnetron. *If the Germans get this, they'll win the war. We will lose.*

"It doesn't turn all the way around," he remarked to no one in particular.

"What?" Osten probed.

"The radar antenna. It doesn't go around three hundred and sixty degrees. It only scans out to sea and partway back over land on each side."

The captain gave him a questioning look.

"Our own radar antennas go all the way around now, but they haven't always. We developed a rotating electromagnetic coupling so that our antennas make complete circles without cables getting in the way. If the Germans' systems are going only partway around, they must be using coaxial cables to communicate. That means—"

Jack jumped up excitedly and was immediately pulled down by two of his bodyguards. "Are you daft," one growled. "That's a good way to get shot."

"Thanks," Jack muttered. He sat in the grass cross-legged, holding his head in his hands while he pondered.

"What are you thinking?" Osten demanded.

"Sir," Jack began slowly, still formulating his thoughts. "Until a few months ago, our radio listeners along the coast picked up transmissions from this and other stations routinely. They forwarded them to our codebreakers, and from those transmissions we learned a lot about German improvements."

Osten harrumphed. "I didn't know our codebreakers were that good." He laughed and then winced against the pain of his wound.

"They are, sir. Believe me. A few months ago, those communications suddenly ceased. Since before the war, messaging from our radar antennas and the operations rooms that control them and send information to the analysis rooms have always been done by telephone cable. The Germans did it by radio, relying on their codes.

"When their radios from the radar stations suddenly went dark, we thought that maybe they had gone to cable as well, but what we didn't think about was that perhaps the radar signal was also being passed by cable instead of by rotating electromagnetic coupling like we have."

The captain stared uncomprehendingly at Jack. "Look, Spook, I'm not understanding any of this. Can you or can you not complete your mission." He shrugged impatiently and winced again. "I've got a hole in my shoulder, I'm bleeding, and I'm almost out of men to lose. If you can't do what you came for, I'll start recalling Company A to the beach to be evacuated."

"I can, sir," Jack exclaimed, his excitement mounting. "I can do it alone, and without physically examining any of the equipment."

Osten's skepticism showed. "I'm not asking you to go up there alone—"

"But I should," Jack replied. "Look." He pointed to the antenna. "They're defending the front. They have a blind spot at the back where the cable runs from the antenna down to the control room. If two of us or more maneuver up there, we're likely to be seen. All I have to do is get up there and cut the cables. Once we do—"

"You *are* daft," Osten said, coughing. "What's that going to do? Knock them out for a few hours."

"Yes, but in that time, they'll be forced to go to their radios. Look." He pointed skyward where the air battle continued unabated. "Those chaps are still fighting, and we've just invaded Europe with the biggest force in this war. All of that is being communicated to Berlin. They need this radar, so they'll use their—"

"Radios," Osten breathed. He studied Jack. "Calm down, soldier. If you do this thing, you'll need your wits about you."

"Yes, sir. And when radio communications come up, our listeners will pick up the transmissions, our decoders will break the messages, and I am positive that we'll get the information I came for."

"And you think you can do that?" He glanced around soberly at the bodyguards still surrounding Jack. "You know we'll have to keep you in sight."

Jack followed his glance. "I know. And I have my cyanide right here in my shirt pocket." As he looked from face to face, he gasped as an awful realization dawned. Only six of the original eleven bodyguards remained.

His reception among the group had been tentative at first, even aloof. Jack supposed the reason for the distance was the requirement to shoot him if the time came. As the days passed, they had become more friendly. They had called him "Spook" and he had given them nicknames. If today was not a bonding experience, then none existed. *When, where did we lose them?*

Osten read Jack's expression. "This has been a costly raid," he said softly. "Do you still think you can do it? When you start up that hill, the Nazis will cut you down."

Jack grinned. "And if they don't, our chaps will. I don't suppose it matters who delivers the *coup de grâs*." He took a deep breath. "I just need two pairs of wire cutters."

Jack lay flat on the grass and peered through twelve-foot-high coils of rusting barbed wire. Inside the perimeter, single lines of wire had been stretched between wooden poles around an octagonal concrete structure. He saw only one entrance, and it faced him, but a wing of the blast wall screened it. Above the concrete, a massive grid of metal, the aerial, turned and alternated direction.

Inside the concrete building must be a control room with operators staring into screens, a bearing operator reading off ranges, a plotter relaying information via a dedicated mic feeding into a direct telephone line to a distant headquarters, and at least one person designated to keep records.

Jack crawled through the tall grass on his stomach, pulling with his forearms and pushing with the sides of his boots. When he reached the edge of the barbed-wire perimeter, he took a moment to surveil the compound again, looking for the communications wires that must be there.

And then he saw them, eight of them in two sets of four. They jutted out of the rear concrete wall through a square frame suspended twenty feet in the air by their connection to a three-legged mast. One of the legs was shorter than the other two because of the slope of the hill.

He would have to climb to cut the wires. His saving grace was that on this side of the compound, no defenses existed. Apparently, attacks had been anticipated to come only from the direction of Pourville or along a service road on the opposite side.

His heartbeat thumped in his ears and his hands sweated as he lifted the barbed wire and slid under, and then did the same at the inner band of wire strands. From far overhead, he heard the continued buzzing of fighter engines as the air battle raged on.

Then he was inside the inner perimeter and at the concrete wall. Taking a final look around and still seeing no sign of defenses on this side of the compound, he picked up his pace, staying low and scurrying to the mast. To cut the wires, he would have to climb.

Hurrying to the mast's short leg, Jack pulled the larger of the two sets of wire cutters from his pocket and started to climb. He dared not stop now, and so he lifted one leg, planted his foot, lifted the other, and ascended rapidly. Then he was above the concrete building's roof and exposed to any patrols in front of it.

He kept climbing, reached the top, and saw that clipping the first six wires would be easy. He reached out and clipped the first, then the second, and then the next four in succession, and they dropped to the ground. However, the seventh and eighth ones were too far to reach.

Suddenly, he heard the hiss of bullets breaking through the air next to his head and then the loud reports of multiple weapons, and then more poured in. He hoped they were from the German side and not from his bodyguards who might now be worried that he could not be rescued. The same deadly end could result regardless.

Stretching himself out as far as he could, he grabbed the next wire and let his feet go. Dangling from the cable, he reached up, cut the second of the remaining two wires, and held onto the last one as he squeezed the cutters.

The wires gave, and Jack dropped. As he hit the steep hillside, he rolled and rolled as gunshots resounded and bullets peppered around him.

49

Bletchley Park, England

Claire knocked on Commander Denniston's office door and then burst in without waiting for a response. "Sir, I think you should hear this."

He looked up, surprised at the intrusion, but gestured toward the chair in front of his desk. "What is it? You look distressed."

Claire nodded. "Definitely anxious, sir. There's something going on along the north coast of France at a place called Dieppe, and Berlin is going wild over it. Apparently, our commandos are raiding there as we speak, but I have the impression that we're not doing well." She paused, and her expression turned hopeful. "But I think we might have an opportunity."

Denniston steepled his hands under his chin and leaned back. "I'm aware of the raid. What makes you think that it's not going well? And what opportunity?"

"The tone of the Berlin messages. They're ebullient. They mention bodies strewn across the beaches at several landing points. Apparently, a German patrol boat crossed the path of a group of commando landing craft on the eastern flank pre-dawn, shot them up, and raised the alarm. The *Wehrmacht* suffered significant damage on the opposite flank where a gun battery was destroyed. But aside from that, the tide of the battle seems to have gone in Germany's favor.

"Reports have come in about fierce fighting at six landing sites, particularly at a town called Pourville. German high command was worried at first that a radar station there might be broken into and their technology exposed or stolen. They poured reinforcements into that location and are celebrating that no breach occurred, and our chaps are now attempting a hasty retreat."

"What's the opportunity?"

"I'm a little bewildered about it myself, but just a few minutes ago, one of our coastal listeners started relaying radio traffic to us that they'd intercepted from that radar station in Pourville. The thing is that the station had been silent for months. Now the volume of traffic is sudden and immense. If I had to guess, I'd say that Pourville converted from radio to telephonic communications when it went silent, and that during the raid, their lines were cut, so they've gone back to radio.

"That's why I came to see you immediately and was rude enough to all but break down your door. Sir, we should assume we're right about the radio transmissions and alert all of our coastal listeners within the reception area to home in on Pourville for at least the next few hours before the station goes dark again. We're doing that in our section that monitors Northern France. We could learn a lot about their current radar operations."

Denniston took to his feet rapidly. "I'll let them know

upstairs and get the order issued.”

50

August 24, 1942
London, England

"It's good to see you," Paul greeted Stephenson in the main foyer of Whitehall, "though I don't know why I'm here." They walked hurriedly through the halls to a conference room near Churchill's office in his capacity as war minister.

"I requested your presence," Stephenson said. "I'm supposed to attend a debriefing. There's no reason why you shouldn't be there as well. I wanted to catch up."

"May I ask what the debriefing is about?"

Stephenson glanced at him with a sardonic expression. "I suppose you know of the doings at Dieppe?"

"I've seen the newspaper reports depicting a resounding success."

"It was that," Stephenson replied, "but not for the reasons given. If you poll the Canadian public right now, you'll find them very angry and particularly upset with Lord Mountbatten. This debriefing is at the request of Lord Lovat through the commando chain and the chief of staff, General Brooke, to Churchill himself."

"Will the prime minister attend?" Paul asked, surprised.

"I suppose he could be called to something more pressing at the last minute, but as of a few minutes ago, he expected to attend." Stephenson shook his head. "I'm afraid the operation was more of a cockup than most people know about, and the Canadians took it in the shorts. At least one of their general officers will see no more command time during this war."

"That serious?"

Stephenson had no more time to respond before they reached the conference room and entered. A very somber atmosphere greeted them. Already present were Lord Mountbatten and General Brooke, both with neutral expressions and whispering between themselves, Lord Lovat showing suffused anger, and Dr. Jones looking bewildered. They greeted Stephenson and Paul with nods but otherwise said nothing.

Presently, Churchill entered and took his seat. Wasting no time, he rested his eyes directly on Lovat. "I understand you requested this meeting, and you were noisy enough about it that General Brooke recommended we conduct it. So please, Lord Lovat, tell me what's on your mind." His expression then softened. "I apologize. Your heroism is known, and you're here out of concern for the men in your command, many of whom gave up their lives in the operation at Dieppe. Say your piece."

Lovat stood slowly and took a deep breath. "Where to begin?" he said, looking across the faces of his audience. "I want to make sure that what happened at Operation Jubilee never happens again." He took another breath, and when he spoke again, his voice shook. "We sustained sixty-five percent casualties. Broken down, that's over fifteen hundred killed, more than twenty-four hundred wounded, and nearly two thousand captured. That's a casualty rate of more than 25%. Of the six thousand who went across the Channel, only about twenty-five hundred came safely home."

He took a deep breath to curb his exasperation.

"I assure you," Churchill broke in softly but firmly, "I know the numbers." He indicated General Brooke sitting next to him. "And so does my chief of staff and Lord Mountbatten."

"And what about that Canadian general who assured his soldiers that it would be 'a piece of cake?'" Despite himself, rage flashed across Lovat's face. "He committed reserves from behind a smoke screen where he could see nothing, and neither could the Royal Marines he sent in before they broke through to a pitiless wall of steel. Those men were chewed up and spat into the ocean like so much—" He caught himself and stopped speaking momentarily. Regaining control, he continued, "Why was there no pre-raid aerial attack on defensive positions? Where was the naval bombardment and support? Out of sixteen objectives, only two were met: subduing the guns at Orange Beach and doing something with that radar station at Green Beach."

"I heard that you were also put out of commission for a short time," Brooke interjected.

Lovat nodded. "A knock on the head was all. I don't know from what. My men took care of me. But I almost lost Captain Porteous as well. Our medic injected him with plasma. He's recovering nicely.

"As I was saying, the raid failed to destroy the airfield at Saint-Aubin; we didn't seize the guns on the left flank at Yellow Beach, although we did manage to get the first American killed in action in the European theater. A Ranger:

Second Lieutenant Edward Loustalot, I believe, from Franklin, Louisiana, in the USA."

Lovat's voice cracked, and he inhaled deeply. "Loustalot took over command and was wounded three times after our British Captain Richard Willis was killed. And of course, forty-seven others met their demise along with the lieutenant on Yellow Beach, but they did manage to subdue the gun battery there even if they were unable to destroy it. In doing so, they saved some lives at Dieppe. My point is that the failures of the raid were not for a lack of courage, tenacity, or perseverance from our men. From where I stand, they were let down by our leadership."

Lovat's last comment caused a stirring among the three principals, but they remained silent. Watching the drama, Paul tried to imagine the horror that Lovat and the forces at Dieppe had endured.

Lovat continued, a note of disgust in his voice. "I understand that in the case of the radar station at Green Beach, all that was achieved was cutting its communications temporarily." His exasperation grew. "That could have been a successful operation, but we achieved nothing other than getting a lot of our own soldiers killed."

At Lovat's last comment, Churchill, Brooke, and Mountbatten exchanged glances. "Your points are well taken," Mountbatten said. "The operation was my idea. I did the planning, and I take full responsi—"

"Let me say something," Brooke broke in. "I understand your frustration, but family lineage aside, don't forget yourself. You're a lieutenant colonel in the army addressing superior officers."

Greater anger crossed Lovat's face, but he locked his heels at attention and muttered, "Yes, sir."

"Relax, Colonel," Brooke said. "You asked to be heard,

and that's why we're here. You're owed as much explanation as we are at liberty to divulge. Every soldier is."

He took a breath. "Let me tell you that the points you made about aerial and main gun naval support were raised by Lord Mountbatten during planning. He was overridden, first by the RAF for fear of blowing surprise. We still do not enjoy air superiority over the French coast, and the plan did not include engaging in a large air battle.

"Secondly, the navy balked at providing heavy gun support for concern of losing more capital ships. God knows we've lost a good many in the Atlantic and in the Pacific, and our fleet has been greatly weakened. If Hitler resumes his assault on our island by air or sea, we'll need all those remaining ships.

"In retrospect, I quite agree that denying the air and sea support was a major shortcoming, although I'll stop short of calling it an error for the reasons I stated. I will also tell you that the Canadian general who committed those reserves will command nothing else for the duration of this war."

Looking unsure of whether to be mollified or not, Lovat relaxed his stance and searched the faces of the three most senior leaders. "May I know what the overall objective was?"

Once again, Churchill, Brooke, and Mountbatten exchanged glances. "You must have heard," Churchill said, peering at Lovat, "that an invasion of Europe is in the offing at some point." He shrugged. "That's no secret. The Germans expect it. Lord Mountbatten, with his raids in Norway, at Saint-Nazaire, Bruneval, and now at Dieppe, has convinced them that it will happen. Some Americans still push for it to happen now, and for that matter, so does Joseph Stalin. If nothing else, the failure of this raid, as you describe it, should convince them that we are not yet ready for the decisive invasion that must take place if we are to liberate Europe. But I believe you have mischaracterized the operation as a failure."

Taken aback, and looking uncertain, Lovat asked, "May I ask what succeeded?"

Mountbatten leaned forward. "I'd like to respond, if I may," he said, addressing Churchill and glancing at Brooke. When they both nodded, he continued, "Given what you saw of our preparedness for Jubilee and assuming an equal state of readiness, what do you suppose would have happened if we had invaded France across a broad front with an intent to stay? Do you think the slaughter of our men would have been greater or lesser?"

"Of course, they would have been greater."

"Exactly. The point is that we had lessons to learn, and there is no teacher. We learn by going in and doing. Out of this operation, we've learned about the design and construction of the Atlantic Wall and how it is defended. We learned that we have the wrong landing craft for the operation, and they must be redesigned. We learned that, as you pointed out, aerial and naval bombardment *must* be a major part of the initial offensive and must be sustained. We now have floating harbors being developed to be moored along secured beaches to bring in tanks, supply trucks, and more troops and equipment—we learned that seizing an existing harbor is much more difficult and costly because they are more heavily defended. We're also developing diversionary and intelligence operations tactics."

With a quick glance at Churchill and Brooke, he added, "The fact of those floating harbors is classified, so keep it under your hat. The reason is simple: the beaches where we'll park them will be lightly defended."

"So, the raid was a dress rehearsal?" Lovat broke in.

Mountbatten shook his head. "I wouldn't call it that

simply because a dress rehearsal assumes everything is ready. We are far from that point. However, we had to find out what we don't know. In that, I think we succeeded."

He took a deep breath. "I feel the losses, Colonel, I really do, and I know the prime minister and General Brooke do too. I've been to more funerals than I ever care to think about. I've been under fire and seen friends and men under my command die, and I was present offshore on a ship during Jubilee. I was ordered not to go ashore, or I would have been there." His eyes bored into Lovat. "All of that is to say that the men who died at Dieppe did not die in vain. For every one of them, ten will be saved when the big invasion comes about because of what we learned in Operation Jubilee."

Lovat stood silently, not moving for a few moments. No one else stirred. Finally, he lifted his head. "I suppose you're right. I hope you are." His face grew taut, his mouth quivered, and his eyes misted. He tried to say thank you, but his voice was lost in a hoarse whisper.

"Colonel Lovat," Brooke said. "You commanded one of the units that had unmitigated success—"

Lovat regained control and straightened. "I wouldn't call it that, sir. We just had more luck. We were almost on the beach before surprise was blown and we landed in the right spot. Those two factors were as much a part of our success as anything, and my men know it."

"Point taken and another lesson learned, Colonel," Brooke said. "I was going to say that there is another invasion brewing ahead of the one into Europe, and given your experience, I'd like to offer you a command of one of the units, if you'll take it."

"Of course, I'll do it," Lovat said without hesitation. "When and where?"

Brooke shook his head. "Not at present, but it's coming up soon."

"Sirs," Mountbatten broke in, speaking to Churchill and Brooke. He swung around to glance at Dr. Jones, who had sat quietly, listening. "We did have a notable success at Dieppe with far-reaching positive implications—"

Brooke shook his head. "We've divulged as much as we need to for one day." He turned to Lovat. "Have we satisfied you, at least for the moment."

"Yes, sir. I have to be able to tell my commandos and the rangers attached to my command that the sacrifice was not for nothing, and to be convincing, I must believe it."

"All right, then. Thank you for coming. You may go."

Thinking the meeting was ending, Paul started to rise as well, but Stephenson touched his arm and indicated for him to keep his seat. He noticed that Mountbatten motioned to Jones to also remain behind as Lovat made his exit.

"I want to know about Jack Nissenthall, our radar genius," Churchill said, addressing Jones after the door had closed. "Did you get as much information as you needed, and did he make it back safely?"

"Yes, on both counts," Jones replied. "And more. As soon as Jack cut those wires, our coastal listeners' radios sparked with huge volumes of German communications coming from the Pourville station. Our people recorded it all and sent it off to be decoded. We discerned immediately that the Germans do not have a jamming technology in use, nor do they have a backup communications system beyond the radio when the telephones go down. We've been able to determine the improvements made to the radar itself, and we're developing countermeasures. If we keep our own jamming technology under wraps until the ultimate invasion into France, I think we'll have a good chance of getting our forces close to shore before they're detected. Our bombing flights over France and Germany will also enjoy a tremendous advantage."

"That's good to hear," Churchill broke in. "And what of our chap, Jack. Will he be able to continue his job in radar?"

Jones chuckled. "I don't think anything will keep him down, sir. He came to see me two days after the operation. He'd had to prove his identity when he came ashore. Fortunately, one of his bodyguards made it back with him and still had his own ID. The security forces let him vouch for Jack. At the time, Jack was wearing an oversized Royal Marine uniform, but when asked, he told the security forces that he was a flight sergeant in the RAF, and of course, the bodyguard knew him only as Private Jack with no name."

"Why was he wearing a Royal Marine uniform?"

Jones laughed again. "It's quite a story. I'll give you the highlights." He related how Jack had carried out his mission.

When he had finished, Churchill said, "He rode the last wire to the ground?"

"I'm not sure on that point. I think he just held onto it as he fell. Fortunately, it was only fifteen feet, and on a slope, so he rolled, and kept rolling until he was out of the line of fire. Then he ran back to his bodyguards."

"How did he get to the beach and across the Channel?"

"He fought his way out. He took a rifle from a dead soldier, and became a combatant, and from what I can tell, he assumed a leadership role, which the others in his group acceded to with no argument. In a house just before he got to the shore, he and one of his bodyguards stripped down to their skivvies, ran to the water, and swam out into the ocean where they were picked up by a landing craft. It was promptly hit by enemy fire and sunk, so he had to look for another. Fortunately, he made it back, joking about whether his cyanide pill had been deactivated by the sea water and that his bodyguard's pistol had been rendered useless because it had rusted."

Listening to the exchange, Mountbatten asked, "How many bodyguards did he have?"

Jones' face turned somber. "He started with eleven, sir. One made it back."

The room descended into silence. Churchill broke it. "Thank you for coming, Dr. Jones. I'm glad things worked out." He gestured toward Stephenson and Paul. "I have business still to do with these two gentlemen, so we'll stay here, and you may go."

As Jones made his way out of the room, Mountbatten remarked, "Those men on the raids were incredible. One officer, Lieutenant Colonel Merritt, crossed a bridge four times under fire. His was the unit in charge of Jack's radar mission. His troops took out four pillboxes, and when it was over and he had put his remaining soldiers on landing craft to evacuate, he stayed behind to set up a rear guard. He was last seen picking up Sten guns for the purpose.

"He was wounded three times before it was all over, and he was captured. We got word through the Red Cross that he's receiving competent medical care."

"Hmph," Brooke groused. "Let's hope so. There was one of our chaplains too, Weir Foote. He went in with our chaps and was working with the wounded on the beach, helping the ones who could be evacuated get on the landing craft. When the last one was full and leaving, he refused to go with them, insisting that his place was with those still needing care and stranded on the beach." Brooke sniffed. "Magnificent fellow, and now in a POW camp."

"Let's be sure he and this Colonel Merritt are properly

recognized," Churchill said. Then he indicated Stephenson and Paul. "Have you met these gentlemen? Bill Stephenson and Major Paul Littlefield."

At that, Mountbatten studied Paul's face. "Aha, I know of you," he said. "A young WAAF worked in my control room. Flight Officer Ryan Northbridge. As I recall, she was quite keen on you." While the others enjoyed the levity, Paul turned crimson. "She is quite pretty," Mountbatten added. "And capable. I was rather upset when she transferred to ferry airplanes, though that is also a critical function."

"Thank you, sir," Paul replied. "I'm fortunate."

"Shall we get back to business?" Churchill said, turning to Brooke. "I mentioned that I want a personal liaison between General Eisenhower and me when he goes to set up his headquarters in Gibraltar for Operation Overlord, and this young major has shown himself to be quite adept in similar roles. Please attach him to Eisenhower's staff immediately. I want him to stay fully abreast of the process and report to me regularly."

Stunned, Paul could only stutter, "Sir, are you sure? I'm flattered, but—"

"Don't waste your modesty here," Churchill said gruffly. "Just get on with the job." He put his hands flat on the table to support rising to his feet and then stopped. "One other thing I should mention if you haven't heard the news. Hitler's begun his assault on Stalingrad." He started rising again, and once more paused. "Meanwhile, the Americans have engaged in land battle on Guadalcanal. It's a bloody mess. But on a good note, the M4 Sherman tanks they promised are on their way to Egypt."

51

September 7, 1942
Guadalcanal, Solomon Islands

Lieutenant Colonel "Red Mike" Edson, United States Marine Corps, studied the ground around him for defensibility from atop Hill 123 while in deep discussion with six other men near the center of a ridgeline on the Island of Guadalcanal. The crest stretched north roughly five hundred yards to the southern edge of Henderson Field and south an equal distance. The airstrip, located inland of Lunga Point on the island's north coast, was named for the first Marine-aviator killed during the Battle of Midway.

From his vantage, the airfield was in full view beyond lush foliage. Farther out, visible as a blue sliver in a faraway mist, was a narrow stretch of the Pacific between the Solomons that had become known as the "Slot." Against the far horizon beyond, the low silhouette of the Florida Islands rose up from the ocean, and just in front of them, the much smaller Tulagi.

This group of islands belonging to the Solomons were a

thousand miles northeast of Australia's northern coast and had been a British protectorate since 1893 with its capital at Tulagi. The archipelago had abounded with headhunters and cannibals before the work of missionaries and other civilizing influences had turned them into peaceful oases with all the beauty and serenity of the tropics.

Then, the Land of the Rising Sun began its imperial drive.

The Slot, running east and west for miles through the archipelago, had gained its moniker from attempts by the Japanese navy to supply, reinforce, and expand its holdings among the islands and the determined opposition by force of the Allies. The contests had culminated in multiple naval battles, sunken ships, and drowned sailors on both sides. With their commanding positions along the Slot, both Guadalcanal and Tulagi provided strategic positioning among the Solomons to whichever side controlled them.

The grassy ground cloaking the coral crest where Edson now stood, officially named "Lunga Ridge," had been dubbed "Edson's Ridge" by his command. Surrounded by thick, seemingly impenetrable jungle, it ran directly south from and perpendicular to the Henderson Field runway and spread east and west a short distance at the south end. Along its eleven-hundred-yard-long spine, four distinct spurs jutted out on either side of the crest and protruded through the morass of thick vegetation. Aerial photographs of the geological formation showed it to look like a centipede. If left undefended, it offered ease of movement to the airfield along its crest. Hence, it was a natural avenue of approach for enemy forces attempting an assault from the south.

A month earlier as part of Operation Shoestring, the 1st Marine Division, under Major General Alexander Vandegrift, took Guadalcanal from the Japanese with minimal contact. He had been warned that an airfield was under construction on the island.

If allowed to become operational, the airfield could operate as a base to cut vital communications and supply lines between the United States, Australia, and New Zealand, the precise result that Operation Shoestring was designed to prevent.

On the same day that Vandegrift moved onto Guadalcanal, Edson and his Marine Raiders, a new special ops unit trained along the lines of British commandos, conducted an amphibious assault on Tulagi. Taken by surprise, the Japanese had attempted to strike back immediately with a massive bombing raid from their airbase on Bougainville, an island to the west at the head of the Slot. It failed.

Vandegrift's Marines came ashore at Guadalcanal, their main resistance thrust on them by the thick jungle terrain, suffocating heat, and confusion among inexperienced Americans offloading men and supplies. Nevertheless, they quickly occupied the airfield, encountering light enemy resistance, and captured surprised construction workers farther inland before establishing a position eight thousand yards wide and fifteen hundred deep.

Two and a half miles across the waters of the Slot at Tulagi, Edson's Raiders found very different circumstances. Along with 1st Battalion, 2nd Marine Regiment; 2nd Battalion, 5th Marine Regiment; and 1st Parachute Battalion, they slogged through three hard days of combat before routing a determined veteran Japanese unit while encountering a new level of ferocity beyond their comprehension: wounded but unvanquished enemy soldiers waited until Marine medics came to render aid. The Japanese wounded released hand grenades to blow themselves up with their enemies.

During this battle, Edson, already revered by his command as a competent leader who cared for the Marines in his charge, further established his reputation as a fierce warrior, leading from the thickest part of battle, contemptuous of enemy fire, unremitting, relentless, and prescient in guessing Japanese moves.

The incursions onto both islands constituted the first American ground warfare in the Pacific. Shortly after securing Tulagi, more Marines assaulted and secured the neighboring islands, Tanambogo and Gavutu. Work then began to transform the anchorage at Gavutu into a giant naval base and refueling station and Tulagi's harbor into a temporary repair center for damaged vessels.

After Tulagi, Gavutu, and Tanambogo were firmly in American hands, the Marines who had wrested the islands away from the Japanese were transferred to Guadalcanal to help defend Henderson Field. Because of its strategic position, no doubt existed that Japan would attack again with all ferocity to recapture it.

The information about the airfield that had compelled the Marine assaults had come from Allied intelligence, Section C, also known as "coastwatchers." The unit had been formed by the Australian army twenty years earlier over concern for Japan's expansive ambitions. Initially, it started with plantation owners whose properties lay in strategic areas of northern Australia and who reported sightings of Japanese movements to the Australian army as they occurred. As Japan began its war of conquest, Section C expanded with four hundred additional coastwatchers recruited from among Australia's and New Zealand's military servicemen, and Pacific Islanders.

The Japanese bombing run on Guadalcanal had failed because Paul Mason, a coastwatcher on Bougainville, observed the bombers take off from a well-hidden position and radioed a warning. With two hours to prepare, Allied forces were ready and turned back the Japanese aircraft.

However, shortly after midnight two nights later, on August 9, a Japanese naval task force sailed into the Slot. In short order, it sank four Allied cruisers. Vandegrift was sure that the naval battle had been a prelude to a massive Japanese assault to re-take Guadalcanal and Henderson Field.

Admiral Fletcher, whose task force had transported the Marine amphibious assault force with its supplies and equipment to Guadalcanal and Tulagi, and in light of the destruction to his ships in the Slot, withdrew the remainder of his group, leaving twelve thousand Marines on the beach in Guadalcanal with only half of their provisions and no naval gunnery support.

Before Pearl Harbor, Australia had sent troops to defend its motherland, Great Britain. Now, with furious combat on its doorstep, it had to look to its own defense. That such was the case had become clear when, on January 23, the British naval base at Rabaul had fallen. Japan was rapidly building it into a major offensive platform for further conquest.

Within the next six weeks, aerial photos showed that the Japanese had established additional outposts among the islands of New Guinea north of Australia and west-northwest of the Solomons. Then on May 3, they had taken Tulagi, and three days later, they seized the last American stronghold, Corregidor.

Amidst those events, the coastwatchers had melded into the jungles of the South Pacific islands with radios and self-defense weapons but minimal support, and reported on the doings of Japanese forces. Though their jobs were grueling and dangerous, Vandegrift and Edson considered their intel reports to be as good as radar sightings.

Japan's attempt to re-take Tulagi had been long and fierce, with much blood spilled on each side. But three weeks later, Edson, his Marine Raiders, and the other assault elements had secured it, turned it over to an Allied relief force, and joined Vandegrift and the 1st Marine Division to reinforce and fortify defenses at Henderson Field. Five days earlier, the Japanese had attacked in force on the north coast of Guadalcanal east of Point Lunga to re-take the airfield.

Vandegrift had deployed his forces on the perimeter of this strategically crucial position and fought off the Japanese. But the battle had left the beach strewn with dead Americans and Japanese, their bodies lying in blood-soaked sand within inches or atop of each other in horrific repose, testifying to their last actions with faces frozen in expressions of determination, resignation, pain, fear, or emptiness.

The general was Edson's commander and one of the men in deep consultation with him on the ridge. Vandegrift was tall and broad-shouldered with a bald head and a no-nonsense demeanor. His courage and leadership during a three-day Japanese assault to re-take Henderson Field had won the hearts of his men, who whispered among themselves that he should be awarded a Congressional Medal of Honor.

Vandegrift expected further Japanese assaults with the same objective, as did the other men conferring on Edson's Ridge. Their discussion revolved around how best to defend against it.

"They'll come through here," Edson stated matter-of-factly. Ordinarily a man with a bulldog countenance, the privations of battle had thinned his face. Like Vandegrift, he was bald. When the idea had surfaced about training a special section of Marines for deep penetration into enemy territory *a la* commandos, the general had selected Edson to recruit, train, and lead it. At Tulagi, Edson and his Raiders had proven their worth.

"I'm not convinced," Vandegrift replied. "Coming from the sea is a much easier operation, and they'll soften us up with naval and aerial bombardment. They underestimated our strength before, but they have better information now."

"They'll expect us to be resupplied and reinforced, sir," the general's operations officer, Colonel Gerald Thomas, interjected. "I have to agree with Edson. We took them by surprise when we arrived; we beat the tar out of them at Tulagi, Tanambogo, and Gavutu; and you embarrassed them in their assault here a few days ago. If they had any doubts about American resolve or fighting ability, that's been answered. Their best bet now is an attack, and that's from the south, through the jungle, and along this ridge. They'll figure that, in addition to surprise, they'll occupy the high ground, and they can still be supported from the sea."

Vandegrift rubbed his chin. "I'm not convinced. Edson's raid on Japanese positions near Tassimboko yesterday brought back lots of documents. Our Japanese language man analyzed them. He agrees that the Japs are staging for a major attack." He shifted his eyes to two other men in the group. "Do either of you have insights?"

Martin Clemens spoke first. He was a big man with a good-natured smile and a high forehead, but many weeks of hiding out and spying on the Japanese had reduced his weight so that he now appeared gaunt. Born and educated in Britain, he had come to the Solomons as a district officer of the protectorate government. The Japanese had begun their foray into these islands as he was returning from leave.

At the time, residents who could were evacuating, and native islanders headed to the bush, out of the way of Japanese soldiers. Clemens had volunteered to stay on Guadalcanal as a coastwatcher, hiding out in the island's many caves and surviving on rations gleaned from the jungle or provided by native islanders.

With him was Jacob Vouza from Tassimboko, a village a few miles east along the coast from Point Lunga and Henderson Field. Tall, dark-skinned, with full, wiry hair, he had been the chief constable in the village, carrying the rank of sergeant major. Educated at the South Seas Evangelical Mission School, he had joined the Solomon Islands Protectorate Armed Constabulary upon graduation. When he retired after twenty-five years, which coincided with Japanese incursions, he had joined Clemens, and the two of them had become the main organizers and trainers of the coastwatcher teams on Guadalcanal. The enemy had become aware of their presence and capabilities and had searched for them. No doubt if they were caught, their lives were forfeit, and probably painfully so.

"We're hearing about lots of Japanese near Jacob's hometown. They started the construction on the airfield in early July, so they had plenty of time to reconnoiter the island for overland routes, and they're thorough enough to do just that." He looked at Vouza. "Jacob?"

Vouza nodded. "We've set listening posts along the major trails and the minor ones that could be useful. If they come this way, we'll be able to give early warning."

"Sir," Colonel Thomas cut in, "even with early warning, we won't have time to react if we're not already in place up here. This terrain is defensible to the force that occupies it. That had better be us, or we'll be handing off a critical advantage."

Vandegrift moved his eyes to take in each man. When he glanced at the sixth one, he chuckled. "What about you, Commander Littlefield? Do you have any insights?"

Josh grinned slightly. "No, sir. I'm here for liaison. Or at least that's why I *was* here until the fleet went off and left me. Jungle warfare is new to me. I can't fathom taking an overland route when the ocean is right there. But then, I'm not a Marine."

Vandegrift laughed, apparently welcoming the light humor. "Yep, you're stuck with us, and by the time this is all over, you'll either be a qualified infantryman or—" He paused to choose his words and muttered grimly, "Something worse."

"Sir, I have a suggestion," Edson cut in, grinning. "My men are tuckered out after weeks of combat. What about if you allow us to do some rest and recuperation up here? We can stay in commo with these coastwatchers." He indicated Clemens and Vouza. "They'll let us know if they hear anything—you too. If the Japs attack here, we'll be ready for them, or if they assault the beach, we can hurry to reinforce. It's a lot easier to reinforce downhill than uphill."

"I concur," Thomas said. "That allows flexibility and keeps our rear covered."

Vandegrift took a deep breath. "All right. You've convinced me, at least on the need for flexibility. We're supposed to be resupplied and reinforced tomorrow, so we should be talking about holding them off only one night before we see relief." His eyebrows creased. "Then again..." He let the thought trail off, unspoken.

Turning to Edson, he said, "I'll bring my headquarters up here and set up behind yours. I'm tired of the constant bombing. It's a nuisance, and if you're wrong about the direction of attack, we won't be overrun; but if you're right, we can shift more easily." He turned to Josh once again with a half-smile. "You're somewhat of a free agent. Pick your poison—my headquarters or Edson's."

Before Josh could respond, Edson spoke up again. "I could use him, if you don't mind, sir. I'm not up to full strength. I need another officer in my operations center." He glanced at Josh. "You can handle that, can't you. I heard you ran some of the operations at Midway. We're moving men and equipment around on land like you run ships and aircraft around at sea. We track it all on maps."

"I'll give it my best shot, if the general is fine with it."

"He's all yours," Vandegrift told Edson.

52

September 10, 1942

Josh slogged up to Hill 123, the tallest hilltop on Edson Ridge, to look around. In the distance, the ocean glimmered and, closer in, the aircraft at Henderson Field reflected the morning sunlight. Between him and the airstrip, a knoll stood astride the main approach to the airfield. Several hundred yards behind him to the south, Hill 80 protruded up through thick jungle.

Josh had accompanied the combined units of the Marine Raiders and the 1st Parachute Battalion, or "Chutes," as they snaked their way through the jungle to Edson's Ridge. "There's too much bombing and shelling close to the beach," the Marine Raiders' commander explained as they set out on their uphill march amidst much moaning and groaning, at yet another set of hot jungles to squirm and scrape through, and more hills to climb. "We're moving to a quiet spot."

Tromping with them through the narrow passages amid occasional subdued clanking of equipment and low-voiced whispers and commands, Josh wondered how a unit so large could move so quietly. Contrasted to the din of ocean wind and spray, the roar of engines, the ring of metallic tools striking together, and the constant, low vibration of a ship's motor, aside from insect sounds and bird calls in the distance, he thought the jungle to be unimaginably quiet.

From conversations with the men, he sensed that despite their griping and fatigue after a month of combat, each knew to a man that they must hold this position on Edson's Ridge, or the battle for Guadalcanal was lost. He wondered whether they understood how pivotal the larger strategic threat would be from losing this battle: Japan's expansion into the South Pacific would go unchecked.

He watched as the Raiders, on reaching the ridge and without further instruction, established a line beginning at Hill 80 and stretching toward the Lunga River. The Chutes set up on the left flank. The combination created a perimeter nine hundred yards long. Almost as soon as they reached their positions, individual Marines and Chutes pulled out machetes and entrenching tools and started digging foxholes. The sun had traveled high in the sky, insects buzzed in profusion, but still they worked.

"Yeah, this is real peaceful, Colonel," one Marine called with a jocular tone as Edson and Josh passed by. "Real restful, too."

Edson laughed. "Make that foxhole deep enough so's all I can see is the tippy-top of your helmet."

"This is the line we have to hold," he told Josh. "If the Japs break through here, our guys will be scattered in the jungle, not knowing who's friend and who's foe in that foliage, with everyone ducking for cover." He puffed up his cheeks and blew out the air. "We could wind up with a lot of casualties from friendly fire, and a bunch of us could be trying to survive on coconuts."

He pointed out the topographic features as he explained his defensive plan. "We put the Chutes here to protect our flank. If I'd put the Raiders up here alone, we'd have no protection on that side, and if we'd dug in on the front slope, the Japs would have probed until they found a weakness in the line."

He pointed toward the airfield. "I've put my reserves, 2nd Battalion, 5th Marines, down there between Henderson and the foot of the ridge behind that knoll. Our forward observers have already registered targets with the howitzer crews, and our 1st Pioneer and 1st Amphibious Tractor battalions are working hard on defensive lines to the west."

Edson watched a line of Marines trundle by, members of Vandegrift's headquarters on their way to set up the general's command post. "I'm not real crazy about that idea," he said. "The boss still thinks the main attack will come on the beach. I don't." He shrugged. "But he's the big gorilla and gets to sit wherever he wants."

Josh took his turn at watch in the operations dugout, a small space hacked into the side of the hill with a flap to cover the entrance. On schedule, he tried to rest on the hard ground in a secluded corner, but sleep would not come. His mind kept flitting between his current circumstance and his last insertion into combat at Midway. How different that had been.

His last memory of that event was a series of shockwaves that reverberated through the ocean's surface as his shot-up Dauntless settled into the water. His next memory was waking up aboard the *Enterprise* and seeing a blurry face leaning over him. As his vision slowly cleared, the face became no more familiar, but it had grinned down at him.

"Radioman Ben Crenshaw. Pleased to meet ya," the man had enthused, grasping his hand. "I thought I should introduce myself formally; and it's a good thing I didn't take you up on that first name BS cuz it looks like we might both survive this war a tad longer."

Josh grunted and smiled weakly. "I hadn't seen your face—"

"Yep. I was already in the plane when you crawled in, but we had our backs to each other. Since we're combat buddies now, I thought we should get acquainted."

Josh tried to turn his head and groaned as pain shot through his neck, and a brace held it still. "How did I get here? I thought I was done for."

Another face had appeared over him and a hand clapped Ben's shoulder. "This man saved your life," a voice boomed. "He managed to wriggle free and got the life raft out of the back before the plane started sinking. You were still strapped in as it was going down, and he dove in after you and dragged you out. A Catalina picked you both up and brought you in." While the man spoke, he took a stethoscope looped around his neck and put the two listening beads in his ears. "Be quiet a moment while I check your heart." When he had finished, he said, "You'll be fine. You're pretty bruised up from the rough landing and probably from the shockwave of the bombs, but nothing's broken and no internal damage. You'll need to rest up a while."

As the medic continued to check Josh's vitals, the sense of how close Josh's life had come to ending gripped him. He shifted his eyes, trying to see past the medic, but could not.

Then he realized that he still grasped Ben's hand. He clasped it more firmly.

"Thanks, buddy," he murmured.

Josh had rested, but the medical people decided that he should not fly for a while until his body was fully functional. A replacement already filled his duties in the operations center, so he was transferred to Admiral Fletcher's task force to liaise with General Vandegrift for the assault into the Solomons.

Josh smiled at the irony. Then, someone stirred in another part of the dugout, bringing him back to the present atop Edson's Ridge on Guadalcanal. Giving up any notion of sleep, he clambered to his feet and stepped through the flap into the cool pre-dawn air. He found the quiet almost incomprehensible. Being within a perimeter watched by eight hundred and forty warriors, alert yet silent, with weapons ready in the darkness of night, was an experience he had never imagined. From the jungle below, the sounds of daytime animals beginning to stir ruptured the quiet, but at a distance.

He stepped back inside the operations dugout. The inside was dark, with dim, hooded lights over maps and charts.

The canvas swished back, and Edson entered. "G'morning. Are we ready to do this thing?" he asked no one in particular. "If it happens, it'll be soon."

"Hoorah," someone exclaimed, but Josh could not see who.

"Is that patrol out?"

The operations officer approached. "Yes, sir, and we're tracking. It should be in the assembly area now and will cross the perimeter at first light."

Platoon Sergeant Joe Buntin from A Company led the twenty-five-man patrol into the jungle along the Lunga River on a probing mission to detect if the enemy was approaching from the south toward Lunga Point and the airfield. Treading softly, his Raiders made their way in radio silence, using hand and arm signals to communicate as they progressed.

Early morning turned to mid-morning, and the chill dissipated until, by noon, blazing heat and high humidity had set in. Then, with the sun high in the sky, they heard men speaking. In Japanese.

Suddenly, the air hissed around them followed by the loud reports of automatic weapons. Small puffs of dirt burst into the air, and all around were sounds the Marines had come to know too well: bullets striking trees, limbs, bushes. The patrol dropped to the ground, maneuvered on their bellies to firing positions, and returned fire.

The gunfire subsided. The infantrymen waited.

Then they heard another, more terrifying noise: the growl of twin-engine Mitsubishi G4M Betty Bombers, and the first bombs falling. Amid thunderous explosions, the munitions continued to drop in a line as the bombers headed toward the ridge. Sergeant Buntin felt the concussive power of a bomb as it lifted him into the air along with a crewman on the automatic rifle team and dropped him yards away.

The bombers finished their run, and the Japanese ground soldiers must have expended their first load of ammunition, resulting in a lull while they reloaded. Bruised and battered but resilient, Buntin used the pause to lead his men back to the ridge.

When the bombs hit, Josh started outside to look. Someone from behind tripped him and shoved him to the ground. "Are you trying to get killed?"

Beyond the canvas flap, munitions exploded, automatic weapons and small arms fired, the tranquility of the morning was replaced by the noises of raw violence.

When it subsided, Josh stepped through the flap to a scene of horror: debris had been thrown about in such a short time, some of it recognizable, some not. Shredded canvas that had been the sides of tents and lean-tos were strewn about. Guns, parts of guns, machine gun links, kitchenware, canteens, and other sundry items had been tossed in impossible places. Vegetation had been thrown up from the jungle in large and small chunks and lay scattered about.

Already, Marines, Raiders, and Chutes scurried to adjust to the damage before the next attack. Men hurried by toting empty stretchers, and as Josh watched, they crouched beside wounded comrades. Most of those writhed in pain, but two lay still, and as their stretchers were lifted into the air, their faces had been covered with blankets. Stepping inside the operations dugout, Josh saw the casualty count being posted: ten wounded and two dead.

As the day wore on, the men repaired what they could, absorbed their losses with stoic faces, and prepared for the next phase of their defense. Afternoon turned to evening, and a light mist spread over the ridge as darkness descended.

Then, late at night, offshore Japanese destroyers commenced a bombardment along the ridge, but the gunners misaimed, and the missiles screamed by overhead, striking in the jungle beyond the perimeter. When the shelling ended twenty minutes later, flares shot skyward in front of their positions. The Japanese were about to assault.

They struck first by a lagoon at the south end of the ridgeline in front of Company C. Jabbering and shouting to draw fire and thus discover Marine positions, they were thwarted by veterans who had already beaten their tactics on Tulagi.

Nevertheless, Japanese probes found gaps between the lines of two platoons on the left flank and breached them. Forced to withdraw, the two units attempted to link up with Company B on Hill 80.

A Marine machine gun fired steadily, its tracers lighting up the sky, but the tenacious Japanese attacked relentlessly until the position was overrun and the gun silenced. Then, enemy soldiers attempted to swim the Lunga to envelop Company C's right flank. Its commander ordered what was left of his company to fall back and close up the perimeter.

Some Raiders did not receive the order to withdraw and waited until Japanese soldiers came within feet of their positions and blazed away with .30-cal. fire. Then they tossed all of their grenades in front of the remaining enemy in their sector to halt the advance.

Josh watched the battle on the map inside the dugout as reports poured in, and when he stepped out occasionally, screams of Marines under torture just beyond the defensive line filled the night. The horror mixed with gunfire and explosions caused rage to well inside, and for the first time he knew viscerally the meaning of hatred.

As daylight approached, the Japanese were beaten back and retreated. Touring the battlefield with Edson, Josh viewed their overrun positions with intense disgust. The

Japanese had hacked Raider captives with bayonets and swords.

American fighter aircraft joined the battle as soon as daylight filtered over the ridgeline. Squadrons of Curtiss P-40 Warhawks and Grumman F4F Wildcats screamed over Japanese positions, strafing them while Marine howitzers and mortars rained down volleys of steel that fragmented into shrapnel and sliced through anything in their path.

Word reached Edson from Vandegrift's Japanese language analyst that enemy shortwave communications with its higher headquarters at Rabaul had been cut, and interceptions of frantic radio transmissions at brigade level indicated that subordinate units were scattered and disorganized. They had not expected the ridge to be so heavily defended. Now, they intended to consolidate their battalions and rush Henderson Field.

Edson took the intelligence reports and prepared to counterattack Company C's former positions and re-take them. Gathering his company commanders at his command post, and while eating cold hash from a can, he told them, "They were testing. They'll be back. Improve your positions. Double up the wire lines. Get the men a hot meal. Throughout the day, dig, wire up tight, get some sleep. We'll all need it."

At dusk, the enemy struck again. Moving under cover of the jungle and dwindling daylight, they attacked, pushing through B Company's positions on the open ground of the ridgeline. Despite depleted strength resulting from battle losses and illness, and ignoring bone-depth fatigue, the company's remaining men joined with Company C and shored up the defense before the enemy realized and exploited the opening it had created.

Monitoring the ebb and flow of battle at the operations

dugout, Josh heard the flap at the entrance pull back, and a moment later, Edson was at his shoulder, peering at the map. "Is that up to date?"

"Yes, sir," Josh replied. "As accurate as we can make it."

"I have a dilemma. Should I shift my reserve to bolster Companies B and C? If I do that, I'll weaken my perimeter on the other side."

At that moment, radio reports from the Chute companies started pouring in. The Japanese had started a new attack at the center and were breaching the defensive line between the Chutes' Bravo and Charlie companies. Their commander ordered them to regroup on Hill 123, but that left Raiders' Company B isolated. Sizing up the situation, Edson called in artillery for close targeting in front of the Marines to provide them a protective umbrella.

Soon reports included instances of Japanese soldiers diving into Marine foxholes seeking relief from flying shrapnel delivered by the artillery. They were seized and bodily tossed back into the barrage.

At the height of battle, someone in Raiders' Company C area screamed, "Gas attack!"

Men scrambled out of their positions and ran for the rear. But Major Ken Bailey, their commanding officer, stopped them. "It's a trick," he yelled. "There's no gas!" The Marines stopped, scurried back to their positions, and resumed the fight.

"Close this place down," Edson ordered Josh. "We're moving down the hill."

As units converged on the knoll just south of the airfield and set up a hasty perimeter, Josh watched Edson with awe. The lieutenant colonel seemed to be everywhere at once, moving to the thick of battle, taking two bullets in his chest, and when his command was about to be overrun, he stood erect on the knoll and directed the battle with an innate sense of the high stakes and what needed to be done.

Henderson Field was less than a half mile away.

Then, when all seemed lost, Edson called out, "Raiders, parachuters, engineers, artillerymen, I don't give a damn who you are. You're all Marines. Come up on this hill and fight!'"

The beleaguered Company B finally reached the knoll and joined on a new U-shaped defensive line, and the field artillery kept up a constant barrage, landing their lethal fire within two hundred yards of the combined units' forward line.

Two more hours of intermittent night combat continued, and then red flares shot high in the night sky, announcing the start of another frontal assault. Suddenly, thousands of screaming voices, as if ascended from hell, cut through the eerie light of the flares. "Banzai!"

Josh heard the bloodcurdling battle cries. He had taken an M1 rifle equipped with a bayonet from a dead Marine, and now, he too crouched on the perimeter as the hordes tramped toward them. Their screams rent the night, but they were not yet visible.

Then the Japs ran across the open ground under the waning light of the flares. Every weapon inside the Allied perimeter opened up, and as enemy fell, many more appeared and kept coming, with their hair-raising war cries.

And then they were at the perimeter, in hand-to-hand combat, and Josh found himself slashing and slicing, and turning to slash and slice some more. Men bumped against him and dropped, but whether they were friend or foe, he never knew.

A Japanese soldier with wide, wild eyes and a fierce grin leaped high in the air at him. Josh shoved the bayonet high, impaling the soldier on it. The light went out of the Jap's eyes.

Japanese mortars targeted both sides of the ridge, cutting communication lines to the division command post. A Marine forward observer raced to the 11th Marines fire direction center with instructions to "drop five and walk it back and forth across the ridge."

The guns of the 5th Battalion, 11th Marines complied, sending huge numbers of rounds flying through the night, alternating their direction of fire in a crisscross pattern in front of the perimeter on the knoll, delivering a cloud of flying shrapnel against enemy soldiers entering the maelstrom.

And then, it was over. As dawn approached, the Japanese fell back. Edson ordered the Chutes' Baker and Charlie companies to advance against them, mopping up rear-guard positions, stragglers, and wounded. The Allied soldiers maneuvered forward gingerly over bloodstained ground with corpses lying all about. They used automatic weapons and tossed grenades ahead of them when encountering resistance. Soon, they returned to their positions on the perimeter.

Edson's command post was now a box on the low hilltop with a field phone line. Josh watched as the commander, "Red Mike" to his men, called the division operations officer, Colonel Thomas.

"My men are exhausted," Edson said. "Can we get some reinforcements and relief."

As daylight broke, the sound of aircraft approached. Almost too numb for concern, Josh looked up to see US Army Air Corps gunships fly over. They strafed the ridge and the jungle with .30- and .50-caliber machine guns, and soon, the last of Japanese resistance had either faded back to their own lines or had dropped dead in place.

The requested replacements arrived and began relieving the men on the perimeter. The battle for Edson's Ridge was over.

"Let's go," Edson called to Josh, setting down his phone receiver. "We're relieved. Our units are heading to Kukum for rest and recuperation. That's down a ways from the airstrip by the coast."

As they walked along, Edson gave Josh a sidelong glance. "I guess this combat is a little different than what you've seen before."

Josh took his time to respond. "The combat is up-close, and when an enemy is in your face—" His mind went to the Japanese soldier he had impaled with his bayonet. "It comes down to him or me. It's personal.

"In the air, we see the faces of the enemy too, but the fight is from a distance. Then again, when you lose friends and comrades, it's just as personal either way."

"I get your point."

"Sir, do you mind if I ask what the losses are? Do we know the numbers yet?"

Edson sighed. "We do, and that fight was costly on both sides. I don't have estimates of Japanese casualties yet, and ours are subject to being updated, but the 1st Raider Battalion lost a hundred and thirty-five men. The 1st Parachute Battalion lost another hundred and twenty-eight. Of those, fifty-nine Marines are dead or missing. Of the three hundred and seventy-seven Chutes who had landed here on August 7, about eighty-six remain. My Raiders came ashore with seven hundred and fifty, and we sustained two hundred and thirty-four killed, wounded, or missing." He took a deep breath. "As you say, it's personal."

They walked on in silence, and behind them, Marines, Raiders, and Chutes followed. After some time, Edson said, "By the way, you've got orders. Colonel Thomas told me over the phone. He'll send a runner with them to the bivouac, but apparently they're on a short suspense."

Surprised, Josh asked, "Any idea what's in them? Am I leaving?"

Edson shook his head. "No idea."

The runner was already at the bivouac site when the tired warriors arrived. He sought out Edson, who pointed to Josh. A pit formed in Josh's stomach as he watched the runner approach. He took the two pages handed to him, scanned them, and dropped his head in dismay.

Edson sidled alongside of him. "What are your orders?"

"I'm headed to London. They want a naval officer with amphibious and air operations combat experience. I'm assigned to the planning staff of some army general by the name of Eisenhower."

Edson grunted. "Good luck. Never heard of him."

53

October 13, 1942
***Oflag* IV-C POW Camp, Colditz Castle, Germany**

RAF Lieutenant Pat Reid stepped into the room where Sergeant Lance Littlefield bunked and caught his eye. Motioning for Lance to follow, he went back out into the hall. "There's been a change of plan," he said as they set out for a secure room high inside the castle.

Lance noticed that stooges had taken up positions along the way. "You're taking no chances," he observed.

Pat nodded. "We don't want to be overheard, not at this point."

They entered the attic, removed a false wall, stepped behind it, and replaced it. "It's always good to have reliable stooges," Lance observed. "Now, what's this about?"

"Let's deal with the bad news first. Last week, on the 7th, seven commandos arrived here at Colditz."

"I didn't hear anything about that."

"Most of the POWs didn't. The commandos were locked

in the guardhouse overnight and kept away from the rest of us. We found out about them only because Peter Tunstall and Scorgie Price happened to see them from above the main hall. They guessed new POWs were coming in and called to them. That's how we learned that the men they saw were POWs and commandos, but then their guards scurried them away. Barry Rupert bribed one of the guards to find out their names, and we sent a coded message back to MI-9 in London to inform them.

"For reasons we don't know, SBO Stayner was not allowed to visit them, which, by the Geneva Convention, he has a right to do. The two commando leaders, Captain Graeme Black and Lieutenant Joseph Houghton, were transferred to the jail in town—probably to prevent organizing an escape.

"One of our chaps, Peter Storie-Pugh, was interned there for one of his many bouts with mischief—the cooler was already full. He managed to speak with the commandos through the walls—"

Pat interrupted himself and took a different tack. "Let me give you a little background." He lit a cigarette and continued. "You know about the raids that the commandos pulled off in Norway and France, the biggest one being at Saint-Nazaire and then one at Dieppe."

Lance nodded, and Pat went on. "All the raids angered Hitler, and he was furious about Saint-Nazaire, but he seemed to think he'd contained the damage that commandos could do at Dieppe. According to German newspapers, he celebrated the British defeat there."

"The one at Dieppe?"

"Yes. Well, last month, the commandos pulled off yet another raid in Norway, Operation Musketoon."

"I heard something about it, but I don't know any particulars."

"This one infuriated Hitler beyond belief. It was at a powerplant in a place called Glomfjord. Two officers and eight men from No. 2 Commando and two from the exiled Norwegian Armed Forces planted explosives and blew up the place. The Norwegians operated under SOE."

"My, my, we do have a myriad of resources these days, don't we? I must say, I'm quite pleased, but why would that raid cause Hitler any more angst than the other?"

Pat shrugged. "I suppose part of it is that there have been so many of them, and Dieppe aside, they've been successful, and this one particularly so."

"Really?"

"That plant supplied electricity for an aluminum production plant, and the raid was so successful that it will take years to repair. Damaging it the way it did, the raid put a big crimp in German weapons production needing aluminum."

Lance smirked. "I can see where that might annoy *Herr* Hitler."

Pat agreed. "Half of the raiding party got away, but these seven were captured; and here's the thing. Captain Black told Peter that they are to be executed, and this morning they were taken out."

Lance's head popped up, and his brows arched. "Why? They were wearing uniforms, weren't they? They weren't spying."

Pat nodded. "The rumor is that Hitler has declared all commandos to be outlaws and thus outside the protections of the Geneva Convention. That's only rumor right now, but he's expected to put it in writing soon."

Pat and Lance stood in silence a few moments. Then a

puzzled look crossed Lance's face. "I feel sorry for those poor blokes, although I'm glad their mission succeeded. But what does any of that have to do with our escape? How does it change things? We're still on for tomorrow, right?"

Smiling, Pat nodded, and then his face turned serious again. "Your younger brother, Jeremy, is a commando. He participated in the raid at Saint-Nazaire."

Lance stared at him in astonishment. "My little brother did what? You're talking about little Jeremy, the baby of the family?"

"I confirmed that tidbit with Lieutenant Commander Stephens. He was on that raid."

Lance shook his head in wonder. "I'd heard that Jeremy escaped a shipwreck and rescued a baby boy, but that's a far cry from going on a raid at a submarine base in German-occupied territory." He stopped short. "I guess when I get home, I'd better make sure he doesn't go on any more such raids."

"Spoken like a true big brother," Pat said, laughing. "Yes, that Jeremy. He sounds to have grown up a bit since you went away. We received the information a short while ago. We had sent a coded message to London about our plans—we needed them to provide various items, including forged identification and travel documents." He reached into his pocket and pulled out a carefully folded handkerchief. "I didn't know your brother was a friend of Lieutenant-Colonel Crockatt who runs MI-9." He chuckled. "There must be something to this notion of your being a *prominente*—knowing people in high places."

Surprised again, Lance muttered, "I didn't know that either. I'm not acquainted with any Major Crockatt." He recognized the handkerchief as an element in a clever MI-9 method to send detailed messages to POWs without the need to code and without being scrutinized by censors.

Essentially, senior POW officers received pairs of innocent-looking handkerchiefs as part of ostensible packages sent from home. One of the handkerchiefs would be trimmed with red, and the other with green. On receipt they were handed over to the POW officer in charge of cryptography. He would first plunge the handkerchief with the red border in a glass of water. When he then immersed the green-trimmed handkerchief in the same glass of water, the chemical reaction produced an easily read complete message on the cloth.

Even the way the packages were obtained without being searched had amazed Lance. Among the French POWs was a master locksmith, Lieutenant "Fredo" Guiges, a man of remarkable talent. Not all the prisoners knew of his skill, but of those who did, his reputation was that no lock existed that he could not pick. He had proved his skill by using razor blades to carve a key that unlocked a cruciform device the Germans had developed to preclude picking a lock. This particular one was on a secured room that held incoming packages requiring inspection prior to distribution.

Once the key was made, sneaking into the room at night, taking out packages, and replacing them with dummy ones was not difficult, and to date the subterfuge had not been detected. In this way, the POWs were able to get almost anything requested, including forged documents.

Lance read the message and glanced up with bright eyes. "Is this a joke?"

"No joke." Pat reached for the handkerchief, and Lance gave it to him with no objection. "We have to burn this, and you have a choice to make. Our escape plans, cover stories, routes—everything is ready for you, me, Wardle, Stephens, and Littledale. If we get to Switzerland, we'll stay there for the duration of the war. That's a requirement in the Geneva Convention to prevent combatants from re-entering the war. But you're being offered a different plan. If you take it, you'll travel much of the way alone—we'll be in close proximity and will take steps so that you're not always observed by yourself, but your journey won't end in Switzerland."

He paused to be sure he had Lance's full attention. "If you take that second route, some of your paperwork will have to be re-done by our forgers here, and in short order. Your risk goes up considerably."

Lance was listening, but a faraway look in his eyes belied his concentration. When Pat finished speaking, he jostled Lance's shoulders. "Keep your mind in the game. You can dream of home when you're safely in Southern France. Do you understand me?"

Lance gave several short, quick nods. "Yeh, yeh, I understand. You *know* which choice I'll take."

"Are you sure? Take an hour or two to think it through if you'd like."

"I'm sure. Tell me what I have to do."

Pat laughed. "I anticipated your answer. The forgers are at work already. We need to revamp your cover story, but we'll leave on schedule."

Lance stared at the silk escape map without seeing it. The notion that he would soon be free, and that a way had been established to take him home instead of being interned in Switzerland for an indeterminate time, seemed surreal. More than two years had passed since the debacle at Dunkirk...

Pat interrupted his thoughts. "Bring your mind back to earth, Sergeant," he chided. "Let's go over the plan once more before we put the map away." They were seated at a table in one of the rooms occupied by flight officers, Pat being one of them. With them were Flight Lieutenant Hank Wardle, Major Ronnie Littledale, and Lieutenant Commander "Billie" Stephens. Also present was Dick Howe, who would assume the mantle of escape officer upon Pat's departure.

"I heard you might know my brother," Lance said when Stephens entered.

"I did, and a good man too," Stephens responded. "I don't know why I didn't put it together before Pat asked about him. Different context, I suppose, but now I can see that the family resemblance is striking." He slapped the table. "Let's hope this works and you get to see each other again soon."

The map Pat had referred to was one showing escape routes and the defenses along the German border with Switzerland. Both had arrived in Red Cross packages containing the popular American Monopoly games produced by the British licensee, John Waddington, Ltd. Cleverly hidden inside some of the games were a map, a compass, and a file. Careful review with recaptured escapees returned to the prison camp had revealed that being found with a map led to additional interrogation regarding how it was obtained, hence Pat had forbidden escapees from carrying any with them. Instead, he required them to memorize routes and pertinent map details.

The particular area along the border was near Singen, on the German border with Switzerland. An earlier escaped POW from Colditz had gone that far. He was captured and returned to the castle, but not before he noticed a wide gap in German security in that area. When interviewed by the escape committee on his return, he gladly divulged his observation, remarking regretfully that he wished he had noticed it prior to his recapture.

"Now we've all agreed," Pat went on with a smirk, "that this escape plan has no chance of succeeding, and that's exactly what gives it its greatest chance of success. The Germans will never expect what we're getting ready to do.

"The main problem is that we've had no ability to check some of the key elements for getting out of the castle, so be prepared to improvise." He turned to Stephens, the senior officer in the group. "And from here until we arrive at our destination, there's no more rank. So, Billie, you start out with the first step."

"Right, Pat—"

"Wait. Excuse me, Billie. One more thing I want to say. Look at each other, and at the other men in the room. Think of the other POWs here. We're thin and gaunt from meager diets and vitamin deprivation. We need to think of that as we travel across Germany. One thin, undernourished man traveling alone might be noted. Two such men traveling together would probably be overlooked if all other things are in order. But five skeletal men traveling in a group will certainly draw the attention of train passengers as well as authorities, particularly when news breaks that five POWs escaped. The point is, stay in pairs, but the pairs should keep apart.

"With Allied bombing in Germany now and the pressures of supporting an army in North Africa and all parts of Europe, the populace is tightening its belt too, so that's less of a factor than it was back in January when Airey Neave made his homerun, but it's still important to keep in mind."

He glanced at Lance. "We've made special provisions for the sergeant."

When finished, Pat nodded at Billie to begin again. "We go out through the kitchen window," Billie said, "climb down bedsheets tied into ropes onto the roofs of the low sheds on the side of the castle where the guards are housed. Then we drop into their courtyard at the west end across from the *kommandant's* headquarters."

"Right," Pat broke in. "I've sawed through the rivets that secure the bars in the kitchen window. We made clay ones to hold them in place. The bars bend easily out of the way, enough for a man to get through." He turned to Wardle. "Ronnie, what's next?"

"When we're down, we tiptoe across the courtyard at a right angle to and behind a guard as he starts his trek across the courtyard. We go to an open pit that's in deep shadows. We'll wear socks over our shoes to muffle our footsteps."

"Yes, and don't forget that the entire courtyard is in full view of every window looking out from the guards' quarters. How do we know when to go?"

"Wing Commander Bader's room overlooks the courtyard. For the past several nights he's had musicians with their instruments 'rehearsing' for a concert. When we're in place, he'll start the music, and when it's 'safe' for us to go, he'll stop."

Lance had to smile. Wing Commander Douglas Bader was a British legend. A daredevil as a young pilot, in his first year after commissioning, he had flown too low over some roofs in an aerobatic maneuver resulting in a crash, costing him both legs.

Retired medically against his will, when war broke out and the RAF was desperate for pilots, he had convinced the senior staff that, with his steel prosthetic legs, he could still be effective as a fighter pilot, and he had become an ace credited with twenty-two kills before his capture. When he was shot down, his artificial legs had become entangled in the cockpit as he bailed out. His German captors were astonished to find a legless pilot sitting in a field waiting to be captured. So respectful were the *Luftwaffe* officers of his pluck that they arranged through Swiss emissaries for a British plane to be granted safe passage to fly a set of legs and drop them by parachute in the vicinity of the POW camp where Bader was then held. One German-celebrated ace, Adolf Galland, had even made a point to visit the camp and befriend Bader. Despite his limitations, at previous camps, the British fighter pilot had attempted several escapes that failed. Thus, he was brought to Colditz, but he was allowed his own room, and he helped others' escape plans enthusiastically.

Pat continued. "Right, we stay put when the music plays, and we move when it stops. Next, Hank?"

"We break into the tall building where Dominic Bruce made his escape two months ago," Wardle said. "Too bad he was recaptured."

"Remember that his mistake was leaving his sheets in place and a village *hausfrau* saw it and alerted the officer on duty. He might have had a few more hours and made good his escape but for that. So, we've enough sheets for twice the length of rope we need, we loop it around a bar in the window, and simply pull the sheets down when we're all on the ground. Lance, brief us on the rest of the way out of the castle."

"Once we've descended, we still have three terraces to scale down. Each is about six feet wide, and the next level down is about twelve feet. Once we've navigated those, we'll be by the river with one more wall to scale, after which we'll be outside of prison security."

"Good," Pat wrapped up. "We have six ghosts in place to cover our absences." He checked his watch and looked up. "It's time. Make your final preparations, and we'll meet in the kitchen in fifteen minutes."

54

October 14, 1942
***Oflag* IV-C POW Camp, Colditz Castle, Germany**

The kitchen was dark when Lance entered. Pat was already there and had removed the clay rivets and bent the bars back. Dressed in civilian laborer's clothing, Pat would travel with Hank Wardle, both of them posing as Flemish workmen. They spoke German, but not well, and they hoped that those roles would explain away their poor use of the language.

Their clothes were remarkable, given the circumstances. Their work trousers had been dyed and altered from RAF uniforms. Pat had a cloth cap and a wind jacket. He also carried an overcoat that he had bought from a French officer who had purchased it from an orderly with access into the village. Wardle was similarly dressed, and they both wore black shoes.

Stephens and Littledale arrived with another POW, Malcolm McColm, who would remove any trace of the escape through this window upon their departure. By the light thrown from an outside lamp, Pat checked each man one last time, inspecting their papers and clothing. Each carried a cardboard box fashioned to look like a leather suitcase. The bags were cumbersome and added to the difficulty of scaling down walls, but once they had cleared the castle and mixed with the public, the luggage would add an element of authenticity, causing them to look less like fugitives.

"All right," Pat said as he checked out Lance. "Time to reverse roles."

Lance grinned. He was dressed similarly to Pat, but in his cardboard suitcase, he carried a business suit brought in by the same orderly who had obtained Pat's overcoat. It had been tailored to him by a Polish POW on an improvised sewing machine and came with a thick winter overcoat and appropriate shoes, shirt, and tie. His paperwork showed him to be a French functionary from an arms factory in Occupied France, and his role was to escort two Flemish workers with specialized skills in furnace construction through Germany back to the plant. He expected his fluency in German to compensate for Pat's and Wardle's deficiency in that regard.

Lance pulled himself to full height. His face straightened into stone. He leaned forward so that his nose almost touched Pat's. "You swine," he muttered fiercely, "when I tell you to move, you move." He pulled an authentic-looking plaster of Paris Mauser from his pocket. "If you give me any more trouble, you will learn what this will do." He jammed it into Pat's waist.

Pat lifted his hands shoulder high and chuckled. "All right, you've convinced me." He listened. "The music's playing. Next time it stops, we go."

They made it down onto the roof of the sheds and to the ground without incident. There, they waited, but something was not right. Pat peered around the front corner of the shed. The guard stood there, but he was not alone. His supervisor was with him, and they both looked up at Bader's window. Something about the irregular starts and stops must have gained the attention of the two Germans. Or maybe because Bader's group had played for the last several nights, the Germans had grown tired of it.

Regardless, the escape group was frozen in place, able neither to go forward nor retreat.

Minutes passed, and then loud voices resounded from Bader's room. The German noncom had apparently entered and ordered the music to cease.

The escapees sat against a back wall in the shadows. A few moments later, Pat returned to the front corner and peeked around. The sentry was near the far end of his walk and would soon turn around.

Pat hurried back to where the others waited. He pointed to Littledale and Stephens. "Get behind me," he whispered. "When I tell you, run to the pit."

Holding their suitcases close to prevent sound, they crept behind Pat to the front corner. He watched the guard coming their way, and when the man reversed direction not more than thirty feet away, Pat signaled to Littledale and Stephens. They scurried across the courtyard.

Lance and Wardle went next. No alarm had been raised, so Pat assumed that the first two had reached the pit safely. This time, as he sent Lance and Wardle over, he waited and watched. They disappeared into the pit just before the guard turned.

Pat's heart beat rapidly and he sat against the wall, regulating his breathing while he listened to the sentry's boots clomp on the hard courtyard surface.

The sound of the boots halted and scraped the ground as they turned and clomped away.

Peering around the corner one last time, Pat grasped his suitcase and raced across the courtyard. He reached it and climbed in, ducking his head. The others were there, peering anxiously into the night. Still no sound of alarm.

"I'm going to the tall building now," Pat told the others. The door he would need to unlock was fifteen yards away. "I won't be able to see the guard. Nudge me when he's looking away."

Moments later, Lance prodded his arm. "Go."

Pat reached the door and started work on the lock. It would not give. He kept working on it, with no luck, and then he heard voices of soldiers returning from the town. Pat recognized one of them. It belonged to *Leutnant* Priem, the camp's security officer.

He scurried back to the pit and waited with the others.

When the voices had waned to silence, he returned to the lock to try again. Sixty nerve-racking minutes later, he returned to the pit. "It's no good," he whispered. "We'll have to try something else."

"That dark shadow over there is the mouth of a tunnel," Lance whispered, pointing. "We couldn't see it from the windows, but I went down it a bit while you worked on the lock. It leads to a tunnel, but I don't know where it goes."

Pat shrugged. "Let's find out."

The tunnel led into darkness, and they felt their way along, reasonably sure now that they would not be heard if they tripped. The group came out under a veranda, and there they found an unlocked door into a cellar.

At the far end was a chute of some sort at the top of which was a barred window. Lance wondered if the others felt the same despair that came over him. In the dark, he could not tell, but then Pat started stripping off his clothes. When he was done, he climbed up the chute to the window.

Moments passed. And then he called down, "One of the bars was loose. I pulled it out. If we each strip down naked, I think we can wriggle through."

Two hours later, the five erstwhile POWs lay sprawled on their backs in the grass at the base of the castle. The first twelve-foot drop-off to the next terrace was only feet away.

Weary, but with no time to waste, they dressed, pulled the sheets from their suitcases, made ropes, and started descending. Going down the three levels took an additional hour, and an hour after that, they had scaled and descended over the outer wall just before the first rays of dawn stretched across the sky.

Now, their journeys' most dangerous legs could begin in earnest: traveling across Germany amid a hostile population while a search would include dogs and orders to shoot to kill. In early morning light, Lance, Pat, and Wardle bade Littledale and Stephens best wishes and went their separate ways.

October 19, 1942
Zurich, Switzerland

Unkempt from days of travel on short rations, Lance sat alone on a bench inside the train station. His instructions had been to be here at this appointed hour where he was to receive additional direction, although by what means, he did not know. The note on the handkerchief that he had read back at Colditz Castle said only that his brother, Jeremy, would be there to collect him. No date was specified, presumably because exactly when Lance would arrive in Zurich was unknown, so Lance had to believe that someone must be watching this spot daily.

Saying goodbye to his two traveling companions had not been easy. The transit had not taken long: four days with only minor troubles along the way. Their papers had held up through multiple checkpoints, and on two instances when an extra degree of arrogance and authority seemed called for, Lance rose to the occasion.

But Pat and Lance had become close chums in their months together at Colditz, Pat as escape officer, and Lance as his assistant. They had shared childhood stories, anecdotes about their families, and ambitions for when the war ended.

Crossing the Swiss border had been easier than either of them had expected. The German checkpoints were exactly as shown on the memorized map, and the lay of the land as described by the failed escapee. Between two of them lay a wide gap created by a ridge near enough to one guardhouse to block sight of a shallow ravine from the other one.

The re-captured escapee had realized as he was being taken away that if he had entered and stayed low in the ravine, the guard in neither checkpoint would have seen him although they could see each other. The imperative was to approach the ravine in darkness, which was what Pat,

Lance, and Wardle had done. Once inside the Swiss border, however, Lance had split from the other two. They would surrender to Swiss authorities to be interned at Davos. Lance would evade and continue on to meet Jeremy.

He stood and paced. Despite no longer being in enemy territory, he was operating outside of local law, and uneasiness mounted. Besides, as Pat had pointed out during their last briefing, he was gaunt, and now he was alone—exactly the situation the escapees had hoped to avoid.

Given the ravages Lance had encountered during battle north of Dunkirk, his trek across France until he was captured, and the stoic demeanors of Germans as he traversed their country on this escape, the relaxed atmosphere of the Swiss people moving about in well-fed comfort in beautiful and well-kept surroundings astonished him, generating a sense of having entered another dimension.

Thinking that pacing might draw unwanted attention, Lance sat back down. He glanced at the enormous arches and the engineering masterpieces that adorned the interior of the station, admiring them and wishing that more talent was applied that way and less to the business of war. He sighed. *Evil will never leave us.*

A stirring among passengers off to his right caught his attention. A man strode briskly toward him in military attire, a black leather coat over black trousers and leather boots, and he wore a high-peaked black service cap with silver braiding along the brim and a silver eagle at the top, the unmistakable uniform of a Gestapo officer. He wore dark wire-rimmed glasses, and he was surrounded by nervous-looking Swiss cantonal police officers who apparently felt helpless to intervene.

Almost before Lance could assess what was taking place, the Gestapo man advanced on him. Without speaking, he thrust a piece of paper next to Lance's face and whirled to the lead Swiss policeman.

"Look," he snarled in German. "It's this one."

Lance looked up in shock.

The Gestapo man pointed to a photo on the paper which had Lance's likeness and those of his fellow escapees. "He entered your country and did not surrender himself as he's required to do by the precious Geneva Convention. Therefore, he has surrendered his rights. And then there's this." He shoved another photo against Lance's chest. "He's wanted for murder in France." He stepped close to the policeman and thrust his nose close to the man's face. "Now, either you escort me and my prisoner to the train, or you can cause a diplomatic issue with the Third *Reich*. Which is it going to be?"

Lance sat in stunned silence, surrounded by policemen, barely aware of the crowd of passersby who paused to gawk and then move nervously away. *What murder is the man talking about?*

The Gestapo officer grabbed him roughly by the shoulder and jerked him to his feet. "Let's go."

Without waiting for an answer from the police, he shoved Lance ahead of him toward a platform where a train waited for departure to Geneva. The Swiss policemen hurried nervously behind them, uncertain about what to do. Within minutes, Lance sat next to the Gestapo officer in a private car on the train with no other passengers. He stared out the window, his heart sinking lower as he watched passengers go by.

A porter stopped by. He looked inside the car but, sensing the cold stare behind the Gestapo officer's dark glasses, he closed the door and hurried about his business. The train's whistle squealed. Steam hissed from released brakes; the train jerked and began to roll. It trundled beyond the station, between low green hills, traveling west and slightly north before gently curving in a southwesterly direction.

55

October 20, 1942
HMS *Seraph,* off the Coast of Gibraltar

"Glad to have you with us," General Clark said as Paul reached the bottom of the steel ladder in the submarine and turned to greet the general.

"It's good to see you again, sir," Paul replied, "and that you remember me, though I'm not quite sure why I'm here."

Clark chuckled. "That was Ike's doing. You're uniquely qualified as a British intelligence officer who's moved about the world, rubbed shoulders with Yanks, and is fluent in French. The idea is that you'll lie low and watch for anything that seems amiss. Are you read in on what we're doing?"

"I am, sir, and I hope it works."

"Me too. Go on forward to the officers' mess and try not to bump your head. Things are tight in here. Have you ever been on a submarine before?"

Paul shook his head. "First time."

"Well, they're crowded, stinky, and wet, but if we avoid

getting sunk, they get us from here to there." He chuckled. "When you get to the mess, you'll find another Littlefield waiting there. Who'd've thunk I'd get two in such a small group. Maybe you're cousins or something. The other one's my new special aide for this mission, and he just joined us. You can fill him in."

Startled, Paul did as instructed and made his way through the cramped boat.

He found the mess and was astounded to see his cousin, Josh Littlefield, sitting at a small table and drinking a cup of coffee.

Josh looked up and his eyes widened in astonishment. "How in hell did the two of us end up on the same submarine in the Mediterranean?" he exclaimed.

Paul clapped an arm around his shoulders. "The notion defies the odds a bit, doesn't it? What a surprise. I was assigned to liaise between General Eisenhower and Prime Minister Churchill. This mission seems to stray from that, and I never expected to find you here."

Josh laughed. "And to think that the last time we saw each other you passed yourself off as a British passport control officer. As I recall, I was somewhat patronizing. Sorry about that, I should've known better."

Paul shook off the comment. "We all have secrets to keep." He found a cup, poured himself some coffee, and sat down across from Josh. "What are you doing here? I thought you were off in the Pacific."

"I was, and then I got transferred to Eisenhower's planning staff with almost no notice. I just got to London a few days ago, and General Clark grabbed me for this mission."

"What's your function, if I'm allowed to ask?"

"It's a strange one," Josh replied. "I'm supposed to be on hand to talk about amphibious operations if the occasion arises, but I don't even know much about what's going on in this theater. I haven't been here long enough. The general told me that a British liaison officer would fill me in. I guess that's you."

"Yes, that's me, and now it's my turn to patronize," Paul said, chuckling. "You'll do fine. And I'm happy to fill you in. In addition to Clark and his entourage, we have three British commandos on board, but none of them speak French. My job is to lie low in the background and watch for indications that things are not what they seem."

He paused to gather his thoughts. "Let's see, where to start. I suppose you should know who's going along if you don't already. You can stop me if I'm going over beaten ground, so to speak. There's BG Lyman Lemnitzer, head of Allied Force Plans; Colonel Hamblem, a shipping and supply expert; Captain Jerauld Wright, a Navy liaison officer—"

Josh interrupted, "Why couldn't he handle my job?"

"I suppose because he's occupied with larger-picture concerns, or he hasn't been around amphibious operations. Anyway, there's one more senior officer on this trip, Colonel Julius Holmes, who heads the civil affairs branch for Operation Torch.

"I'll tell you what's a little puzzling to me is that Clark is on this mission at all. He's Eisenhower's deputy and head of planning for Operation Torch, so he knows more about it than anyone. If he's captured, the results could be catastrophic. It's some small relief that he intends to wear the insignia of a lieutenant colonel when we go ashore." *The general must be carrying his own cyanide pill.*

Josh blew out a rush of air. "Risky." He shook his head. "I just got put on the planning staff for Torch, and I haven't been here long enough to know much about it. I was brought over because of what we did at Guadalcanal, but I'm a fighter pilot and air operations officer. I arrived on the island after amphibious operations were complete, and I was a liaison officer at the time. At best, I observed the amphibious operations from afar and from behind."

"Well, as you Americans say, you go with what you've got. I'm sure you'll be looked to for expertise in only those areas where you're competent. We were told that the officer being sent came with Admiral Halsey's high recommendation. He wouldn't have given it or sent you if he lacked confidence in you."

Josh shot him a skeptical glance. "I was shot down at Midway, and Halsey liked the guy who replaced me while I recovered. I was the easiest of the two to let go. I understand we're going to invade North Africa?"

"That's the plan. This will be the first very large-scale combined-arms operation. That's a concept that Lord Mountbatten developed that's proven itself in several raids. Operation Torch anticipates three landings. The Eastern Assault Force, commanded by Major General Doc Ryder, will land at Algiers with approximately twenty thousand troops. It'll capture the port of Bougie and then advance toward Tunisia.

"The Central Assault Force, under Major General Lloyd Fredendall, will land at Oran with eighteen thousand troops. Its objective is to capture the city and the airfields at Tafaraoui and La Senia.

"The third group, the Western Assault Force, commanded by Major General George Patton, will land at Casablanca, Morocco, with twenty-four thousand troops. It will counter any German or Spanish action and drive east."

Josh whistled. "That's a lot of troops under fire. I hope

our guys are ready. I've never heard of any of those generals. Have you?"

Paul shook his head. "It's a tricky operation with a lot of political overtones. The main objective of this mission we're on now in this submarine is to remove a lot of enemy combatants without firing a shot."

"I'm all for that," Josh said, lifting his brows. "How do we pull it off? I've seen enough bloodshed to last several lifetimes."

Paul took a deep breath. "It's complicated. I'll try to simplify. You know that Germany took over much of Northern France and her Atlantic coast."

Josh nodded. "And the French run what was left of the country out of a town called Vichy, so they call it Vichy France."

"Correct, and by the armistice agreement, Vichy kept all the French colonies, including those in North Africa. This is where it gets dicey. Churchill and Roosevelt agreed to defeat German forces in North Africa as a necessary prelude to invading Europe. There are pros and cons to doing that rather than invading Europe first. I'll go over those with you at another time if you like, but the decision's been made. Torch is going forward, and as you know, the planning is in progress.

"The Vichy army controls a lot of the western and northern coasts in North Africa, from Morocco to Algeria and beyond. We'd like to avoid fighting them if we can."

"How do we do that?"

"The problem is a lot of bitterness flying about. Some Vichy military members support the bombing the British did to the French navy because they saw the need to keep those warships out of Hitler's hands. Others want nothing to do with us, and they will happily turn their guns on us.

"The French forces in North Africa still belong to Vichy. And General Pétain, as head of state, has collaborated with the Nazis. As things are, if the Brits go ashore, the Vichy forces will fight unless ordered not to. Pétain will not give such an order. On the contrary, he's likely to order those troops into open combat against us.

"General Charles de Gaulle would no doubt like to be in on the invasion, but he's neither invited nor kept informed on its progress. I'm not even sure he knows about it. President Roosevelt has a particular dislike for him and his Free French, which results in deep distrust."

"Why?"

"De Gaulle was highly critical of Roosevelt when the president recognized the Vichy government after Germany invaded France."

"I recall that. I wondered about it at the time."

Paul thought back quickly over the meetings he had attended with Churchill, Roosevelt, "Little Bill" Stephenson, and "Wild Bill" Donovan. If he had learned nothing else, it was not to second-guess their good intentions and actions. "I don't know any of the particulars surrounding that, but most Vichy North African forces don't trust de Gaulle either. They resent that he went to Britain, the country that bombed their navy, to set up his Free French Resistance. So that rules out having his group join the operation.

"And of course, too many Vichys would be more than happy to shoot at us Brits, so that rules us out for the landing force. We'll take a support role instead, with our big navy guns and aerial bombardment."

"So that puts our American boys at the front all by themselves."

"Yes, it does," Paul said solemnly. "I'm sorry about that. All that said, Vichy forces at the ground level have no love for Germany and are repulsed by being under the Nazi thumb. But they still like Americans, so maybe General Clark can work out a deal that will save face and save lives. In any case, threading this needle won't be easy."

Josh listened without comment while sipping his coffee.

"Anyway," Paul continued, "while General Clark was in DC two weeks ago, your American expert on North Africa, Robert Murphy, who's also your counselor to Vichy, reported that Major General Charles Mast, chief of staff of the French Nineteenth Corps, was willing to entertain talks with military representatives about cooperating with the Allies.

"Murphy had previously been in touch with General Alphonse Juin, the commander of French forces in North Africa, known to be sympathetic to the Allies. Murphy had also communicated with General Henri Giraud.

"You might have heard of Giraud. He recently made a spectacular escape from a German castle, the Königstein Fortress. He was already a hero from the last war, and this latest escape burnished his reputation. The Allies, particularly Roosevelt, think he could rally Vichy forces to fight with the Allies. Giraud named Mast to represent him.

"So, this mission is to meet with Mast to explore the idea of transporting Giraud to Algiers to wrest control of the colonial government from Vichy, take command of the Vichy army in North Africa, and order it to stand down while the Allies invade. Hopefully, they'll even join us. Thousands of soldiers' lives would be saved."

October 22, 1942
Off the Coast of Algeria

Paul and Josh sat near the rear of a dinghy bringing them to shore. The boat scrunched against the beach, and they scrambled over its side with the rest of General Clark's entourage. A tall man, whose high forehead gleamed in the ambient light, met them, and led them quietly through the sand.

The *Seraph* had arrived early that morning offshore from an isolated white house with a red-tiled roof along the beach ninety miles west of Algiers, but when the submarine rose to periscope depth, the captain spotted a fishing boat within two hundred feet and ordered a slow descent to the sea floor. When they checked again two hours later, the area was clear, but already a glimmer of daylight cast silver highlights across the uninterrupted skyline and sea to the east. Not wanting to risk discovery, Clark's contingent waited until the next nightfall to go ashore.

When they were finally safely inside the house, Clark introduced his group. The tall man turned out to be Robert Murphy. He was broad-shouldered with dark, thinning hair and the soft demeanor and serious face of a diplomat. Courteous to a fault, he introduced General Mast, a trim, dignified man with a stern look and direct manner.

"I want to know," Mast said, when they were seated, his aide sitting behind him taking notes, "can you expand your proposed invasion to go into southern France?"

Clark quelled the urge to take a deep breath. "I would be lying to you if I said yes, General. At the moment not only is that logistically impossible, but our troops are not ready yet. I'm sure you'd agree that storming France is going to be much more difficult than storming North Africa, and our soldiers had better be ready for a fight much tougher than the one here. They need to gain experience."

"Can you tell me the general plan?"

Watching Clark, Paul was sure that he had seen a fleeting, wary expression in the American general's eyes. *He anticipated the question. But he can't reveal the plan.*

Clark leaned toward Mast and looked directly in his eyes. "General, we're bringing in half a million troops with up to two thousand planes and plenty of US Navy."

Paul was glad for his training on maintaining a neutral expression. He stifled his shock. Clark was bluffing. No more than a hundred and twelve thousand troops were planned for the invasion force.

Mast eyed Clark with barely disguised skepticism. "What you're intending, if I read between the lines correctly, is an amphibious assault. The Allies' history in that regard is dismal. Mr. Churchill's incursion at Gallipoli in the last war was a disaster, and the operation at Dieppe two months ago wasn't any better."

Clark took his time to respond. "Your point about both operations is well taken. I'd like to believe that we learned valuable lessons from both. But the British are our valued allies, and if you know about those two operations, you must also know about their successful raids in Norway and at Saint-Nazaire. Regardless of how you might feel about what they did at Mers-el-Kébir, the fact is that when we go into France to take it back, the British will be there with us. We won't succeed without them.

"Now, regarding our knowledge of amphibious operations, I've brought with me a naval lieutenant commander who just arrived from the war in the Pacific, specifically at Guadalcanal. Have you heard of our progress there?"

Mast nodded. "I read the stories coming from your own captive press corps."

Startled at the response, Clark sat quietly a moment. Then he nodded. "Healthy skepticism is good." He turned to

Josh. "Commander Littlefield, tell us about your experiences in the Solomons."

Josh stood, but before he could speak, Clark added, "Commander Littlefield is a fighter pilot who also fought at Midway and was shot down, but not before he made a bombing run on the *Hiryu*. His next action was in the Solomons, and he was there for the defense of Henderson Field." He turned back to Josh. "Go ahead, Commander."

Josh glanced around at the faces peering at him. "As the general told you," he said, addressing his remarks to Mast, who returned a stolid stare, "I was there for the operations in the Solomons. Initially, we went in at Tulagi and Guadalcanal. The fighting at Tulagi was fierce and we took three days to consolidate that objective.

"Initially, our operations were much easier on Guadalcanal, but the Japanese counterattacked..." As he continued to relate what had taken place in defense of Henderson Field, vivid images of the horror he had lived through seemed to materialize in front of him. The Japanese soldier diving through the air to be impaled on Josh's bayonet appeared so real that he could almost reach out and touch the dying soldier.

He continued speaking, but his voice and eyes took on haunted overtones, and when he had finished, the room remained silent for a spell.

At last, Mast said, "But you held."

The images vanished as Josh brought himself back to the present. "We did, sir."

"If I may ask, what did you learn during those assaults."

Josh's eyes narrowed and he cocked his head while he gathered his thoughts. "We learned, sir, to prepare carefully, to use every asset to soften the enemy with aerial bombing and naval big guns, and to keep those assets in support during and for the duration of the assault until the objective is taken. And we learned to go in with overwhelming force, to continue the drive until we've overrun and secured the target area, and to rely on the training, skill, and tenacity of our individual fighters."

Mast continued to observe Josh a few moments longer and then turned to Clark. "This man has seen war up close. He is a soldier."

Clark shot Josh an appreciative glance and then replied to Mast. "Yes, sir, and as we speak, our Marines are assaulting the beaches all over the Solomons. The final battle of Guadalcanal has not yet been fought—the Japanese want it back—but the fact is that the battle is one we must win, or the twin threats of German Naziism and Japanese imperialism will destroy civilization as we know it."

Mast nodded and leaned back in thought. More discussion ensued, and then Clark said, "Our resolve is set in stone, General Mast. As you must know, we delivered three hundred new M4 Sherman tanks and a hundred 105 mm self-propelled guns to the Brits at El Alamein last month. The next battle there is likely to be very different from the one back in July. There won't be another stalemate. My point is that we're coming in, and we'd rather not fight your French soldiers.

"Assuming we reach an agreement, what can you do to help us? I'll tell you now that President Roosevelt has authorized me to assure you officially that, if you join with us, we will restore France to her pre-war borders. Further, your officers will lead your countrymen in this war, and the Allies will view France as an equal partner."

Mast's reaction was immediate and emotional even as he maintained dignity. He wiped moisture from his eyes and sniffed, and when he responded, he seemed barely able to restrain enthusiasm. "If you deliver to us two thousand rifles with ammunition and grenades, we'll take control of communications centers and troop barracks, we'll arrest pro-Vichy commanders, and we'll seize public buildings. That's what we can do.

"We'll also do our best to prevent our navy from firing on your invasion forces, but that will take more finesse."

"That's crucial."

"It is, and we want this to succeed as much as you do, so when I tell you that we will do our best to bring that about, you can believe it. But the French navy is not under our authority."

"We'll need to work on that."

Mast leaned back again and contemplated before responding. Then he sat forward. "I need to be sure that you understand the extreme risk we are taking in meeting with you. If anyone who works with me in this plan is found out, we will be executed for treason. Of that there is no doubt."

"You mean like the risk this party took to come here?"

Mast furrowed his brows. "Touché, General. But if our forces refuse to fight yours, Germany will occupy the rest of France. And they will seize our fleet at Toulon."

Clark nodded solemnly. "I see the difficulty. Can you get word to the commanding admiral in Toulon? Would he be amenable?"

Mast shrugged. "I don't know. But I assure you that we'll work on it."

Clark chose his next words carefully and spoke in a low tone. "If the French navy fires on us, you know what we will have to do."

Mast nodded without speaking. Silence descended.

After a few moments, Clark said, "My last order of business regards who will command French forces. If you are agreeable, our president will designate General Giraud as the commander of French forces in North Africa."

Mast's eyes brightened, and a broad smile crossed his face. "Of course, that will certainly be agreeable to General Giraud. Can you bring him to Algeria?"

"We'll be happy to." Clark took in a deep breath and let it out. "Now, General, if you don't mind, I'd like to go for a walk on the beach while my staff works out details with your aide. I've been cooped up in that submarine for a few days and I've got more to go on the return trip."

Mast chuckled and made a slight hand gesture. "I wouldn't recommend you go out in that uniform. I'll loan you a French one."

After Clark's return from his walk, Mast met him at the door. "We will have the opportunity to see if your prediction concerning El Alamein is correct. The second battle there has begun."

Back aboard the submarine, Clark congratulated Josh on his delivery and then took Paul aside. "Did you notice anything of concern?"

"Not in the way the engagement took place or in Mast's conduct. In that respect, things went remarkably well."

Clark peered at him. "But—?" Recognizing Paul's reluctance to speak, he said, "Tell me what's on your mind."

"Some things became clearer during the meeting. For instance, General Mast is a chief of staff, not a commander, and despite the risks he took, we don't know that anyone will sign up to his plans to arrest pro-Vichy officers. Since his own commander was not present, I'm assuming that his boss might be one of the detainees."

"Hmm. Good point. Go on."

"There's the issue of the fleet at Toulon. Who's going to give the order to scuttle or surrender it to the Allies. That's going to be a tricky issue and a crucial one, and the fly in the ointment might be Pétain's own deputy, Admiral Jean Darlan."

"Explain. I know who Darlan is. His reputation as a high-level collaborator with the Germans is worldwide, but I've never dealt with him. Murphy's been secretly in touch with him, and Darlan told him that when we have three thousand tanks, six thousand planes, and half a million men to bring to Marseille, to let him know. Then he'd welcome us. Give me the rundown."

"He's Pétain's bulldog," Paul began. "As minister of the interior, he heads his intelligence apparatus, and he's also minister of defense and commander in chief of the French navy. Essentially, he runs his own Gestapo, and he's tried, unsuccessfully to date, to convert the *gendarmeries* into something like the SS. He's rounded up Jews and shipped them off at the behest of Berlin, and he's arrested Resistance members aggressively. Pétain gives him free rein on any and all matters that catch Darlan's interest. He's known to believe that the Nazis will win the war, and he sees a future in which France is an important vassal state to Germany. His way to satisfy personal ambitions is to join them. He even offered Germany raw materials from within French colonies. Base rights too. Recall that in February of last year, he was named as Pétain's successor, and last October, he ordered his navy to fire on an Allied ship at Dakar. If he's not under control before we invade, he could cause us problems, including ensuring that the fleet at Toulon *is* used against us."

Clark listened intently. "Interesting. Glad I asked." He frowned. "We can't trust Darlan, but maybe we could use him. Murphy thinks we could turn him. The man is obviously driven by how to impress whoever has the biggest and most guns. We'll have to convince him that's us."

56

November 5, 1942
Marseille, France

"I don't mind going, but I don't understand the mission," Jeremy said, not hiding his impatience. "The man has already shown extraordinary aggrandizement beyond reality, and I don't see why we're catering to him at all. Escaping from a POW camp is one thing. Commanding troops in the field is another. You yourself diverted attention away from General Giraud rather than let the Allies know his true response."

Fourcade smiled gently in agreement. "Yes, I did that. But the powers that be decided to bring him on board. Our job is to get him to the submarine to take him to the meeting."

"But he doesn't even like us. Is it a British submarine?"

"I expect that it is. You know that I'm only given the amount of information I need to complete a mission. You've made the mental leap to the conclusion that the Allies intend to install him in some sort of leadership position, but all we really know is that we've been tasked to get him to the sub. You're taking him because he already knows you from when you attended his meeting with Duke McMahon. I gather he's nervous about the trip and wants to deal only with people he already knows. Your *bona fides* were established when the duke introduced you. Not that he's enthusiastic, but he finds you acceptable."

"Hmph. Lucky me."

Fourcade laughed in her musical way. "Jeremy, this isn't like you. You'll usually take any assignment without complaint."

Jeremy chuckled and hung his head. "I apologize." He looked up with pleading eyes. "I haven't seen Amélie in months, and I'm always worried about her. Chantal is safe here with Maurice, but you won't even tell me where Amélie is."

"And that's for her own safety as well as yours. She's on an extended mission. How's your brother, Lance?"

Jeremy scowled. "You know how he is. And where's Horton? Is Chantal still besotted with him?"

"Well, you've asked me two questions. To answer the first, Horton is still doing his job up in Loire—"

"At least someone has some stability in his life," Jeremy growled.

"My, my, you are a handful today. And yes, Chantal is still dreamy-eyed about him, although she's still mad that he wouldn't kiss her." Seeing Jeremy's puzzled look, she added, "Remind me to tell you that story sometime."

Jeremy laughed. "Sorry for being difficult. All right, I'll take the general. When?"

"Tonight." Fourcade leaned toward him and touched his hand. "And when you get back, I might have a surprise for you."

Jeremy's eyes brightened. "Amélie? Is she coming here?"

Fourcade grimaced over a smile. "I shouldn't have said anything. You keep your mind on your job tonight. It's easy enough, but you don't want to do something inadvertently to mess things up, like I might just have done. You'll meet the general. You already know where. Guide him to the boat, go out with him to meet the sub, and then return here. Your role tonight is basically a hand-holding one."

Jeremy grinned. "Are you sure this is the same general who escaped from Königstein Fortress?"

"Just remember to speak to him only in French. As you stated, he doesn't like you Brits, and it's one of your subs that's coming to get him. But he thinks it's American. Even the officers and crew will be dressed in American uniforms." She pursed her lips. "And that's the sum total of what I know."

Fourcade need not have worried that Jeremy would be distracted on his mission. Giraud became so fussy that Jeremy feared at one point that the general's greatest physical threat might come from Jeremy himself as he fought an urge to throttle the man.

They met in a barn a few hundred yards from the embarkation point, and at first, the general was fully courteous, although Jeremy doubted that Giraud could ever dispense with his sense of pomp and self. Basking in the historic moment that would be his, the general strutted, becoming impatient when the submarine was delayed.

The Resistance group that was to ferry him into the dark waters in the very early morning hours knew not to ask questions, but some shot him furtive glances, seeming to have recognized him. The light in the barn was dim, but the general's uniform was distinct, and his portrait had adorned walls and newspapers across the country.

Before the appointed time, Giraud kept checking his watch and asking if the scheduled time was correct. When the sub was late, he paced and muttered such that the security team worried that he might arouse unwanted attention.

The first time Jeremy had rendezvoused with a submarine had been well over two years ago. Back then, he was to be a passenger on the vessel with no choice but to rely on the Resistance members to bring him to the correct coordinates on the dark, tossing sea at the appointed time. The same was true this time, but he noticed a level of confidence that had been absent before. He had no way of knowing if any of the Resistance men were the same as those of two years ago, but these moved about with awareness and ease, men who knew their jobs and their teammates, and communicated with each other silently through gestures or in very low voices.

At last, they signaled readiness. The submarine was in position. Jeremy escorted the general to the beach and climbed into the boat with him. The Resistance crew rowed through the dark waves, and when they were away from shore a few hundred yards, they stopped and waited.

Moments later, with a barely audible whoosh, the sub surfaced, invisible but for the barely gleaming reflection of ambient light. Using dim lights as a guide, the dinghy closed the distance, and Jeremy helped the general across to the deck. Then he settled back on his seat and folded his arms. His excitement grew as he focused all his thoughts on Amélie.

On reaching shore, he thanked the crew and the security team in the dark, hardly having seen their faces. Then he set off again to the villa in Marseille, trying not to forget security measures as he went.

He arrived shortly before dawn, and on seeing the gates facing onto the street in front of the main house and gardens, a smile formed on his face and broadened the nearer he came. Once inside the gate, he could no longer restrain his eagerness. He broke into a dead run and threw the front door open.

The foyer was empty. The house bore an unusual coldness about it.

Jeremy hurried to the terrace.

Fourcade sat there alone. She held her forehead in her hands, and when she heard Jeremy, she looked up. Dark rings circled her eyes.

"Where's Amélie?" he asked.

Fourcade took a deep breath. "She's not here."

57

November 7, 1942
Sark Island, Guernsey Bailiwick, English Channel Isles

Marian and Stephen sat close together on the stack of suitcases in the storage room at the back of the house. It was cold and damp for the lack of heat and time of year, and they squeezed next to each other to share the headphones to listen to the BBC.

The announcer was introducing President Roosevelt in an address to the French people. When the president commenced his speech, Marian pulled back and looked at Stephen in astonishment. “Good heavens, he’s speaking in French.”

“And his accent isn’t bad either. Let’s listen.”

“My friends, who suffer day and night,” Roosevelt said, “under the crushing yoke of the Nazis, I speak to you as one who was with your army and navy in France in 1918. I have held all my life the deepest friendship for the French people —for the entire French people. I retain and cherish the friendship of hundreds of French people, in France and outside of France. I know your farms, your villages, and your cities. I know your soldiers, professors, and workmen. I know what a precious heritage of the French people are your homes, your culture, and the principles of democracy in France. I salute again and reiterate my faith in Liberty, Equality, and Fraternity. No two nations exist which are more united by historic and mutually friendly ties than the people of France and the United States.

"Americans, with the assistance of the United Nations, are striving for their own safe future as well as the restoration of the ideals, the liberties, and the democracy of all those who have lived under the Tricolor.

"We come among you to repulse the cruel invaders who would remove forever your rights of self-government, your rights to religious freedom, and your rights to live your own lives in peace and security.

"We come among you solely to defeat and rout your enemies. Have faith in our words. We do not want to cause you any harm.

"We assure you that once the menace of Germany and Italy is removed from you, we shall quit your territory at once. I am appealing to your realism, to your self-interest and national ideals. Do not obstruct, I beg of you, this great purpose. Help us where you are able, my friends, and we shall see again the glorious day when liberty and peace shall reign again on earth.

"Vive la France eternelle!"

When Roosevelt had finished speaking, Marian stared into Stephen's eyes with an odd mixture of hope and horror. "Oh my God, Stephen. The United States is getting ready to do something. It sounds like they might invade somewhere. Do you think it's France?"

"That's as good a guess as any, though why they would

announce such an intention before they do it is beyond me. That doesn't sound like good military practice."

Marian curled her hand in front of her mouth, ignoring how bony it had become under the sparse rationing of the Nazis. "I'm sure you're right, although his speech was a warning to the French people to seek cover and stay out of the way of military operations. That's the way I saw it."

She suddenly flung herself on the shrunken form of her normally tall husband. "Oh, Stephen. Do you think there's hope for us? Do you think the Allies can defeat these Nazis and drive them out of our lives?" She sobbed into his chest. "Do you think we'll ever see our children alive again?"

She took her seat again on the suitcases and clasped her hands together. "I so much want this invasion, if that's what it is, but I'm so afraid that one of our sons might wash up on a beach in his own blood." She dropped her head in her hands. "I'm scared."

Stephen stood and leaned over to console her. "There, there," he said, gently rubbing the tears away from her eyes. "Stiff upper lip—"

Marian laughed, a spontaneous guffaw. "And all that other British rubbish." She stood. "Let's put this away and go have some of that awful ersatz tea."

58

November 9, 1942
Over the Mediterranean Sea

Paul leaned back in his seat on a transport plane and closed his eyes, wondering at the events of the past four days. Juxtaposed against each other, they could not seem more surreal. Today was Sunday.

As the Torch landings began, President Roosevelt released a press statement, which Paul held in his hand. He opened his eyes, glanced down, and re-read it.

"In order to forestall an invasion of Africa by Germany and Italy, which if successful, would constitute a direct threat to America across the comparatively narrow sea from Western Africa, a powerful American force equipped with adequate weapons of modern warfare and under American Command is today landing on the Mediterranean and Atlantic Coasts of the French Colonies in Africa.

"The landing of this American army is being assisted by the British navy and air forces and it will, in the immediate future, be reinforced by a considerable number of divisions of the British army.

"This combined allied force, under American Command, in conjunction with the British campaign in Egypt, is designed to prevent an occupation by the Axis armies of any part of Northern or Western Africa, and to deny to the aggressor nations a starting point from which to launch an attack against the Atlantic Coast of the Americas.

"In addition, it provides an effective second front assistance to our heroic allies in Russia.

"The French Government and the French people have been informed of the purpose of this expedition and have been assured that the allies seek no territory and have no intention of interfering with friendly French authorities in Africa.

"The government of France and the people of France and the French possessions have been requested to cooperate with and assist the American expedition in its effort to repel the German and Italian international criminals, and by so doing to liberate France and the French empire from the Axis yoke.

"This expedition will develop into a major effort by the Allied nations, and there is every expectation that it will be successful in repelling the planned German and Italian invasion of Africa and prove the first historic step to the liberation and restoration of France."

Paul took a deep breath and let it out slowly. The Torch landings were underway and going well, and he was on his way to Algiers with General Clark to meet Admiral Darlan. Further, the general had just delivered some news personal to Paul that had come out of the blue.

On the previous Wednesday, attracted by the sudden ringing of many church bells clearly heard through windows of Whitehall, he had raised his head to listen, double-checking his calendar to be sure that the day was, in fact, not Sunday. Around him, others exclaimed in surprise, and then someone called, "It must be the news coming out of El Alamein. Tune in the wireless."

Moments later, the familiar voice of BBC war correspondent, Bruce Belfrage, had rang across the room, his tone tinged with enthusiasm. "Here's some excellent news which has come during the past hour. The Axis forces in the Western Desert, after twelve days and nights of ceaseless attacks by our land and air forces, are now in full retreat. It's known that the enemy's losses, in killed and wounded, have been exceptionally high."

Cheers broke out across the room. "This is sensational," a young officer had called out. "This is our first victory against Germany's field army in the entire war so far, and we're beating them badly. We knew the Desert Fox would get his comeuppance once Monty was on the job."

Paul had smiled. Lieutenant-General Bernard Montgomery, popularly known to the public as "Monty," had been the general whom Churchill had put in command of British forces in Africa in place of General Auchinleck at the beginning of August during the trip to Cairo. The change had yielded the desired result. *Then again, Monty had the new American Sherman tanks.*

Then on Thursday, the 5th, Paul had flown with Eisenhower's headquarters group to establish the command and operations center for Operation Torch at Gibraltar. His escort had toured him over the strategically located peninsula at the mouth of the Mediterranean where it spilled into the Atlantic only twenty-four miles across the strait from Morocco, clearly visible across the blue water. From the top of the iconic "Rock," he had gazed down on the flat ground far below that jutted into the sea. On this wide piece of land, an airfield had been constructed, and on its edge was a massive naval base.

"What's happened with the civilian population," Paul had asked.

"Some were evacuated to Britain and French Morocco before the French surrender, and I suppose they're still there. Others went to Madeira and Jamaica to wait out the war."

As their Land Rover started down the mammoth slab of granite protruding into the sky on their way to St. Michael's Cave, Paul jerked his head around and stared back along the road at a scampering animal. "Did I just see a monkey?"

"You did, sir, a macaque from the Atlas Mountains. They were brought over centuries ago and have thrived here ever since. Gibraltarians kept them fed, but this war interrupted that. The military does its best to look out for them. The Rock has been attacked several times, first by the French air force two years ago in retaliation for our bombing their navy at Mers-el-Kébir. They didn't do much damage, but the macaques suffered.

"The Italians bombed us several times this year, and of course that's done the monkeys no good either. The Italians also sent in frogmen to sink our ships. They were successful in September last year when three mini subs sank thirty thousand tons of goods on merchant ships at anchor here. And of course, they keep trying."

They came to a checkpoint where credentials were checked, and then entered the eerie, artificial half-light of a vast natural cavern inside the Rock. It rose many stories high and disappeared into darkness, and Paul gazed in wonder at the odd shapes and colors of gigantic icicle-shaped stalactites still dripping their mineral deposits onto the mirror-image stalagmites below, all of them glowing when struck by light.

"This cave has an extensive tunnel system," the escort said. "Much of your headquarters' staff is set up in here. I should tell you that we have an elaborate defensive plan in case we're ever overrun. Of course, if the Germans or Italians ever do that, the Mediterranean would be closed to the Allies. Most of us would evacuate, but we'd leave behind a unit of specially trained soldiers hidden behind false walls around the Rock with food, water, arms and ammunition, and radios, to subsist for an indefinite time. Their jobs would be to spy on the occupiers and report back to headquarters."

"Are you serious?"

The escort had merely nodded.

Then, late in the afternoon on the night before last, just hours before the Torch landings were to commence, Paul had been summoned to General Eisenhower's office with instructions to wear an American uniform. Paul knew his role under those circumstances: speak French only and watch for subtle undertones that might indicate the ulterior motives of someone else in the meeting.

On entering, he was astonished to be introduced to General Henri Giraud. The general also did a double-take on seeing Paul, exclaiming, "I swear I just left your brother, or someone who looks enough like you to be your brother. He escorted me out to the submarine."

Paul laughed off the coincidence. "I don't know who that could be, but of course I know of you from the news reports of your famous escape." Then, while the general basked in the glow of his achievement, Paul wondered about Jeremy's whereabouts.

Three hours of discussion ensued regarding the timing

of Giraud's return to North Africa. Then, the French general dropped a figurative landmine.

"I will not go," he informed Eisenhower, "until I have been named as supreme commander of all Allied forces for all military operations in North Africa and France."

Paul locked his attention on Eisenhower, whose eyes had opened wide. Paul then shifted his attention to Clark, whose face had turned red with fury.

"We would like the Honorable General to know that the time of his usefulness to the Americans for the restoration of the glory that was once France is now nearing an end," Clark had said, his voice rising. "We do not need you after tonight."

Flustered but undeterred, Giraud had frowned angrily and persisted, "What about the prestige of Giraud? What would the French people think of me?"

"We are at war, General," Clark barked, his voice rising further. "Our concern is winning it and sparing as many lives of our soldiers and your people as possible."

As if not hearing Clark, Giraud repeated, "What about Giraud's prestige? The French people would think poorly of me, and what about my family?"

As Paul watched in stoic amazement, the argument continued. At one point, Giraud requested a break to use the restroom. While he was absent, Eisenhower turned to Paul. "You've watched. What do you think?"

"He's stalling, sir. He knows that Torch is about to execute. If the landings go well, he'll want in. If they go poorly, he'll want out."

"You nailed it," Clark growled, bordering on sullenness. He turned to Eisenhower. "Sir, he might not be our man."

Eisenhower agreed. "When he comes back, say your worst."

"With pleasure."

Giraud re-entered the room. He looked across the faces of the other three men and started across to his seat.

"Before you sit down, General Giraud," Clark told him, "if you don't go along with us, you're going to be out in the snow on your ass."

Startled at Clark's brusqueness with Eisenhower's evident approval, Giraud had left the room and returned to his guest quarters. Excusing himself, Paul went to the operations room to bring himself abreast of the current situation.

Taking a seat before a huge map of the Mediterranean spanning its north and south coasts from west of Morocco to east of Algiers, he watched as the clock ticked down toward zero hour.

Warships had arrived on-station from Great Britain and the US, assembled in two places north of Algeria. Recalling the conversations in Florida between Churchill and Stephenson, Paul noted with interest that Brazilian ships, both cargo and troop carriers, were part of the invasion force, and yet more ships streamed across the Atlantic from other South American ports to deliver vital supplies.

Troop transports arrived from United States' eastern ports and held steady off the west coast of Morocco and south of British and American aircraft carriers and gunships inside the Mediterranean. Then, as the hands on a clock over the map moved past the appointed time, map plotters pushed small markers across it, first representing masses of fighters, bombers, and naval guns delivering deadly ordnance along the North African coast, and then thousands of US soldiers storming the beaches at Casablanca, Oran, and Algiers. Paul wondered how many already lay maimed or dead in the sand.

As Paul slept on a cot behind the operations room, a young captain rushed in and shook him awake. "Sir, the commanding general wants to see you ASAP."

Paul sat up abruptly, stretched, and wiped the sleep from his eyes. "How long have I been out?"

"Not long, sir. Maybe an hour. But you needed the rest. You've been up all last night and today."

"How's the invasion going?"

"Very well, sir. We've taken Algiers."

"Already?" He looked at his watch. It showed 1930 hours.

"Yes, sir. It's just happened."

General Clark was with Eisenhower in the latter's office when Paul arrived. "President Roosevelt's already heard from Marshal Pétain," Eisenhower said, holding up a message. "The marshal condemned the invasion. He told the president that he would defend against any attack." The general's forehead furrowed. "Our response? We severed formal relations with France."

"And now that Giraud sees the invasion is a success," Clark chortled, "he wants to play ball."

"There's more," Eisenhower said, glancing at Clark. "Tell him."

"You predicted trouble with Darlan," Clark said. "It might have arrived." In his animated style, Clark explained that Darlan had, coincidental with the start of Torch, arrived in Algiers to see his son who was dying there of polio. "He learned of the invasion from his agents an hour before execution, and he wants to meet with us again. He outranks Giraud and Mast, and the Vichy troops respect him. I'm casting no aspersions about his love for his son, but he's a blatant opportunist who's made overtures to us.

Still, he could blow the whole works irrespective of Giraud."

Eisenhower grasped Clark's shoulder. "Mark, you know my thinking. Get to Algiers and fix this thing. Torch is going smoothly. The question now is how many Americans and Frenchmen will die unnecessarily.

"You'll have to fly since we don't have time for a submarine." He glanced at Paul with a crooked grin. "Take Littlefield with you. He'll be your interpreter and, besides, he's had a cogent thought or two."

As the transport plane winged over the Mediterranean under fighter escort, Paul contemplated the journey he had traveled in the past two years, but seemingly over a lifetime. He recalled that back then he had bemoaned to Claire over lunch that his contribution to the war as a junior intelligence analyst paled by comparison to those that she made at Bletchley, and that Jeremy and Lance had made at Dunkirk.

And since then, the places, events, and people I've seen are beyond comprehension. Meetings with Churchill and Roosevelt. Flying to survey the battlefields in Greece and Albania. Traveling to Moscow with the prime minister. Camp X. The shipyards in California. The tank factory in Michigan. If I ever write this up, people will think it's a novel.

He felt Clark watching him. "You got any ideas? I'll tell you honestly, I'm fresh out of them. How do you deal with a man who'll sell out his country to the highest bidder?"

"Sir, I wish I had some insights. I'm still grappling with the notion that I'm on this plane headed to Algiers."

Clark grunted and reached into his jacket pocket. "By

the way, the boss called over to your PM before we got on the plane. I'd told Ike about your analysis of Darlan. Since you're coming along as my primary aide on this junket, he thought you might need some added pull." He drew out a folded sheaf of papers and handed them to Paul. "Congratulations, you just made lieutenant colonel. I brought along the shoulder boards, too." He pulled them from another pocket and handed them over.

Paul took them in shock. "Sir, two years ago I was a lieutenant—"

"And now you're a lieutenant colonel. You came up fast. Learn to live with it. Anyway, when the war's over, your highers will probably take most of it away. Keep in mind, this isn't a reward. Our military gives medals for that. Yours does too." He chuckled. "You can't buy much with 'em, but they look pretty hanging on a wall. Anyway, we need you to carry a certain level of authority. You'll live up to it."

When he and Clark met Darlan at the St. Georges Hotel in Algiers after ducking German Junkers 88 bombers overflying the city as they landed, Paul was surprised by the admiral's diminutive height. An assassination attempt had been made on his life shortly before the invasion started, so he was angry, nonplussed, and required to look up physically at the tall American general towering over him. Nonetheless, he carried himself well with classical good looks, a firm jaw, straight nose, graying hair, and blue eyes. He quickly asserted his perceived French authority in the opening discussions.

"I'll bring in my own interpreter soon," Darlan told Paul when the fact became apparent that neither Darlan nor

Clark spoke each other's language. In the meantime, Paul translated for them. "Tell the general that I received his terms of armistice and forwarded them to Vichy, but I am here in private capacity to visit my son. I did not come with any portfolio to negotiate, and anything we agree on here must be passed in front of General Pétain before being formally accepted."

"I understand," Clark replied. "I hope you understand that time is short, and I need to get straight to the point. America has broken formal relations with France. I need to know if you're ready to sign our terms of armistice."

Darlan let out a breath. "We will have no decision on that until after the Council of Ministers meets in Vichy this afternoon."

Clark stood impatiently. "I'm a ground commander. I don't have time to go back and forth for authorities. Our troops east of here must pass through your army's positions in Tunisia to meet our common enemy in Libya. I don't want them fighting each other. If you can't act, I'll have to find another French commander who can."

Darlan's face grew taut with controlled anger, and he drew back. "You must do what you must do. I've ordered the French troops in Algiers not to resist, and they've obeyed. Your soldiers have our guarantee of security here. But, as I told you, I sent your terms of armistice forward and must await a response before I can issue such an order for the rest of North Africa."

"That doesn't work. You've got thirty minutes."

Darlan's eyes opened wide in astonishment. "I'll need to tell my government what is taking place."

Clark jutted out his chin in unbridled obstinacy. "That'll take too much time, in which case I'll have to detain you under protective custody. Why can't you issue the same order for the rest of North Africa as you did for Algiers? What answer would you expect from Pétain, keeping in mind that we broke off formal ties?"

"I sent my recommendation," Darlan stated in clipped terms as the color in his cheeks rose with increased anger. "I explained that you came here with overwhelming force, that we cannot expect to defeat you, and that continued fighting would be stupid."

Clark rose to full height and placed his curled fists on his hips. "Then issue the order to your troops for a ceasefire so they don't shoot at our soldiers. If you don't, I'll get General Giraud to do it."

Darlan scoffed. "He has no authority here, and our armies know it. I'm not sure they will obey his order. We'll lose time, the fighting will continue, and we'll see more loss of blood." He reached to the collar of his tunic to loosen it.

"Then you issue the order."

Darlan took a deep breath and kept his seat, but he stared at Clark with piercing eyes, and the rims of his eyelids had begun to turn pink. "General Clark, if I do that, the *Wehrmacht* will immediately occupy the rest of France."

Clark folded his arms. "General Darlan, we both know the danger to Southern France, but that occupation is going to occur regardless of what we do here. If the *Third Reich* wins this war, Southern France will cease to exist as will the nation of France. For you personally, it boils down to this: are you going to stay with Vichy or cooperate with us?"

Moments passed in silence, the French admiral and the American general contemplating each other. "I made an oath to obey the orders of Marshal Pétain," Darlan said in a low voice, and Paul thought his demeanor showed diminishing resolve.

"I can't take responsibility to issue the order you want."

"This is no time to obey those orders," Clark growled. "You took your oath at the point of a loaded gun, and your country is under foreign domination. Pétain is considered by many of your countrymen to be a traitor. You have the opportunity to rally Frenchmen to win this war. This is your last chance."

Darlan heaved a sigh. "I could send an urgent message to Pétain recommending a ceasefire for Algeria and Morocco."

"You've already done that."

"Not in specific terms."

"I don't have time," Clark yelled in exasperation. "Your soldiers and ours outside of Algiers are shooting at each other. Frenchmen and Americans share the same interests at heart, and we're wasting time fighting among ourselves."

Once more, the room descended into silence. Then Darlan sighed again. "May I confer with my staff?"

"You have five minutes, but neither you nor any of them will be allowed to leave or communicate with anyone outside of this suite. Is that clear?"

"Perfectly."

"What do you think?" Clark asked Paul while Darlan conferred with his subordinates in another room.

"He's between a rock and a hard place, sir, and he knows it. I think fear is beginning to overtake his arrogance. He must know how much he is despised in France, but he's right that the Vichy troops in North Africa support him. Given that they might have to fight the Americans if he does not come to an agreement, it's anyone's guess how long they would continue that support if he does not cooperate with us.

"You've essentially told him that Vichy France no longer exists as a political entity and that German occupation of the rest of France is inevitable. He's been speaking to us, so he can't go back to France—the Gestapo would arrest and interrogate him immediately. He might not like it, but in the end, he'll do as we ask. I don't see that he has any other choice."

Clark peered at Paul with a discerning expression. "Remind me never to play poker with you."

Paul chuckled. "General, you dealt the cards, and from a stacked deck. I was just looking over your shoulder."

When Darlan re-entered the room, his attitude had softened to become more conciliatory. He handed Clark a sheet of paper. "Here is my message to Pétain."

Clark took and read it. "This just tells Pétain that I won't accept your refusal to declare an immediate armistice, that further battle will be fruitless, and that blood will flow. You're telling him that fighting us will result in the loss of your African colonies, and to forestall that you want to cease hostilities and declare neutrality."

He shook his head. "This doesn't cover the waterfront, and we don't have time for it. I want an order from you to your troops for a ceasefire. Now."

Darlan stared around the room, cornered, with no escape. At last, he nodded reluctantly. "I'll send one out to Generals Juin, Nogues, Barres, our air force, and our navy."

Clark nodded. "I'll instruct our major commanders to decide the local terms of armistice. They'll negotiate with their counterpart French commanders. General Patton will meet with General Nogues. When your troops cease firing, the terms will go into effect for the entire area."

"I assume there will be no hostilities in Tunisia?"

"That's right."

"What about Giraud? I sent out an order to have him arrested. He's been in hiding from me. And now we're supposed to fight side by side?"

Clark took a deep breath. "General Darlan, Giraud wants the same thing you do, a free and sovereign France. There's room for everyone. At the moment, I just want to stop the fighting between us. Let's get that order written and sent out."

To Paul's great relief, Darlan acquiesced. The two generals hunkered next to each other over a coffee table with pens and paper. Fifteen minutes later, Clark straightened and read the draft out loud. "Effective immediately, all land, sea, and air forces under French command are ordered to cease firing on all American troops and their allies. You are ordered to return all forces under your command to your bases and observe strict neutrality." It was addressed to the major French commanders in North Africa over Admiral Darlan's signature.

"So, General, is it over now?" Paul asked Clark when they were alone. "The French are neutralized in Africa?"

Clark cocked his head to one side. "I'd like to think so, but the situation is fluid. Ego is as much in play now as anything. Look at that arrogant Giraud wanting to be named supreme allied commander, and what was his chief concern? What Frenchmen might think of him if he were not awarded the title. Meanwhile, he's commanded nothing of significance lately.

"And you were right about Darlan. His main priority is saving his own skin, and soon his only avenue to accomplish that is to deal with us. Mark my words. We'll have more unpleasant dealings with him, and we still have that fleet in Toulon to worry about.

"But at least for the moment, a hundred and twelve thousand French soldiers across North Africa won't be shooting at our guys. I'd call it success."

Paul stood and stretched. "Agreed, sir. Not bad for a day's work."

59

November 10, 1942
Marseille, France

"No word yet?"

Fourcade shook her head. "I'm sorry, Jeremy, no."

"Can't you at least tell me where Amélie was? I could go look for her."

"You know you can't do that. She was deep in Occupied France. To tell you the truth, against my better judgment, I let her come back to see you. She needed a break." She sighed. "For what it's worth, if we find out where she is, we must rescue her. She knows too much about a specific operation. We can't let it be tortured out of her."

Jeremy grimaced at Fourcade's last comment as she went on. "We know she can't be far away because she had checked in as she traveled. Maurice has people out now tracing her movements."

The door on the veranda opened, and Maurice emerged. Usually, his big, grizzled face carried a warm smile that masked his clandestine purpose as he made his rounds as a vendor of vegetables to major hotels and restaurants where influential people gathered and talked. On this evening, however, his wide eyes and tight lips foretold high anxiety. Even before exchanging greetings, he blurted, "You must leave, at once. Everyone. Take only what you must and burn everything else."

"What? What are you talking about?" Fourcade exclaimed in shock. Maurice was not a man given to panic, which was one of the reasons he seconded as her security officer and ran the local Resistance organization in Marseille. "Why?"

"The Allies invaded North Africa. French forces refused to fight them. Hitler is furious and announced he will occupy the rest of France. Our friends in the north sent word that German units are already assembling to invade the south. By this time tomorrow, they will likely be here."

Jeremy listened, aghast. "What about Amélie? We can't forget about her."

"No, we can't, for personal and strategic reasons. Maurice? Anything?"

Still struggling to catch his breath, Maurice nodded. "She was picked up by pro-Vichy *gendarmes* in Valence. I don't know why. I suspect they'll hold her until the SS and Gestapo make their way south and let them deal with her."

Jeremy stood, his face a mask of fury. "I'll get her out."

Maurice raised his palms in a placating gesture. "We have Resistance fighters on the way there to rescue her."

"I'll join them. I'm trained for this."

Fourcade smiled gently. "And you, Horton, and Kenyon, God rest his soul, trained our Resistance fighters well. We have to trust them."

"Too late anyway," Maurice broke in. "Jeremy, Valence is thick with Resistance activity. The fighters there know what they're doing, and they're on their way. You wouldn't have time from here." He turned to Fourcade. "We got a message from MI-9. They want you to escape to England. They're sending a Lysander to pick you up tonight." He returned his attention to Jeremy. "You have to be on the plane as well. Horton was ordered back too. He'll get on a Lysander flight in the Loire Valley." Pausing as a thought struck him, he asked, "Didn't you just see him recently?"

Jeremy stared distantly but nodded. "A couple of weeks ago. I stopped in there on my way back from Switzerland."

"That's right. You went to rescue your brother."

Jeremy ignored the comment.

Meanwhile, Fourcade put her hand to her head. "I can't just leave here," she interjected. "What about the Alliance?"

"I won't go without Amélie," Jeremy said firmly. "I'm staying until she's safe."

"Madame," Maurice replied to Fourcade, "if they capture you, the Alliance is finished. You're the brains and heart of it. You built it. The leaders in the network trust *you*." He heaved a sigh. "You can come back when things settle down."

He turned back to Jeremy. "You need to think with your head, not your emotions. When we rescue Amélie, she will say that she won't leave without Chantal. We are having to move quite a few people out of France. We'll get Amélie and hide her. We can't let her be interrogated.

"But Jeremy, if you're still here when the Nazis roll into Marseille, you'll be detained even if for no other reason than that you're of military age. At best, chances are you'd be sent to Germany for forced labor. The country is draining its young male population for enlistment in the *Wehrmacht*. At worst, you'll be interrogated—and strong men have broken in great numbers."

He shook his head sadly. "We expected the Nazis to occupy Southern France at some point, and our local Resistance was ready to give them a rough time, but we didn't expect this. The Nazis are angry, unopposed, coming in force, and they'll be suspicious of anything that moves. It's best if you get out of the country, let things settle, and then come back. I'll keep Amélie and Chantal safe, you have my solemn promise."

Unmollified, Jeremy only stared with a sullen expression.

"Jeremy," Maurice said. "I'm your friend. There's more to the message, and it comes directly from Lieutenant Colonel Crockatt." He pulled a note from his jacket and read, "'Reminder. You are a soldier. We are at war. You are ordered home.'"

Maurice put his big arm around Jeremy's neck. "At the end of the war, you don't want to be hunted as a deserter. What good will you be to Amélie then?"

60

November 10, 1942
Valence, France

Amélie stared at the bars in the window on the opposite wall of her cell. Dusk was settling in. She still did not know why she had been detained. Something to do with her papers, but they had served her well going and coming from Paris through myriad checkpoints. A local functionary at the train station had almost let her through, then something on her travel document caught his eye, and suddenly she was surrounded by *gendarmes* with barking dogs, placed in handcuffs, and led away to this jail.

She worried about how she would hold up during interrogation. Her training at MI-6's spy school outside of London had been rigorous in techniques on resisting giving up information, with the admonition that the longest time for holding out that should be expected of anyone undergoing Gestapo torture practices was forty-eight hours, but that would give allies sufficient time to control any damage resulting from information that might be divulged. *Then what?* She blocked the thought.

Her job in Paris had been to liaise clandestinely with Jeannie Rousseau, a French woman from Dinard in the north of France who had worked at the *Wehrmacht* headquarters that had been responsible for planning the aborted invasion of Great Britain. The Gestapo there had suspected Jeannie of spying and had arrested her, but so great was the respect for her by her German army bosses that they refused to believe the charges and forced her release on condition that she leave France's Atlantic coastal regions where Germany had built up huge military facilities.

Amélie had facilitated Jeannie's linkup with the Resistance in Dinard and her passage south upon release from the Gestapo, and when Jeannie subsequently decided to ingratiate herself into the German high command in Paris for intelligence collection, Amélie had volunteered to be her courier.

Jeannie was an unusually gifted woman, beautiful, graceful, intelligent, highly educated, and fluent in five tongues, including German. Her language ability had been her entrée into German higher headquarters, being called upon to interpret during meetings between German commanders and French civil authorities, and to translate documents. She had cultured an ability to be coquettish, and she used a combination of charm and intelligence to lure information from unwitting senior German officers. Complementing her many talents was her most formidable weapon: a photographic memory.

At Dinard, while moving about conference rooms where classified documents were left lying about and discussions centered on secret matters, Jeannie listened and saw what she could but took no notes. In her apartment, when key information needed to be passed along, she reproduced it in detailed reports.

On arriving in Paris a year ago, Jeannie had cultivated acquaintances carefully, slowly making her way into German military circles until landing a job with an arms contractor. Then she had gradually accepted greater work and responsibility, always pleasant, lighting up rooms with her smile, and was soon invited to cocktail parties where German generals gathered. They took notice of her.

Amélie, for her part, had moved to Paris shortly after Jeannie had begun work for the arms contractor. Careful not to be seen around each other frequently, they had worked out their methods of communication, and Amélie had carried documents spirited to her to their final destination. Although Amélie was careful not to learn too much about what she was carrying in order to have as little knowledge as possible that could be coerced from her, she could not help becoming aware of bits and pieces now and then.

One tidbit she had overheard when delivering her most recent documents had terrified her. The knowledge of its release beyond the confines of the German High Command would send shockwaves through the Third *Reich*, result in a purge from the headquarters in Paris, probably cost Jeannie her life, and rip into the Alliance Resistance network.

The information was described in three small words: Drones. Rockets. Bombs.

Those were the only three words that Amélie had overheard, but she understood the terrifying implications, and she suspected the target: London.

Now, sitting in the jail cell, Amélie knew the implications of the Gestapo learning of that particular secret being out. She could not let it happen.

She fingered along the seam of her sweater. There, sewn

in, was a pill provided to her at the end of her London training. "You can hold it in your mouth, and it won't melt," her trainer had said. "To activate it you must bite down."

She had wondered then if she would have the courage to use it. That worry thundered in her head and her heartbeat pounded in her ears now as she contemplated that the time might have come.

Thoughts of her deceased mother and father came to mind, and she smiled slightly thinking that soon she might see them. Images of Chantal came next. The younger sister had been so scared as a fourteen-year-old girl when the Germans had first invaded their hometown of Dunkirk. She had since grown up fast into a cunning and adept fighter.

Amélie's tears had already started to fall when she thought of Jeremy, and she fought back sobs. Then she took a deep breath, and a stubborn expression crossed her face. "They won't see me cry."

With trembling hands, she began to pick at the seam of her sweater.

A sound at the window, and then another, arrested her attention. As she stared at the small glass letting through the last glimmers of daylight, a small piece of gravel struck it, making the same sound, and falling away. Hurrying over, Amélie tried to reach the bars to look out, but the window was a little higher than her arms. She jumped, and on the third try, managed to get her hands around the bars and pull herself up far enough to see over the sill.

Below, hidden from view in the opposite direction by a row of bushes, a small man squatted. He made eye contact, smiled as if to encourage her, and pointed into the interior. Almost immediately, she heard the rapid footsteps of more than one person hurrying through the hall.

Seconds later, two men appeared at her cell door. One

was a *gendarme* officer, his eyes wide with fear, a kerchief pressed tightly against his mouth and tied tightly at the rear. Another man stood immediately behind him with a pistol pushed against the soft place where the *gendarme's* skull met his neck.

Keys jangled in a shaking hand, the lock clanged, and the door opened. The man with the gun shoved the *gendarme* inside the cell and motioned for Amélie to exit. "*Allez, allez*!" he hissed. "*Vite!*"

In the hall, another man waited. He grabbed Amélie by the hand and ran with her through the corridor.

As she reached the end, a gurgling sound caught her ear. She glanced back. The man with the pistol had not yet left the cell. Her guide tugged her hand, and she ran with him through the remaining passages to the front of the building. Along the way, other armed men stood in doorways, and once she and her escort had passed, they fell in behind and protected her from the rear. Moments later, she was in a truck and disappeared into Valence night traffic.

61

November 11, 1942
London, England

Dawn was just breaking as the Lysander carrying Jeremy and Fourcade floated down to the runway at RAF Tangmere. When it stopped in front of the terminal, Jeremy clambered down the attached steel ladder and helped Fourcade to the ground. A car waited for them, and as soon as they had freshened up and were prepared for the next leg of their journey to London, they set out.

Neither had spoken much during the flight, Jeremy because he did not care to, and Fourcade because she respected his wishes. "Go straight to MI-9 at the old Metropole Hotel building," he told the driver.

"I'm supposed to take you to Whitehall, to MI-6."

"I work for MI-9," Jeremy retorted irritably, "and I'm in no mood to argue."

"Do as he says," Fourcade told the driver, and the soft, commanding edge in her voice convinced him to follow their instruction.

Jeremy's mind remained numb during the two-hour drive to London, but he noticed that more traffic appeared on the roads since he had flown out of this same airfield during the Battle of Britain. That seemed so long ago, and so many mates were lost in the interim. *And now, what will become of Amélie—*

He blocked the thought and tried to admire the passing countryside, but most of the leaves had fallen from the trees, the fields were bare, and the sky overcast. Watching him, Fourcade reached across and squeezed his hand. "She'll be all right," she tried to comfort, "Maurice will see to it."

When Jeremy did not respond, she said, "Look, Jeremy. Maurice put a plan into place before we even knew what had happened to Amélie. We've built a competent organization. Our people know what to do. They don't know Amélie's mission, but they know it's a critical one. They'll rescue her, protect her, and get word back to us. Remember, she is also an MI-9 asset."

Jeremy turned his face toward her and squeezed her hand. "Thanks, Madame—"

"Oh, stop with the 'Madame,' would you? In times like these, we're friends—more like family. Call me by my first name, 'Madeleine.'"

"It's the not knowing," Jeremy rasped. "I can face just about anything else, but the idea of Amélie in Gestapo hands." His voice trailed off and he turned back to stare out the window. "And I left her there."

"I know, Jeremy. I know how you feel."

Jeremy turned back to her. "You're thinking of Major Faye?" he asked softly.

She nodded and fought back emotion. "I don't know where he is either."

"I'm so sorry. I knew the two of you liked each other. I hadn't realized the affection had gone that far."

Fourcade laughed and wiped her eyes. "We're not as young as you. We don't wear our feelings on our sleeves, but we're serious about each other."

Jeremy sat back in his seat. "This war is so evil. It interrupts every part of life. No one can be normal. Amélie didn't grow up intending to be a spy behind enemy lines in her own country. Chantal—"

Fourcade shook her head. "It's not the war that's evil. It's the people who conspire to rule the rest of us. All we want is to live our lives without interference. Evil people do anything to gain power, including letting loose the worst of what war brings. We're left with no alternative but to fight back."

They rode the rest of the way in silence, and when reaching the Metropole building and checking through security, Jeremy led Fourcade through the maze to Crockatt's office. Vivian greeted them, thrilled to see Jeremy safe at home again, and was pleased to meet Fourcade. "You're an icon," she said. "You've built the most effective Resistance organization in Europe."

"You flatter me," Fourcade said. "We do what we can."

Crockatt was also pleased to see them. "Come in, come in. Others will be happy you made it safely—"

Jeremy interrupted him with an edge in his voice. "Sir, why was I ordered home?"

Crockatt studied him. "The Germans executed Operation Attila, Jeremy, to take over the rest of France. Things are in flux there, worse than ever. We needed to get key people out until we have a better grasp of the situation. We intend to go back in."

"I'm hardly key," Jeremy retorted. "Meanwhile, Amélie—"

"I have some news, Captain," Crockatt said, a touch sternly. "Come into my office, sit down, and I'll tell you about it. That's not a request." He turned to Fourcade. "Please join us. You might want to hear this too." To Vivian, he said, "Would you bring some tea."

When they were seated, Crockatt started. "I won't bandy about. Amélie is safe. The Resistance in Valance got her out. She's on her way to Maurice's farm now."

Seeing Jeremy's sigh of relief, he smiled slightly. "There was a price to pay. The *Wehrmacht* moved in an hour after her rescue, and the Gestapo with them. The Resistance left their calling card at the *gendarmerie*."

Jeremy's eyes narrowed.

Fourcade sucked in her breath.

"They left the on-duty guard in the cell with his throat slit and with a sign hanging around his neck written in his own blood. You can guess what it said."

"*Collaborateur*," Jeremy breathed.

"Were there reprisals?" Fourcade asked softly.

"I'm afraid so," Crockatt replied, frowning grimly. "As I mentioned, the Nazis arrived an hour after Amélie's rescue. The Gestapo rounded up twenty people on the street and shot them against a wall."

Jeremy's head sagged backward. "She'll know that, and she'll blame herself." He stood and pointed a finger at Crockatt. "Get her out or send me back."

The lieutenant colonel took to his feet, controlling his anger. "You forget yourself, Captain. This is not a private war, and you are still a soldier talking to a superior officer. We've all had terrible circumstances to deal with. If you'll recall, the reason that you're still in this world and emotionally wrapped up with Amélie and her family is that she and her father went out into a storm to save you. Should you be blamed for that or for the horrible events at Dunkirk? One notion you've convinced me of is that you are in no emotional or mental state to go back to France now, and there'll be a delay before we start up those flights again. Which is the reason why we cannot pull Amélie out now."

Jeremy listened, at first furious, but deflated by degrees as Crockatt spoke, and when he had finished, Jeremy was shamefaced. "I'm sorry, sir. I was out of line."

Crockatt waved off the apology. "Everybody's under stress." He paused, and a slow smile crossed his face. "I have some good news; that is, aside from Amélie's rescue. I wanted to get the bad news over with before I mentioned it. You have people waiting to see you in the conference room. Horton made it back just before you—"

"Horton's here?" Jeremy blurted excitedly.

"Yes, and—"

Before Crockatt could continue, Jeremy bolted out of the office, flew down the hall, and entered the conference room. Crockatt chuckled with amusement and continued conversing with Fourcade. "It's such a pleasure to finally meet you," he said as Vivian brought in a tea tray.

Stony Stratford, England

Claire was about to put Timmy to bed when she heard pebbles scrunching in the driveway from a car driving over them. Her stomach sank. She thought of stopping at the cabinet for a stiff drink before answering the door, but instead she held Timmy tightly and went to look out through the window.

The sedan looked as if it could be the same two-door that Paul had driven up on occasion, but in the last light of dusk, she could not be sure. Two people emerged from the front, a man and a woman, and they both turned back to let two more passengers out of the rear. Claire's heart sank further.

Then as the four began walking up the garden path, she held her hand to her mouth and let out an excited squeal as she recognized the broad shoulders and the gait of the man in front. "Jeremy?"

She rushed to the door, and by the time she flung it open, Jeremy stood there grinning. He embraced his sister while she wept happy tears into his shoulder. Then he stepped aside and introduced Madeleine Fourcade. "I've invited her to stay for a few days, if you don't mind."

"Of course," Claire said enthusiastically, and stopped herself from saying that she knew much about Fourcade and Alliance from reports she had read at Bletchley.

"I've heard so much about you," Fourcade said. "Jeremy thinks the world of you."

"He thinks the world of my place to stay when he comes home," Claire said, laughing. "I just can't believe you're both here."

"Horton too," Jeremy said, and stepped aside to let the sergeant through.

"Derek Horton, savior of my middle brother. I haven't seen you since you went back to France right after Dunkirk. This is a surprise, and a welcome one." Claire handed Timmy to Jeremy to hold while she embraced the sergeant. The tyke stared at Jeremy and then wrapped his arms around Jeremy's neck while Jeremy squeezed him.

After Claire let Horton go, Jeremy looked at her with an indefinable expression. "I have one more surprise." He moved aside to reveal the fourth person, a thin man who had stood in the shadows. As he stepped into the light, Claire saw that his face was very thin and his eyes sunken. But she recognized the impish expression behind them, and the mischievous grin.

"Lance," she gasped, as brother and sister gripped each other in a tearful embrace.

EPILOGUE

"I was so afraid I'd never see you again," Claire sobbed softly as she walked with her arm around him into the living room, joined by the others.

"What happened to 'things will get better, you'll see,'" Lance teased, while squeezing her.

Claire didn't reply; instead, she continued holding onto Lance, trembling as they sat together on the sofa. She relaxed and wiped her eyes while the others took their seats. "I'm so happy to see you," she told Lance while staving off more emotion. She suddenly pulled back and stared at him. "How did you get here? Did you escape?"

Lance grinned. "Guilty," he said, "but I didn't do it alone." He pointed at Jeremy. "I had some help from my little brother, the Gestapo officer."

Claire's eyes shifted back and forth between her two younger brothers. "Explain."

Jeremy, still holding and playing with Timmy, rocked back and forth. "I didn't do much—just usurped a little authority is all."

"Yeah, that's all," Lance quipped. He turned back to

Claire. "I got out of Colditz with four other POWs. We got word to Crockatt about when we would be coming out through those nonsensical messages I'd sent you. He was able to get some forged documents to get us into Switzerland." He shifted his gaze once again to Jeremy. "Little brother here had already done a scouting trip into Switzerland and learned that the country had a treaty with the Third *Reich.* The agreement allows free passage of German trains through Switzerland to the occupied zones in France. The same is true with official German passengers on Swiss trains.

"Again, through the good graces of MI-9, Jeremy had excellent papers forged showing him as a Gestapo officer and went to Zurich to wait. Crockatt got a message to me to go to the Zurich station. Local Resistance members kept an eye on the station. When they spotted me, they let Jeremy know, and he escorted me out of the country."

Lance grinned. "The surveillance team recognized me easily by the family resemblance, despite my emaciated state. Simple as that." He laughed. "I'll tell you that Jeremy gave me quite a start. When I first saw him, I thought I was headed for Gestapo torture. It took a moment to recognize him and then I could hardly hold down my excitement."

"It wasn't all that simple, mum," Horton broke in. "Jeremy was a bit worried that, once in France, he might trip up in the Gestapo disguise, so he switched to another one. But he thought the resemblance between him and Lance might raise curiosity. So instead of going on to Marseille, a Resistance group brought Lance to me in the Loire Valley while Jeremy continued south." He shot a crooked grin at Lance. "If you think this former POW looks skinny now, you should've seen him then. We fattened him up a bit.

"But he wouldn't leave." Horton opened his eyes wide in

mock exasperation. “Lance was supposed to get right onto a Lysander flight, but he got interested in our operations and wanted to stay, until Crockatt ordered us both back to London.”

Claire listened in amazement, and when Horton finished, she shook her head. “What an unbelievable story. I’m just glad you’re home.”

“Madeleine had a hand in it too,” Jeremy said, gesturing toward Fourcade. “She cajoled Crockatt to get my documents done, and her networks provided safe passage.” He set Timmy down and walked over to put an arm around Fourcade’s shoulder. “We couldn’t have done any of it without her.”

He felt a tug on his trousers and, glancing down, found Timmy gazing up at him with big, rounded eyes. “Jermy,” the little boy said, “will you play with me and my trucks?”

While Jeremy sat on the floor with Timmy and his toys, Fourcade and Horton sat in facing overstuffed chairs. Lance, still sitting next to Claire on the sofa, turned to her. “How are Mum and Dad? Any recent news.”

Claire shook her head sadly. “Nothing beyond what we’ve known. They’re alive. Rations are short. Life for them is miserable. They haven’t said so about the rations and the misery, but that’s the inescapable conclusion.”

Lance closed his eyes as the images of his parents and Sark under German occupation floated through his mind. “And Paul?”

Claire sighed. “I haven’t the faintest notion of what he does or where he is. It seems that every time I have one of you home, another brother disappears. You know Paul’s serious about a girl he’s met, Ryan Northbridge, and I know she’d like to hear from him too.”

“Paul is serious about a girl?” Lance said, chuckling, his

face showing his skepticism. "He's always had his head too buried in books to take notice."

"They met while working on something together, but neither can say what it was. She's beautiful and very nice, but she's as elusive as he is, ferrying fighters and bombers all over England." A note of stridency entered her voice. "I dream of the day when I'll have you all together again in one place, with Mum and Dad."

She stood and crossed to the cabinet. "Drinks, anyone?" Then she whirled around and fixed her eyes on Jeremy. "Little brother, I heard about Germany's occupation of the rest of France. How are Amélie and Chantal?"

A dark expression crossed Jeremy's face. "I'd rather not talk about it," he replied without looking up.

Fourcade left her seat and joined Claire at the cabinet. "I'll fill you in."

Marseille, France

Amélie had stopped shaking by the time she arrived at Maurice's farm in the early morning hours of the day after her escape in Valence. Her rescuers had brought her to Maurice in a small backroad warehouse at Chabeuil, a village eight miles southeast of Valence. Still in shock from her horrific ordeal, she had clung to him as they drove through the night on a circuitous route through Serres, Sisteron, and La Brillane.

"Where's Jeremy?" she had asked several times when waking up from fitful dozes. Each time, Maurice assured her that he was safe. "Will I see him?"

He patted her head back into his chest. "I'll explain when we get to my farm."

On their arrival, Chantal rushed out to the little car, embraced her sister, and helped her into the house. Maurice's wife made hot coffee, and they gathered around the table in the kitchen. Maurice explained about Jeremy.

"I'm glad he's safe," Amélie whispered.

A tear ran down her cheek and Maurice was taken by how small and vulnerable she suddenly seemed. He glanced at Chantal and had the same perception. *They're young girls. They shouldn't be in this war.* Then he thought of his own children asleep upstairs. *And neither should they.*

"We need to get you both to Pau," he told the sisters. "Phillippe Boutron still runs the diplomatic pouch through there from the Vichy embassy in Madrid, and he's still one of our staunchest members of the Resistance. We'll get word to him to meet you there and give you safe passage out of the country."

Amélie nodded. "I'll be glad to see him again. And then we can come back?" She raised her chin and gazed into Maurice's eyes. "We're not giving up this fight."

He smiled. "And neither is Fourcade, Jeremy, me, or the Alliance, I promise you. We'll re-constitute and carry on." He chuckled. "Nothing will keep Jeremy away. I thought I was going to have to beat him over the head to keep him from going to look for you. He couldn't have done anything. By the time he found out you'd been arrested, it was too late. And it still took a direct order from Crockatt with a threat of court-martial to get him on the plane back to London."

Amélie smiled shyly and averted her eyes.

Chantal broke in. "And what about you and your family, Maurice?"

He smiled. "We'll be fine. I've lived here all my life. I'm a simple country farmer who runs a vegetable vending business. Half of Marseille's upper class would starve without me to bring their vegetables, and I'm sure that when the Germans arrive, they'll find that they need my produce." He grinned slyly. "And I'll be happy to sell to them and take away whatever information I can."

St. Georges Hotel, Algiers, Algeria

Hearing a knock on his hotel door, Paul opened it and was startled to find Josh standing there, looking tired, but with a sadness about him not explained by combat operations. Although he had not expected to see his cousin there, he was not surprised that Josh was in Algiers. Darlan's orders had taken hold. Vichy resistance to the invasion had stopped, and US forces were now firmly in control of Algiers and consolidating.

"Come in," Paul said. "I hadn't expected to see you."

"I came in with the headquarters group to coordinate air cover." Josh's face quivered. "I'm sorry. I won't stay long, but I wanted to see family."

Paul saw that Josh fought back intense emotion. "What is it? What's happened."

Josh took a deep breath and gasped, "My mother died last night."

"No," Paul exclaimed in shock. "Aunt Della? Are you sure?"

Josh nodded. "I got the word a few minutes ago."

"Do you know the cause?"

"Old age, I expect." Josh shook his head sadly. "And loneliness."

Paul eyed him compassionately. "You must go home—"

Josh shook his head. "In the middle of a combat operation? I won't even ask. She wouldn't want me to. With a hundred and twelve thousand of our men now in combat, I won't be the only one dealing with bad news." He breathed a forlorn sigh. "My brother and sister, Zack and Sherry, will be there for the funeral, I'm sure."

Thoughts of his own parents flashed through Paul's mind. How were they faring under Nazi occupation and the awful privations of war? Despite the strength of their characters, Stephen and Marian were advanced in years and must be struggling terribly just to survive. He drove their skeletal images from his mind.

"I should get back," Josh said. "Thanks for listening."

"Of course, we must see each other as often as possible for the duration. As you say, we're family."

November 10, 1942
London, England

Lance entered the old Metropole Hotel and stopped at the security desk. After a brief call to the MI-9 office in Room 442, the security attendant instructed him to take a seat. Moments later, Vivian appeared to escort him to Crockatt's office.

"I can't tell you how relieved we are to have you back home and out of that dreadful POW camp," she said as they maneuvered through the corridors. "From the first time Jeremy came to see us, he was intent on getting you out of there. Your family must be thrilled."

"They are. I've enjoyed visiting with Jeremy and Claire the last couple of days. I wish Paul could have been with us."

"All in good time. I'm sure he's doing important work."

They reached the MI-9 office, and Vivian showed Lance in to see Crockatt. "This *is* a surprise," Crockatt said by way of greeting. "Please, sit down. What can I do for you?"

"Please, sir," Lance said without taking a seat. "I could use your advice and guidance."

Taken aback, Crockatt hesitated. "All right. What is it?"

"Sir, I can't sit on the sidelines. I need to be back in this war. I know you're not the right person to ask, but I thought you could possibly point me in the right direction."

Crockatt stroked his chin and furrowed his brow. "And which direction would that be?"

"Sir, I want to join the commandos."

RIDING THE TEMPEST

Book #5 in the After Dunkirk series

As the chaos of World War II spreads from Europe to Northern Africa and the Pacific, one family fights for their freedom against impossible odds...

Led by the US and supported by Britain, the Allies invade North Africa. Promoted within the British intelligence service, Paul is sent to Algiers during a ceasefire announced by French General Darlan. But when a deadly new assignment pushes his skills to the limit, will he step up to the challenge of his new role?

At Bletchley Park, Claire and her team of analysts discern from decoded messages that the Germans have employed a new type of radar that is decimating RAF bombers. And the messages she decodes grow more troubling by the hour as the war heats up in Northern Africa.

Lance is sent to Colditz, a special prison for recaptured escapees. He will risk everything to make his escape to join the commandos back in England, where his brother Jeremy is enlisted in a daring raid.

With fighting ongoing at Guadalcanal and in North Africa, the Allies gain strategic ground in both the European and Pacific theaters—but determined enemies on both fronts strike back with furious counterattacks.

JOIN THE READER LIST

Never miss a new release! Sign up to receive exclusive updates from author Lee Jackson.

Join today at severnriverbooks.com/authors/lee-jackson

AUTHOR'S NOTE

Hopefully you will recall the episode in the seventh chapter with Corporal George Peel and the raid at Vågsøy, Norway. One segment that I could not put in the story but should be told is that, years later, George (that was his real name), visited the village to return the silver box to its rightful owner. He met a lady at the house where he and his companions had taken refuge and eaten Christmas treats. George had taken the tiny silver box with the scripture verses.

The meeting was tearful. She told him that she had been three years of age at the time of the raid, and it was probably she who had made the muffled, fearful cry that George had heard. He tried to return the box, telling her, "I did a terrible thing."

She refused, saying, "It's all right. That was my grandmother's. You needed it. Please keep it."

My throat gets tight telling the story and recalling the heartwarming video of their meeting. The lady's name was not mentioned.

The other element of this book that should be discussed is the inclusion in the story of Ian Fleming, author of the James Bond series of books and movies. Fleming was a British intelligence officer during the war.

While researching, I ran across the incident recounted herein in which Fleming deals with an enemy agent who has broken the US codes and was preparing to deliver them to the Japanese. Per my studies, the operation occurred as I described it with the exception of Paul's participation. My practice is, when I know the name of a person who performed a heroic deed which I include in my books, I use the actual name. It is my way of honoring the true heroes.

In this case, Fleming's action, if occurring as written, contributed immensely to success in the Pacific Theater. Reportedly, there was another participant who carried out assistance actions as I described. Obviously, that was not Paul, but I could not find the individual's name, so I inserted Paul.

Included in my inquiries was a mention that the above-described scenario was depicted in a scene in one of Fleming's books and a movie based on it, *Casino Royale*. After *The Giant Awakens* had gone to proofreading, I received a note from one of my beta readers who had run across opposing research stating that the operation had not been carried out as described, and that instead, the movie scene had transmuted to urban legend and the actions retrospectively attributed to Fleming. Since both sources are credible and I have no way of knowing which is correct, I've included this explanation. However, in support of the story as described, I offer the following two quotations: